PRAISE FOR

The House on Prytania

"Expertly packed with suspense and family secrets, and soaked in New Orleans atmosphere, *The House on Prytania* is Karen White at her best. This twisty, satisfying tale will keep readers up far too late."

—Simone St. James, *New York Times* bestselling author of *The Sun Down Motel*

"An exciting psychic mystery best enjoyed by veterans who've read all the previous entries in both series." —*Kirkus Reviews*

"An excellent story, with a fabulous heroine in Nola, in a town that has so much history, with ghosts, mystery, suspense, and historical homes." —The Reading Cafe

"The characters pull you in just as much as the mystery. White brings New Orleans and its history to life, from Jackson Square to shotgun houses." —Caffeinated Reviewer

PRAISE FOR

The Shop on Royal Street

"A complex mystery that's appropriately goose-bumpy. Not just fans of the Tradd Street series, of which this is a spin-off, will look forward to seeing more of Nola." —*Publishers Weekly*

"White has added another page-turner to her repertoire of haunted houses and ghosts who won't stay put." —*The Times* (Munster, IA)

"White has a knack for combining ghostly shenanigans with charming Southern settings and you'll want to add *The Shop on Royal Street* to your spring reading list." —*The Augusta Chronicle*

ALSO BY KAREN WHITE

The Color of Light
Learning to Breathe
Pieces of the Heart
The Memory of Water
The Lost Hours
Falling Home
On Folly Beach
The Beach Trees
Sea Change
After the Rain
The Time Between
A Long Time Gone
The Sound of Glass
Flight Patterns
Spinning the Moon
The Night the Lights Went Out
Dreams of Falling
The Last Night in London

Cowritten with Beatriz Williams and Lauren Willig

The Forgotten Room
The Glass Ocean
All the Ways We Said Goodbye
The Lost Summers of Newport

The Tradd Street Series

The House on Tradd Street
The Girl on Legare Street
The Strangers on Montagu Street
Return to Tradd Street
The Guests on South Battery
The Christmas Spirits on Tradd Street
The Attic on Queen Street

The Royal Street Series

The Shop on Royal Street

THE HOUSE ON PRYTANIA

KAREN WHITE

Berkley
New York

BERKLEY
An imprint of Penguin Random House LLC
penguinrandomhouse.com

Copyright © 2023 by Harley House Books, LLC
Readers Guide copyright © 2024 by Penguin Random House LLC
Excerpt from *The Lady on Esplanade* copyright © 2024 by Harley House Books, LLC
Penguin Random House supports copyright. Copyright fuels creativity, encourages diverse voices, promotes free speech, and creates a vibrant culture. Thank you for buying an authorized edition of this book and for complying with copyright laws by not reproducing, scanning, or distributing any part of it in any form without permission. You are supporting writers and allowing Penguin Random House to continue to publish books for every reader.

BERKLEY and the BERKLEY & B colophon are registered trademarks of Penguin Random House LLC.

ISBN: 978-0-593-33463-8

The Library of Congress has cataloged the Berkley hardcover edition of this book as follows:

Names: White, Karen (Karen S.), author.
Title: The house on Prytania / Karen White.
Description: New York : Berkley, [2023] | Series: [A Royal Street novel]
Identifiers: LCCN 2022054568 (print) | LCCN 2022054569 (ebook) |
ISBN 9780593334621 (hardcover) | ISBN 9780593334652 (ebook)
Subjects: LCGFT: Novels.
Classification: LCC PS3623.H5776 H66 2023 (print) |
LCC PS3623.H5776 (ebook) | DDC 813/.6--dc23/eng/20221109
LC record available at https://lccn.loc.gov/2022054568
LC ebook record available at https://lccn.loc.gov/2022054569

Berkley hardcover edition / May 2023
Berkley trade paperback edition / May 2024

Printed in the United States of America
1st Printing

This is a work of fiction. Names, characters, places, and incidents either are the product of the author's imagination or are used fictitiously, and any resemblance to actual persons, living or dead, business establishments, events, or locales is entirely coincidental.

To my family—without whom I would have
finished this book much sooner. I love you.

CHAPTER 1

The Crescent City, with its long and tangled history, its glorious architecture and subtropical allure, along with its inarguably dark past and requisite restless spirits, is a forgiving place. A city with accepting arms for society's lost and hungry souls, and a haven for people like me who'd stumbled and fallen yet managed to pull themselves back up. People who were brave enough to try again in a place known for its extremes, or simply too hardheaded to admit defeat.

As the St. Charles streetcar I'd just exited waddled its way down the tracks toward the river bend, I listened to its clanging and jangling. It had become the soundtrack of my life in a new city, much as the church bells chiming their holy chorus in my hometown of Charleston once were.

Slowly walking down Broadway, I enjoyed the afternoon air of an early-October Saturday. The oppressive humidity of summer had lifted, giving us a reprieve, and although the temperature was nowhere near what anybody up north would call cold, it was cool enough that I wore a sweater over my T-shirt. Even my fingers felt chilled as they gripped the straps of my backpack.

I considered slipping on the gloves that my stepmother, Melanie, had sent me—along with typed instructions on how to care for them. I was due a visit from my family—my parents and my twelve-year-old half siblings, Sarah and JJ—the following week, and I didn't want to register Melanie's disappointment at seeing my dirty gloves. Exactly the reason why I wasn't wearing them. Because absolutely nobody in real life had the patience to clean their gloves to Melanie's specifications. Unless they were Melanie.

I lived on Tulane University's so-called fraternity row, my upstairs town-house apartment sandwiched between two fraternity houses, so I was prepared to dodge the street football being played as I made my way down the sidewalk. The days were shorter now, the rose-tinted dusk sky hovering over me as I walked, the growing dimness darkening the shadows between houses and behind unlit windows. Not for the first time, I was grateful that I had only five senses and couldn't see anything within the shadows. But just because I couldn't see anything didn't mean that nothing was there.

I climbed the steps to my apartment, enjoying the drifting scents of something spicy and pumpkin-y baking in the oven. Being greeted by fresh baked goods was just one of the perks of having the Southern version of Martha Stewart as my roommate. A version that sported flame red hair and had a skill set that included all things domestic as well as the ability to change a tire while wearing high heels, and had an accent as thick as the Delta mud from her home state of Mississippi.

Jolene McKenna was a force of nature whose turns of phrase could be simultaneously head-scratching and profound, and whose sweet nature hid a backbone of steel mixed with concrete. Jolene had been my roommate during my abbreviated tenure at Tulane, and when we'd run into each other in New Orleans seven years later, I had needed a roommate, and she'd needed an apartment. It had seemed serendipitous.

As soon as I opened the French door at the top of the stairwell and threw off my backpack, I was attacked by a small gray and white fur ball with two dark button eyes and a matching nose and a wildly waving plumed tail. He was wearing yet another fall-themed dog sweater courtesy of his favorite aunt, Jolene. Although Mardi was technically *my* rescue dog, Jolene had taken over all his accessorizing, something my stepmother, Melanie, could appreciate. I had drawn the line at monogramming, but little by little I'd noticed *MLT* (Mardi Lee Trenholm) appearing on bowls, bedding, and his dog-sized bathrobe.

At the tap-tap sound of approaching high heels, Mardi and I looked up to see Jolene. As usual, her hair and makeup were perfect, and she wore a *Wizard of Oz*–themed apron over a cocktail dress. At her look of disappointment, something clicked in the back of my mind. "Oh, no. Did I forget . . . ?"

"Yes. Tonight is the big welcome-home party for Sunny Ryan. I've been texting you for the last hour, but you didn't respond." Her eyes widened as they settled on my unruly hair, which had had only a glancing swipe from a brush earlier that morning before I'd left for work. "I'm not sure if we have enough time to make you presentable, but I've never been called a quitter."

She took Mardi from my arms. "Sorry—I was catching up on Beau's podcast and my battery died. Really, Jolene, there's no reason for me to get all gussied up." I used one of her words to placate her. "It's just a small gathering of family and close friends."

Jolene grabbed my wrist and began pulling me toward the bathroom. "I've already drawn your bath. It's grown cool, but that means you won't lollygag. And of course you should get gussied up. Beau will be there."

I blinked at her. My relationship with Beau Ryan was complicated. Which was a lot like saying the levee system in New Orleans might have a few flaws. I hadn't the energy or the time to hash it all out now. Instead, I said, "Well, Beau is Sunny's brother, so it would be strange if he wasn't. And I'm sure his girlfriend will be there, too. Besides, I haven't heard from Beau since Sunny showed up the night of Mardi's gotcha party. He's obviously moved on now that he doesn't need my help finding his sister."

Jolene stopped at the threshold of the bathroom and pulled off my baggy cardigan before gently pushing me inside. "For someone so smart, you sure can be ignorant. Now hop in the tub and do the best you can with that shampoo. You have exactly five minutes, and I'm timing you. Starting now." She tapped the screen of her smart watch before closing the door in my face.

One hour and fifteen minutes later, we were in Jolene's relic of a car—named Bubba by its owner—and headed down Broadway on our way to the Ryans' historic family home on Prytania in the Garden District. Mardi, wearing a celebratory yellow kerchief that matched his sweater, sat dutifully in his car seat in the back, the air from the vent blowing his fur from his face like in a shampoo commercial. The heater in the old car apparently had only two settings: off and full blast. I wanted to crack open my window to let in fresh air but was scolded by Jolene, who warned me that the three layers of Aqua Net she'd applied to my hair could go only so far.

A silver platter filled with Jolene's pumpkin nut muffins sat on my lap. Apparently, she had the hearing of a bat, because despite the volume of the heater and the rumbling of the tires passing over the ubiquitously uneven paving of New Orleans's streets, she heard me carefully lifting the plastic wrap to grab a pinch of one, and she slapped my hand.

"You're worse than Mardi," she scolded.

"I'm starving. I've been cutting bathroom floor tiles all afternoon. Thibaut is teaching me, and he's very patient, but it takes forever. I didn't want to take a food break and disappoint him."

Jolene swerved around a giant pothole in the middle of the road, causing me to grab the platter to keep it from sliding off my lap. "You do know that Thibaut works for you, right?"

"Yeah, that. I keep forgetting." Thibaut Kobylt was a master of all things construction related and led the two-man crew—including another jack-of-all-trades, Jorge—helping me restore my first home, a Creole cottage in the Marigny neighborhood. He was talented, smart, funny, and had the patience of Job. His only flaw was that he'd done time in jail for the manslaughter of his wife. I'd left out that little detail when telling my parents about Thibaut. There were some things they were probably better off not knowing.

Regardless, I was lucky to have Thibaut on my crew, which was a very small one, owing to the not-unfounded rumor that my house wasn't "right." Meaning it was haunted, possessed, or cursed. Or maybe just possessed or cursed, since it shouldn't still be haunted. With the help of a reluctant Beau Ryan, who still hadn't reconciled himself to the idea that he could communicate with ghosts, we had eradicated two spirits bound to the house—those of Beau's grandfather and his grandmother's best friend, Jeanne, who'd been murdered in the house in 1964 by her own father.

But in the weeks since, it had become clear even to me that things were still not right with the house. Judging from the fact that neighbors and most workmen continued to refuse to set foot inside, and from the regular delivery of gris-gris bags to my front porch, I wasn't the only person who thought so. Even when the house was empty, the atmosphere was like that of a suspended breath, the air thick with the sort of tension that precedes the whistling of a teakettle.

I had even thought I'd smelled a hint of pipe tobacco, the telltale sign that Beau's grandfather was nearby. But he couldn't be. Beau had sent him to the light. Maybe he just wanted to hang on for a little while longer to get to see Beau. Or maybe they didn't allow smoking in heaven. Any reason other than the nagging thought that Charles Ryan still had something to tell us.

"How long do you think we need to stay?"

Jolene sighed as she turned onto Prytania, rolling over the curb and jostling the platter on my lap. "Don't you want to get to know

Beau's long-lost sister and find out where she's been for the past couple of decades? I mean, the last time they saw her, she was just a baby. That's a lot to go over."

"I agree. And I'm interested in hearing her story. Yet from what she's already told us, all she knows is that she was adopted when she was a toddler and raised by a loving family in Edina, Minnesota. Curiosity about her birth parents brought her back to New Orleans."

"So what's bothering you?" Jolene asked.

"I didn't say something was bothering me."

"You didn't have to. You're snapping that rubber band on your wrist, which is something you've started doing when you've got something stewing inside your head."

I thought for a moment, trying to pinpoint exactly what was bothering me. "Don't you think it odd that Sunny showed up when she did? Right after we'd uncovered the truth about Antoine Broussard and his connection to her kidnapping?"

"But now that Sunny's shown up, none of that matters anymore," Jolene said as she slid into a driveway and flipped down the car's visor—bravely hanging on to the ceiling with duct tape and a prayer—and began reapplying her lipstick.

"Exactly," I said.

She carefully closed the visor, then turned her gaze to meet mine. "What are you saying?"

I shrugged, not really sure what I was saying. "I don't know. It just seems like such a . . . coincidence."

"And there's no such thing as coincidence," she said slowly, echoing the oft-repeated mantra of my father, Jack Trenholm. He was an international bestselling author of true-crime books, and it was something he'd discovered in his research and that had been proven time and time again.

Jolene shifted in her seat so that she faced me. "Sometimes, Nola, we are handed miracles disguised as coincidences. For over twenty years, Sunny had no idea that she had a family looking for her, and that family had no idea that she was even alive. Then suddenly, for reasons beyond our comprehension, all the stars aligned, and the pieces fell into place, and Sunny and her family are together again. I don't think it's fair for us to question it. I think all we need to do is rejoice in this miracle."

When I didn't respond, Jolene squeezed my hand where it rested on the seat. "I don't blame you for questioning it. It's your nature to question things. I'm sure you can't help but compare Sunny's story with your own and how you had no one looking for you after your mama died. But that was only because they didn't know you existed." She squeezed my hand again, then sat back in her seat. "But now you are loved to pieces by your family and friends, and that's the most important thing. Even if that little green face of jealousy pops up every once in a while, you can just whack it on the head with the full knowledge that you are deeply loved and cherished."

"You're right," I said, my eyes open but seeing nothing except my thirteen-year-old self on a cross-country bus from California to South Carolina, with all my hopes and fears confined to a single piece of paper crumpled in my pocket, on which my mother had scribbled the name of the father I had never met.

"And I know you don't want to talk about it, but I think your heart is still hurting because of Michael. He's a weasel and he betrayed your trust, and it takes the heart a lot longer than the brain to get over that kind of hurt. Just thank your stars that it was short-lived and you didn't have to eat the whole egg to know it was rotten." She gave me a sympathetic smile to soften her words. "I think that might be the reason why you can't feel the kind of happy you should at Sunny's reunion with her family."

The mention of Michael Hebert shook me out of my reverie. I widened my eyes, finally registering where Jolene had parked the car. "Where are we? This isn't the Ryans' house."

"I know that. I just didn't want anyone seeing me fixing my makeup."

By "anyone," I knew she meant Jaxson Landry, a local lawyer and the object of her unrequited love. He was dating her friend Carly. She had told me that Jaxson had bought a ring for Carly, and I didn't want to rub salt in the wound. Pressing hard on the pedal, Jolene backed out of the driveway, oblivious to the blaring horn of an oncoming car.

"Maybe I need to stop looking at everything like a crime novel and just be happy for Beau and his family," I said.

"I think that's a very good plan. Besides, Sunny looks like Beau and is cute as a button. Except for the blond hair. It's completely the wrong shade."

"What do you mean? You think she highlights it?"

Jolene pulled up onto the curb behind a line of cars parked in front of the Ryans' Italianate house. With an aggrieved sigh, she put the car in park. "Nola, I thank my lucky stars that we found each other again. There is so much I need to teach you. Sunny, despite her name, is no more a natural blonde than Dolly Parton is. And I adore Dolly, so you know that I'm not throwing shade on anyone's character."

"Of course not. And dyeing your hair isn't a crime."

"Although in some cases it should be. From the pictures we've seen, Sunny was blond as a little girl and it just darkened over time. It happens a lot—both ways. My second cousin twice removed on my mama's side was born with a whole head of jet-black hair, and let me tell you that all that tongue wagging almost did that poor baby's mama in. Luckily, it all fell out when she was two—or maybe it was three—but it all grew back just as blond as can be. We think it's because her granddaddy was part I-talian. . . ."

I made a big show of unbuckling my seat belt and gathering my backpack, eager to distract Jolene before she gave me another lesson about her family tree. Jolene pushed open her door with a soft grunt before walking around the car to open my door. She took the platter of muffins. "I think these will be safer with me until we get them inside. You can bring Mardi."

Mardi pulled at his leash as we headed toward the gate with the hourglass in the middle. It was a nod to the Ryans' antiques shop, called the Past Is Never Past, on Royal Street in the Quarter. I held the gate open for Jolene, doing my best to restrain Mardi on his leash.

I wasn't sure whether he was excited about the muffins or because he loved visiting Beau's grandmother. They had bonded at his gotcha party, and Mimi Ryan had included Mardi's name on the invitation to Sunny's welcome-home party. I just hoped no food would be left on low tables, because Mardi's name should have been Hoover.

Despite Mardi's hard tugging on the leash, I slowed my walk, never tired of seeing the glorious architecture of what I thought was one of the prettiest houses in a neighborhood famed for its beautiful houses. As we approached the marble steps and arched colonnade of the front porch, the massive wooden double doors opened and Christopher Benoit, a longtime Ryan family friend and employee, stood in the entranceway with a welcoming smile.

I'd started to greet him when Mardi gave one more tug, pulling the leash from my hand. He raced around Jolene and up the steps. After briefly and enthusiastically greeting Christopher, he ran behind him into the foyer. I hurried to catch up, expecting to hear the sounds of crashing china and crystal, but by the time I'd reached the foyer, all I could hear were Mardi's soft whimpers of pleasure coming from the front parlor. I stopped abruptly on the threshold, taking in the small gathering of familiar faces, along with a few new ones, and Sunny Ryan sitting between Mimi and Beau on the sofa while my dog—previously known as my fierce protector—rested his head on Sunny's chest, licking the bottom of her pixie-like chin while staring up at her adoringly.

"See?" Jolene whispered in my ear. "Would Mardi steer us wrong?"

I recalled how Mardi had never liked Michael and would greet him with bared fangs. Granted, fangs that resembled tiny pillows, but the intent had been clear. My shoulders relaxed as I looked at the glowing, happy people assembled in the Ryans' parlor. The scene reminded me of my last birthday party in Charleston, where I'd been surrounded by the family and friends who loved me unconditionally. Even with the lopsided and barely edible cake that Melanie had made for me with her own hands, I'd felt cherished—the same emotion I recognized on the pink and now slightly wet face of Sunny Ryan as my traitorous dog continued to bathe her with affection.

I had the sudden feeling someone was watching me. Slowly, I turned to find I was in the direct line of sight of the large portrait of Dr. Charles Ryan hanging in the foyer, the end of his pipe sticking out from his jacket pocket. The light and shadows of the painting made the eyes appear to follow me. When I turned back toward the roomful of people, my attention was drawn to two small puddles of water in the distinctive shape of a woman's feet in front of Beau.

Jerking my gaze away, I looked up to discover Sam, Beau's girlfriend and podcast partner, looking at me, a curious expression on her face. She motioned for me to stay where I was, as if she had the intention of speaking with me. I wasn't sure what it was she wanted to say to me, but I was fairly certain it had something to do with Beau. I pretended I hadn't seen her and I stepped backward into the small crowd, hoping to disappear long enough to call an Uber and leave. I still hadn't emotionally recovered from the whole Michael fiasco, and I was in no mood for more drama.

I had made it into the dining room, where the table sat covered with all kinds of food on platters and in bowls, including Jolene's muffins. She'd already dusted them with powdered sugar from the little dispenser she'd brought in her purse (because Jolene). I'd hit the Confirm button on my Uber app when I heard Sam call my name.

I gave a quick wave in her direction as I headed toward the door. "My Uber's here—I've got to go."

Jolene sent me a questioning look, and I held my hand up to my head like an old-fashioned telephone—something I'd seen Melanie do frequently—to let her know I'd call later.

Sam followed me out the door, then stopped on the porch as I jogged down the path toward the gate, silently hoping that the approaching car actually was my Uber.

"We need to talk," she shouted as I clanged the gate shut behind me. "I'll text you."

I gave a thumbs-up as I opened the car door, pretty sure that Sam didn't have my number. I paused to verify that I was in the correct Uber, then slid inside. I wasn't sure if Sam wanted to talk about the footprints or Beau—or both. I wasn't interested in discussing either topic with anyone, especially Sam, for reasons I couldn't explain even to myself.

I shut the car door without glancing back, feeling her gaze on me long after I lost sight of the house on Prytania.

CHAPTER 2

I stood under an awning near the corner of Canal and Royal in a misty drizzle, watching my young friend Trevor riding my bike toward me. For a small fee, the twelve-year-old entrepreneur guarded my bike each night so I didn't have to ride it all the way uptown after a long day. In the mornings I worked at my office on Poydras as an architectural historian for a civil engineering firm, then in the afternoon shifted to the renovations at my new house, leaving just enough energy to bike to the streetcar stop and hand over my bicycle to Trevor.

He had sold me the bike, the basket, and several other essential items—including a Super Soaker to deter the more aggressive flying cockroaches—for what were clearly inflated prices for used items. Trevor insisted I was paying a convenience fee for having him source the products and hand deliver them, and I couldn't say that he was wrong.

"Hi, Miss Nola. Sorry I'm late. Meemaw forgot to make my lunch last night, so I tried to make it myself. 'Cept we didn't have no bread, and it made me late for school. I didn't have time to get your bike out of my hiding place before school, so I had to get it after."

"So you didn't have anything for lunch?"

"No, ma'am. But my best friend, Gary, always has somethin' for me. His mama likes me and says I'm too skinny, so she packs extra."

After digging into my back pocket and pulling out a five, I handed it to him. "Use this to buy a hot lunch the next time that happens, all right? For emergency purposes, and only for food, and get an extra dessert for Gary. Do not use it to buy anything you plan to resell, all right?"

"Yes, ma'am," he said, eagerly taking the bill and shoving it into his pocket. As with every interaction with Trevor, I chose to trust him. His charm and smile always overcame any second thoughts.

"I've got something for you from Miss Jolene." I slid off my backpack before pulling out an oddly shaped yet beautifully wrapped gift complete with an extravagant bow.

He reached for it, but I held it back before carefully placing it on the ground. "All you have to do is peel off that small strip of tape at the top and it will unwrap itself."

With cheeks puffed out with anticipation, Trevor carefully removed the tape. The paper fell away like a flower blooming, leaving a decoupaged clay pot at the center. I was pretty sure Jolene had both spun the pot and decorated it herself, but I hadn't asked because I didn't want to hate her. Trevor lifted the pot and studied it, not quite sure what to say.

"It's for your home computer fund," I explained. "I figured all the money you earn from working at the antiques store and from your side business can be put in here. Christopher said he'd be happy to keep it locked up at the shop to keep it safe."

Trevor nodded to show that he'd heard me, but his eyes were fixated on the pot. "Why's it got a rainbow?"

"Because at the end of every rainbow is a pot of gold. Jolene loves rainbows because of the song 'Over the Rainbow' in her favorite movie, *The Wizard of Oz*."

He squinted at me with his dark brown eyes, not understanding.

"You know—Dorothy and the Tin Man, Scarecrow and Lion?"

"Huh?"

I blinked a couple of times, wondering if he might be kidding, because, to my knowledge, I'd never met anyone who wasn't familiar with the movie or the books. I squatted down to get a better look in his face. He was small for his age, and I got down to his level only when it was for something important.

"Trevor, do you mean to say you've never seen *The Wizard of Oz* or read the books?"

He shook his head. "No, ma'am."

"No flying monkeys or the Wicked Witch of the West?"

He narrowed his eyes again, but this time to clearly show that he doubted my sanity.

I stood. "Well, we're going to fix that right up. Now that you have a library card, you can check out *The Wonderful Wizard of Oz* by Frank Baum. Just ask the librarian."

"Can't I just watch the movie?"

"Sure. But only after you read the first book—there are fourteen in the series. Everybody knows the book is always better than the movie. Besides, reading makes you smarter."

"Huh," he grunted, clearly not convinced.

"Guess what Jolene's favorite book in the whole world is."

His eyes brightened, and I knew I had him. Ever since he'd met Jolene and had become the recipient of her baked goodies, he'd been a devoted admirer. He wasn't alone in that regard, since she seemed to have that effect on everyone. Everyone except Jaxson Landry.

"*The Avengers*!"

At my look, he burst out in his contagious laugh. "I'm just punkin' you, Miss Nola."

"Yeah, well, Jolene would be very impressed if you read the first book in the series. I bet—with your meemaw's permission—we could have you over to our apartment to watch the movie after you read the book. Jolene makes the best popcorn."

A frown appeared and he focused his gaze on the pavement at his feet. "Don't know about that."

"I hope you're not thinking that the book will be too hard. Christopher or I would be happy to help if you get stuck."

He looked up with an expression I couldn't read, but it quickly faded before I could overthink it. He tucked the pot under his arm while I folded up the paper and placed it carefully inside. "I gotta go—Christopher's waiting for me. I'm supposed to be at the shop now to sweep the back room."

"Don't let me keep you. He says he doesn't know how he did it all without you."

His small chest expanded like that of a robin preparing to sing. "My meemaw taught me how to clean right. Between you and me, Miss Nola, some of them corners at the shop hadn't seen a broom or rag since Jesus was a baby."

I hid my smile. "Well, then, you'd better hurry."

He didn't budge. "You owe me a dollar."

"A dollar? What for?"

"'Cause I brought you your bike in the rain. It's an extra fee."

"I don't remember ever paying that before."

"It's a new policy." He grinned so big that I could see the pink of his gums. "You told me to look for ways to earn money so I can buy myself my own computer."

I fished a dollar bill out of my pocket and handed it to him. "I've created a monster."

"Yes, ma'am," he said. His grin never dimmed as he said good-bye and began jogging toward the Past Is Never Past, carefully cradling the pot against his chest.

In the upstairs bathroom of my Creole cottage I sat up on my padded knees and rubbed my back. I'd been painstakingly applying thin-set mortar to the membrane I'd helped Thibaut install the previous day, and I had lost track of time while placing black and white octagonal floor tiles in a design I'd found in *Preservation Resource* magazine.

I had appreciated Thibaut's agreeing that laying individual tiles was a lot more time-consuming and difficult than laying sheets of tile but way worth it in the long run. Which was always the way with historic restorations. My back and knees currently disagreed, and my mind was beginning to concur with my body when I looked up to realize that I had backed myself into a corner. My only way out was to step on the newly laid tiles with their even rows of meticulously placed spacers, which would erase all my hard work.

I groaned out loud when I spotted my phone lying out of reach on the other side of the doorway, where I'd placed it because it kept falling out of my back pocket when I leaned over. Melanie had sent me a lanyard designed to hang a phone around a person's neck. She'd sworn by it, saying she didn't lose her phone in the house anymore. I'd laughed at it as something only old people would need and shoved it into the back of a drawer. Someone was laughing now, but it definitely wasn't me.

Thibaut and Jorge had long since left, their misplaced confidence that I could get this one job done before they returned in the morning sitting like sour milk in my stomach. I stood in my small untiled corner, wary of the waning of the light as I counted how many rows I needed to leap over. And how many rows I would likely destroy and have to replace before tomorrow morning.

The sound of a vehicle pulling up outside and then the slam of a door gave me hope. Maybe Thibaut or Jorge had forgotten something and had returned to the house. Holding my breath, I listened to footsteps climbing the porch while my nostrils flared at the unmistakable scent of pipe tobacco. A loud knock sounded on the front door, and my surprise expelled air from my lungs in a deep cough.

"Nola? Are you still here?"

I recognized Beau's voice and felt relieved and horrified at the same time. I was glad to be rescued but would have preferred it be by anyone but him. We had a long history of me being the unwilling rescuee while Beau Ryan swooped in to play my unwanted hero. Melanie and Jolene kept telling me that I needed to reanalyze my feelings on the subject, but that would be like blowing into a hurricane to change the direction of the wind. I'd come by my stubbornness honestly, and I wasn't likely to change anytime soon.

My phone, its ringer silenced, vibrated on the floor. I found it easier to concentrate when I wasn't being interrupted by calls and texts. Although I was beginning to think that if I had been interrupted, I might have noticed my error sooner.

"I'm upstairs," I shouted. "If that's you calling, I can't answer my phone right now. But if you could come up, I'd appreciate it."

"Why are you shouting?" Beau's head appeared in the doorway.

I started at the sound of his voice, causing me to drop my trowel into the bucket of thin-set with a soft *plop.* I pressed my hand against my pounding chest. "Because I thought you were downstairs."

"I was, but now I'm here." He grinned as he eyed my predicament. "You know, Nola, it's usually recommended that when you're putting down any kind of flooring, you should start on the far end and work your way toward the door so you don't get trapped in a corner."

"Gee, thanks for that clever observation. It would have been more appreciated four hours ago, when I started."

"I bet," he said, nodding sagely. "What are you going to do now?"

"Oh, I don't know. Learn how to sleep standing up, I guess."

The smell of tobacco was even stronger now, the scent concentrated around Beau. "Do you smell that?"

"Yes," he admitted, showing how far he'd come in accepting his psychic abilities. He might not be shouting from the rooftops his aptitude for communicating with ghosts now, and he was still debunking fraudulent psychics on his podcast, *Bumps in the Night and Other Improbabilities*, but acknowledging it to me was a huge step forward.

As if reading my mind, Beau said, "Let's discuss my grandfather's pipe smoke later. I figure we have more pressing issues." He indicated where I stood, in my little corner. "Have you come up with any ideas?"

"Yeah, but none that wouldn't involve ruining at least two rows of tiles. Probably more if I fell backward after I leapt. Which I'm prepared to do without your help."

He crossed his arms. "Sure. And I'm happy to watch. And I'll even hold a flashlight while you pull up the crooked tiles and replace them before the mortar dries. Or," he said with a wide grin, "you could leap toward me and I'll work with your momentum and pull you forward. I bet you could clear all of the tiles and go home at a reasonable hour."

I wanted to refuse, just for principle's sake, but my stomach was already grumbling and my eyes could barely focus from the strain of the exacting work of getting the rows of tiles perfectly straight.

I sighed loudly. "All right. You win."

His grin faded. "It's not about winning or losing, Nola. It's about accepting an offer of help. Without any expectations of payment or me thinking less of you because you needed help." He held out his hands, palms up. "Come on. Take one huge leap toward me and I'll grab you. And I promise not to tell anyone."

I wanted to roll my eyes, but I was too grateful to show any attitude that might make him rescind his offer. "Fine." Without warning, I sprang forward in an awkward version of a grand jeté that I'd once watched my little sister do in a ballet recital. From my gawky movements it was clear that I'd never taken a single ballet lesson, but the aim of my front leg and the forward propulsion were all I needed to clear the tiles. And collide into a surprised Beau, who plunged backward, breaking my fall as we landed together with an inelegant thud on the hard cypress floor.

We both lay there in stunned silence, catching our breath and checking to see if we still had sensation in all parts of our bodies. I soon became aware of the solid feel of him beneath me, and of the warmth of his arms, which had found their way around me. It was all too familiar, reminding me of the night he'd been sick and had slept on the couch in my Uptown apartment and had sleepwalked, alert enough to have a phone conversation with his dead mother and then kiss me. Both events that we had studiously avoided mentioning since.

I rolled away, his arms seemingly reluctant to let me go. I jumped up and brushed off my jeans even though the only thing they'd touched was Beau. He was looking up at me with a slightly stunned expression, but I knew better than to offer my hand and touch him again.

"Sorry," I said, handing him the bottle of water that I'd left with my phone. "I thought you were ready. Are you all right?"

He pulled himself up and stood, rubbing the back of his head with his free hand. "I don't think I damaged the floor, if that's what you're worried about."

"Funny. Seriously, you could have a concussion. Are you dizzy? Feeling sleepy?" I recalled when Melanie had been pushed down a flight of stairs by an unhappy spirit and the doctor had forced her to stay on bed rest, but not before he'd made her stay awake for a period of time just to make sure she hadn't suffered any brain damage. I picked up my phone, noticing that I had five unread texts, and turned on the flashlight. Standing on tiptoe to shine it in his eyes, I said, "Let me see your pupils." I had no idea what I was looking for, but it seemed like something I should be doing.

He gently pushed my hand away, a grin forming in the corner of his mouth. "I'm sure they're still there. I'm fine—I promise. I'll probably have a nice knot on my head tomorrow, but that just means I'll think of you stuck in the corner of your bathroom every time I comb my hair."

I snatched the water from his hand. "I hope it gives you a headache each time." I turned and walked out to the landing and began making my way down the stairs. "I trust you didn't drop by to give me another driving lesson. I'm way too tired and annoyed right now."

Since having a disastrous accident with lots of repercussions while still a student driver, I'd been determined to give up driving forever. Until my new job in New Orleans required me to get to places that were too far on foot or by bike, and too expensive to hire a rideshare. Beau had taken it upon himself to teach me, an effort that could only be called heroic—but not by me. His reassuring words had been that New Orleans wouldn't even notice one more bad driver. And if I got a truck or a big enough car, like Jolene's, it wouldn't matter who was the worst as long as I was the biggest.

"No, actually. About other things. You left Sunny's party pretty early, so I didn't get the chance to talk with you."

I stopped at the bottom of the stairs and glanced down at my phone in an attempt to buy time as I searched for a response. I was surprised to find that one of my texts was from Sam.

Meet 4 breakfast tomorrow? We should talk. Horns 7:30?

My thumbs hesitated for a moment as I wondered how she'd gotten my number. My phone vibrated as I held it.

Jolene gave me ur number.

"Great," I said under my breath, my thumbs flying over my screen as I replied. I said yes because I had a strong feeling that she would keep asking until I did. It wasn't that I didn't like Sam. I didn't know her well, but what I did know, I liked. We might even have been good friends if it weren't for the fact that she was dating Beau. And it wasn't as if I wanted to date Beau, either. It was just . . . well, I wasn't sure. I knew only that Beau and I weren't a good fit because of reasons I preferred not to analyze. It could be because I didn't like being beholden to anybody. Or maybe it was because of what I'd overheard him telling his dead mother over the phone. *I want her too much. She's dangerous. I can't afford to lose my focus. I can't ever let that happen again.*

Its important

"Is there a problem?" Beau said, indicating my phone.

I shook my head, then placed my phone in my back pocket. "No problem. Just . . . stuff."

The pungent scent of pipe tobacco drifted past us, too heavy to ignore.

"We need to talk," Beau said.

For someone who was attempting not to cause any drama while she focused on her new job and restored her Creole cottage, I had a lot of people who seemed eager to talk to me. "Okay," I said slowly.

"Mimi wanted me to invite you and Jolene to dinner on Friday night to really meet Sunny. We figured you'd have questions. And we thought you might want to know each other better, considering we'll all be working together at some point."

"Sure. Just let me know the time and I'll tell Jolene. Is that all?" A soft exhale came from behind me, enveloping us in a veil of pipe smoke.

His gaze drifted over my head before returning to my face. "Not quite. There are a couple more things we need to discuss."

Knowing I didn't really have a choice, and because I had no plans for the rest of the evening, I opened the front door to the only spot in the house containing chairs. As I stepped onto the porch, I heard two sets of footsteps following me outside into the cool, crisp air.

CHAPTER 3

I settled myself into one of the two worn lawn chairs I'd found beneath the overgrown foliage in the backyard. It creaked in protest when I sat, and I wondered how much longer it would last before someone fell through the frayed plastic onto the floorboards.

Beau carefully sat in the other chair, gingerly sliding back as if testing his weight. "You should probably go ahead and get porch furniture now. These chairs are gasping their last."

I met his gaze, wondering if he was aware that he'd read my mind. Again. It was like our brain waves were always moving in tandem, sometimes separating around rocks in their path, then meeting up again. Looking away, I said, "Yeah, well, I guess I got what I paid for." I wiggled back and forth, making the chair squeak like hungry mice. "Jolene is already shopping around for vendors who are willing to give us a huge discount in return for being featured on our Insta and YouTube pages. She's got over two hundred thousand followers already, so she's got a lot of clout."

Beau nodded. "I'm not sure if they tune in to see Thibaut and Jorge's acrobatic and juggling acts or just to hear what comes out of

Jolene's mouth next, but the combination is gold in terms of free promo."

The deal I'd worked out with Beau's company, JR Properties, was that he would act as my licensed contractor for my home restoration project in return for publicity. We'd hit the jackpot by putting Jolene, who already worked for Beau, in charge of the company's social media. As a bonus for Jolene, Jaxson was acting as our photographer and videographer. It was a hobby for him, and he and Beau were childhood friends, so it made sense. Especially because it was easy on the budget, since he was doing it for free, and because nobody else could be hired to come to the house for any amount of money.

I was beginning to take the rejection of my house by just about everybody very personally. I'd even had a loud argument with my UPS deliveryman, who never came to a complete stop but rather rolled the boxes out of his truck to land on the walkway in front of my house. No matter how many times I chased him down the street yelling for him to stop, he always pretended he couldn't hear me.

"How did you know I was here?" I wasn't sure why I was avoiding whatever Beau wanted to talk to me about, but experience had taught me that when someone warned you that a talk was coming instead of just telling you outright, it wasn't going to be good.

"When my calls went straight to voice mail and you didn't answer my texts, I called Jolene, and she told me you were still here. So I drove by and saw your bike on the porch. It's not locked, by the way." He leaned forward to get a better look at it. "Maybe because you decided it's too ugly to steal."

I watched him closely, wondering if he'd added that last bit so I wouldn't ask if he'd been worried about me. "Very funny. I think the cute flowered basket on the front makes it almost couture. And despite appearances, the bike is completely functional. Trevor keeps it in tip-top condition. Besides, Thibaut, Jorge, and I have figured out that anything that's been left on the porch is off-limits to thieves.

Maybe the good gris-gris bags someone keeps leaving on the porch actually work."

A coil of tobacco-scented smoke drifted around us before quickly dissipating. Beau didn't pluck at the rubber band on his arm, which he did to fight his fear—something he'd taught me when he'd given me my own rubber band.

"You're not afraid?" I asked softly.

He shook his head. "It's my grandfather. I'm not afraid of him."

"But why is he back?"

Beau took in a deep breath, then exhaled slowly. "It's one of the things I wanted to talk with you about."

I shivered in my shirtsleeves. I'd been warm enough upstairs while I worked, but the evening had turned chilly, and I'd left my sweater inside. It was a cute pink and white Lilly Pulitzer cardigan that Melanie had sent to me in an attempt to elevate my look (Jolene's words). She'd bought a matching one for Sarah, which had made me roll my eyes. At least she hadn't bought ones for our dogs, Porgy and Bess, too—as far as I knew. It wouldn't have surprised me if she had.

Beau slid off his jacket and held it out to me. "I don't need it. I'm hot natured."

I shivered again, recalling why I didn't need him to remind me. An uncomfortable silence fell as we both became aware that he'd broken our unspoken agreement that we never mention again the night he'd spent on my sofa.

Leaning back, I said, "So, spill it."

He thrummed his fingers on his jean-clad thighs. "Michael Hebert."

Anger pulsed through me at the mention of his name. He'd feigned a romantic interest in me to gain access to the Ryans and the secrets his family suspected were hidden in my Creole cottage. Secrets that would reveal Michael's great-grandfather's guilt in the murder of Michael's grandaunt, Jeanne Broussard, which was also connected to Sunny's disappearance. It would have been easier to forgive Michael for being unwilling to resist the pressure from his powerful family if only I hadn't fallen so completely for him. I still felt the bruise around my heart every time I thought about him.

I looked at Beau, hoping to see a grin to show me he was joking. But even in the dim light, I could see the firm set of his jaw and the straight line of his mouth.

"Seriously, Beau? I thought I made it clear that door is closed. Permanently. I still can't even believe that you asked me to rekindle my relationship with Michael for some misguided sense of revenge. But there's no reason for us to even have anything to do with Michael or his extended family. Sunny found us, so there's no more need for me to do the one thing I told you I wouldn't do. I understand your desperation, but I don't think I can forgive you."

His fingers stopped tapping. "Yes, well, I'm not asking you for forgiveness."

I froze, afraid of what he would say next. Almost unaware, I began snapping the band around my wrist. He reached over and pressed his hand against mine, stilling the movement.

"I'm sorry."

His words didn't alleviate my fear and doubt. Because it was abundantly clear that he wasn't done.

"Sorry for asking me in the first place, or sorry because you're about to ask me again?"

"Both." He looked at me without moving, the only sound that of the wind chime singing out in the tranquil night. Even the ever-present Christmas trees, now decked out in full Halloween regalia in their coffin planters in the yard across the street, remained still. Their orange twinkling lights highlighted the plastic ghosts and flying witches on broomsticks with a firelike glow.

"You can't possibly think . . ."

"I know. And I've been trying to work out in my head if there might be a better way. But the bottom line is there isn't."

"But Sunny is back. We know Michael's great-grandfather was responsible for her kidnapping, even though we can't prove anything because all the evidence we have is contained within a door now floating in a swamp. And it can only be revealed by someone like Mimi, with psychometric abilities. Which, I can only imagine, is worthless in a court of law."

"You're right," he agreed, surprising me.

"Then why are you asking me to reach into my heart and rip it out again? Are you trying to drive me back to drinking?" Beau was one of the few people who knew about my inner demons and my ongoing struggle to keep them at bay. I was sober now, for good. I hoped.

"I understand. I do. And I won't force you into saying yes."

"But what would I be saying yes to? As much as I loathe Michael, what he did isn't a punishable offense."

Beau leaned forward, clasping his hands between his knees. "No, it's not, although it probably should be. But what his family has gotten away with for years definitely is. Including driving my grandfather into an early grave and making my grandmother and me suffer for over two decades wondering what happened to Sunny." He drew a deep breath. "I want to bring them down."

"With what?" I wasn't following his line of thought. "There's no real evidence of wrongdoing. And the family still wields enough power to discourage even retired cops like Jaxson's uncle Bernie from participating in any dirt digging. He told us that himself."

Beau faced me, his pupils reflecting the orange lights. "I think there is real evidence. There's a reason why my dad stored the Maison Blanche door here instead of destroying it. Probably the same reason he saved Jeanne's clientele book and the other items in the hatbox hidden behind a sealed closet door."

I thought about the tie clasp and pipe that had belonged to his grandfather, as well as the photograph negative and yellow hair ribbon that could have been used as evidence if the case had ever made it to court. But it hadn't. Hurricane Katrina and the years since had intervened, and the case had been conveniently closed.

The faint scent of pipe smoke once again flitted through the air, my skin responding with goose bumps rippling down my arms beneath Beau's coat. "Your grandfather isn't alone."

"I know." He studied his clasped hands before turning his attention back to me.

"I'm pretty sure it's your mother," I added quietly.

He nodded slowly. "Yeah. I've seen her footprints. I thought they would both go once we found Sunny."

"Me, too. You should ask her why she's still here."

Beau sat up in his chair, the metal frame groaning in protest. "No. I can't. I'm still so . . . angry with her. For leaving me."

I knew that wasn't the whole story. I'd heard too much of his conversation on a disconnected landline phone with Adele, his mother, who was presumed dead during Katrina. Either he didn't remember asking her for help or he didn't want me to know he had. *Can you help me find her? I know she's alive, or she'd have told me. I've been searching for so long and I can't do this on my own.* And then his response to her unheard question. *Not her. I want her too much.* I'd known he was talking about me.

I wanted to take his hand, to let him know I understood. I had been angry at my own mother for a long time after her death following a short life full of bad choices. I kept my hands in my lap, not wanting to complicate our already complicated relationship. But I'd learned a few things from my therapist and the never-ending road to recovery.

"Forgiveness doesn't mean forgetting, Beau. Loving someone and being angry with them at the same time is actually a thing. Maybe your mom is still here because she needs to know that you've forgiven her."

I heard the sound of him swallowing, then waited for him to speak. "It's more than that. And I think there's something else, too. I think it's the same reason why my grandfather is still here."

I took a deep breath, needing to voice the one thought that hadn't left me alone since I'd first smelled the pipe tobacco long after I thought Beau had sent the restless spirits in my house into the light. "Maybe they're still here to make sure you don't do anything stupid. Like poking a stick in the lion's cage."

He exhaled, a small puff of air rising from his mouth. "Or maybe he's here to protect me while I expose the truth and see that someone is punished. Antoine Broussard got away with murdering his own daughter while incriminating my grandfather for the crime. And his family is still benefiting from his evil deeds from decades ago. I want justice. Accountability. Even now, the family business, the Sabatier Group, goes against everything you and I believe in. Tearing down older buildings to replace them with cheaply built, less sustainable structures. Why should they be allowed to have any say in the rebuilding of the vernacular architecture of New Orleans when they've been sucking this city dry of everything of value for generations? Their greed is why they're where they are now, and it seems I'm the last man standing who can bring them down."

"That's admirable, Beau. Really. But the Sabatier Group is huge, and the family behind it is very powerful in ways Uncle Bernie is afraid to tell us. You can't do it alone."

He paused. Took a deep breath. "I know. I wasn't planning on it."

I studied him with growing incredulity. "You're serious, aren't you?"

"I realize this is a big ask. . . ."

"A big ask? That's like calling Katrina a little storm. I never want to see Michael again." I paused, needing to redirect the conversation before I lost my self-control. Forcing a smile, I said, "Not to mention that if something happened to you, I'd have to find another general contractor to manage my renovation, and that could slow me down a bit. A good contractor is hard to find."

He didn't smile. "Have you ever wondered about Michael's parents? I've been doing a lot of research on the Broussard-Hebert-Sabatier family connections. Michael's father, Marco, is Antoine's grandson and worked for Antoine for a number of years. And then, suddenly, he and his wife decide to become missionaries and pack up to go live on the other side of the world. They left their children in the care of Marco's sister, Angelina, and her husband, Robert Sabatier. This same arrangement stipulated that Michael and his sister, Felicity, be educated up north. Both were sent to boarding school, and Felicity decided to stay. I know I'm not the only one to find that not only weird but also highly suspicious."

"Sure, that's strange, but not inconceivable. A lot of kids go to boarding school away from home."

Beau's gaze held mine. "That's not the part that confuses me. It's the fact that Michael's parents apparently suddenly found God and decided to devote their lives to saving souls on the other side of the world, leaving their children behind. There is nothing that I have found in any of my research that hints at anything more religious about Marco and his wife, Theresa, than dutifully bringing their children each week to Sunday mass at Holy Name. That's it. And then boom, they're off. There's a story here, just waiting for someone to crack it open and expose all of their dark secrets."

A cold chill swept over me, raising the hair on my scalp. "Don't do this, Beau. Please. You have Sunny back. Can't you just leave it at that? No good can come of you dredging up the past."

"I'm not so sure." He turned away from me and stared across the street at the festive trees in their odd coffin planters, each washed with pinpoints of orange lights. "Could you at least think about it?"

"I already gave you my answer—"

"Just think about it, okay?" he said, cutting me off. He stood, holding out his hand to help me up.

I hesitated before slipping my hand into his, preparing myself for the jolt of warmth and that unnamed spark that I refused to identify. I dropped his hand as soon as I could.

Beau's face remained serious as he spoke. "You've had a long day. I'll help you lock up, and then drive you home."

"I've got my bike. I've already texted Trevor to let him know I'd be late for the drop-off."

"It's dark, Nola. And the flashlight duct-taped to your handlebars will only give drivers something to aim for when you attempt to cross Esplanade."

Too tired to argue, I let him help me lock up and load my bike into the back of his truck. I kept Beau's jacket around me the entire drive, shivering despite the heat blasting from the dash vents, aware of the glow of a pipe from my front porch and a pair of unseen eyes following us until we turned the corner out of sight.

CHAPTER 4

Jolene chased after me as I attempted to leave the apartment the following day.

"If you'd just hold your horses, I can do a nice French braid. . . ."

I turned around, blocking her brush-wielding arm with my own, like we were two fencers getting ready to face off. "Stop it—I'm going to be late. And I'm just going to meet Sam. Beau won't be there."

"Lorda mercy, Nola. I did not just hear you say that. We don't make ourselves look good for men. We do it as a form of self-respect. When we know we're put together, it shows off our most intelligent and confident selves. It's about winning friends and influencing people, and you can't do that looking like something swept up on the curb by the street cleaner. Besides, it's always better to arrive late than ugly."

I stared at her blankly.

"That's an expression, Nola. You couldn't be ugly if you tried. And you do seem to try quite a bit with some of your outfits, but we don't have time for that now." She held up her brush again and I turned, resigning myself to her ministrations.

"So, what does Sam want to discuss with you?" she asked, pulling my hair back so tightly it made my eyes water.

"I have no idea. She couldn't have a bone to pick with me. My relationship with Beau has been strictly platonic." Except once, but that wasn't something I was going to share.

At the word "bone," Mardi lifted his head from the sofa pillow that Jolene had embroidered with his name and a cute paw motif.

"Strictly platonic," Jolene repeated in her slow Southern drawl.

"Exactly. Just like your relationship with Jaxson."

She gave an extra-hard tug on my hair. "Sorry. Your hair needs extra taming today."

I tried to turn to face her, but she kept such a firm grip on my braid that I was afraid of scalping myself if I moved. "I'm sorry. I didn't mean to say that."

"You shouldn't apologize for pointing out the truth. I deserved that. And I'd much rather hear it from a friend than anyone else."

Jolene relaxed her hold on my hair, and I breathed a sigh of relief that my eyes had stopped watering. When she was done, she grabbed my shoulders and spun me around. "Much better, but there's still something missing." She regarded me critically. "Where are your pearls?"

"Seriously? I'm wearing jeans and a sweater. I don't think . . ."

"Perfect," she said, unclasping her own set from around her neck before settling it on mine. "All you need now is a bit of color. . . ." Jolene reached into her pocket to pull out her ever-present tube of lipstick.

At that, I stepped away from her, grabbing the worn and grubby backpack that had seen me through a lot of things. "I have to go. I'll see you later."

"Hang on—I have something for you!"

I hoped it wasn't another big Barbie head. Or another monogrammed anything. My room and closet already looked as if a monogram machine had run amok, spewing my initials like beads from a Mardi Gras float. Jolene ran to the kitchen and emerged with a gift bag exploding with metallic tissue paper and extravagantly tied bows. I knew better than to ask if she'd done them herself.

Jolene handed it to me with a bright smile, keeping her hand on the bottom. "Careful—it might spill. I wanted to make sure it was good and hot before I gave it to you."

Curious now, I moved the bow-festooned handles aside and parted the paper to reveal the top of a travel coffee cup. I carefully pulled it out, then read what had been printed on the front and smiled.

CALIFORNIAN BY BIRTH, SOUTHERN BY CHOICE.

"I thought when you learned to drive, you'd want something to put in the cup holder of your car. But for now, you can take it on the streetcar on your way to work." Beaming, she added, "And I already spoke to Trevor about finding a cup holder to attach to the handlebar on your bike. He said he didn't think it would be safe, but I assured him you wouldn't take a sip unless you were at a full stop. And that you're more dangerous to society if you're caffeine deprived."

I grinned. "This is perfect—and so thoughtful. Thank you."

"I was going to get one that said 'Bless Your Heart,' but I figured you wouldn't want people to think you were cussing them out."

"Good choice. Thank you—really. For the hot coffee, too." I hugged her, careful not to tilt my new cup. "Why are you so nice to me?"

"Because you're my friend. And because you deserve it. Probably more than most people."

I pulled back, unable to speak past the frog in my throat. She followed me through the French door at the top of the stairs, tugging on my backpack briefly. "I'm just sticking in a tube of my favorite lipstick in case you change your mind." Leaning over the banister to watch me descend past the landing, she called after me, "Don't forget to be polite."

I paused on the bottom step to look up at her. "Of course I'll be polite. Why wouldn't I?"

Her eyebrows rose, but I didn't stick around long enough to hear anything else.

I stood outside the small bungalow that housed Horn's Eatery on the corner of Dauphine and Touro, not far from my cottage in the Marigny. Despite the cooler air of fall, the sidewalk was full of diners with their dogs sitting outside and enjoying coffee and breakfast.

A sign over the glass double doors read THE GARDEN OF EATIN', and a chalkboard stand in the middle of the sidewalk read *Wisdom says that if you're hungry, you should eat.* Although the thought of having a private conversation with Sam had stolen my appetite, the delicious smells of the food on diners' plates made my stomach grumble. Taking a deep breath, I opened the door and stepped inside.

As usual, my historic-house-loving self noticed the architectural elements first. An original dark wood-planked ceiling covered a large single room containing booths along the sides with small tables placed in the middle. A full bar dominated one end of the room. Out of habit, I diverted my attention away from the glass bottles lined up on the shelves, focusing instead on the diners.

I spotted Sam immediately, sitting in a booth next to the window. Her head was bent toward her phone, so she didn't see me, giving me the chance to take in her coordinated jacket-and-sweater outfit, her smooth dark hair falling in gentle waves around her face. She looked like she'd just stepped out of a J.Crew catalog. Self-consciously, I looked down at my worn jeans and the oversized, holey sweater that I'd had since high school. I stopped a server walking past me. "Excuse me—where's the ladies' room?"

Checking quickly to make sure that Sam hadn't spotted me yet, I ducked into the bathroom and headed straight for the mirror. I pulled out the tube of lipstick Jolene had given me, a muted pink with "blue tones," which, according to Jolene, flattered my coloring. She kept threatening to bring me home with her on her next trip to Mississippi so her aunt Janie could do my colors. I had no idea what that meant, but I wondered if it would hurt.

After carefully applying the lipstick just like Jolene had shown me, and then using a square of paper towel to blot my lips, I could only hope that I didn't resemble a circus clown. I stepped back from the mirror, reluctantly appreciating what Jolene had done to my hair. And the pearls. Although I couldn't help comparing the pearls with my outfit to the floral basket on my bike. Whatever. With a deep breath, I pulled my shoulders back and faked confidence as I strode to Sam's table.

Sam smiled warmly as I slid across from her in the booth. "Hi, Nola. It's so good to see you." She shifted her gaze briefly and gave a nod to someone out of my line of vision. Before I could say anything, a server placed a steaming-hot cup of coffee in front of me. "I've heard that it's best to keep you caffeinated."

I laughed, immediately put at ease. "I drank an entire travel mug full of coffee on my way here, and I was just now feeling the need for another infusion."

Holding up her own cup of coffee, she said, "This is my third and I'm definitely not done yet." As she sipped from her cup, I noticed her unpolished and seriously gnawed fingernails. It was somehow reassuring to know that she wasn't perfect.

Sam handed a menu to me. "Are you hungry? I'm afraid that there's not a lot of healthy options. . . ."

"Good," I said, my stomach grumbling as I watched a plate full of something yummy being carried past us, the trailing scent of bacon and melted butter making my mouth water. I looked down at my menu. "What do you recommend?"

She grinned. "How hungry are you?"

"Very."

"Great, then. You like corn bread waffles, pulled pork, chimichurri sauce, and pickled peppers?"

I nodded enthusiastically. "You had me at 'corn bread.'"

"I've got you covered." Sam signaled for the server and placed an order for Waffle Cochon and a Creole Slammer. "Those are my two favorite things on the menu, so we can split and share—that's what Beau and I usually do. I hope you don't mind me ordering for you, but everything's good and I know you don't have a lot of time, and I really wanted to talk with you about something important."

"No worries." I took a sip of coffee, hoping it would reach my brain before I needed to answer any questions about Beau.

"It's about Adele."

"Adele?"

"Yes. Beau's mother?"

"I know who she is," I said. "I'm just . . . surprised. I don't know a lot about her, except that she's presumed dead."

Sam cleared her throat. "Yeah, well. That's the thing." Sam put down her cup and focused her gaze on it as if searching for words among the coffee grounds. "I think Beau talks to her." She paused, waiting for me to bolt. When I didn't, she said, "Every night. At least, every night when he stays over at my apartment, which is a lot. I have an antique phone—you know, one of those old wooden box phones with the crank and handheld earpiece? My great-aunt left it to me, and I kept it because at the time I thought it was pretty cool. It's not even plugged into anything—just a few nails to hook it onto the wall."

Sam stopped talking to allow our server to refill our cups. Once he was out of earshot, she said, "But it rings. Never when I'm there alone, but every night when he's there. We'll be in bed asleep and it rings. The first time it happened I got up, but Beau told me to go back to sleep, that it was just an odd malfunction, and we let it ring a few more times until it stopped. But then . . ."

I raised my eyebrows and didn't say anything, to show that she still had my full attention. Or at least most of it, because part of my mind was squirming at the thought of the two of them in bed together.

Sam continued. "I'm assuming that since you were with Beau when he cleared the spirits from your house, you're aware that he has . . . abilities that he's still reluctant to explore. Working with you was sort of a turning point for him, but he's not there yet. We're still doing the debunking-psychics podcast—which is still valid, I think—but I feel he's also more open to exploring legitimate ways to help trapped spirits move on."

"He admitted that to you?"

"Not in so many words. But you know how when you're in an intimate relationship with someone you can understand things about them without them saying them?"

I nodded, even though I had no clue what she meant. My mind was too busy trying to dart around the word "intimate" in relation to her and Beau to try to figure it out.

"Anyway, the next time the phone rang, I pretended to be in a deep sleep when he got out of bed to answer it. It hangs on the wall outside the bedroom, and even though he closed the door, I could hear him through the cheap particleboard walls. I'm sure you know all about the shoddy construction found in modern buildings." We rolled our eyes together, and I felt as if we had just bonded.

The server came with our food, and as much as I was dying to hear the rest of Sam's story, I had to interrupt her long enough to divide each plate of food in perfect halves using the ruler Melanie had engraved with my name and given me. I was unsure if the look on Sam's face was one of surprise or appreciation, but I was too hungry to care.

We each devoured the first few forkfuls of food on our plates, then grinned at each other like kindred spirits. "Nothing like a healthy appetite, right?" she said. "Are you a runner, too?"

I nodded, my mouth already full with my next bite. After swallowing it down with water, I said, "I've been a runner since I joined the track-and-field team in high school. But now I have to run because Jolene loves to bake, and she's really good at it."

Her lips turned up in a lopsided grin. "Yeah, I know. Beau's brought some of her creations home. Let's just say they're worth running that extra mile. Or two."

"True." I leaned forward. "So, you were saying about the phone ringing in your apartment . . ."

"Right." She swallowed another bite before continuing. "So, while I faked being asleep, I could hear Beau picking up the earpiece. I'm pretty sure he wasn't sleepwalking, since I've never seen him do it before, but he was definitely having a two-way conversation." She paused. "With Adele."

"His mother."

Sam nodded.

"Who has probably been dead for over twenty years. On a phone that probably hasn't actually worked for at least a century."

"Right." She tilted her head, studying me. "Why aren't you acting very surprised?"

"Because it happened before—the night he was sick and slept on my couch. I heard him on the unplugged landline phone then, and I was pretty sure he was talking to his mother."

She pulled her eyebrows together. "And you didn't think this was worth mentioning?"

I managed to maintain my neutral expression as I recalled his exact words. "I thought he was sleepwalking. When I asked him about it the next day, he claimed he wasn't a sleepwalker, so I left it at that."

Sam put her fork down and folded her hands on the edge of the table. "Nola—can I be honest?"

"Of course." My breakfast settled uneasily in my stomach, threatening to come back up.

"It's no secret to you or me that Beau has psychic abilities. Like your stepmother, Melanie. He always holds her up as being the real thing, which I'm sure you know. She's one in a million, according to Beau, which is why we still do our debunking podcast."

I relaxed a little. "I know. He's mentioned that. Why are you telling me this?"

"Because I thought that once Sunny came back home, Adele could rest in peace. But she's still here. That night—after the phone call—

Beau fell back asleep but I was wide-awake. I went into the room with the phone and switched on a lamp to read. That's when I saw a set of wet footprints on the floor next to the wall by the phone. I'd seen them before occasionally but had always brushed them off as something explainable. But this time . . ."

"I know. I've seen them, too," I said. "When I knew him in Charleston. So did Melanie. And a couple of times since I've been here."

"Right. Me, too. I assumed she was hanging around to remind Beau to keep looking for his sister. But Sunny's back now. So why is Adele still here?"

The server reappeared to take our empty plates. After he'd left, I said, "There must be a reason why she's still here. According to Melanie, there's always a reason."

"And Beau won't talk to Adele about it," Sam said. "He'll answer the phone, but it's only to let her know that he's fine on his own, and then he hangs up." Sam chewed on her thumbnail, but quickly dropped her hand when she spotted me watching.

"I know. It's because he's still too angry with her for leaving him. And he doesn't want to actively channel her because he's afraid of who else will come in. He hasn't had enough experience to regulate who he allows in, so he tries to block out everyone."

Sam's eyebrows shot up. "He told you that?"

Not exactly. I nodded, not wanting to go into detail about the midnight conversation I'd overheard between Beau and Adele. "So we're at an impasse."

"Not necessarily."

Her tone reminded me too much of Melanie when she decided to do something despite everyone—including my dad—telling her not to. "What do you mean?"

"That you and I need to take matters into our own hands and go right to the source. Otherwise, Adele will never find peace, and neither will Beau."

I stared back at her. "Unless you have psychic powers that I'm not aware of, neither one of us can go right to the source."

"True. But we know someone who can." She gave me a meaningful look.

I glanced around the room as if to find answers from the other diners or the paneled ceiling. My head swung back to Sam when I realized whom she meant. "Melanie?"

"Exactly. Isn't she coming to visit next week? It shouldn't take her very long to figure it out and send Adele home, right?"

I shook my head vigorously. "No. Absolutely not. I moved to New Orleans to prove to my family that I could survive on my own, without their help. Even with something like this. If I ask just once for anything, they'll assume that it's okay to jump into my business at any time. It's just how they are. I know they love me, but . . ." I stopped, not sure how to explain.

She looked deflated. "Not even . . . ?"

"Nope."

Sam sat back against her seat, her shoulders slumped. "Fine. I get it. And from what Beau has told me about you, I'm not completely surprised." Her mouth turned up in a quick smile. "I meant that in a good way."

"Thanks. I think."

"That's why I came up with a plan B, in case you said no."

"A plan B?

She paused, taking a deep breath. "If we go on the theory that Adele and Beau's grandfather are still here to protect Beau because he won't drop his digging into the Broussard family, then we'll need to find out the truth before the Broussards even know that someone's poking around and they start looking at Beau. And the only way to do that is to use the only key to their front door that we have."

A twinge of uneasiness tickled my spine. "We have a key?"

Sam's light brown eyes considered me for a moment. "Michael Hebert."

I was shaking my head before the name was even out of her mouth. "No. You don't have to go any further. My answer is no where he's concerned." I leaned forward, pressing the heels of my hands into the edge of the table. "Did Beau put you up to this? Because he just asked me the same thing, and my answer was no then, too."

"He didn't—I swear. But that shows just how desperate he is to see someone punished. He's also really angry. Having Sunny back has only reminded him of how many years were stolen from them. Desperation and anger are a combination that never ends well."

"Then let's go to the police. That's what they do, right? Investigate crimes."

"Nola," Sam said with the patient voice Melanie had once used to explain to me that tofu wasn't, in fact, an adequate substitute for steak. "The Ryans have tried that route—remember? And none of the case files survived Katrina, and what remains is circumstantial. Or paranormal, which doesn't count. What's missing is an 'in' into the Broussard family—and that would be Michael. Through you. Maybe even his parents. Did you know that they left New Orleans shortly after Katrina? They're a huge missing piece in this puzzle."

"A lot of people did," I countered.

"True. But I don't know many who still had their homes and livelihoods and chose to pack up and leave for the other side of the world. It's curious, is all I'm saying."

A coincidence. I mentally batted the word away. "Look. Even if I suddenly went insane and agreed to see Michael, I'm not even sure how I'd find out anything about his parents. It's not like I could ask them."

"No. But Michael could. Or his aunt and uncle. Someone knows something. And through Michael you might be able to find out what."

I shook my head. "If his feelings for me were real and not manufactured, I could maybe imagine him doing that for me."

"And you really believe that Michael didn't have feelings for you?"

I looked away for a moment. "I really don't know. I find it hard to believe that anyone can be that good of a liar. But his initial intentions were to deceive me, and he did. Completely. If he developed feelings for me, it doesn't matter. He's a lying snake and I want nothing more to do with him."

"Not even if it means saving Beau's life?"

"That's not fair. And I think you're being a little overdramatic. Besides, if you're so worried, why don't you approach Michael yourself?"

"Because I have a boyfriend."

"Ouch."

Sam clenched her eyes shut for a moment. "I'm so sorry—that's not what I meant. What I meant to say was that Beau is my boyfriend, and it would look suspicious if all of a sudden I showed interest in Michael Hebert."

"True," I admitted. "But you have no idea what you're asking."

"No, I don't. But could you live with the guilt if something happened to Beau? I know I couldn't."

"Great. So now you're playing the guilt card."

She grinned. "I'm Catholic. I can't help it."

I rolled my eyes. "Well, I'm not. Although I do have Melanie as a stepmother."

"I don't think I follow, but whatever. My point is I don't think either one of us is the type to look the other way and let bad things happen. Not if there's a chance we can do something about it."

"What are you proposing? Joining forces with Beau?"

Shaking her head, she said, "Absolutely not. That would put all of us in danger. He can't know."

"Oh, I see. So we just lock Beau in his bedroom until we've figured all of this out."

Sam's mouth twisted in a half smile. "I'd be lying if I said I hadn't seriously considered that."

The waiter approached with the check and Sam took it. I didn't fight her for it, since I felt at this point that she owed me and I should probably consider ordering a to-go bag for lunch, too.

"So what are you suggesting?"

She grinned, and once again I wished she weren't dating Beau, because I thought we could be really great friends. "We have Mimi on our side. She doesn't want him going after the Broussard family any more than we do. She's just got Sunny back, and she doesn't want to lose another grandchild now. She'll help. I know she will. She'll find projects for him that will take him out of town or just bog him down to such a degree that he won't have any time to dig into things he needs to stay away from."

"While we look for things we have no idea are what we're looking for."

"Maybe. But who knows what we might find while we're searching for answers?" Glancing at her phone, Sam said, "It's late. We both need to get going. We'll talk later and come up with a plan of action, okay?"

"I haven't agreed to any of this. I haven't even said I'd think about it." We both stood and walked toward the door.

"But you will," Sam said as she returned her wallet to her purse. "I thought you might be a little more enthusiastic about getting back at Michael for what he did to you. I mean, do you really want to wait for karma to take care of him? You know, like him getting hit by a streetcar?"

I winced. Despite everything, I didn't want anything bad happening to him. Just an attack of chicken pox. Or hemorrhoids. Or even a month of sleepless nights. I pulled the door open and held it for Sam. "Not really."

"Yes, well, try to remember that some wise person once said that revenge is sweet. And I know you do like dessert."

She promised to call me, and then we said good-bye. We began walking in opposite directions, my mind swirling over our conversation before finally settling on a remembered quote I'd once read on a poster on a dorm room wall: *Before you embark on a journey of revenge, dig two graves.*

CHAPTER 5

Two nights later, on Friday, as I was dressing for dinner at Mimi's, I was equally excited and worried that Jolene hadn't come into my room once to hijack my getting-ready process and prolong it indefinitely. I could go from start to finish in about five minutes, something Jolene said I shouldn't be proud of.

I heard her on her phone, and I figured she was speaking to either her mother or her grandmother by the number of times I heard "Bless 'em" and "Lorda mercy." By the time she'd emerged, hair and makeup in place but otherwise looking a little flustered, I was already dressed and ready to go in my best jeans, sweater (the Lilly Pulitzer one that Melanie had given me), and ankle boots. I'd even brushed my hair.

"Everything all right?" I asked.

"I hope so. My whole town is in a tizzy because the mayor died from a heart attack and now everybody's fighting over his funeral."

"Did he not have a wife or significant other?"

"That's the thing. They were hitched but not churched, if you know what I mean, so his sister wants to take over. The girlfriend wants him buried in his favorite Ole Miss game-day outfit, including a bag of chips and a bowl of dip in case he gets hungry."

"That's insane."

"I know, right? What if Jesus is an LSU fan? Anyway, as the town's funeral director, Grandmama is fit to be tied trying to get all sides to agree so they can finally lay poor Mr. Tyson to rest."

While I searched for something to say, she examined my outfit choice. "You look nice, Nola, but are you sure you want to wear that?"

I looked down at my sweater. "What's wrong with this? I thought you said you liked it."

"Oh, I do. I even want to borrow it. But hasn't Beau already seen you in it?"

I grabbed our coats from the rack by the door and tossed Jolene's to her. "Even if he has, I don't care. Besides, he's a guy. I'm sure he couldn't recall what he wore yesterday, much less what I did."

She pulled a silk scarf from her pocket and draped it around my neck before knotting it at my throat. "I think you'd be surprised what Beau notices about you." Smoothing the scarf, then patting it gently, she said, "There. Now you're ready." Jolene opened the door at the top of the stairs. "Please grab that plate of pralines on the coffee table and bring them."

"I thought Mimi said that you didn't need to bring anything."

"Really, Nola, have I taught you nothing? I'd rather my hair catch on fire than arrive at a party without bringing something."

I grabbed the plate and led us down the stairs.

It had started sprinkling while I was getting dressed, and it was now pouring. I stopped on the first outdoor step, protected from the elements by the small arched overhang. "We should take an Uber. Since you don't like driving in the rain." I looked at Jolene hopefully.

From her other coat pocket she'd pulled out one of those plastic hair bonnets that I'd seen only in documentaries from the sixties and seventies, when big hair and bouffants had been in fashion, and she placed it on her head, tying the clear plastic straps in a pretty bow beneath her chin. Jolene's grandmother had purchased the world's supply of rain bonnets before they'd gone permanently out of style, and she'd made sure her granddaughter had her own stash. It would have been comical if Jolene didn't take her hair so seriously. Or mine. But I had drawn the line the first and only time she'd tried to put one on me.

"Don't be silly," she said as she stepped out next to me, pulling the door closed behind her and locking it. "We're so much safer in Bubba, because he's so big and made of steel. Unless I hit a truck carrying something flammable, we'll be fine." She moved to the next step while snapping open her umbrella. Looking back at me, she said, "You coming?"

Not feeling reassured, I walked with her to the car and got in while she held her umbrella over me. Then she moved to the driver's seat and gracefully sat while simultaneously closing the umbrella without splattering water anywhere.

"One day you'll have to show me how you do that," I said.

She smiled at me and turned the key in the ignition. "Baby steps, Nola. Baby steps. Let's work on proper mascara application and accessorizing first, and then we can move on to more advanced things."

I wanted to laugh, but I didn't think she was joking.

I didn't release my hold on the door handle until she'd safely parked Bubba in front of the Ryans' house on Prytania, not seeming to mind that both right-side tires were on the curb.

Jolene looked at me in the dim light from the ceiling bulb and frowned. "I told you that you should have worn one of Grandmama's bonnets. Your hair looks like you stuck your finger in a light socket."

"Thank you," I said, staring back at her. "And you look like you're auditioning for the matchmaker part in *Fiddler on the Roof.*"

"True," she said, unlatching her seat belt. "But when I get to the front porch and take it off, I won't look like roadkill dragged in by the dog."

Beau met us at the door and took our coats, his eyes lingering on my hair briefly before he showed us into the front parlor and excused himself to hang up our coats. Christopher stood by the bar while Mimi and her newfound granddaughter, Sunny, sat close together on the settee, deep in conversation, their hands clasped together between them. They both looked up and smiled but didn't move apart or stand.

"Thank you both for coming," Mimi said. She indicated two velvet salmon-colored Biedermeier chairs by the white marble fireplace. "Please have a seat and let Christopher know what you'd like to drink."

Beau returned to the room and leaned an elbow on the marble mantel. "I told Christopher that I'd be happy playing bartender, but he's a little territorial, so I'm not going to argue."

"I'm not territorial. I'm just better at mixing drinks than most people." Christopher turned to Jolene with a smile. "How about a Sazerac?"

"No," Beau and I said in unison at the same moment that Jolene said, "Yes, please."

"It's just that last time . . ." I started.

Jolene smiled sweetly, the same smile she would use right before she said *Bless your heart.*

Christopher grinned. "One Sazerac and one water with lemon coming right up."

I sat next to the fireplace, for the first time noticing, perched on top, a small bust of Bacchus, the Roman god of wine and revelry. It corresponded with the Bacchus orgy irreverently painted on the dining room ceiling—a family legacy of sorts, initially meant as a taunt from one brother to the other, and now a point of pride for the Ryan family.

"So," I said, directing my attention to Sunny, "how are you settling in?"

She looked at Mimi. "Really great. I had no idea when I started my search that I'd find an entire long-lost family who'd been looking for me all these years!"

I listened to her speak and tried to place her accent. I remembered it from the first time we'd met, when she'd shown up at my apartment looking for Beau. She was blond and petite, and when she smiled it was clear why her family had nicknamed her Sunny. "Your accent . . ." I began.

"Is from all over," Sunny said. "My dad—I mean, my adoptive dad—was in the Air Force, so I moved around a lot. He retired about ten years ago and moved back to his hometown in Minnesota. I went to high school there, so I probably sound more Midwestern than anything else."

I nodded, although I didn't completely agree. During my time in California I'd met lots of people from all over the country sucked in by the lure of fame and fortune on the West Coast like lint to a dryer vent—my mom included. They erased their accents faster than their savings, so that they sounded like they were from everywhere and nowhere at the same time. My gaze slid down her arm, where I'd seen a small fleur-de-lis tattoo the first time I'd met her.

She saw me looking and turned over her wrist so we could all see the pale, blue-veined skin where the small iconic symbol of New Orleans sat like a brand. "I got this as soon as I found out about my real family." Sunny smiled at Mimi. "It's funny, really. I've always felt a tugging feeling whenever I would see a fleur-de-lis. My mom said that I would be obsessed with any news story that showed Mardi Gras footage of the floats and the crowds and all the crazy costumes and beads. For my first Halloween after I was adopted, I wanted to be a Mardi Gras queen." A small smile graced her pixie-like face. "Mom had no idea what a Mardi Gras queen costume was. She ended up getting a Disney princess dress and putting lots of feathers and sequins on it and making a matching mask. It was wonderful, even if nobody knew what I was supposed to be."

I looked from Beau to Mimi, waiting for one of them to take the lead in the conversation, to put all the missing pieces into some sort of explanation of how Sunny had come to be back in New Orleans, but they both seemed too busy staring adoringly at her. Which, I suppose, made sense. It wasn't exactly how I'd been greeted after being separated from my father for the first thirteen years of my life, but I guess not everybody could be so lucky as to have a family actively searching for them.

Not willing to sit in silence, especially when there were so many questions that needed answering, I said, "So . . ." I stopped, not sure where to start, and chose the most general question I could think of. "What's your story?"

Sunny shrugged. "I've told this story so many times in the last few weeks that it's hard to remember where to begin." She looked at Mimi for support.

"She didn't even know she was adopted until she was in high school," Mimi said, patting Sunny's leg. "Her adoptive parents thought it best. They never wanted her to feel as if she didn't belong."

Her words were like a small sting around the vicinity of my heart for reasons I wasn't yet prepared to fully examine. "How did you find out?" I asked.

Her bright blue eyes were clear as they met mine. "The student council at my school was doing a blood drive, and my friends were all donating blood, so I donated, too. They were giving out coupons to a local restaurant if we brought more people, so I got my parents to donate. That's when I found out that they're both O positives. I'm an AB negative. We'd studied blood types in biology, so I knew that wasn't possible."

"That would do it," I said. "Of course, anyone who watches *CSI* would know that, too, but whatever works."

Beau looked at me and frowned, as if he could see the tiny chip on my shoulder. I was happy that Sunny had found her way back home. It was nothing short of a miracle, which certainly didn't explain my mixed emotions every time I looked at her and saw her bright, sunny smile. Maybe I was comparing her situation with mine, which wasn't fair. She'd been taken and was absent from their lives for all but the first two years of her life.

"Nobody's mentioned your adoptive parents having been arrested, so I'm guessing they weren't involved in your kidnapping."

Sunny looked down at her lap while Beau and Mimi shared a glance, leaving me to shift in my seat and wonder what they weren't telling me. "It was a private adoption," Beau said. "But the paperwork has vanished and the adoption lawyer they used either never existed or did a great job of covering his tracks."

I looked up to find Beau's gaze on me, his thoughts reflecting mine. I thought about my conversation with Sam, and how she wanted me to involve myself with the people who had the power, reach, and lack of conscience to steal a child from her family and leave no trace of their involvement. Or at least knew the right people to bribe. An involuntary shiver blew across the back of my neck as I considered again what that family might be capable of if they discovered anyone digging into a past they preferred to leave buried.

"Yeah, Mom and Dad figured that out, too," Sunny said, her voice just barely audible. "It took me about six months to talk myself into asking to find my birth parents, and that's when we discovered what happened."

I took a slow sip of my water, letting it slide down my suddenly dry throat. "So how in the world did you end up here?"

"Reddit." She lifted her hands, palms up. "I know, right? Who knew social media could actually do something productive?"

"Actually," Jolene said, accepting another Sazerac from Christopher while studiously avoiding my gaze, "I find Instagram a wonderful way to discover new makeup tips, with great tutorials. They're almost as good as a big Barbie head."

"Right," Sunny said slowly. "Anyway, I ended up in a forum that shares information about missing children." Her voice broke, and she dipped her head to regain her composure. "I didn't know that I was missing at that point, but I'd have to be pretty oblivious for the thought not to have occurred to me." She gave me a wobbly smile. "It's actually pretty amazing. I shared that I was looking for information on my birth parents, but all I had was my approximate birth year and a picture of what I looked like right after I was adopted. And then . . ."

Sunny was interrupted by the appearance of a fat black cat, its measuring green eyes taking in the room and its occupants as it stalked onto the Aubusson rug. It paused in front of the sofa, twisting its glossy head before choosing Sunny's legs to rub against, then settling down at her feet.

"I didn't know you had a cat," I said.

"We don't," Mimi said. "It arrived on our doorstep a few days ago with no collar and no chip—just like Mardi. We didn't feed it at first, hoping it would go away, but it took a liking to my back garden. And when no one claimed him, Sunny began feeding it. That very first day when I opened the door to bring out some food, the cat just walked calmly inside as if it owned the place and hasn't left since. Lorda set up a bed and litter box in the kitchen and the cat seems to know what to do, so I suppose we have a cat now. Although it ignores the bed in the kitchen at night and heads to Sunny's room to sleep on the pillow next to her. It's the craziest thing."

"Have you named him?" Jolene leaned over to see the underbelly of the cat. "Or is it a her?"

"Mambo," said Mimi. "Sunny named him." She squeezed Sunny's hand. "It makes all of this so real. As if Sunny has always lived here and been a part of our family."

"Do cats like to wear clothes?" Jolene asked. "I think a bow tie on Mambo would be very distinguished."

"And then what happened?" I asked, as eager to drop the subject of cats wearing clothes as I was to hear the rest of Sunny's story. To discover something in it that would stop my misplaced feelings of what I could describe only as resentment. After all, like Sunny's, my story had ended happily. Eventually.

Mambo jumped up into Sunny's lap, and she began stroking the cat beneath the chin. "In something like two days someone had found a news article from the *Times-Picayune* about my abduction along with a photograph of me from around that time. Compared to the photo my parents had taken, it was almost identical. There was no denying that I was Sunny Ryan."

"And that you had a family in New Orleans who had never stopped missing you."

"And looking for me."

Sunny bent to kiss the top of Mambo's head while Beau's gaze met mine. Mimi had never stopped missing her, but she *had* stopped looking, although only to protect her one remaining grandchild.

"And that's when you got the tattoo," I said.

"Pretty much." Sunny sank back into the sofa, pressing herself against Mimi.

Jolene used her napkin to dab at her eyes. "It really is a miracle. Just like that time my uncle Stubby's prized sow gave birth to a two-headed piglet. You don't see that every day, you know?"

"No, we certainly don't," Christopher said as he stood to refill my water glass.

Jolene placed her empty glass on a low table in front of us, then leaned her elbows on her knees. "What name did they give you?"

"Donna. Donna Marie Mathieson. But I think I want to go back to using Sunny. I think I feel more like a Sunny than a Donna. Even though I guess my real name is Jolie, so I better get used to signing both." She offered a tentative smile.

Jolene thrummed her fingertips against her jaw, her elbows moving side to side with her knees. "Your mama and daddy don't mind?"

"I, um, they . . ."

"They were killed in a car accident shortly before Sunny found us," Beau said softly, his eyes on Sunny as she pressed her face into the cat's neck.

"Oh, you poor thing," Jolene said. "To lose both of your parents."

"Twice," Beau added. "Even though she doesn't remember our parents, it's still another loss."

"Of course it is," Jolene said, dabbing a napkin at the corners of her eyes. "You poor, poor thing. I can't imagine what you've been through. But what a miracle that you made your way back to your other family."

Sunny lifted her head, her own eyes moist. "I don't know what I would have done without Mimi and Beau. They've really been my rocks, dealing with the emotional blow and helping me with my parents' estate and all the paperwork." She shrugged. "Mom always used to say that when a door closes, a window opens. I just wish she and Dad could be here to share this with me. We could all be one happy family." She began crying in earnest, and Mimi pressed Sunny's head onto her shoulder, muffling her sobs.

"I'm sorry," I said, embarrassed to see that I was the only one not crying. Even Christopher had looked away to wipe his eyes.

I waited for the wave of sympathy, and it passed over me like a brief rain burst that was gone before a person had a chance to get wet. It wasn't that I was completely without compassion. What had happened to Sunny was horrible. Maybe even worse than what had happened to me. Life wasn't fair. I knew that. But some perverse part of me clung tight to the resentment that her family had missed her and had wanted her back. Before Jolene had a chance to slap me into next week (her words) if I didn't behave, I doubled down on my efforts to be nice.

"What are your plans now?" I asked with my best kindergarten teacher voice.

Wadding a tissue in her hand, Sunny smiled at me with reddened eyes. "Beau has offered me a job at JR Properties, helping Jolene with some of the scheduling and paperwork, since she's doing so much site work now. He said that I could help you with your renovations, too, sort of learn the ropes. Maybe go back to school and get a degree in preservation or something. I'm a quick study, and I'm really interested in learning."

I managed to keep the smile on my face as I turned to Beau, expecting some sort of recognition or apology for knowingly overstepping into my life. Again.

Instead, he said, "Thibaut and Jorge have already given their two thumbs-up. I brought Sunny to the cottage to meet the team and they're already like extended family. We figured she could do coffee and lunch runs while learning some of the basics, so it's a win-win.

Too bad she wasn't there when you were tiling the upstairs bath. She would probably have pointed out that you were tiling yourself into a corner before it was too late." A chuckle rumbled in his throat as he sat back against the sofa.

I took a generous swallow of water to prevent myself from saying what I really wanted to. "Excuse me for a moment, please," I said as I stood. "I have a horrible headache and need some Tylenol." I smiled briefly in Mimi's direction. "I know where it is."

Jolene reached down toward her feet, to the purse that matched her shoes. "I've got some right . . ."

I sent her a warning glance as I strode past her, hoping she would understand that I needed to leave the room. "I'll be right back." Walking quickly past the portrait of Charles Ryan, I felt his painted eyes following me as I ran up the stairs.

CHAPTER 6

I took the stairs two at a time, then paused when I was halfway down the hallway, in front of the closed door that led into what I mentally referred to as Mimi's storage room (I wasn't sure what she called the bizarre collection of artifacts from unsolved crimes that she stored on endless shelves beyond the locked door). Mimi had the gift of psychometry, which, when she touched objects, gave her insight into what appeared to be unsolvable crimes. Desperate families had come to see Mimi as a last resort, and she'd been able to help many grieving relatives of victims. It wasn't a room I wanted to see the inside of again. I still had nightmares about the Frozen Charlottes in the curio cabinet against the far wall.

Realizing that I actually did have a headache, I walked to the black and white bathroom next door and plucked out the familiar red and white bottle from the medicine cabinet.

"Nola?"

I jerked back, dropping the bottle into the porcelain sink with a loud clatter. Turning, I saw Sunny standing outside the bathroom door with an apologetic smile.

"I'm so sorry—did I startle you?"

I pressed the heel of my hand against my chest, feeling the heavy pumping of my heart. "No, not at all. Why would you think that sneaking up behind someone and saying their name would be startling?"

"I guess I deserve that. I am so sorry. My parents were light sleepers, so I grew up learning how to move really quietly."

I gave her points for understanding sarcasm and for her apology. Shaking out two pills into my palm, I said, "Did you need some, too?"

She shook her head. "No. I wanted to speak with you alone. I hope that's all right."

I hid my surprise. "Sure." I closed the medicine cabinet and faced her. "What about?"

"Can we go into my room? Just in case anyone else comes up. I don't think I want us to be overheard."

"Okay." I caught the faint scent of cigarettes as she stood close to me. "You smoke?"

"Yeah. Trying to quit. Again. I actually did stop before the car accident, and then"—she shrugged—"I started again. Please don't tell Mimi. I don't want to disappoint her."

I thought it was an odd request, but I nodded anyway. My mind was so occupied with reasons why she'd need to speak with me that I almost didn't notice that she was opening the door to the storage room. "Wait—" I stopped at the threshold. Instead of the endless shelves of detritus from broken lives, a mahogany sleigh bed sat against a wall across from a pair of pretty yellow and white toile chairs and matching ottomans. These were placed in front of a fireplace that I hadn't even noticed during my previous visits to the room. Bright light flooded through the tall windows that had been covered with heavy draperies, obscuring all light. The curio cabinet—thank goodness—was gone.

"That was quick," I said. "What did they do with all the . . . stuff that was in here?"

"You mean the excess inventory? They moved it to the shop on

Royal Street. I'm not really sure why it was here to begin with, except that it's a big house and they had the space. Mimi's working really hard to give me a room that I love and has hired a designer. I've never worked with a designer before—it wasn't something my parents ever really considered—but I have to say that I'm having fun with it. Jenny's pretty cool and has lots of great ideas that fit with my personality. It's just that . . ."

I waited for her to finish.

With a tight throat, she said, "It's just that I wish my parents could see it. This house alone would have made my mom swoon."

For the first time, I felt a connection to this lost-and-found girl, felt bonded by our wandering along the same lonely path, searching for the way home. "I get it. My mom died when I was almost fourteen. She was a musician and taught me everything she knew about playing guitar and writing music. There are still times now when I hear a song or think of a lyric and I turn to say something and realize all over again that she's not there."

An odd expression that looked a lot like panic flashed across her face before quickly vanishing. "I want to say I'm sorry, but that's not really enough, is it?"

I shook my head, liking Sunny Ryan a little bit more. "No. I still have my dad and my stepmother, and a brother and sister. They're pretty much an answer to a dream I never thought I'd had. And now you have a brother and a grandmother. They're not a replacement, but they're a great 'instead of,' you know? Even though both your biological parents and adoptive parents are no longer here, you know that you were wanted. And loved." I hoped she hadn't heard the hitch in my voice. I hadn't meant to be talking about myself.

She didn't smile, only nodded, then led me over to the pair of chairs and sat down in one. As I sat, she looked nervously at the closed door behind me. "Sorry—I just want to make sure that nobody can hear."

Sunny sat on the edge of her seat and leaned forward, then waited until I'd done the same before she spoke. With a low voice, she said, "I need your help."

My brows lifted. Of all the things I thought she might say, this wasn't anywhere near the top twenty. "My help? Doing what?" I looked around at the sparse room. "If it's decorating ideas, you're better off sticking with Jenny the designer. Or Jolene. Assuming you want everything monogrammed."

She smiled briefly. "No, it's not that. It's a little more complicated. It's . . . Beau."

I thought she might be joking, so I gave a little laugh and said, "Then it can't be *that* complicated, right? I mean, he's a guy. Definitely not any more complicated than a dog. Or cat. As long as their basic needs are met, they're pretty content."

I sobered when I saw that she wasn't laughing. "He wants to find a way to get back at the people who kidnapped me. But Mimi said they're very dangerous and that he should drop it because I'm back now and it doesn't matter anymore."

"Okay . . ." I said, thinking about the two similar conversations I'd recently had with both Beau and Sam. "And you think I might be able to persuade him not to?"

"Partly." She dropped her eyes to stare at the tattoo on her inner wrist. With her gaze still averted, she added, "But I don't think that would be enough. Which is why I'm asking you to work with me to figure out how to bring them to justice without involving Beau. We can throw him red herrings to keep him busy while we do the real work. I just . . . found him. I don't know what I'd do if something happened to him." Sunny paused, lifted her eyes. "Mimi's really scared me. But I'm not the kind of person to allow the people responsible to walk free, you know? It's not right. I just figured that you and I would have a better chance of getting info than Beau. They're probably waiting for him to do something, so he's already in their sights. But not us."

I narrowed my eyes. "Have you been speaking with Samantha?"

At her blank look, I added, "His girlfriend and podcast partner."

"I know who she is. Why would you ask?"

"Because she and I just had an almost identical conversation. I told her I didn't want to get involved because . . . well, it would mean me rekindling a relationship with Michael Hebert, a close family relation to the people responsible for your abduction. I thought I'd made it clear that I would rather stick knitting needles in my eyeballs than ever speak with him again, but she thinks I'm considering it because I should want to get back at Michael. You can ask Beau if you want to know all the sordid details."

"I know. He told me. Which made me think you might be up for some revenge."

I stood. "Why does everyone seem to think I'm motivated by revenge? I just want to leave it all behind me."

She held my gaze. "Even if it means saving a life? Because Beau's not going to stop until the Broussard family stops him. Permanently. I couldn't live with myself if that happened. Could you?"

I was spared from answering by a soft knock on the door and then Jolene's voice from the other side. "Is everything all right?"

I gratefully opened the door. "Yeah. We were just chatting and getting to know each other." I felt Sunny watching me.

"I've been sent to let you know that supper is on the table. I don't know about y'all, but I'm so hungry I could eat the butt off a hobbyhorse."

Sunny approached, and I smelled the faint scent of cigarettes again. With an accent that mimicked Jolene's, Sunny said, "And I'm so hungry I could eat the paint off the walls."

Jolene sent her an appreciative look. "Well, my goodness, Sunny. You sound just like my cousin Speedy. Her real name is Darlene, but no one has ever called her that, since she's slow as molasses, but she was born and raised in the Mississippi Delta and has an accent to prove it."

Sunny absently rubbed at her wrist tattoo, reminding me of Beau and his rubber-band-snapping habit. "Thank you. I'm a quick study. I guess I had to be. With my dad's job in the Air Force and us moving around so much, I picked up accents wherever we lived, just to fit in. I think I learned that one when Dad was stationed at Barksdale, in Bossier City, Louisiana."

"Well, I'm impressed, and that's saying something." Jolene stepped out into the hallway. "We should hurry. There's nothing worse than cold hush puppies."

Sunny put a hand on my arm, holding me back. In an almost-whisper, she said, "Will you think about what I said?"

She dropped her hand, her gaze lingering on mine for a long moment before she followed Jolene into the hall and down the stairs. I paused in the doorway, her words having hit me like a hard shove. My stomach churned as I saw from Sunny's perspective my reluctance to help—a petty, self-absorbed reaction to a betrayal, and embarrassment about having been played. Yes, Michael had broken my heart and I wasn't completely sure that I was over him. Yet I couldn't dismiss the small tingle of excitement at the possibility of revenge. Or the actuality that I might protect Beau from real harm.

I hurried down the steps to where Sunny and Jolene waited for me in front of Charles Ryan's portrait in the foyer. A cool breeze blew at my face, moving my hair. Sunny shivered, her gaze darting between Jolene and me. "Please don't think I'm weird or anything, but is this house supposed to be haunted?"

We found ourselves gazing at the portrait of Charles Ryan, his painted eyes boring into mine. "Well," Jolene said, "it would depend on how you define the word 'haunted,' but I will share with you two of the most important things my grandmama taught me." She began counting off points, starting with her thumb. "The first is that all old houses are full of memories of those who've passed on, so cold spots and shadows are as much a part of the house as wood rot and creaky floors."

She dropped her hand and headed toward the dining room, and Sunny and I followed her like ducklings waiting for bread crumbs. "What's the second thing?" Sunny asked.

Jolene paused at the threshold. With a serious voice, she said, "Never iron or fry chicken naked."

My feet pounded against the asphalt running path at Audubon Park as I finished my third lap around the lagoon. Because of the whole Michael Hebert thing, I hadn't previously returned to what had once been part of my daily routine. The park was where we'd first met, and he lived across the street, on Audubon Place, making my chances of running into him fairly high. Which was exactly the reason why I'd been avoiding the park until now. I wasn't sure why, since Michael should be the one avoiding me. But the lingering thought that he might *want* to see me made me both hopeful and terrified that I'd run into him. And despite having been given a script from Sam as to what I should say to Michael should I see him, I still wasn't sure what would come out of my mouth if I did.

Jolene had been awake before me, as was her annoying habit—annoying except for the freshly brewed coffee and hot muffin she had waiting for me on the table—and she'd forced me into hot pink running shorts with a coordinating top. Even the socks matched. She seemed to think that I had a better chance of encouraging Michael's attention if I wore something other than my usual running clothes. Which, according to Jolene, were a cross between her grandpa's hand-me-downs and Goodwill rejects.

I slowed my pace to check my fitness tracker, debating whether I needed a fourth lap. Eating baked goods every day, complete with gluten and white flour—previously not words in my vocabulary—was a great motivator. But I was tired, having stayed up too late the night before trying to find the right notes to the song I'd been writing since I'd moved to New Orleans. I'd written a whole line—hardly enough to make the loss of sleep worthwhile.

I pulled my phone from the handy side pocket in Jolene's running shorts and made my way to a bench by the fountain at the front of the park. I opened my fitness app to check on my running partners, Melanie and my aunt Jayne, and noticed that Melanie had again "forgotten" to turn on the app, so nothing had been updated since her last run. She usually made up for this lapse in memory by manually inputting her stats, which always made me roll my eyes. Either she was running both ways between her house and her favorite doughnut shop, Glazed Donuts on King, or she was stretching the truth. Or both.

An incoming text beeped from Melanie. I opened her garbled message, stifling an inner groan as I prepared my brain for a workout. For a person who was otherwise thin, she apparently had very fat thumbs, so her accuracy rate while texting was about five percent, and if she attempted voice dictation, Siri thought she was speaking Swahili, which made for very interesting messages. It had taken me years to be able to translate her texts, but I was an expert now. The biggest challenge was filling in the empty spaces in words where bottom-row letters on the keyboard should be but weren't since she always missed them and hit the space bar instead.

Can't wait to see you! I'll be bringing gifts for your team—I hope that's okay. I had to ask Rich Kobylt how to spell Thibaut and am bringing him suspenders just in case he has more in common with Rich than their last name. Also, Sarah wants to stay all week instead of just the weekend. JJ does, too, but he's got a bake-off competition. It's fine with your dad and me. I'll let you decide. Love you!

Instead of the kiss emoji to end her text, a brown pile of poop smiled at me from the screen. I assumed that was a mistake.

My little sister, so open about her psychic abilities when she was younger, had grown to be a lot more secretive about them once she realized that none of her friends or classmates had entourages of imaginary friends and deceased relatives trailing them wherever they went.

The final blow had come when Sarah's best friend, Lollie, had burst into tears on class picture day when Sarah said that Lollie's grandmother thought Lollie should have worn the bow in her hair like her mother had suggested. This wouldn't have been so upsetting except for the fact that Lollie's grandmother had died the week before.

I'd bent to my phone to respond when another text popped onto my screen. It was from Beau: Are you in or not?

Before I could type my reply, two more texts came in, one from Sunny and one from Sam, both similar messages. Did you see Michael?

My thumbs flew over the screen as I responded to the last two. No

I hit Send, and then thought a moment before sending another message. Is there a plan b

I opened Beau's text again but hesitated before typing anything. It was bad enough that I was conspiring with Sunny and Sam to rekindle my relationship with Michael so I could eke out a revenge I wasn't sure I wanted. But to play double agent and pretend to be helping Beau while actually hiding any useful information made me physically sick. I closed my eyes and took a deep breath, willing the nausea to pass. I would make a terrible spy.

"Nola?"

I kept my eyes closed, unsure if I'd imagined Michael's voice.

"Nola?"

This time Michael's voice was accompanied by a gentle hand on my shoulder. "You okay? Do you need some water?"

I opened my eyes to see Michael Hebert's suntanned face, his hazel eyes full of concern. He placed a purple water bottle sporting the Saints logo into my hand and helped me lift it to my mouth. I took several long gulps, not because I was thirsty but because I had no idea what I wanted to say. Or was supposed to say.

When I'd reached the end of the bottle, I handed it back to him. "Thanks." Well, that was a start.

"Do you need to lie down? You don't look well."

I shook my head. "I'm okay. I didn't pace myself. Thanks for the water."

He looked at me, forcing me to focus my attention on the outstretched arm of the sculpture of the woman in the fountain, a bird perched on her hand.

I felt him sit next to me on the bench. "This is the first time I've come to run in the park since . . ." He stopped. "I figured you wouldn't want to see me, and I know how you love to run in the park, so I stayed away."

I finally met his eyes, and they were the same eyes of the man I'd once thought I was falling in love with. Until the real Michael Hebert had been exposed, and I'd learned that everything had been a lie, his feelings for me manufactured just so he could have access to whatever secrets he thought were hidden inside my house.

"Me, too," I said, my reality check giving me a firm grip on my emotions, helping me remember what I was supposed to be doing. I resisted the need to move away from him on the bench despite the humiliation that hummed right beneath my skin. Facing him now was a lot like I imagined it would feel to walk into a crowded room and fall flat on my face, then have to get up and keep talking as if nothing had happened.

"My jaw still hurts where Beau punched me." He brushed the stubble on the side of his cheek.

"Good."

He smiled. "I guess I deserved that. And the punch."

"You won't get any argument from me. My only regret is that I didn't think to do it first."

He leaned toward me with serious eyes. "Give it your best shot. Whatever it takes to make you understand that I am truly sorry."

"Sorry?" My voice rose. My first impulse was to give him what he was asking for, which reassured me that I still clung to at least a bit of self-respect.

He sat up, his palms facing me in a gesture of surrender. "I know. It's a pathetic word. Not even barely adequate to describe how I feel."

"Then why did you do it?" I wasn't sure if that played into the game set up by Sunny and Sam, but I didn't really care. If I was being forced to head down the path of revenge, I had to get something out of it just for myself. Like an answer.

He took a deep breath, as if trying to figure out where to start, and when he did start, his words surprised me. "You come from a nice, normal family."

I wanted to interrupt to explain that there was nothing normal about a stepmother who could speak to the dead, but I needed him to continue.

"I don't," he said. "I mean, what sort of parents suddenly take off to the other side of the world and leave behind their kids to be raised by relatives? That's not normal. I've seen them about five times in the last two decades, and only because they needed to sign some paperwork for the company or negotiate for more supplies for whatever part of the world they were headed for next."

A snowy egret landed on the edge of the fountain and we watched its yellow feet goose-step around the perimeter, the bird ignoring us. I felt a moment of envy at its confidence.

He looked down at his hands again. "My great-grandfather Antoine Broussard passed down the story of how my grandaunt Jeanne had been murdered by Beau's grandfather, Charles Ryan." He held up his hand when he heard my intake of breath. "I now know that's not true. I think my uncle truly believed it, which made it easier for me to go along with whatever he wanted me to do. And after I met you, it smoothed away some of the guilt I'd begun to feel."

"So why didn't you tell me when you realized what was going on?"

"Because I'm a jerk. Because my family . . ." He paused, then started again. "Since I last saw you, I've been doing research. About my great-grandfather Antoine. About some of the things he was rumored to have been involved in. Most of them are true. He was a really bad guy whose influence is still felt not only in the business he started, but also in my family."

"Well, that's one thing we can agree upon. So, why are you here? You said you'd stopped running in the park."

"I did." He looked down at his hands, now clasped between his knees. "But I wanted to see you. I've missed you. Even if you wouldn't talk to me, I wanted to at least see you. To try to explain my actions. To make you understand my family."

"So you know that Antoine killed his own daughter."

He looked at me with surprise. "I only suspected. But you knew?"

"Let's just say that Beau and I learned a lot about your family while trying to figure out who kept on breaking into my house."

Michael had the decency to look chagrined. "I was told that my job was only to gain access, not to ask questions. I know how lame this sounds, but I only did what I was told."

My phone buzzed in my hand, and I looked down at it to see another text from Beau. Well?

"Do you think we could . . ." Michael shrugged. "I don't know—have dinner?"

When I didn't respond, he said, "Well, that's a relief. I was afraid you'd scream and run away."

"I still might. Why do you think we should have dinner?"

"To talk. Maybe start over?"

At my look of incredulity, he rushed to explain. "I mean as friends. I don't think that even you can deny that we have a connection. We were drawn to each other because we were both abandoned by our parents. The circumstances were different, but we wear similar bruises. And I really like you, Nola. A lot. And I thought you liked me, too. Despite everything, I was hoping there was still that."

He looked at me expectantly. I held my breath so I wouldn't say every vile thing I'd been calling him in my head ever since I'd discovered his duplicity. Because even now, I couldn't completely erase the feelings I'd had for him. And that was why contemplating going out with him should have been an easy *no* but wasn't. But, as I'd discovered the hard way over the last eight years, nothing was ever easy. Even revenge.

Michael tentatively took my hand, and when I didn't pull back, he squeezed it. "I thought we could talk about what happened. Not to excuse what I did, but maybe so I could explain it in a way you could understand."

I stared down at our clasped hands so he couldn't look behind my eyes and see my head and heart playing keep-away with my conscience.

"I know it's a lot to ask, and that I don't deserve five minutes in your company, but I had to try. The worst you can say is no, right?"

I lifted my eyes, and he gave me the devastating grin that had once loosened my bones. "Actually, there are a lot of worse things I could say to you right now, but all of them would make me want to wash my mouth out with soap." My phone buzzed in my hand again, but I didn't look, knowing it was Beau, repeating his question.

Michael looked at me hopefully. "Then how about dinner this weekend? Do you like Commander's?"

It was a rhetorical question. Everyone liked the iconic restaurant, but very few could get last-minute reservations. I pulled my hand away and stood. "I've got to go."

Michael stood, too. "Friday night, then? Pick you up at seven?"

I thought of the repercussions Beau would face if I walked away from Michael now. If I shut the door on this opportunity to get inside Michael's family and make them face justice for the abduction of Sunny Ryan. Beau would stop at nothing to get those answers himself, despite the danger. My phone buzzed again, and I realized that I really didn't have a choice at all.

"Thursday," I said. "My family arrives on Friday. I'll see you then." I hurriedly exited the park, turning left to jog down St. Charles toward Broadway. When I'd reached the next intersection, I slowed my pace to a walk so I could reply to Beau's texts. With my head bent over my phone, I typed, I'm in.

Before I could change my mind, I sprinted across St. Charles Avenue and ran at full speed all the way back to my apartment, my breathing not loud enough to erase the one thought that kept racing across my brain. *Before you embark on a journey of revenge, dig two graves.*

CHAPTER 7

Two days later, I leaned my bike against the front of my house, not bothering with the lock. My cottage continued to be a thief repellent—along with a delivery service, contractor, and visitor deterrent. The only intruders I experienced were the extremely large cockroaches that, according to Thibaut, would survive a nuclear blast and that all the roach bait and poison just made bigger and stronger.

Despite the air's being still, the wind chime of blue glass by the front door swayed, the tinkling breaking the silence that enveloped my house like heavy fog. Even in the middle of summer, the nightly chorus of insects from neighboring yards ended at the perimeter of my property.

The faint smell of pipe smoke teased the air, and I turned my head toward the end of the porch, where I'd once seen the specter of Charles Ryan smoking his pipe. But that was before Beau and I had sent him into the light. It wasn't unheard of for a freed spirit to return occasionally to check on the living. I turned the doorknob and pushed open the front door, pausing as I caught another whiff of smoke. A shudder went through me as I considered the possibility that he had unfinished business. Something that still tied him to my house.

The rousing beat of salsa music thumped upstairs. I closed the door loudly to let Thibaut and Jorge know I was there before climbing up the steps, stopping at the top of the stairs to peer inside the closet that had been nailed shut when I purchased the cottage. The door sat ajar, the vintage clothes, shoes, hatboxes, and Mr. Bingle doll found inside since removed to my apartment.

Jolene had sold most of the clothing items to a vintage clothing store in the Quarter, but the Mr. Bingle doll and one of the hatboxes, with its mysterious contents—a pipe, a yellow hair ribbon, a tie clasp, and an old camera negative—remained in the back room of the apartment along with a clientele book from the now-defunct Maison Blanche department store. Jolene and I had agreed to keep it all hidden, buried under a pile of monogrammed throw pillows, just in case. Not that we expected another attempted robbery, but we'd decided that there had to have been a reason for it all to have been locked in the closet since the murder of Jeanne Broussard in 1964.

Michael's uncle had hired someone to break in and steal the Maison Blanche door we'd stored in my apartment. Fortunately, the thief had been thwarted by Jolene and her well-aimed blow from a large Barbie head. I tried not to think too much about that night, not only in deference to Barbie and the lessons I'd learned from her in terms of makeup application, but also because that was when I'd become aware of Michael's betrayal.

But with the discovery of the truth behind Jeanne's murder and Sunny's abduction, there should have been no reason to keep the hatbox hidden any longer. Unless there was. And it wasn't like we didn't have enough monogrammed pillows. That's why the box remained in the back room, camouflaged as a design statement. At least until I was satisfied that there really was no reason for anyone else to want it.

I continued into the newly studded hallway, listening as the salsa music grew louder. I almost tripped over a tennis ball as it rolled toward me. I stooped to pick it up, then followed the music to its source. I found the eighties-era boom box along with Thibaut and

Jorge in the back bedroom hand sanding the newly patched plaster on the far wall. They both turned when I entered, their attention drawn to the ball in my hand.

"Where'd you find that?" Thibaut asked as he leaned down to turn off the music. "We've been looking all over! We were practicing our juggling routine this morning to warm up our hands, and the darn thing rolled around a corner and disappeared."

"I, um . . . well, I guess it was stuck in a corner and I must have accidentally dislodged it while I was walking." Both Thibaut and Jorge stared at me, neither one reaching for the ball. I walked over to the far corner and placed it on the floor. "It's here whenever you need it." To change the subject, I said, "I hope you saved some of the wall patching for me!"

"Yes, ma'am," Thibaut said, leading me through the hallway to the adjacent bedroom. Holes in the old plaster walls where new electrical outlets and switches had been installed, as well as a few irregular punctures that could have been made by any number of objects that I preferred not to consider, dotted the four walls like a patchwork quilt. "You told me how much you loved patching old plaster, so we saved this whole room for you."

I rubbed my hands together. "I can't wait! I'm taking a half day of vacation so I can really dig in. It's slow right now at the office, and I'd rather be mixing plaster than cleaning the refrigerator." I peered closely at a hole in one of the walls. "And it looks like I have some lath repair, too. That's my favorite part."

The giant of a man smiled, making it easy to forget his past. "It's a bit like that game I used to play with my son—Tetris, I think. Like tile work, too—trying to figure out which piece will fit in where. Greggie was much better at it than me. I don't think I ever beat his score." Thibaut's face softened at the mention of his son. He had never spoken to me about Greg, who had been raised by Thibaut's late wife's family and not allowed contact with his father.

"You must miss him," I said. "How long has it been since you've seen him?"

"Fifteen years. Fifteen very long years. I haven't even heard his voice. I'm not allowed to call him, and I don't even think he knows how to get in touch. If I thought he'd call, I might actually get a cell phone."

"I'm so sorry."

He shrugged his giant shoulders. "Don't be. I made my bed, and now I've got to lie in it. I just wish . . ." Thibaut studied me with eyes that looked suspiciously teary. "I just wish that we could talk about it. About what happened. I need to make sure that he's in a good place about it. That he understands that I still love him."

I wondered at his choice of words, not completely sure what sort of good place there was for a boy whose father had killed his mother. And why Thibaut was worried about his son wondering if his dad still loved him instead of the other way around.

He turned his head while he rubbed his eyes with the back of his hand. With a forced cheerfulness, he said, "I don't think I've complimented you yet on the excellent job you did on the bathroom floor tiles. I don't think I could have done it better myself. Most beginners tile themselves into a corner and then have to wreck the floor to get out."

"That's crazy," I said, faking a chuckle. "What kind of a clueless amateur would do such a thing?"

"I can't imagine." Beau's voice came from the doorway. "Hopefully nobody who works for JR Properties. I'd like to think I did a better job of hiring."

Avoiding Beau's gaze, I made to move past him. "I'd better get started mixing that plaster—"

"Hang on a minute."

I stopped, waiting for him to humiliate me in front of Thibaut by telling the whole story.

"I need a favor."

"A favor? In return for . . ." I glanced at Thibaut, who seemed to be focused on checking out the extent of missing lath behind the plaster holes.

Wearing a grin, Beau shook his head. "Just a favor. You're even allowed to say no. But I don't think you will."

"Okay," I said, curious but wary. This would officially be the very first time he'd asked me for help. I gritted my teeth, waiting for it. Because no exchange between Beau and me had ever been straightforward or without risk.

"Mimi's got it into her head that we need to expand the renovation part of our business."

"But that's already the core of JR Properties, right?"

Beau nodded. "Yeah, but this idea is more about a niche market. She says she got the idea from you."

"Me?"

"You. And the whole murder-house angle."

"The murder-house angle," I repeated slowly, just to make sure I'd heard him right.

"Mimi's been doing some research and found that there are a lot of potentially valuable properties in the New Orleans metro and beyond with the same kind of . . . background as your house. You know, where unfortunate incidents have occurred in the recent or not-so-recent past."

"You mean murders."

"Sure. Or unexplained deaths, disappearances, bodies left behind because nobody thought to check on them. That sort of thing."

"Right. And I made her think of all that."

Beau smiled. "Yeah. Pretty much. She showed me a listing for a house on Esplanade selling for basically peanuts despite the houses in the neighborhood all being valued at far more, and it has been on the market for eight years without a single offer."

"I probably already know the answer, but why?"

He smiled again, probably knowing how it affected most women. Including me. "Single-victim homicide, and the disappearance of the family of three who lived there, a mom, dad, and their thirteen-year-old daughter. No sign of them has ever been found, and they've been officially declared dead, which is why the house is for sale. The relatives of the family held on to the hope they'd return but decided eight years ago to settle the estate and put it on the market."

"So, what's wrong with the house?"

Beau sent me a meaningful glance. "Besides looking like an eighties décor bomb exploded inside? Nothing." He paused as Thibaut left the room.

"Go on," I said.

"So, Mimi has been looking at all the social media Jolene has been uploading all over the place and how the number of subscribers on the YouTube page multiplies every week."

"Well, that has nothing to do with me. It's mostly to do with Thibaut and Jorge and their Three Stooges act."

"True. But it seems that if viewers tune in to see their routine, they stay to watch the instructional video that follows. And Jolene answers every question from viewers, which always makes it even more entertaining. But I really think it's her new title idea that's bringing in viewers."

"Her new title idea?"

"Yeah. Didn't she mention it to you?"

"No, actually. She didn't. And I've been too busy to watch, so I'm clueless." I crossed my arms, knowing there had to be a reason why Jolene hadn't told me. "I'm almost afraid to ask, but what is it?"

He smiled like a little boy revealing his latest Lego masterpiece. "*Murder House Flip*."

I stared at him, sure that I must have misheard. "I'm sorry, what?"

"*Murder House Flip*!"

At my confused look, Beau rushed on. "DIY shows are really popular, but for a new one to stand out in the crowd there needs to be an added twist. True-crime podcasts, shows, and YouTube channels have really exploded, too. So why not marry the two and do a channel all about renovating houses where murders—old or new—have occurred? Brilliant, huh?"

When I didn't respond, Beau pressed on. "I guess Jolene wanted to test the title first to see if it worked, and judging by the growth in numbers, it's working. In fact, it's working so well that Mimi is hoping to attract the attention of one of the DIY networks."

"That's ridiculous," I said.

"No. *Keeping Up with the Kardashians* was ridiculous. This makes sense. People are obsessed with home renovations, and with true crime. Why not give them both, with the added bonus of highlighting a house with a history?"

"A house with a history? That would be the White House. Or Buckingham Palace. What you're talking about is a whole different ball game."

"Mimi's point exactly. It's a whole new concept in the DIY world. I think it's an idea whose time has come."

Because it was Beau, I would have preferred to find a headless cockroach in my salad than to say that he was right, so instead, I said, "Mimi might be onto something."

"She definitely is. And I'm glad to hear that you agree. Otherwise, I'd be thinking that Mimi was just trying to distract me."

His eyes were blank as he regarded me, making me wonder if he'd already guessed the truth about his grandmother's subterfuge, but I decided to move ahead. I quashed my tinge of guilt by reminding myself that it was for his own good. Just like when I'd hidden Melanie's doughnuts and replaced them with organic breakfast bars.

If I'd been the sort of person who could learn from her first mistake so she wouldn't repeat it, I would have seen the opportunity then and confessed everything to Beau. But I didn't. I could only hope that Sam, Sunny, and I could find the answers Beau needed before his own digging caught the attention of Michael's family. Or at least before he discovered our complicity. I wasn't sure which would be worse.

"You said you were here to ask me for a favor?"

He smiled in the way a nurse does before plunging in a needle. "Well, since we've proven that we work well together and both bring something to a restoration project, this might be a great professional relationship."

I screwed up my eyes, trying to envision what he was seeing. "Like that snarky couple on *Love It or List It*?"

"I was thinking more like Chip and Joanna Gaines, but snarky could work."

"Except they're married, with about a ton of kids, and genuinely like each other."

He drew back as if offended. "Harsh. It's not my fault that I have the skills necessary to help you out of your occasional mishaps, but I'm always happy to be there. Even without an official thank-you."

"If you're wanting me to go along with your plan, you're not saying the right thing. It's not *my* fault that you leap in even when your help is clearly not needed." I shook my head to make him stop talking. "And who in the world even gave you the idea that we could work well together?"

"Sam."

"Sam," I repeated, wondering if this might be part of her grand plan or if she seriously thought Beau and I could make a nice, platonic team.

"Yeah. So, before you say anything else, why don't we go check out the house and see what we think, okay?"

I tried to come up with a reason why this was a very bad idea, but there was nothing in my vocabulary that could translate *I have a serious crush on you and I heard you tell your dead mother that you want me too much*. "Sure. Just know that I'm not agreeing to anything except to look at the house."

He smiled again, as if he knew exactly what it did to my knees. "Great." He held out his arm. "After you."

I walked into the hallway, then turned to face him. "Have you considered that the chance of there being hangers-on in these 'murder houses' is pretty high?"

Beau gave a sharp nod. "I'm aware."

I frowned. "Are you prepared to deal with whatever repercussions that might mean?"

"Not yet, but I plan to be. Mimi has spent her life trying to help people with her gift. Could be that's the only way I can come to terms with my . . . problem. Mimi has to be very careful with curating her surroundings so she can control who she lets in. Maybe that's what I need to learn."

"Why is this suddenly important to you?" I didn't need to involve myself with Beau's personal life. Yet our lives had run in tandem for so long, I couldn't feign indifference.

His gaze skittered away from mine. "Honesty. With myself, mostly. But with others, too. I mean, I spend a lot of time debunking things I'm not totally sure aren't real. And Sam goes along with it as my sidekick. Sometimes I find myself wondering if she and I . . ." He shrugged. "Anyway, I was hoping to talk to Melanie while she's here. Hopefully get some pointers from her."

I welcomed the abrupt conversation turn away from Sam and Beau. "You'd better start brushing up on ABBA lyrics. Especially 'Dancing Queen.'"

"Whatever it takes." He dug into his back jeans pocket and pulled out his keys before tossing them to me. "You're driving."

My satisfied smile at the image of him belting out ABBA music quickly died. He and Jolene had conspired to take me to the DMV to get my permit on a Saturday-afternoon trip to get beignets. "But Esplanade has a neutral ground. What if I go the wrong way?"

He moved toward me and gently pushed my back to propel me toward the stairs. "If you can't tell your left from your right by now, you have more problems than not knowing how to drive." I headed down the stairs, with Beau following close behind, as if he was afraid that I might bolt—a thought that had crossed my mind.

Beau shut the front door behind us and moved past me down the porch steps, but I stopped, absently plucking at the rubber band on my arm.

"You got this, Nola. And I'll be in the seat next to you. If it makes you feel any better, you can even imagine me facing some vengeful spirit while singing 'Dancing Queen' at the top of my lungs."

I gripped the keys as I made my way to the driver's side. "I hope we live to regret this."

"What? You behind the wheel or the two of us flipping murder houses?"

I met his eyes. "Both." I unlocked the doors and climbed behind the wheel, aware again of the scent of pipe smoke that followed us out of the house and of the bright green tennis ball now rolling down the steps, then stopping in front of the truck as if to make sure it was seen.

CHAPTER 8

Beau pointed at a spot on the curb directly across the street from the Past Is Never Past. "How's your parallel parking?"

I wanted to look at him to see if he was joking, but I was too busy avoiding hapless pedestrians and the ubiquitous orange cones marking cavernous potholes while dodging other vehicles as we headed down Royal Street. It wasn't on the way to Esplanade, but Beau said he had to stop by the shop to pick up props for that evening's live-stream episode of *Bumps in the Night and Other Improbabilities.* "Probably about the same as your skill in putting on a pair of Spanx. Why don't I drop you off and go around the block a few times . . . ?"

"It's two spaces, Nola. Plenty of room."

"Right. For my bike, maybe. There are people behind me, which makes me nervous. There is no way I'm going to do this without serious carnage. . . ."

Beau reached across me and flipped on the turn signal. "Just pull up next to the car in front and I'll guide you through it. You'll lose sleep torturing yourself over me witnessing you quitting."

"I seriously hate you right now."

I heard the smile in his voice, and I would have hit him if my hands hadn't had the steering wheel in a death grip. "It wouldn't be a relationship if one of us didn't say that at least once. Now, as soon as my door reaches the back bumper of the car in front, turn hard right."

After several near misses, close calls, and honking horns, I somehow managed to wedge Beau's truck into a spot at the curb. Cold sweat beaded on my face, and I wasn't sure I could ever straighten my fingers again.

"See? That wasn't so bad, was it?"

I swallowed to get moisture back into my mouth so I could speak. "Right. And the iceberg that sank the *Titanic* wasn't so big."

Beau reached over and pulled my fingers from the steering wheel. "But you did it. Best way to get over a fear is to keep doing the thing you're afraid of so it doesn't scare you anymore."

"Did your dad tell you that?"

"Nope. Henry Ford. Christopher gave me a paperweight with that quote on it for my sixteenth birthday. I keep it on my desk as a reminder." He unbuckled his seat belt and leaned back but didn't make a move to exit the truck.

I used the time to unclench my jaw and peel my shoulders away from my neck before breathing in and out slowly, like Melanie's best friend, Dr. Sophie Wallen-Arasi, had shown me. She was usually too granola for Melanie, but except for her drastic adherence to renovation purity, she was pretty cool. And the breathing really did help in times of stress. Like now.

"Okay," I said. "I'm ready."

"Good. I'm not. I'm going to need another minute."

I watched as he closed his eyes and began plucking at the rubber band on his wrist.

After several long moments Beau opened his eyes and turned toward me. "Being in an antiques store never used to bother me. That's how I was able to work here and in your grandparents' store. But ever since that night in your house, it's getting harder and harder."

"Harder for what?"

"To block them out. The unwanted ones. My old techniques aren't working, and if I'm going to move forward with this new idea, or come into the store, I have to figure things out."

I unbuckled my seat belt. "Yep—that's a problem. I'm sure Melanie won't mind you asking for help. I just hope you like ABBA. Otherwise, you might decide that letting all the spirits in might be easier to take."

We exited the truck and met on the sidewalk in front of the shop. "What's not to like?" Beau asked. "I have a couple of songs on my playlist—and that's from before I met Melanie."

"Lies. I'm not seeing how a fan of random indie bands and jazz can also love ABBA."

"And I don't see how a musically gifted songwriter doesn't understand their genius. Their music is accessible to both casual and informed listeners, but their songs are very personal. Like they're singing to each other, but also directly to every single member in the audience. It didn't hurt that they adopted Phil Spector's Wall of Sound so they always sounded polished and big."

"Who knew?" I said. "You'll have to tell Melanie. But if you make 'SOS' your ringtone, I'll know you've been taken in by the dark side."

A bicyclist pedaled past while clutching an old cassette player, a familiar song blasting. "The Smashing Pumpkins," I said.

"That's '1979,'" he said simultaneously. "Jinx."

"Not really," I said, walking into the cold air that persisted inside the antiques store throughout the year, regardless of the outdoor temperature. I no longer believed Mimi's claim that it was an air-conditioning problem.

"I heard you have a date with Michael on Thursday. I thought you might have mentioned it by now."

His abrupt change of topic left me stumbling for words. I glanced behind Beau to where I could see Christopher speaking with two middle-aged women at the desk in the rear of the store. "I, uh . . ."

"So you've decided to help me."

I looked at him in surprise. "I told you I was in."

"Actually, you texted me. And 'I'm in' is an incomplete answer. I've been waiting for you to elaborate. But I guess a date with Michael means you're *all* in."

I hadn't considered until just then that by helping Sam and Sunny, I'd also have to do a lot of lying to Beau. And I was a terrible liar. I'd learned that the first time I'd told my dad I was going to bed early, only to find him waiting in the backyard after I'd shimmied myself out of my window and climbed down a drainpipe.

"I guess it does. How did you find out about the date?"

He slid his backpack off his shoulder and rested it on the floor. "Trevor. I ran into him here, at the store, and he mentioned that he was looking for a mace key chain for you for your dinner with Michael at Commander's. He's a great information resource."

"Yeah, well, I need to tell him to be more discreet. I was going to tell you myself afterward, but only if I had any information to share."

"Uh-huh. The mere fact that you have a date with Michael should have been worthy of a mention." He glanced over at Christopher, who was still talking with the same customers. "Wait here while I go in the back room and get the stuff I need. I'll be right back."

I found myself watching Christopher and the two women. One of them was sobbing into a handkerchief and the other was holding her hand. On the desk between them sat a gold birdcage inside of which perched a small blue parrot preening its wings. Eventually the women stood, and Christopher rounded the corner of his desk. He picked up the cage and carried it with him as he escorted the women to the door. Beau returned, and we both stayed back as I lowered my eyes, uncomfortable witnessing the grief of a stranger.

"I am so very sorry for your loss," Christopher said, his voice gentle. "I do promise to speak with Mrs. Ryan on your behalf, but as I mentioned, she's on hiatus right now. Her skills are in high demand, and they do take a toll on her well-being, as you can imagine. I have your information, and I promise to be in touch as soon as she is able to resume her work."

"Thank you," one of the women said. I looked up to see Christopher handing the birdcage to the woman who'd been sobbing into a wadded-up handkerchief.

Red and swollen eyes met mine briefly as she took the cage, giving me the chance to see her better. She appeared to be somewhere in her mid-sixties, but her slender figure and stiff spine lent her an air of dignity. Her natural light blond hair was cut in an attractive bob and streaked with sparkling strands of pure platinum. The fingers that held the birdcage were devoid of polish or rings except for a cushion-set solitaire sapphire ring worn on her right hand. I knew even before I looked that she'd be wearing tasteful Ferragamo flats on her feet. She reminded me of the well-heeled women I saw when strolling through Saks or any of the other high-end stores at the Canal Place mall. I had neither the desire nor the money to shop there, but I'd attended a few movies at the theater on the third floor and would sometimes cut through the beauty department at Saks to see if I could be tempted into buying my own tube of lipstick. So far, I hadn't.

I glanced over at her slightly younger companion, similar enough in appearance that the two women had to be sisters, although this woman wore large, dangling earrings and her platinum hair was worn long down her back, a purple silk headband holding her hair from her face. It matched her purple tunic with yellow embroidered dragons and the gladiator sandals that exposed black-painted toenails.

"Thank you, Mr. Benoit," the younger woman said, offering her hand to Christopher. "I apologize for the tears, but I'm sure you can understand. It's been eight long years, and this is our last option."

Christopher nodded solemnly. "I do understand, Mrs. Meggison. I will let Mrs. Ryan know."

Mrs. Meggison took hold of Christopher's hand and squeezed, giving him a warm smile. "I know you will. And please call me

Honey," she drawled. "Everyone does. Mrs. Meggison was my mother-in-law."

Christopher smiled. "Of course." He opened the door. "I hope to see y'all soon."

"Us, too," Honey said, stepping past her sister and out onto the sidewalk. "Good-bye for now."

The older woman held out her hand to Christopher in a formal handshake and didn't invite him to call her by her given name. "Mrs. Wenzel," he said, shaking her outstretched hand. "Until then."

As she turned to leave, I had an up-close view of the pocket-sized bird, with its azure feathers and striking cobalt wing tips like the markings on a commercial jet. It had stopped preening and was now fixated on Beau, its head twitching from side to side as if it were trying to form a question. It opened its yellow beak and let out a shrill squawk, its round black eyes staring unblinkingly at Beau.

Mrs. Wenzel stopped and pressed her hand against her chest while lifting the cage to eye level. "Well, my goodness. That's the first sound I've ever heard him make."

I couldn't pretend anymore that I hadn't been listening. "But don't all parrots talk?"

All eyes turned to me, including those of Honey, who remained just outside the doorway.

"Not necessarily," Honey said. "This is a parrotlet. Just like their larger relatives, parrotlets are certainly capable of talking if their owners take the time to teach them. Except we've only had Zeus for eight years." She raised her handkerchief to her nose and sniffed. "We acquired him from our younger brother, Mark, after he . . . disappeared. Zeus hasn't made so much as a peep ever since."

"That's fascinating," I said, ignoring cautioning looks from Christopher and Beau. I seemed to have inherited my novelist dad's dogged determination to get to the bottom of a story, and despite my years in the South and tutelage from Melanie and my two Southern grandmothers, that determination had not been softened in any way. It came in handy when I dealt with contractors and suppliers.

"We don't even know his real name," Mrs. Wenzel said as Honey dabbed again at the corners of her eyes. "We named him Zeus as a lark, seeing as how he's just this little thing, and left all alone after . . ." She stopped.

"So you never saw the bird when you visited?" I asked. There was a story here. If not for a book, then maybe for a song.

"We and our brother were . . . estranged," Honey added between sniffles.

Mrs. Wenzel nodded. "Not through our choosing, you understand. Mark was the son of our father's second marriage and was a good deal younger. But we had a wonderful relationship with him until . . ."

"Until his marriage to Jessica," Honey finished. "We were so happy for him, and then when little Lynda was born we were over the moon. We just don't know what happened. That's why we were here—"

Christopher opened the door wider. "I am sure you ladies need to get going. But thank you both again for coming. I will certainly speak with Mrs. Ryan, and I'll be in touch."

"Of course," Mrs. Wenzel said, and gave me a closed smile. Then she turned toward her sister and, clutching the bird cage, gingerly stepped down onto the sidewalk.

Zeus twisted his head to stare at Beau while continuing his high-pitched chirping, which was still audible after the door was closed behind the bird and the two women. I turned to Christopher to apologize, but I stopped when I noticed that Beau's pallor now blended with the white wall behind him.

"That bird . . ." Beau began.

"Seemed to have something to say to you," I prompted.

He stared at me blankly before quickly shaking his head. "I forgot something from the storeroom. I'll be right back." Beau left us watching after him, his movement blowing the price tags of the chandeliers that hung from the ceiling.

I waited for Christopher to say something about the women or the bird, but instead he said, "I don't think I've thanked you enough for introducing us to Trevor. He's become a customer favorite and has earned a lot of money in tips. We have to empty out the tip jar Jolene decorated for him just about every day. I helped him open up his own checking account and showed him how to go online to see his balance. He's really got a good head for numbers. And salesmanship. I really do think he could sell ice to polar bears."

"I can't tell you how happy that makes me. Have you met his meemaw or brother yet? He talks about them a lot, but I've never met them."

Christopher shook his head. "Not yet, but I did get a note from Meemaw thanking me. At least I think that's what it was—the handwriting was pretty bad since she has arthritis."

I looked past him toward the door to the secret back room from which I'd been forbidden but hadn't given up trying to find an excuse to see inside. "Maybe I should go see if Beau needs my help," I suggested.

When Christopher didn't say anything, I looked at him, surprised to find a bemused smile on his face. "Oh, what a tangled web we weave . . ."

A jolt of alarm ran through me. "Excuse me?"

He crossed his arms. "Mimi told me everything. And I'm going to tell you exactly what I told her. Lying to someone, even if you think it's for their own good, never ends well. I haven't figured out exactly what else you're planning, but my advice is that you come clean to Beau now, before you're buried so deep that you can't climb your way out. I don't know if you've noticed, but Beau holds on to a grudge like a dog with a bone. It could ruin your relationship forever."

I felt the heat rise to my face, a sign of the familiar obstinance that reared its ugly head whenever someone tried to tell me what to do. "I don't know what Mimi told you, but I'm just here to help Beau with a new project so he won't have the time to stick his nose into the Broussard family and get it cut off. Or worse. That's all. Besides, Beau and I don't really have a 'relationship.' We're just work partners."

Christopher stood with his arms folded, like a parent patiently waiting for a guilty toddler to confess taking the last cookie from the jar. His amber eyes remained on mine, and I refused to be the first to look away. "Mimi hasn't shared anything with me—I simply guessed. You just confirmed. And I'm coming from a position of friendship for you and Beau, and a genuine desire to help you both. Which is why I'm suggesting that you tell Beau everything. Now."

"Tell me what?" Beau shouted across the empty shop from where he stood locking the outer storage room door.

"That we need to hurry. I think it's going to start raining in a minute." I felt Christopher's odd eyes on me, but I kept my own averted.

"I got what I needed," Beau said, holding up a small corrugated box before placing it in his backpack on the floor. "Let's go."

I felt Christopher watching me as I passed through the door he held open, but I didn't look up.

"Webs can get sticky," Christopher said.

"I don't intend to find out." I hustled across the street toward Beau's truck, barely avoiding an oncoming car whose dead aim was thankfully derailed by a cave-sized pothole.

CHAPTER 9

It was a short drive over to Esplanade, an eclectic treasure trove of nineteenth-century architectural designs. The oak-lined avenue bisected by a neutral ground was decorated with multihued homes of all styles and sizes, the once iconic street still elegant despite the ravages of time, its houses like too-bright rouge on an aging madam.

Since its beginning, Esplanade had been home to a diverse community of residents. On both sides of the avenue, majestic mansions rubbed shoulders with modest shotguns and squat Creole cottages, all nestled close together along the grand boulevard. As we neared the odd chicken-wing intersection with Bayou Road, Beau indicated a bright blue shotgun house on my right. Without adequate warning, I swerved toward the curb in front of its tiny front yard, eliciting an angry honk from the pickup truck behind me.

Beau caught my hand before I had the chance to show the impatient driver a rude finger gesture. "I'm not sure what the speed limit is, Nola, but I'm pretty sure it's more than fifteen miles per hour. I'm actually surprised it took him this long to honk at you."

I sent Beau a withering glare. "I told you I wasn't ready for public roads."

He unbuckled his seat belt and stepped out of the truck. "You did great. You just need to practice going a little faster. I think you're ready for I-10."

I climbed out, then slammed my door. "You have a death wish or something? Personally, I'd like to make it to thirty."

Beau stepped in front of the truck, his gaze intense, his expression a mix between anger and . . . something I couldn't name. Whatever it was made a cold sweat break out along my spine. "I'm not sure who you're trying to fool, Nola—you or me. You were born to defy any fear that dared to stand in your way."

I took a step toward him, ready to challenge his assumptions about me, especially anything related to the first thirteen years of my life, but paused as I caught the scent of a woman's perfume, strong and pungent, wafting across the porch, as if the lady of the house had just come out to greet us.

"Do you smell that?" I asked quietly.

Beau nodded before we turned in tandem to look at the house. We stood on the narrow strip of yard in front of the one-room-wide house posed on squat, sturdy brick piers. The six-paneled sun-faded yellow door sat beneath a rectangular transom in a Greek key surround, welcoming visitors and the home's owners alike with an elegant flair. Despite the home's small stature, the Classical Revival architectural details, including dentils and a low parapet, and four Doric pillars holding up the front gallery, made it seem much bigger. Almost like a young girl dressing up in her mother's clothes. Full-length six-over-nine double-hung windows, each with full louvered shutters, opened onto the front porch.

Two missing slats in one of the louvers gave the facade a gap-toothed expression that added to the sense of benign neglect corroborated by the flaking paint and overgrown weeds. I bent to peer through the opening between the louvers and immediately jumped back as a shadow moved just past my sight inside the room beyond.

"I thought the house was empty. Is someone meeting us here?"

"Nope. At least, no one I was expecting." Beau snapped the rubber band on his wrist and began climbing the porch steps just as a door slammed somewhere inside the house. Our eyes met. "Stay here," he said, motioning me to stay behind him.

"Seriously?" I stepped up on the porch to stand next to him. "Either we go in together or we stay out on this porch and call the police."

The unidentified scent once again floated around us. Or, more accurately, fell on us, as I could feel tiny droplets of moisture on my bare arms as if I'd just been spritzed with a perfume bottle.

"Do you recognize the fragrance?" Beau asked.

"Not really. Although . . ."

He raised his eyebrows.

"Although it's similar to a fragrance my grandmother Amelia wears. Sort of old-lady-like. Not that she's an old lady," I said quickly. "Well, she's not *that* old. But there's definitely a similar note. Like tea rose or something else that's appealing to, well, women of a certain generation. It's not exactly threatening, is it?"

"No. It's not." He snapped the rubber band one more time before pulling a key from his pocket. The slide and click of a door being unbolted came from inside as the handle turned and the door swung slowly open.

We stood without speaking for what seemed like a full minute, peering at the interior, which was darkened by closed drapes and dark brown wood. Beau began humming, and it took me a moment to realize the song was "SOS."

"Really, Beau? ABBA?"

"I figured, if it works for Melanie, it might work for me."

"And is it working?"

"Let's find out." He pushed the door all the way open, then stepped inside. "Hello?" he called out. Only a heavy silence answered. Not that an intruder would respond, of course, but if there was someone in the house, hopefully hearing Beau would encourage them to leave through the back door. Assuming that the possible intruder was the living, breathing kind.

Without waiting for him to invite me to join him, I followed him into the front room. Shotgun houses were designed with an economy of space in mind in order to fit multiple houses on a single street. They were built cheek by jowl in working-class neighborhoods in New Orleans and across the South. It took my eyes a few blinks to get accustomed to the dimness. Because shotgun houses were typically built close together, windows were rarely installed on the sides. They were a frequent addition during renovations, but in this front room none existed, all the light coming from the two floor-to-ceiling windows next to the front door and from the transom window.

Oversized and overstuffed furniture crowded the twelve-foot-wide room. A hand-carved rocking chair sat next to a laminate side table with a missing leg that had been replaced by a sawed-off baseball bat. A floor lamp had a homemade rubber band–and–paper clip contraption holding the broken lampshade onto its base.

"I hope it's not all like this," I whispered.

"Why are you whispering?" Beau whispered back.

Annoyed because I didn't have an answer, I asked, "How many rooms?"

"No idea. There's very little information on the listing site—I don't think anyone's been here for a long time to update the listing. It looks like a typical shotgun, which means the next room is probably the dining room, then the kitchen, then a small bedroom, then a bigger bedroom at the rear. Somewhere there's a bathroom—hopefully two. And hopefully in better condition than the ones at your house." He gave an exaggerated shudder.

"Funny. But yeah."

The sound of small feet running from somewhere in the back of the structure made us freeze.

"Just this once, Nola, could you please stay here in case I need you to get help? I'm just going to check the back of the house to make sure there's no one here."

"But . . ."

"Nola, please. I know you're more than capable of protecting yourself. But I'm bigger than you."

I hated to tell him that he was right, so I didn't. "It sounded like a small child," I said.

"I know."

I watched as he headed into the next room—the dining room, judging by the table in my line of sight. Single shotgun houses were designed without hallways, each room leading to the next, allowing for lots of family togetherness whether you wanted it or not. If the front and back windows were open at the same time, a breeze could run the length of the house as natural air-conditioning, the lofty ten-foot ceilings adding to the ventilation. Front porches were mandatory for hot summer days, lending themselves to general community socialization. They weren't used as much since the invention of air-conditioning, but porches were still a staple in New Orleans.

Beau's footsteps faded away as he disappeared into the back of the house; then he quickly returned. "It's a camelback," he said. "Can't see it from the street, but there are stairs off the kitchen to the second floor." He held out his hand palm up, just like I did for Mardi. "Stay here," he reminded me.

"Whatever," I said, keeping my hand on the doorknob, the door open just in case. "And I'm not a dog," I added to his departing back.

"I've noticed," he said, as his footsteps disappeared again. Before closing the door I waited until I heard the slow progress of his steps.

I began pulling aside the heavy velvet drapes on the tall windows, coughing as the layers of dust complained by erupting into clouds of thick motes that coated my nostrils and throat. Undeterred in my quest for brightness, I yanked open the shutters, allowing in streams of sunlight diluted only by windows that hadn't been washed in years.

He returned quickly. "Did you see anything?" I asked, fiddling with the puddled fabric at the bottoms of the drapery panels.

"Nothing. All the windows and the back door are locked. There were only small footprints in the dust on the floor on the stairs and in the apartment on the second floor."

"Did you . . . ?" I stopped, unsure how to continue.

"Talk to him? I mean, I think it's a boy, but I can't be sure. But no. I need to know he's the only one here before I attempt to communicate. Maybe you can help me figure that out."

"All right," I said slowly.

"See what I did there?" I could hear the smile in his voice. "I just asked nicely for your help, and neither one of us burst into flames. That's a good sign, right?"

"A good sign of what?"

Beau turned and yanked aside the curtains on the second window. With a sidelong glance and an arched eyebrow, he said, "I have no idea."

The sounds of a car engine and then slamming doors brought our attention to the front of the house. Peering through the murky windows, we spotted a dark maroon late-model Buick sedan and two women who studied Beau's truck before approaching the house.

"Isn't that . . . ?"

"It is." Beau swung open the front door and stepped out onto the porch. "Can I help you ladies?"

They looked at him with varying expressions of surprise. Mrs. Wenzel pressed her lips together before lifting the bird and its cage from the car. "Are you the buyers?" Honey asked excitedly.

"Potentially," Beau said. "Or, at least, my grandmother, Mrs. Ryan, is. She sent my associate Nola Trenholm with me today to get a deeper understanding of any restoration work needed."

They joined us on the porch, Mrs. Wenzel frowning deeply, scoring ridges on either side of her mouth. "The house is in perfect condition. I myself have seen to the upkeep over the last several years, so I would know. Ever since our half brother and family disappeared." The small blue bird flapped its wings in agitation. Mrs. Wenzel leaned down to peer into the cage. In a sweet, high-pitched voice that seemed out of place on the elegant woman, she said, "I know, sweet baby. They left you behind, didn't they? All alone with no one to care for you." She straightened, the frown back on her face. "Zeus doesn't like to be alone, so he goes with us everywhere now. This was his home. I thought he might want to see it one last time."

"Mrs. Ryan is your grandmother?" Honey asked with a hopeful note.

"Yes," Beau said, eyeing the bird with caution, his curious stare thankfully not reciprocated. "And I agree that the house appears to be in great shape. It's just a bit dat—"

"Beau means to say that the décor is a bit too sophisticated for today's buyer," I interrupted. "That could be why you haven't had any takers despite its having been on the market for so long."

"And not having central air," Honey added, looking like she almost believed it.

Mrs. Wenzel looked at her sister and shook her head. "Or," she interjected, "it has more to do with the unsolved murder of our stepmother in the house, and the disappearance of our brother, his wife, and their young daughter. They call houses like this—"

"Murder houses," Honey whispered loudly, leading her sister inside the house.

"We know," Beau said. "Which is such a shame, because it's just a gorgeous specimen of early twentieth-century architecture. We plan to really make it shine for today's buyer."

"Do you really think you can?" The older woman peered into Beau's face. "Some people say these houses carry some very bad juju. You might want to focus on the out-of-towners, because anyone from here knows better."

"It's a shame," Honey said, moving toward a stuffed floral armchair with a yellowed lace doily on the headrest. "It's been in our family since it was built. Our grandfather worked on the docks and raised his eight children here, and our father chose to leave it to our half brother when he died." Her lips tightened. "Joan and I spent a lot of happy times here as children visiting our grandparents. The kitchen was updated in the fifties by our grandmother, but I don't think it's been touched since, and most of the furniture is original."

I bit my tongue before I could comment on the cracked-leather footstool with what appeared to be real alligator feet, or on the collection of taxidermied animal heads hanging on the walls. "How long did your brother and his family live here?"

The two women shared a look. "Jessica—our sister-in-law—moved in here first with our niece, Lynda, when she was just a baby. Our stepmother lived here alone after our father died, but apparently she and Jessica were very close. We think Jessica might have needed her mother-in-law's help caring for Lynda. Jessica and our half brother, Mark, also owned a beautiful lakefront mansion, but I think she found it too big to manage. I believe she lived here with Lynda most of the time. As I mentioned earlier, we were estranged, so we have no idea what was going on with her and our brother, but that's how I understand it. And then one day . . ." Mrs. Wenzel's voice trailed off.

"Your stepmother was murdered, and your brother and family disappeared and haven't been seen or heard from since," Beau said.

Mrs. Wenzel's lips tightened again. "Yes." She pressed her hand against her heart. "Honey and I were interviewed by the police as if we had something to do with it." Her crepey eyelids shuttered her eyes for a moment. "It was upsetting and humiliating. We were cleared, of course, but it was very traumatic for both of us."

"So you and your husband aren't planning on living here?" Honey asked with a sweet smile.

Beau and I stared at each other in mutual horror. "No," we said in unison, shaking our heads.

"I mean, we're not together," I explained. "And definitely not husband and wife."

"Such a shame. Y'all make such a cute couple."

"No, we don't," I said at the same time Beau said, "Don't give her any ideas."

I glared at him, but he was distracted by his phone vibrating. While he stepped back to respond, Honey said, "If it's all right, we're going to take one last look and then be on our way. It's time to say good-bye."

"What she means to say is that we're also hoping that Zeus will finally talk to us. He was the only witness to what happened."

"Let us know," I said, wondering what sort of bad juju the family had been given for such a tragedy to occur with only a mute parrot as witness. Sort of like being put on a diet and living in New Orleans. Or being a recovering alcoholic. Although this last had been self-imposed, so I had no one else to blame.

With the small cage held high to give the bird the best vantage point, the two women headed toward the dining room. Beau slid his phone into his back pocket. "Let's go out onto the porch. I don't want the women to hear us talking about what we're going to be gutting, so we'll wait until they leave before we do our walk-through. Sunny will be here by then, so we can do it together."

"Sunny?"

"Yeah." He opened the front door and led me outside to the porch steps. We sat at the top, both of us making sure there was enough room between us so that our shoulders wouldn't touch. "That was Sunny texting me. She heard Mimi and me talking about this project and she thought it would be a great way to get her feet wet and see what JR Properties is all about. She's eager to learn, and I think she could be a big asset to our team. Besides, she's got skin in the game. Her name *is* the company."

"*Our* team? I haven't said yes yet."

He gave me that grin—the one I was beginning to suspect he knew had an effect on me. "Was there ever any question? It's a win-win for both of us. You get more experience, and the company gets more exposure." His expression sobered. "It's especially important now, when companies like the Sabatier Group just want to tear down and build new because it's easier and quicker. Some are companies led by people who aren't from here but after Katrina saw land-grab opportunities. But others, like Sabatier, are native New Orleanians and have no excuse for erasing our heritage and collective history one building at a time. The bigger JR Properties becomes, the more assets we'll have to devote to renovation and rebuilding." He grinned at me again, and I had to look away. "And, as you've reminded me numerous times, you're smart. You graduated number one in your grad school class, so at least you look good on paper. All you need now is more hands-on stuff. So you don't do things like tile yourself into a corner."

"Seriously?" I stood. "You need to work on your sales pitch, Beau. That was the most backhanded compliment I think I've ever heard. Just ask Thibaut and Jorge—nobody can reglaze a window better than me. Or strip years of paint and varnish from wood. I wasn't good at any of that until I started working with them, and I've learned because they're patient teachers. They never *once* laughed at one of my mistakes."

Planning to make my grand exit, I took a step down before I realized that we'd come in Beau's truck and he had the keys. I groaned in frustration, but at least I restrained myself from stamping my foot. "Ask them," I said. "I am more than qualified to lead this project. And I *definitely* look better than just on paper."

He stood slowly, his face serious. "Believe me, I've noticed."

The front door opened and Honey poked out her head. "Mr. Ryan? Joan and I realize that a building inspection is required before any transaction can be completed, but just in case this is a problem, we thought we might mention this now."

Beau turned his back to me and I saw his shoulder muscles tense through his shirt. "What problem?"

"Well, we don't know if it actually is a problem. There appears to be water on the floor in the rear bedroom, but there's nothing on the ceiling and we can't figure out the source. We thought you might come look at it. We'd hate for there to be a water problem somewhere and all the furnishings ruined."

I bit my lip so I wouldn't make an inappropriate comment about how the furniture was beyond ruining, and water, or perhaps a gas can and a match, might be a good thing.

Beau's muscles remained tense as he nodded. "Sure. I'll go look." Turning back to me, he said, "Wait here for Sunny, and you can give her a rundown of the history of the house and any ideas you might have for the renovation."

I opened my mouth to argue, but he'd already followed Honey back inside. A cool breeze swept through the porch, making the palm fronds in the small front garden rustle. An errant leaf dislodged itself from the gnarled live oak near the street, and it swirled in an erratic pattern until it reached the porch, rocking back and forth like a feather before settling at my feet. I bent to pick it up, stopping midway. Next to the fallen leaf sat two puddles of water, perfectly formed in the shape of a woman's feet.

CHAPTER 10

I sat in the backseat on the drive home, Sunny up front with Beau. I wanted to ask Beau about the puddles of water found in the house and the footprints on the porch, but knew he'd be as forthcoming on those topics as I'd be about my thoughts on what he'd meant by *Believe me, I've noticed.* I was fairly confident that he hadn't been referring to my brilliant intellect and proficiency in historic preservation.

As I climbed out of the backseat, Sunny rolled down her window. "I'm so excited to be working together." She winked, so I wasn't sure if she was talking about the Esplanade project or our side game of saving Beau from himself.

"Me, too," I said. I didn't move away from the truck, a stray thought plucking at my brain. "Just a quick question—when you were at the house today, did you smell or see anything unusual?"

"Besides those two women with the bird in the cage?" She giggled. "No. Why? Should I have?"

"No reason. Beau and I thought we smelled a woman's perfume—that's all."

"Ooh—maybe it's haunted," she said with enthusiasm. "That could make some great social media posts. We can ask Mimi to lend us some of her Frozen Charlotte dolls to decorate with during the renovation. How cool would that be?"

I kept my grin in place, avoiding looking at Beau. "That's certainly an option. We'll talk about it later." I stepped back from the truck as Sunny started rolling up her window. Beau called out through the narrowing crack, "Let me know when you're ready to tackle the interstate, Nola. I'm ready when you are."

The window closed, and I had to mouth, *When hell freezes over.*

I let myself into the apartment, listening to laughter from upstairs and aware of the absent scent of food cooking in the kitchen. I'd begun to salivate like Pavlov's dogs whenever I climbed the stairs to our apartment at the end of the day. It wasn't that I expected Jolene to make dinner or bake something for me every day, but she always did. Obviously, something was horribly wrong.

I ran up the rest of the stairs and flung open the door, panting from the exertion. Jolene and Jaxson sat in front of her open laptop on the couch, the only two fixtures in the room that weren't bedecked in purple, gold, and green Mardi Gras colors. Even Mardi wore a tricolor jester collar that had along its pointed edges bells that jangled as he bounced over to say hello to me before promptly rolling onto his back to show his belly.

"Was I abducted by aliens and skipped a few months? Last time I checked, it was still October."

Jolene stood and smoothed her hands on her skinny jeans. As she approached I stared, taking in the ballet flats and her messy bun. The only way I recognized her was by her full face of makeup and her flaming red hair. And her smile as she approached me.

"Who are you and what have you done with Jolene? The Jolene I know doesn't own jeans. Or flats."

Jolene hugged me. "You're such a silly goose. Still the same Jolene, I promise." Jaxson stood, wearing jeans, too, and tennis shoes, but the starched collar on his golf shirt told me that he hadn't also been abducted.

"I asked Jolene for some remodeling advice for my apartment, and instead she took a day off from work and spent it with my landlord and me, going over how to do some upgrades while being sensitive to the historic elements of the property. She also gave me free advice on redecorating my own apartment. Carly has been meaning to redo it for a while now, but she's always so busy. I'm a guy, but even I was getting tired of the frat-house décor. And I knew Jolene had a great eye just from seeing what she's done to this apartment."

"Please don't tell me that she re-created the *Wizard of Oz* set." I said that as a joke, but I wasn't completely sure until Jolene laughed.

"Very funny. To be honest, I considered it, because anything would be better than what's there now. I just about near fainted when I saw the beanbag chairs and the milk-crate furniture. It's just wrong for a grown man to be living that way." Jolene beamed. "I'm just happy I could help out a friend." Her voice sounded a little more high-pitched than usual, but Jaxson didn't appear to notice.

"She wouldn't let me pay her, or even reimburse her for a bedside lamp and an extra throw pillow she had and claims she wasn't using. I declined to have it monogrammed, although she would have done that, too, if I'd said yes."

"Nothing's safe," I said. "Just look at Mardi."

Mardi looked up at the sound of his name, and we all admired his rugby-striped sweater with *MLT* monogrammed on the back.

Jaxson grinned. "I'll be sure not to stand still long enough. Anyway, I thought I'd thank her by taking her out to dinner, but first she asked if I could help her with some of the 'Welcome to New Orleans' décor for your family's visit."

I walked toward the dining room, admiring Jolene's use of foil streamers hanging from the doorways and the impressive amount of confetti sprinkled on top of the furniture.

"We also had balloons," Jolene said. "The kind with all those glittery sparkles, but Mardi got rid of them quicker than a hiccup, so I figured we'd skip them for now. There will also be a king cake I've already ordered from Randazzo's, and pralines from Aunt Sally's. Those are the only things I won't be personally making."

"Jolene." My eyes felt warm and watery. "This is the nicest thing. You didn't have to do this. I think it's already enough that you're allowing my little sister to move in for a week and you even seem excited about it."

"Oh, I am! I've even got a little surprise for her."

"Is it monogrammed?" Jaxson asked.

Jolene's smile faltered. "No, it's not. I didn't even think about it." She brightened. "But thank goodness it's not too late."

"Thank goodness." I reached up and twirled a bouquet of feathers and masks hanging from the ceiling light fixture and tied with an extravagant bow of purple velvet ribbon sprinkled with what appeared to be hand-sewn gold and green sequins. Turning back to Jolene, I said, "I'm sorry I missed the filming today at the house. I meant to be there to demonstrate the authentic way to patch plaster walls, but Beau dragged me away to look at a house on Esplanade for his new venture."

Jolene and Jaxson shared a glance as Jolene retrieved the laptop from the coffee table. "Actually, that's what we were laughing at when you came in. I brought Mardi with me to the house because I just can't take that abandoned look he gives me every time I leave him by himself, and Thibaut and Jorge used him in their act! Mardi is quite the acrobat and enjoyed showing off his skills. I only just posted it, and we already have over one thousand views. Here—come look."

She placed the laptop on top of a gold-and-green-striped linen tablecloth on the dining table. I'd been so distracted by the streamers and glitter that I only just then finally caught sight of the centerpiece. I stifled a small scream as I remembered the last time Jolene had gotten creative with a centerpiece and how the fright had taken five years off my life.

"I told her we should warn you first, but we weren't expecting you so soon," Jaxson said.

"Don't you just love it?" Jolene said.

While my heart slowed to a normal rate, I examined the disembodied, oversized Barbie doll head in the middle of the table, the golden blond hair piled high in a mass of curls, colorful jewels, and glitter, all tucked beneath a tall crown of heavy gold filigree with a clear stone the size of a child's fist in the center. Over her eyes, Barbie wore a glittering mask of purple satin embroidered with the words *WELCOME TRENHOLM FAMILY!* in green lettering around the top and bottom.

"You made all of this?" I swallowed down a lump in my throat.

Jolene nodded. "I wanted to re-create a Mardi Gras float in the living room, but since we're just renting, the landlord wouldn't have allowed me to put holes in the plaster, and I don't think the electrical system could handle the animatronics. Which is a shame, since I already scavenged two mannequins from a dumpster . . ."

"A Mardi Gras float?"

"I know. I'm disappointed, too. But I did my best with what I had."

I shook my head. "No, really. This is . . . perfect. I couldn't have asked for anything more. It's really amazing. My family will be . . . amazed," I said for lack of a better word. I hugged Jolene. "You're the best. I have no idea where you found the time to do all of this, but everything is just beautiful."

"To give credit where credit is due," she said, "I borrowed the crown from Carly. She was Queen of Carnival a few years back and said if I was very careful I could borrow the replica of her crown that her parents had made for her. She said it was just catching dust at her parents' house, and when she heard that I was going to make one and Jaxson said he would help—he knows how to use a glue gun; isn't that wonderful?—Carly said it was ridiculous when she had one already made. Isn't that sweet?"

"That's probably not the word I'd use, but it does make a good conversation piece."

"It sure does," Jaxson said, attempting not to smile.

Trying hard to ignore the Barbie head, I leaned over the laptop and hit Play on the video Jolene had pulled up on our YouTube channel. In addition to the usual intricate juggling routines with various tools and the occasional pratfalls involving tripping, stumbling, and falling headfirst into paint buckets, the highlight of the reel was my sweet Mardi sailing effortlessly through a hula hoop held a few inches off the ground.

Jolene leaned forward and pressed a few keys on the laptop. "Look at it in slow motion and tell me that's not cuter than a bug's ear!"

I watched again as Mardi stretched out his fluffy front and back cankles like a capeless Superman and sailed through the circle with ease. Jolene backed it up and showed it to me three more times in slow motion so I could admire the way his soft fur floated around his head and body, his plumed tail wagging with delight at the end of his trick.

"I'll admit that's pretty cute. And they can continue teaching Mardi tricks as long as Mardi enjoys it and they don't start lighting the hula hoop on fire."

Jolene scooped up Mardi and gave him a big kiss on the top of his head. "Do you think I would allow that? We're just about as close as sisters, Nola, but Mardi and me, well, we're tighter than bark on a hickory tree. I think of him as my own and I wouldn't allow any harm to come to him." She pressed his head against her chest, covering his ears. In a low voice, she said, "I don't want to hurt his feelings, since he thinks he's the protector."

She moved the cursor back to the beginning of Mardi's trick and hit the Play button again, and this time my focus strayed to the background of the scene, to the open closet door at the top of the steps. Saliva evaporated from my mouth as I watched a dark shadow slither across the doorway. Filmy edges of viscous black ink surrounded the opaque center of the humanlike shadow. The flash of movement disappeared so quickly that I almost doubted I'd seen it at all. But my dry mouth and nausea told me I had.

Jolene reached over to close the laptop.

"Hang on. Can I see that again in slow motion?" Without waiting for a response, I adjusted the speed of the video, then pressed the Play button. This time, I focused all my attention on the closet, needing to reassure myself that it was the shadow of a tree outside or an actual person walking in the upstairs hallway. But there it was again, with the bloblike movements of an undulating inkblot. I leaned closer, a dense ache of fear pulsing in the pit of my stomach. Despite the blob's strange consistency, the shapes of a head, arms, and legs were clearly those of a person. Or what might have once been a person. Or . . . something humanlike.

I straightened and closed the laptop myself. "That's great. I can't wait to see what they come up with next." I reached over and scratched Mardi under the chin to hide the shaking of my hand. I wasn't ready to share what I'd seen. Not yet. At least not before I'd had a chance to figure out what I thought I'd seen.

"Well, now that you're here, why don't you join us for dinner?" Jaxson said. "It was sort of last-minute, so nothing fancy, but I love Pascal's Manale. They're known for their barbecue shrimp, and if you've never tried their white chocolate bread pudding, you haven't lived. It's one of Carly's favorite places, but she's in Dallas for work, so it'll just be us."

My stomach had been grumbling for almost an hour, and the mention of the bread pudding had me salivating. "I would love to—" I stopped as I caught Jolene's gaze. Even though I didn't agree with her pining over someone who was practically engaged to someone else, I also knew that I didn't want to be the source of her disappointment. Or subjected to her form of revenge, which included no fresh baked goods or morning coffee. She could be hateful like that.

"But unfortunately," I continued, "I have a lot of catching up to do since I was out of the office today. Lots of prep work for another field assignment. I'll just order a pizza or something."

"Well, only if you're sure—" Jolene began.

"Absolutely. You two go on and have fun. You've worked so hard today, and you deserve it."

"That settles it, I guess," Jaxson said. "We'll bring you back some of that bread pudding. I'll make sure it's vegan first." He winked.

"Don't you dare."

"Just give me a sec," Jolene said, already turning to plump the pillows on the couch. "I need to quickly run the vacuum before I leave. In case I missed some of that glitter the first time."

"It's spotless," I said. "If I see any loose sparkles or glitter, I promise to suck them right up."

Jolene hesitated. "Grandmama said to always make sure my house is clean when I leave, in case I don't come back. And she should know. She's had to go into some homes to pick out clothes for the deceased, and the stories she could tell you would give you heart palpitations."

"Besides that being more than a little morbid, I don't think that's something you need to worry about." I took hold of Jolene's elbow and led her in the direction of her room. "I've got it all under control, promise. And Jaxson will drive carefully and make sure you're wearing your seat belt, all right? Now just skedaddle into your room and put some color on so you can leave."

She beamed at me. "I do think I might have taught you a thing or two, Nola. Including a new word."

"Make that two. I said 'cattywampus' the other day to describe the proximity of two buildings. I guess I've had a good teacher."

"Well, you're an excellent student. And after your family leaves and I can reclaim the Barbie head, we'll work on more lessons. We haven't gone over workout makeup yet."

I gently pushed her into the room. "Later," I said, grabbing hold of the knob and pulling the door shut. "Much," I added quietly to the closed door.

"I heard that," Jolene shouted from inside her room.

My laughter was cut off by the shrill ring of the phone sitting on the edge of the teacher's school desk I'd inherited with the apartment. I grabbed the receiver before it could ring a second time, confetti flying as I lifted it to my ear. "Hello?"

The crackling sound of endless space filled my ear as I strained to hear through the static, anticipating the high-pitched tone of

Melanie's long-dead grandmother. Instead, I heard a low rumble, something otherworldly. Something between a growl and a laugh.

"Hello?" I repeated, hoping it was just a prank call, even while knowing that no calls, prank or otherwise, could come through a nonfunctioning phone. The sound diminished into a low guttural snarl from a thick-necked beast—worse, somehow, than the initial noise. Like a whispered threat instead of a scream. My hand began to shake enough that I had to hold the phone with both hands.

The sound ended abruptly, as if it had been sucked into the black hole from where it came, and it was replaced by the soft voice of an old woman. "Nola." I pressed the receiver to my ear to hear better. The background static almost overcame the treacly voice.

"Yes. I'm here."

"Adele. Adele is—"

The last word faded with a pop. "Adele is what?"

"Heeeeeeerrrrrre." The word started softly before amplifying at the end, reminding me of the frightening Edison doll found in my aunt Jayne's inherited house. *That* was a nightmare I wouldn't be forgetting anytime soon.

I swallowed. "Okay . . ." I began, my voice flung out into open space.

"Help . . . Beau." This was another voice, the voice of a young woman. More distinct than Grandma Sarah's. But maybe that's how it worked on the other side—you're left with the voice you leave the world with. Yet there was something odd about it, too. I had a strange flash of a memory of a family vacation on the Isle of Palms, and then I was back in my apartment, holding a phone while talking to dead people.

"I'm trying," I said, hoping I'd understood.

"Help . . . Beau," repeated the same voice, followed by another loud popping noise that could have been a word, then "Sunny."

"Help Beau and Sunny?" I shouted, hearing the dial tone, and just my voice speaking into the receiver. "Hello?" I said, even though I knew no one was there. Maybe I'd been imagining the whole thing.

"Everything all right?" Jaxson asked, glancing at the phone, then back at me.

"Yeah. Everything's fine."

"Can I get you a Coke or something? You look like you've just seen a ghost."

I met his eyes, wanting to laugh. But I only nodded, knowing that if I opened my mouth a wild, maniacal sound would emerge.

As Jaxson headed for the kitchen, I stared at the phone in my hand, and I knew it was unplugged without even looking. I slammed the receiver back into the cradle, the flash of memory clear now. My sister and I used to sit in the shallow surf and talk underwater to see if we could understand each other. That's the voice I'd just heard. A voice speaking from beneath the waves. *Adele.*

CHAPTER 11

I sat on the couch in the living room, Mardi sitting on the cushion next to me, his dark, soulful eyes staring up at me with concern. Jaxson placed a glass filled with ice and Coke into my hand. "Thanks." My hands shook, rattling the ice, so I lowered the glass onto the Cowardly Lion coaster.

I motioned for Jaxson to sit next to me. Keeping my voice down, I said, "Would you mind if I asked you for another favor?"

He didn't hesitate, which made me like him even more. "Sure, anything." He put on the serious lawyer face that I always had trouble reconciling with the smattering of freckles on the nose that made him look like a perpetual boy.

"Actually, this is probably more of a favor from your uncle Bernie, if he's up for it," I said, referring to his retired-police-detective uncle, who'd played a huge part in discovering the story behind Sunny's disappearance.

"Uncle Bernie's itching to come out of retirement. He feels a little cheated not being able to close Sunny's case."

"I know. I think we all do."

"But Sunny's back now, so it all worked out in the end."

"Did it, though? Yeah, Sunny's back and everyone's happy. But it's not exactly the end, is it?"

Jaxson shook his head. "If you mean because no one has been convicted for her abduction, then no. But as Uncle Bernie said, the Ryans need to let it go. They got what they wanted. Messing with the Broussard family isn't a good idea."

"I know, and I agree—mostly. But Beau won't let it rest. He wants to keep digging for evidence so that the truth about the Broussards' involvement in Sunny's abduction is out. And Jeanne Broussard's real killer is exposed. You and Mimi and I all know that's not in anyone's best interests. Especially Beau's, but I might as well be talking to a rock to get it to change its mind."

Jaxson pressed his elbows into his thighs and leaned forward. "It's not just a bad idea, Nola. It's stupid, for all the reasons we already know. Antoine Broussard might be dead, but he has enough powerful friends and family who wouldn't want his reputation sullied, regardless of the truth. I can have Uncle Bernie talk to Beau if you think that would help."

"If I thought it would help, I'd ask. Instead, Sam, Sunny, and I have come up with another idea."

He raised his eyebrows. "And Beau's okay with this?"

I grimaced. "Beau doesn't exactly know. Which means you can't tell him, all right? Mimi's in on it, too. She's distracting him with another project while I . . ."

"While you what?"

I hesitated too long while I tried to make up an answer he'd believe, and that wouldn't make me look overly naïve and ignorant.

"Oh, no. Let me guess: while you pretend to want to get back together with Michael so you can get inside the family circle."

Jaxson sank back into the couch and blew air out between his lips in a sharp whistle. "Oh, boy. I've heard a lot of crazy ideas in my line of work, but—I'm not going to lie—that's probably the craziest. And dumbest." He sat up straight again. "And definitely too dangerous. You could get hurt, Nola." He attempted a smile. "Jolene would never forgive me."

"Which is why I'm not telling her everything. I've already told her that I'm having dinner with Michael tomorrow night, but not everything else. I'll be really careful, and if it looks like things aren't going well, I'm outta there before anyone gets hurt."

"I'm guessing there's no way to talk you out of this, is there?"

"No. Trust me, if Beau would just be grateful that he has his sister back and let it go at that, I wouldn't be doing this. But since I've already committed, I've been thinking about all the loose ends that were just swept under the table when Sunny reappeared."

Jaxson straightened. "Like what?"

"Well, the locked closet, for one. Inside, besides a pristine Mr. Bingle doll, there were a bunch of hatboxes." I held up my hand the way Jolene did, counting off with each finger, starting with my thumb. "In one of them, there was a tie clasp and pipe that had belonged to Charles Ryan, a yellow hair ribbon that had been worn by Sunny, and a film negative showing Sunny's abduction. In another was Jeanne's clientele book from Maison Blanche. We get that all of it could be used as physical evidence if the Ryans ever decided to pursue a case against the Broussards. Which is why Mimi wanted Beau's dad, Buddy, to destroy it all in the first place. To protect her family. If the Broussards knew that stuff was still around . . ." My voice trailed off, the consequences settling uneasily on my shoulders.

Jaxson thrummed his fingers on his leg, thinking. "And then Buddy disappeared, and we can't ask him why he didn't get rid of it all, but my guess is that his idea was to convince Mimi and the Broussards that he had destroyed everything, planning to wait until he had more evidence for a solid case. But then he—"

"Disappeared, presumed dead, another victim of Katrina," I finished.

Jaxson steepled his fingers, something he probably did when working out the logistics of a case, which definitely made him look more lawyerly. Except for the freckles. "Which is why after Michael's uncle found out about the office door still being at the house where Jeanne had been killed and that you'd bought the cottage, he sent Michael to discover if there might be more incriminating evidence that had survived."

At my look of distress, he said, "Sorry. I know it's a sore subject."

"Like sliding down a razor blade and landing in alcohol. But Beau is determined to see justice served. Unfortunately, to get to the bottom of all of this I'm going to have to spend some time with Michael."

"You can't be serious."

"As a heart attack. We figure if I can find out the truth before Beau has a chance to stick his nose into places where it will draw attention, we can see justice served and everyone can sleep at night without keeping one eye open."

"But did Beau toss all of the hatbox contents into the Manchac Swamp along with the Maison Blanche door?"

I looked away, unable to meet his eyes. "Um, not exactly."

Jaxson's brows shot up. "Not exactly?"

"Let's just say that they're in a safe place. There were too many questions without answers, and Beau and I thought that it would be . . . premature to destroy everything. I mean, why was Jeanne's clientele book saved? Jolene and I have gone through it dozens of times to see if we could find anything that might incriminate her uncle." I swallowed with distaste. "The one who was sexually abusing her and the reason why she was murdered."

"By her father." Jaxson shook his head. "This is all so disturbing. But okay. The clientele book is obviously important. It could have been kept for the same reason the door was. So Mimi could . . ." He stopped, searching for the right word.

"It's called psychometry. The Broussards know about Mimi's abilities, which is why they wanted to destroy the door, and would want to destroy anything else that ties the Broussards to Jeanne's murder if they knew it existed."

"Have you asked Mimi to see if she can read the items from the hatboxes? Or whatever it's called that she does."

"Reading objects. Touching them. I'm not sure what she calls it. But no. We, uh, can't."

Jaxson drew his eyebrows together in question before realization came to him. "Because she thinks Beau destroyed everything."

"Pretty much."

"Let me get this straight—you and Mimi are working on your own plan to keep Beau occupied while you are also working with Sam and Sunny to figure things out before Beau can, while at the same time you're pretending to be interested in Michael Hebert so you can get inside the Broussard family and see if you can find out anything to help them. Sounds perfect to me. I mean, what could go wrong?"

"I know, right?"

For a long moment he stared at me with a look of unflattering surprise. "I'm kidding, Nola. This sounds like a *Scooby-Doo* episode. You know, where there are lots of really bad guys dressed as monsters chasing and attempting to kill all the characters until at the end the monsters are revealed to be the bad guys and the police show up to make the arrest and nobody gets hurt. But this isn't an old cartoon, Nola. This could end very, very badly."

"I understand your concern, Jaxson. I do. And I appreciate it. Just know that I won't do anything stupid, I promise."

"I think it's too late for that."

I frowned at him. "You're not going to tell Beau, are you? Because you and I both know that I have a better chance than he does when it comes to covert activity."

Jaxson hesitated for a moment before giving a single reluctant nod.

"Good. Because I need your uncle Bernie's help. He thinks like a cop and knows all the players. But I wanted to ask you first because Bernie's not as young as he used to be, and I don't want him to get involved unless you think he's healthy and strong enough. And if you think we can protect his identity. I really need his help, but I won't ask him if you don't think I should."

He gripped his knees and looked down at the rug, his brows knitted. Eventually, he looked up and met my eyes. "I guess I'll have to ask him."

I felt my ribs expand, releasing some of the stress I'd been feeling ever since my conversation with Sam. "Thank you," I said. "I really appreciate it."

"Is there anything specific you're thinking about?"

"Right now, I was just hoping he could look at the clientele book. Maybe with his professional eye he can figure out something we haven't been able to."

Jaxson surprised me with a wide grin. "You really are your father's daughter, aren't you?"

"Why do you say that?"

"Your attention to detail, for starters. And your tenacity at digging out crumbs that other people might dismiss as irrelevant. Or coincidence."

"Because there's no such thing as coincidence." We turned at the sound of Jolene's voice. Her hair had been brushed and sprayed, and her lips shone with a fresh coat of lipstick, but she wore the same jeans and flats. This, and the clientele book she carried, meant she'd probably been spending most of her time listening instead of primping. "I figured I'd save you some time and get this for you to take to Uncle Bernie."

Jaxson immediately stood and took the book, then placed it on the coffee table. With a grin, he said, "You heard every word, didn't you?"

Jolene looked offended. "Is a frog's butt watertight? How else was I supposed to know what's going on with the two of you whispering in here like two snakes in the grass?"

"I was hoping to spare you from getting involved." I crossed my arms. "If I'd wanted you to know, I would have already told you."

Smiling cheerfully, Jolene said, "Well, it's too late now. I guess you can call me a coconspirator."

Jaxson turned back to me. "There's something else that you're not telling me, isn't there?"

"What makes you think that?" I swallowed as I pushed aside the memory of the creepy black shadow I'd seen in the video, not sure I could explain that to anyone. Except Melanie. Or Beau. And not sure I even wanted to. Besides Melanie's love for organization, I seemed to have also acquired her tendency to ignore anything unpleasant in the hope that it would go away. Or until it exploded in my face. Unfortunately, I had to experience everything more than once before I learned the hard way.

"I'm a public defender—remember? I've acquired a sixth sense about people holding back information."

"Fine. There is one more thing." I looked between Jaxson and Jolene. "I'm pretty sure Beau's grandfather is still around. We've both smelled his pipe smoke a few times at the house." I would keep the anomaly I'd seen in the video to myself. For now. At least until I could talk to Beau and make sure I wasn't imagining it.

Jolene rubbed her hands over her arms. "What do you think it means?"

"Either Charles is here just to keep an eye on Beau"—I paused—"or there's still unfinished business that needs to be taken care of before he can move on."

"But Sunny's back," Jaxson said. "And we know who was responsible. I can't imagine that he's wanting Beau to seek justice at this point. Not when it would put him and Mimi in danger."

"That's pretty much what I thought. Which is why I'm agreeing to have dinner with Michael, and also why I need Bernie's help. I'm in way over my head here."

Jolene put her arms around me and squeezed. "Don't forget you've got us. And I think we make a great team." She stepped back. "We should get going. I'm so hungry I could eat my own hand. But first I'm going to grab a heavier sweater. I've got chill bumps all over my arms."

Jaxson picked up the clientele book. "I'll go ahead and take this now. If it's okay with you, I'll go through it before I bring it over for Bernie—assuming he'll agree to help. Which I'm pretty sure he will. I've never known someone to hate retirement as much as he does."

I glanced over at Jolene's half-open door to make sure she wasn't eavesdropping again. "There's something else I wanted to ask you about."

"Sure."

"Have you given Carly the ring yet?"

He didn't drop his gaze. "Not yet. She's been traveling a lot, so I haven't been able to pin her down. But soon."

I nodded. "All right. But I need to let you know that if you hurt Jolene, I will hunt you down along with all three hundred or so of her closest friends and extended family members. You understand?"

I had to admire his ability to hold my gaze. "I do. I have no plans to do anything that would hurt her."

"Yeah, well, planning isn't usually a part of the equation when it comes to matters of the heart. Maybe you need to think of Jolene as a fine bottle of bourbon, and you're an alcoholic trying to stay sober."

"I'll keep that in mind."

"Good," I said just as Jolene reappeared wearing a fluffy pale pink cardigan and another layer of hair spray.

"Keep what in mind?"

Jaxson's eyes met mine again for a moment before he said, "That Pascal's Manale can pack up a bread pudding to bring back for Nola."

"And maybe some turtle soup, too." She leaned down to give Mardi a kiss on his nose and a quick scratch behind his ears. "You be good for Mommy, all right? And make sure she shares some of her pizza with you."

"Don't worry about us—we'll be fine. Just enjoy your dinner."

I opened the door at the top of the stairs to let them through. We said our good-byes and I waited until I heard the door close at the bottom. Then I headed back to Jolene's laptop and typed in her password, MARDI, before opening up the video. I sat down in one of the dining chairs and watched again and again as the dark shadow roiled from one side of the closet to the other. Even looking at it on video made my insides clench with terror. I'd never felt that when I'd been in the house with Charles and his pipe smoke. Or even when the ghost of Jeanne Broussard had pushed me down the stairs. This appeared to be a new entity entirely, its dark aura exuding evil. But if it wasn't Charles or Jeanne, who was it? And why had it chosen now to make its presence known?

I shut the laptop, then drummed my fingers on top. There were only two people I could ask about it, and only one of them lived in New Orleans. I picked up my phone and texted Beau. Can you talk now?

While I waited for him to respond, I opened a food delivery app and ordered pizza, then switched back to my text screen and stared at it for what seemed like five minutes. I was about to close the screen when a bubble appeared with moving dots as Beau texted his response: No.

I stared at my phone for a full minute before turning off the screen and then slowly walking down the stairs to wait for my pizza. Sitting in the halo of the front door light on the outside steps, I tried to force my brain to think about work, about why moths never learned the truth about lightbulbs, about learning to drive, and about Mardi's first Halloween with us. Anything except what Beau might be doing right now, and the unnamed presence in my house.

CHAPTER 12

I pedaled quickly down Dauphine after work the following day, hoping to catch Jorge and Thibaut while they were still at my house, not only so that we could check their progress on their spreadsheets, but also because I didn't want to be alone in the house after watching the video of the thing in the upstairs hallway.

I got off my bike in front of the house and searched for Jorge's and Thibaut's trucks parked along the street. I looked up and down both curbs of the street, and then again just in case I'd missed them. The guys usually left early on Thursdays to attend a Bible study at Jorge's church, but I'd hoped they'd still be there when I finally got away from the office and made my way to the Marigny. The number of people in the city had swelled due to the upcoming Halloween festivities, including the Krewe of Boo parade scheduled for the following day, a whole week before the actual holiday.

Ernest and Bob across the street had already festooned their coffin-planted trees with webs, enormous spiders, and twinkling skull lights. I might have found it cute if I didn't have my own Halloween décor living upstairs in my closet.

I stared up at my house and took a fortifying breath, remembering what Grandmother Sarah had said. *The house chose you.* In theory, I still believed it. But all I had to do was recall what I'd seen in the video and my doubts would return. My phone buzzed as I dragged my bike up the porch steps, then gingerly leaned it against the house. I was never sure which was sturdier, so I treated both bike and house like elderly aunts with brittle bones.

I eagerly checked my screen, hoping the text was from Beau. I hadn't heard from him after our brief text exchange the previous night, and I wasn't sure if I should be annoyed or worried. Instead, I saw a text from Jolene that showed a Bitmoji of a red-haired woman with an hourglass tapping her foot.

After checking the time, I quickly texted back. Date not for 2 more hrs

Her response came as soon as I'd hit Send. U need every minute hurry take uber

I sent an eye roll emoji before replacing the phone in my back pocket, unwilling to admit how tempted I was to simply leave my bike there and Uber back to our apartment, where I knew a warm bubbly bath would be waiting for me. And I would. Just not yet. I sniffed the air, satisfied that I smelled nothing but the usual scents of old wood, drywall dust, and a wet breeze blowing in from the river.

Goose bumps blossomed on my arms and exposed neck as I turned the key in the lock and opened the door. They had to be from the damp air that confused my body temperature, making it unable to distinguish between cold and hot when the temperature hovered between seasons, as if debating with itself. They had to be.

I stepped inside and flipped on the newly installed switch by the front door. Jolene was still brokering a deal with a local high-end lighting supplier, so only bare bulbs currently lit the house, but at least I now had electricity. The late fall day had already begun robbing the sky of light, creating darkened corners logic told me were empty, but my imagination showed me oily shadows with the head and limbs of a person.

I headed toward the kitchen, flipping on lights as I walked, eager to check on the progress. Thibaut was making custom cabinets to match the design Jolene and I had agreed on. She'd originally suggested a yellow-brick-road theme, with the pantry painted like the Royal Palace of Oz. She'd been so earnest that it had taken me ten minutes of trying to say "Hell no" in a polite way so as not to hurt her feelings before she'd told me she was joking and that she was a little insulted that I'd doubted her sense of style.

Flipping on the kitchen light was met with the familiar sound of scurrying as the aircraft-carrier-sized winged cockroaches found their hiding places faster than I could pick up one of the cans of Raid I'd placed strategically around the room. I had finally stopped trying to put lipstick on a pig—Jolene's words—by calling them the more genteel "palmetto bugs," as I'd been taught while living in Charleston. Because whatever you called them, they were large, pervasive, and, according to Jolene, the devil's own spawn. Sadly, pest control wasn't even a glimmer in my eye while construction was happening and doors and windows were constantly open. I looked forward to when I could schedule monthly visits from an exterminator like Jolene probably looked forward to a new lipstick color.

I bit back my disappointment at seeing the empty kitchen walls. Thibaut had promised to show me how to install the glass subway tile backsplash, but that couldn't go in until the cabinets were placed. My disappointment was quickly replaced with surprise when I spotted the large piece of furniture in the center of the floor, still smelling of the fresh coat of black lacquer paint that covered its surfaces.

It appeared to be the bottom half of a breakfront, with heavy carved legs and a bronze lock and key on the two front cabinet doors. The top was missing, allowing me to see inside the cavernous opening of the bottom half, and making me want to rub my hands with glee imagining the options I'd have choosing a surface and how gorgeous this piece would be as my kitchen island.

I walked around it twice, hoping for some clue as to its origin, before pulling out my phone to text Beau. Can u talk? I stared at the words on the screen before backspacing over them. I didn't have time to play another waiting game while my overactive imagination worked overtime as it considered different possible reasons why Beau wasn't responding, all of which involved Sam and none of which involved clothes.

I opened the Uber app, then held my thumbs momentarily suspended as a door hinge whined from somewhere upstairs. I moved as stealthily as I could in my new leather flats—a concession to Jolene that I highly regretted right then—and stopped at the bottom of the steps and looked up toward the upstairs closet. The door sat fully open, the inside shrouded in darkness. I flipped the switch that turned on the upstairs hall light, trying hard to remember if the door had been closed when I'd arrived.

I listened for any further sound of movement, reminding myself that the front door had been locked and that Thibaut was obsessive about checking all windows and doors before he left. His and Jorge's tools were neatly stowed in a corner of the kitchen, untouched, as were the boxes of plumbing fixtures in the front room waiting to be installed.

It was an old house, I kept repeating in my head. Full of weary creaks and groans from simply withstanding gravity and the vagaries of Mother Nature for over a century. Just like Melanie's dad, who sometimes needed my assistance to help him stand after he'd been kneeling in the garden too long, his knees popping as they readjusted to a standing position. It beat the alternative, as he was fond of mentioning. I imagined my house felt the same.

The closet seemed less menacing now with the arc of light spilling into it from the hallway. Maybe what I'd seen in the video had been just odd shadows caused by the too-bright light from a bare bulb. My mom had told me that as a child I would never believe her when she told me something was hot and I shouldn't touch it. I always needed to find out for myself, leaving nasty blisters on my fingers but the odd satisfaction of knowing for sure.

I marched up the stairs with heavy steps, attempting to show confidence either to myself or to anyone—or anything—that might be listening. I flipped on my phone light and gave a cursory inspection of the closet before moving into the two slowly developing new bedrooms and the bathroom. After satisfying myself that I was alone, I headed back toward the stairs.

A soft sound from behind me made me pause. It was the sort of sound made by someone attempting to hold their breath to avoid discovery. I turned around to face the closet, aiming my flashlight into the two back corners. There wasn't enough wall space on either side of the doorway inside the closet for anyone to hide, but I looked anyway. I wasn't going to lie to myself by thinking I'd imagined the sound. Maybe flying cockroaches had evolved enough to make human sounds. As horrifying as that thought was, the alternative was so much worse.

Gripping my phone just in case I needed to use it as a weapon, I turned again to leave. I'd made it to the top of the steps before I was stopped again by another sound. A *tap tap tap* followed by a high-pitched *screeeeech* like a fingernail on an old school chalkboard.

I marched back to the closet and stood inside the doorway, holding my breath and listening. A swoosh of air brushed my back, turning me around toward the stairway just as the closet door slammed shut in my face. I sprang forward and twisted the knob, which wouldn't turn, the rational part of my brain telling me that there was no functioning lock on the new doorknob, that if I kept trying it should turn and open. Except it didn't.

Something unidentifiable brushed my cheek, and I screamed. I swatted with both hands, dropping my phone, the beam of the flashlight now aimed up at the ceiling. A ceiling that seemed to be moving with shiny bits and pieces reflecting the light from the screen. One of the bits dropped onto the floor in front of me, followed by the flutter of an insect's wings passing by my ear. I made a grab for my phone just as the light flickered out and something landed on the back of my neck.

I screamed again. And screamed and screamed and screamed as I pressed myself into as small of a ball as I could and raked my nubby fingernails against my scalp again and again until the skin felt raw. Yet I couldn't stop screaming or scraping, doing anything to keep away the silence that would allow in the thought that I couldn't escape.

The door flew open, and the hall light illuminated a surprised Beau as I threw myself at him. I wanted to keep running, to find the cans of Raid and kill as many of the bugs as I could, but Beau held on to me, his arms tight around my waist, pressing me against him.

"What happened? Why are you screaming?"

I kept my face tucked into his neck and pointed to the closet, my eyes clenched so I wouldn't have to look at what I knew was there and had felt along my arms and the back of my neck and hair. "Don't let them out! They're all over the ceiling. They're falling on me."

"What are? Nola, you're not making sense." He pried me away from him and held me at arm's length. "Open your eyes. Now."

I shook my head, only part of it out of resentment for Beau telling me what to do.

"There is nothing in the closet, Nola. What did you see?"

I opened my eyes, the overhead light blinding me momentarily until they adjusted; then I turned my head to look inside the closet. Empty except for my phone in the middle of the floor. Keeping my arms wrapped tightly around me, I walked inside to retrieve it, looking up at the pristine newly painted ceiling and at the empty hanging rods along the side walls.

"There were—" I began, my attention suddenly drawn to the sound of Beau snapping the band against his wrist.

"It's . . . still here," he said with a low voice.

"It? It wasn't an it. It was hundreds and hundreds of roaches. They were everywhere. On the ceiling. Falling on me. They . . ." I stopped.

Beau was staring behind me, into the closet, his eyes widening in fear. Without turning around to see, I ran at Beau again, and he managed to stop us both from tumbling down the steps. With one swift movement, he grabbed the closet door and slammed it closed before lifting me in his arms and settling us on the floor with our backs against the door.

"I know. I know," he said. His voice was very close to my ear as he patted my back as if I were a small child.

"They were there." My voice shook, embarrassing me. I forced my jaw to be still and repeated it. "They were there."

"I believe you," Beau said, his breath warm on my neck.

Little by little, I felt myself relax, and I rested my head on his chest below his chin, the rhythm of his heart in my ear.

"I was so scared," I muttered sleepily.

"So was I."

I sat up, our faces close together. "What did you see?"

"I'm not sure. It started as a dark spot on the far wall, and then it grew and became three-dimensional and . . . real. Except there weren't any features. And it seemed to move like . . ." His voice trailed away.

"Like an oil slick?"

"Yeah. Exactly. Did you see it, too?"

I shook my head. "I only saw the—" I shuddered, unable to say the word "roaches." "But I saw the shadow. It's on the video Jolene and Jaxson made here yesterday. It's the one with Mardi doing tricks, and it's in the background. Inside the closet."

"Why didn't you tell me?"

I tried to pull away, but his arms held me. "I tried. I texted you. I asked if you could talk and you said no."

He narrowed his eyes as he thought, then opened them again with realization. "Oh, yeah. I remember now. I was . . . busy."

I wanted to ask him what had been keeping him so busy, but my jaw started to tremble again, the shaking spreading through my body like a heat rash. Beau pressed my head against his chest and tightened his arms around me. "I've got you now." He spoke softly in my ear, creating a whole new set of goose bumps on my neck. "I would have been scared, too."

"I wasn't scared," I mumbled into his shirt.

His chest rumbled as he laughed. "I'm sure. It must have been someone else screaming."

I sat up again. "I wasn't screaming. I was just . . . shouting. For someone to open the door, because it was locked."

Beau's eyes were serious now. "It wasn't locked, Nola. I pulled it open without any trouble." He shook his head before I could protest. "I believe you. Obviously, there's something going on here."

"But what? I can't live here with something that doesn't want me here. It was—"

"Terrifying."

"Yeah. That."

He kept looking at me, as if expecting me to say something more. "Oh. Right." I took a deep breath. "Thank you, Beau. For saving me from . . . whatever that was. Even though I didn't—"

"Don't say it. Because that will make you look ungrateful. And then the next time I might not just drop everything to come save you."

"I don't need—"

He put his finger against my lips. "Don't ruin it."

Our eyes met, and I forgot what I'd been about to say. His thumb traced the edges of my mouth, the smell of his skin hauntingly familiar, a ghostly reminder of the night he'd spent on my couch.

"Just when I'm starting to think that you're mad at me or really hate me, I'm reassured when I'm the first person you call when you're in trouble. I'm trying to figure out what that means."

I wanted to give him a few pointed suggestions, but the movement of his thumb against my skin mesmerized me, softening my body so that I relaxed into the curve of him. We fit together seamlessly, without any awkwardness, like solid wooden joists that understood the burdens of time and air and needed no adjustments.

Beau pressed his forehead against mine. "I'm just glad you texted me. I don't want to think about how long you'd have been stuck inside there."

His words shook me from my stupor. I pulled back to look at him. "What? I didn't text you. Not since last night when I asked if you could talk."

"But someone did. From your phone. I could show you, but you'd have to get off of my lap."

Neither one of us moved, too afraid to confirm what we'd find on his phone. Or maybe the way our bodies were nestled into each other was like the force caused by the meeting of two magnets.

My phone rang, and I sprang from Beau's lap to answer it.

"Nola—where are you?" I didn't need to look at the screen to identify Jolene's voice. "I've been calling and calling and I was fixin' to call the police. Do you have any idea what time it is? At this rate we'll be lucky to hose you down outside and slap on some lipstick and heels."

I pushed aside that visual. "I'm sorry—I'll explain later. I'm leaving now." I ended the call before she could make any more suggestions about how to hurry my beautification process with gardening tools.

Beau had already stood. "I'll drive you."

I was still too shaken by my ordeal to argue, so I only nodded before heading toward the stairs. My hand was firm against the banister as I carefully made my way to the bottom.

As we walked out onto the front porch, I paused by my bike. "Hang on. We need to put this in your truck."

Beau kept walking. "I think it's safe, Nola. Even if a thief were brave enough to step up onto this porch, no one wants to be seen riding a bike with a banana seat and a giant basket with flowers."

"Very funny. All I need is one drunk guy to steal my bike and I don't have any way to get around town." When he looked at me expectantly, I added, "Please."

As Beau hauled my bike into the back of his truck, he said, "You didn't ask me what I was so busy doing last night that I couldn't talk when you texted."

I focused my gaze on the door handle of the truck. "I figured it was none of my business."

"Well, it was. Kinda. Christopher, Trevor, and I were installing your new kitchen island. It was supposed to be a surprise, and I didn't want to ruin it."

"Oh. It's . . . amazing. It's so perfect. I saw it when I first got here and I had no idea where it had come from, but I love it. It's only . . ." I bit my lip, hearing Jolene in my head saying something about looking a gift horse in the mouth. "It's only that I didn't put an island in the plans because it was over budget. And that piece, well, it's special, and an antique, and I know I can't afford it."

"I think you can." He closed the truck's tailgate. "Climb in and I'll tell you about it on the way home. Unless you'd prefer to drive."

I quickly hauled myself into the passenger seat and shut the door.

Beau put the truck in drive and pulled out into the street. "Christopher brought Trevor to his first estate auction last weekend, and when Trevor saw the breakfront he said it would be perfect for your kitchen."

I shifted in my seat to look directly at Beau. "Trevor bought it? But where did he get the money? All the money he's making at the store is supposed to go into his computer fund."

"Come on, Nola. Do you think Christopher would allow that?"

"No," I said slowly, already wondering how I could return the breakfront without hurting Trevor's feelings.

Beau slammed on the brakes as a driver ignored a stop sign on a side street and pulled out in front of us. He frequently reminded me that if I could learn to drive in New Orleans, I could drive anywhere. "It was at the end of the auction, and they were going to scrap the breakfront because it was in bad shape and missing its top. Trevor brokered the deal—offering to haul it away for free if some of their guys could put it in the van. That boy's a born salesman."

"That he is," I said, feeling as proud as if he were my own son. "So, who fixed it up and painted it?"

"Trevor picked the distressed black himself. And then Christopher and Jolene showed him the right way to strip the old varnish and use the right painting technique."

I found myself close to tears before another thought occurred to me. "What would have happened if Trevor had suggested orange or purple or some sort of wild design?"

"Then you'd have yourself a hideous island, because there is no way we could have told him he was wrong. I haven't seen that kind of excitement on a kid's face since the Saints won the Super Bowl. Happily, it worked out."

"Happily. I couldn't have found anything else as perfect. I'll have to find some way to pay him—at least for his time."

"Agreed. But I'd suggest not asking him first, or you'll end up paying for a whole lot more than just his time."

We both started laughing, louder and longer than necessary, as if trying to put more than only miles between us and the unknown entity in the upstairs closet.

CHAPTER 13

Despite Jolene's threats, no hoses were used to get me ready for my date with Michael at Commander's. But I'd been wrong to assume that because it was Michael Jolene would allow any shortcuts.

As I attempted to deflect yet another dosing of hair spray, she said, "You need to pick out a signature scent that will make him think of you every time he smells it so that even after you scrape him off the bottom of your shoe the fragrance will torment him."

"I don't know any perfumes. How about Charlie? My little sister used to love that."

Jolene froze, her hand and the can it held mercifully suspended. "A signature scent shouldn't be something your little sister wears or something you can pick off the shelf down at the Walmart." She put the can on her dressing table and began to fluff my hair at the scalp with something she called her teasing comb. "Maybe we can sneak in a visit to Saks this weekend. They have the best fragrance department. But first we have to go check out the Saint Expedite statue."

"The what?"

"It's over on Rampart, at the Our Lady of Guadalupe Church. I've always wanted to see it, and I thought we could squeeze it in during our sightseeing this weekend."

"Saint Expedite?" I said. "Is that a real saint?"

"Sort of. Long story, but Saint Expedite is named after the label on a crate that arrived at the church. It contained only him and no explanation. At some point he became the patron saint of impatience, and there are speed prayers and shortened novenas for his followers, who are always in a hurry. Saint Jude is in the other corner of the church, so we could go see him, too. Saint Jude is the patron saint of lost causes, so I thought I could go have a talk with him."

"But you're not Catholic."

She looked at me as if I'd just told her the sky was blue.

"Whatever," I said, slipping from the chair to make my escape. I was allowed to wait for Michael downstairs, "just this once," since Jolene was still too angry to look at him. I picked up the small bag and cashmere wrap she had loaned me, and I fled toward the upstairs French door.

"Hang on! I forgot the Preparation H!"

I quickly ducked into the upper hallway, making it to the first landing before Jolene could reach me. I looked up in horror as she brandished the yellow and white tube. "I'm pretty sure there is no need for that, Jolene!"

"Don't be silly. It's for that red blemish on your forehead. Just a dab and it will be gone in an hour. It's also good for pores and—from what I've heard, of course—for squeezing into skinny jeans. But that's for times when you're not going to be in a crowd. Everybody will recognize the smell, and heaven forbid they think it's coming from you."

I was more than a little relieved when I heard the sound of a car door closing outside. "Maybe next time. He's here."

Slightly mollified, she said, "Fine. Hopefully, it'll get bigger and redder so that you'll look like a cyclops by the end of the evening and it'll ruin his appetite."

I grimaced up at her. "Gee, thanks. I guess I'll just feel self-conscious all night and hope that nobody calls animal control to come get me."

Jolene laughed. "You really are funny, Nola. I have no idea why Beau says you don't have a sense of humor."

The doorbell rang, and I paused for a moment before opening the door, my hand on the knob as I waited for my heartbeat to slow.

"And remind Michael that I have a Barbie head and I know how to use it!"

She ducked out of sight just as I opened the door and found myself face-to-face with the person I'd once planned to never lay eyes on again.

The bright teal and white Victorian building on the corner of Coliseum and Washington Avenue in the Garden District is a New Orleans icon on the same plane as such lauded landmarks as St. Louis Cathedral and the Superdome. Commander's Palace (just Commander's to locals) is the sort of place where New Orleanians go to sit at favorite tables to celebrate their big and small moments while enjoying some of the best food in the city. It's also where visitors (and uninitiated newcomers, such as myself) go for pretty much the same reason, but sit at less favorable tables.

Michael and I spoke very little on the drive to the restaurant, and even after we were led to a cozy table for two in the back corner of an elegant yellow and cream dining room, we kept our conversation on such fascinating topics as the weather, Jolene's latest culinary masterpiece, and what Mardi was wearing for Halloween. It was as if we'd both agreed on a temporary truce until we were numbed by so much fabulous food that we could speak honestly without worrying about feeling potential barbs.

After a large meal that I mostly couldn't taste, Michael asked for two dessert menus—reminding me that there was a lot to like about Michael Hebert despite, well, my inability to trust him. We each ordered a crème brûlée, even though our server insisted a single order was big enough to share. Something I'd learned from Melanie, and was now relishing as I awakened to the nonvegan world of real food, was that I did not like to share my dessert. I'd yet to stab a fork into anyone's hand, but I had a feeling the first time lay in the near future.

I admired the powdered sugar stencil of a fleur-de-lis on top of each dessert as the plates were placed in front of us. I wanted to snap a photo on my phone to show Jolene, imagining her making a stencil of Mardi's face to use on pancakes and muffins, but I didn't want to be *that* person taking pictures of her food.

"Want me to do it?" Michael said with a grin.

"How did you know what I was thinking?"

His hazel eyes were measuring as he looked back at me. "You're easy to read, I guess."

I glanced away, uncomfortable. Michael reached across the table and touched my hand, misreading my sudden nervousness. "I'm sorry, Nola. I just meant that you're one of those honest and good people who are easy to read only because they're not the type to scheme."

I slowly slid my hand away. My focus turned to the two cups of coffee that had just been placed in front of us. Thinking it would be rude to ignore my coffee or spit it out after a quick taste, I filled half of my cup with cream and sugar just in case it was chicory coffee.

I swished my spoon back and forth, watching as the color in the cup lightened. Despite my assurance that he could drink whatever he wanted, he'd joined me for a virgin sidecar cocktail when we'd first sat down, and seltzer with lime to sip with dinner. "I have to ask. Did you know I was a recovering alcoholic when we first met? Before . . ." I waved my hand, not wanting to relive the horrendous events of the past few months by putting them into words.

He looked genuinely wounded, his eyes lowering to the white tablecloth where our server had already scraped away any crumbs. "No. I swear I didn't. I would never have put you in a situation where you felt like you needed to have a drink. Regardless of what you might think, that's not the type of person I am."

I forced myself to smile despite the unpleasant memories being stirred up along with my coffee. "So," I said, bringing up the proverbial elephant that had been sitting at the table since we arrived, "you wanted the chance to explain why you did what you did. I'm all ears. Just don't expect me to forgive you, whether I understand your reasons or not."

He put his fork down and took a sip of coffee. "That's fair. I just want you to know everything."

I raised an eyebrow. "Everything?"

"Everything I know," he amended. "Which, admittedly, isn't a lot. Because as lame as it sounds, I didn't know at the time why my uncle asked me to break into your house. Or the real reason why he wanted that Maison Blanche door. I swear it."

I chewed slowly, wishing I could enjoy the crème brûlée, but I might as well have been eating toasted cardboard. "I find that interesting. If not just a little suspect. You're a grown man, Michael. Don't you ask questions?"

He leaned forward. "You don't know my family."

"If we're going to be friends, maybe I should."

Michael reached for my hand again and I let him wrap it with his warm fingers. "I do want to be friends, even though I know we can't ever be anything else. I can accept that if you just try not to hate me."

"Why is it so important that I don't hate you?"

He took in a long and slow breath. "You inspire me, Nola. The way you don't let your past dictate your future. Even the way you handle your illness. You stumble, but you get back up. You have done a much better job of recovering from a difficult childhood than I have. So has my sister, Felicity. But she's too busy leading her exciting life in New York to take the time to explain how she faces her world. She's younger, too. She probably doesn't remember our parents, at least enough to miss them. That's why I need you in my life. I want to learn from you."

I kept my hand in his, noticing how different his touch was from Beau's. Not that I was thinking about Beau. He just had an inconvenient way of popping into my head at awkward moments. "Okay," I said slowly, knowing that this was part of the plan, that Michael was exactly where we wanted him. Yet my stomach felt unsettled, deception not a compatible condiment with crème brûlée. I placed my fork on my plate.

Keeping my hand in his, I smiled.

Our server appeared to refill our coffee cups, and Michael relinquished my hand and slid back in his chair. I shook my head, blocking the top of my cup with my fingers. The coffee had been the dreaded chicory, the bitter aftertaste of it like an insult to the wonderful meal I'd just eaten.

Michael straightened his tie repeatedly, something I'd discovered he did when he was nervous. "Thank you, Nola. Thank you. I can't tell you how much this means to me."

He was so genuinely happy that it made me feel guilty. I managed to smile, then quickly grabbed my purse and excused myself to find the ladies' bathroom. I wound my way through the maze of dining rooms until I found myself in the mercifully empty bathroom. The walls were covered with a soft green tufted fabric, almost begging me to stand in front of it to rest my forehead. I wondered if that had been the intention of the designers, knowing intimate dinner conversations could be headache forming.

I breathed in and out, each breath increasing in me the resolve needed for the purpose of being with Michael in the first place. I stayed in that position until another woman entered the bathroom. I stepped back from the wall and approached the mirror to stare at my reflection and wonder why I looked the same as I had in Jolene's mirror. A toilet flushed and I fished out the tube of lipstick Jolene had thoughtfully placed in my bag. I dutifully touched up my lips, then blotted them on a tissue just as I'd been instructed. All my motions seemed so normal. Even when the other woman left, holding the door for me and smiling, I still felt like Nola, and not at all like the kind of person who would seek revenge, no matter how justified.

Michael stood as I approached our table, and he held out my chair as I sat. The plates had been cleared away and replaced with two fresh glasses of seltzer and lemon. I took a long sip from mine, needing to moisten my parched mouth, glad for the lipstick to hide the cracks.

"So," I said, "where do we go from here?" My toes curled inside my shoes as I waited for him to answer.

"I'd like you to meet my aunt and uncle. They'd like to apologize to you in person. And let you hear their side of the story."

"Wow. I didn't expect that at all. Why would they want to do that?"

"Because I told them how special you are." He took a deep breath, considering his words. "They know you're close with the Ryans, and they'd like you to be a kind of ambassador between the two families. My aunt and uncle have been staying out of New Orleans society in deference to the Ryans' loss, but they'd like to reemerge with a clean slate."

"That could take quite a while."

He flashed a warm smile. "Yeah, we figured. That's why we thought we'd invite you to our beach house next weekend. To give us all time to talk and come to an understanding of recent events."

I studied the condensation dripping down my glass, my thumb tracing one of the droplets. "My family arrives tomorrow for a visit. My parents and brother are leaving this Sunday, but my twelve-year-old sister, Sarah, will be staying the week."

"Then bring her. I'd love to meet her. And so would my aunt and uncle. They've always wanted a house full of kids."

"I'll have to ask. It's her last day in New Orleans. But if I agree, I'd also like a friend to come with me. It would make me feel more . . ."

"Secure," Michael finished for me. "I don't blame you. My family and I have done nothing so far to make you feel safe with us, so of course you can bring Sarah or anyone else. As long as it's not Beau Ryan."

I almost laughed. "Don't worry. Beau's not a friend. He's acting as the general contractor for my house project, and we might be expanding our working relationship with a new rehab of a house on Esplanade. But there's nothing . . . romantic . . . between us." Or at least nothing that could be labeled romantic. Whatever it was between Beau and me defied explanation. "I was thinking about asking Jolene."

Michael nodded. "Good choice. I like her."

"It's hard not to. Just a heads-up, but you'll need to work hard to get back into her good graces. As a matter of fact, before I left the apartment this evening, she told me to remind you that she has another Barbie head and won't hesitate to use it."

A startled expression crossed his face. "Duly noted. I'm assuming she'd use it to pummel me?"

"That, or she'd put it in your bed as a warning."

Our eyes met before we both burst out laughing, the tension of the evening melting away until I began to feel as if this were a normal date. Almost. Because the ugly specter of revenge that had been sitting at the table all night was still there, staring me in the face. The dominoes were being stacked in place, and all I had to do was move very carefully so I wouldn't knock the first one over and start an avalanche.

CHAPTER 14

Jolene volunteered to drive us to the airport to pick up my parents and siblings, even though my dad and Melanie insisted that an Uber was just fine. Jolene had nearly had a conniption—her word—at the thought of not meeting my family at the airport, insinuating that only having the plague or bleeding from the eyeballs would excuse me. When I pointed out that I didn't have a car, she looked hurt that I didn't consider her, and therefore Bubba, a part of my family; if I did, I wouldn't have thought twice about asking her to make the airport run. It was hard to argue with Jolene, even though I knew on inspection many of her arguments wouldn't stand up in a strong wind. It was just easier to give in.

The only thing reassuring about driving on I-10 with Jolene behind the wheel was that the lanes were wider than the city streets, giving her more room to maneuver without chipping paint on passing cars—Bubba was larger than every vehicle we passed except for a dump truck and a tractor trailer. Still, by the time we pulled into the passenger pickup area at Louis Armstrong International, my fingers had stiffened into a clawlike shape from gripping the door handle, and my throat and tongue felt like sandpaper from silent screaming.

I spotted my dad first. He was usually the tallest in a crowd, making it easy. Now it was especially easy, since every woman was already looking in his direction, as well as several men. I'd like to think the attention was because he was a well-known writer, and not because of his looks. During the "low period"—what Melanie and I called the time when Jack had been dumped by his agent and was just trying to stay published—his publisher had made him pose shirtless for his back-cover author photo. I thought I'd never be able to show my face in school again and had considered faking my death and moving to another country.

He was in the middle of an earnest discussion with Melanie. At least, she was being earnest; Jack was just giving her that half smile that meant he was irritating her on purpose. It was how they communicated and it seemed to work. Most of the time. There was always a lot of kissing and making up, which would make JJ and Sarah cover their eyes with their hands, but to me it had shown the type of love and permanence I had craved as a child and young adult. And still did. Knowing that it existed gave me hope.

As if he could feel me looking at him, my dad turned and saw me. "Nola!" he shouted. Heads pivoted as Jack, Melanie, JJ, and Sarah all ran toward me with outstretched arms.

"Group hug," Melanie declared as eight arms embraced me.

It was embarrassing and awkward and we were making a spectacle of ourselves, yet I closed my eyes and reveled in that sense of love and belonging that had eluded me for so many years, and that I had treated so casually and irreverently more than once. I hoped I'd outgrow that need, and was unsure if we could all survive intact again.

Each parent claimed a bear hug and a smacking kiss on each cheek before I could disentangle myself. "You look wonderful, Nola," Melanie said, the corners of her eyes creasing with lines I didn't remember. "I love what you're doing with your hair. And are you wearing a dress?"

"Who are you and what have you done to my daughter?" Jack said with mock horror.

"Very funny. It's good to see you, too. Before you give me too much credit, it's Jolene's dress, and she's the one who French-braided my hair. Mom, you two have already met, but Dad, this is Jolene, the one you've been hearing about."

I turned to introduce my friend, now standing between JJ and Sarah, who both looked up at her with apparent adoration, ignoring me completely. I rolled my eyes, something Jolene had told me I needed to stop doing since it would give me wrinkles, but I felt the occasion called for it. "Dad, this is Jolene McKenna. Jolene, my dad."

Overlooking her outstretched hand, my dad gave her the same sort of bear hug he'd given me. "Thank you," he said. "For everything."

She pulled back and shrugged, a pretty pink blush covering her cheeks. "Nola is family. I take care of my family."

I wanted to roll my eyes again, but I couldn't because I felt the surprising sting of tears. I wondered if that meant I was growing up.

"And this is my brother, JJ, and my sister, Sarah." I rubbed their heads like I'd done when they were small, although I was a little startled to notice that they were almost as tall as me now.

Jolene beamed. "As if I couldn't have picked y'all out as being kin. You're all like peas from the same pod as your daddy. My goodness—those are some strong genes."

"Tell me about it," Melanie said wryly. "I was just an incubator for Jack's babies. That was my only contribution to these two." She smiled with warm affection at the twins.

Sarah met my eyes and raised her eyebrows, acknowledging that there was at least one part of Melanie's genetic makeup that had found its way to her biological daughter.

"I like your hair," Sarah said softly. "Is that the real color?"

"It sure is. That's why my mama named me Jolene. Like the song."

Sarah looked at her blankly.

"Don't worry, sugar," Jolene said. "I have Dolly Parton's greatest hits in my cassette player in the car, and we'll listen on the way home."

"I'll sit up front, next to Jolene," JJ announced, and now I did roll my eyes.

I turned to find Melanie smiling at me, which made me nervous. "We have a little surprise for you."

"Yeah?" I said, looking around for a wrapped package and seeing nothing but their suitcases.

I became aware of a man approaching us from behind, someone tall, slender, and handsome, and devastatingly familiar. "Hi, Nola," he said. "It's been a while."

Cooper Ravenel, my best friend's older brother and my first heartbreak, stood in front of us, holding a large suitcase and a backpack as if he was planning on staying awhile. His dark blond hair was a little longer than when I'd known him during his Citadel years, but his smile remained the same.

"Cooper," I said, proud of the steadiness of my voice. It had been years since he'd announced he was moving to California after his graduation from the Citadel and he had left me behind. I was still in high school, and at the time I'd told myself I understood. But my heart didn't believe me, and the bruise was still tender every time I thought about him.

He put down his baggage and took a step forward as if to embrace me, but I blocked him by crossing my arms across my chest. "Surprise," he said.

I looked at Melanie and Jack and then back at Cooper, trying to find my breath. And the appropriate words that wouldn't come out as an accusation or a shriek of anger or a mortifying sob. I managed to swallow down my tangle of jumbled emotions. "Wow. What a surprise. What are you doing here?"

"I've decided that California isn't for me. So I've accepted a great job here as a security analyst with a consulting firm. The job will require lots of travel, but this will be my home base."

"You're moving here? To New Orleans?"

"Yeah. Isn't that great? I mean, I knew you were already living here because of Alston, but then I ran into your family at the Charleston airport and had a nice time catching up."

"Wow." I needed to stop saying that.

"He had reservations at another hotel, but we convinced him to stay at the Hotel Peter and Paul with us, so he switched hotels." Melanie beamed. "It's amazing what you can do with a phone these days."

My eyes met my dad's as we raised our eyebrows in unison, thinking about the one hundred or so apps on Melanie's phone that she had no idea how to use. It was one of her quirks that was endearing and annoying, sometimes both at the same time.

"Amazing," I said, which was better than "Wow," but still inadequate.

"I would say that running into your family was a coincidence, but . . ."

"There's no such thing as coincidence," everyone finished, and then laughed, and the tension and pent-up emotions I'd been holding on to ever since Cooper had exited my life dwindled to a tiny speck—but were not erased completely. I imagined all broken hearts carried lifelong scars.

He smiled, his cheeks creasing in the way I remembered, and I could picture him at the dining room table at the house on Tradd Street, working with my dad and me to decode a cryptic cipher. "I don't start my new job until next Monday, so I'll have an entire week to go house hunting. Melanie said that you could give me some pointers since you've just been through it yourself."

"Oh, she'd love to," Jolene said. "But if we don't skedaddle, we'll spend all week here at the airport." She led us all to Bubba and I noted Jack's dubious expression as he looked at the car and then all of their luggage and then back again.

"Don't worry, Dad. It will all fit—trust me. This trunk is big enough to carry at least seven bodies and the shovels needed to bury them—and with room to spare."

"It's eight," Jolene corrected, oblivious to the side-glances of her audience.

"Her grandmother is a funeral director," I said, as if that explained anything.

Jolene squeezed JJ's invisible biceps. Not quite thirteen, he had yet to hit the growth spurt and begin the filling out that had been threatening for over a year. "Let's allow these strong gentlemen to do all the heavy lifting." JJ blushed and eagerly grabbed one of Melanie's bags, barely lifting it off the ground.

"Your mother packs rocks, son. We might have to call a forklift." Jack grabbed the other end of the case, and the two of them managed to lift it into the cavernous trunk.

"I'll direct," Melanie said. "I'm really good at organizing spaces so that—"

"I think they can manage," I said, pulling Melanie up onto the curb, making sure she didn't trip in her high heels.

To everyone's surprise, there was still room in Bubba's trunk for at least one more body and a shovel, even after we'd loaded Melanie's two large suitcases and her cosmetics bag.

"Where's everybody supposed to sit?" Sarah asked. Like her twin, she had also not yet begun to blossom, but it was clear to everyone that once she did, our dad would have a hard time beating away the boys. He'd already started collecting brochures for all-girls convent schools in Ireland just as a warning.

"I'm sitting next to Jolene," JJ announced, quickly sliding into the middle of the front bench seat.

Sarah rolled her eyes. "I'll sit on the hump in the backseat because I'm smallest. And because it puts me in the right spot to put things in JJ's hair."

"Kids!" Melanie said. "You're supposed to be on your best behavior. Don't make me start singing."

That was enough to make the twins sit back in their seats and not make a sound.

Jack slid next to Sarah in the back, but when I made to get in on the other side of her, Melanie raced around the car to take hold of my elbow. "Why don't you ride with Cooper since we're all going to the same place? You can go with him to pick up his rental car and do some catching up."

I looked at my dad for help, expecting him to do the thing where he'd form a V with his index and middle fingers, point at his eyes, and then redirect them to point at Cooper to make it clear that he was watching. He'd actually done that once when I'd gone on a date with Cooper a million years ago in Charleston. But he didn't do it now. Either he had switched his focus to his younger daughter or he believed I'd be safe with Cooper.

"I mean, I'd love the company if you don't mind," Cooper said.

Feeling everyone's expectant eyes on me, I agreed. I closed the side door, then waited for Melanie to climb into the front seat. Leaning in through Jolene's open window, I said, "Buckle up and hang on tight. Saying a few Hail Marys might help, too."

"But we're not Catholic," Sarah pointed out.

"Doesn't matter. I think Bubba might be."

With an admonishing look, Jolene rolled up her window, and I stepped back to watch them take off with a rumble of the giant engine.

Cooper and I talked of mundane things as he went through the process of picking up his rental, a normal-sized sedan that didn't necessitate my stepping up to get inside (like Beau's truck), didn't have seats and windows that were manual, and didn't have a cassette player. It was also much smaller than Bubba, with bucket seats that were close enough together that I could easily reach over and touch Cooper. I'd accidentally brushed his arm as I was placing his backpack in the trunk, and the familiar zing—now whittled down to more of a buzz—was still there. He'd glanced at me, making me wonder if he'd felt it, too. While my brain and heart busied themselves with a game of tug-of-war, I pressed myself against my door to make sure there would be no more touching, accidental or otherwise.

"Melanie was telling me about a new project you're going to be working on—a shotgun house, I think? I'd love to take a look, if that's okay. I don't think anyone who grows up in an old house in Charleston is comfortable living in anything else—at least for long. Not that I have any dreams of doing any renovations. But if the timeline works out, and I love the house and the location, I could always rent somewhere until it's ready. I think I'd like to live in a house where you had a hand in the renovations."

When I didn't respond, he said, "I mean, if you're okay with showing a work in progress."

"I'd be happy to show it to you. It's just that there are a couple of things you need to be aware of."

"Yeah?" He turned to me with the gray eyes that I remembered, the same ones that would light up when I said something funny or when I just walked into the room. For a long time I had avoided going out with guys with gray eyes just because of Cooper's.

"Well, for one, it's not a done deal yet. Beau Ryan, Jolene's boss and my contractor, and his grandmother are getting into the business of buying old houses with a history, rehabbing them, then selling them. This would be their first project."

Cooper nodded. "And old houses with a history would mean . . ."

"Murder. That's usually one of the reasons why nice houses in good neighborhoods aren't selling."

"I see. I don't think that would bother me—as long as there aren't any visible reminders, of course. Like bloodstained carpet."

"Seriously? Like I would try to sell a house with bloodstained carpets?"

He laughed. "No. Just thought I'd check in case you're not the same Nola I remember."

My own smile faltered, and I looked down at my hands. "I'm definitely not the same Nola you remember. A lot can happen in the span of a decade, you know?"

I felt him turn his head toward me, but I didn't look up. "Yeah, I know. Alston's kept me informed. I wanted to come back home, see if there was anything I could do, but Alston said your parents were handling it and she wasn't sure I'd be a welcome face. But I'm glad you're well." He was silent for a moment, and just when I'd started to relax, he spoke again. "You look beautiful, by the way."

"Thank you," I said. "It's because of Jolene. She's next-level when it comes to what to wear to pick up family at the airport. Or to go running in the park, for that matter."

The side of his face creased in another smile as he kept his focus on the road ahead. "No. It's more than that. You have a sense of . . . maturity about you. You always did, but now it's like you're a little more comfortable in your own skin. Like you shed your old skin and have found the new one a lot more to your liking."

"Great. So you think I'm an old snake. I'll have to remember that the next time someone asks me what's the nicest thing someone has ever said to me."

Cooper laughed and I joined him, happy to have rediscovered our old footing. "Well, glad we got that out of the way," he said, still smiling. "So, what's the other thing? You said there were a couple of things I needed to be aware of."

Knowing I could be honest with him, I said, "How do you feel about ghosts?"

"Well," he said, drawing out the word. "Knowing Melanie and having seen firsthand what she does, I have an enlightened perspective, I think. I grew up in an old house with lots of creaks and groans and cold spots. I never completely believed my mom when she brushed it all off by claiming that all old houses had leaks and drafts and old floor joists, but it helped Alston and me sleep at night. In other words, they don't bother me, so I don't bother them."

"I used to say the same thing."

He turned to look at me, his eyebrow raised.

"My cottage—the one I bought and am in the process of renovating—has a few 'memories,' as Jolene likes to call them. There were two, but Beau and I sent them on their way. But now one of them seems to be back, and there's also a new one now. A not-very-nice one who is difficult to ignore."

"Well, it's a good thing Melanie's here, right?"

"True. Although I really don't want her involved. She needs to know that I can handle things on my own."

"What about Beau? You mentioned that he helped before."

I nodded. "To be honest, I haven't gotten that far. I guess I was hoping that if I ignored it, it would just go away on its own."

"Good plan," he said. "That usually works well."

"I know, I know. I need to talk to Beau. See if we can figure out some kind of strategy."

An SUV going about ninety swerved into the lane in front of us, causing Cooper to slam on the brakes and honk, but the oblivious driver of the SUV simply coasted into the next lane and sped away. "Welcome to New Orleans," I said.

"I've been driving in LA for the last few years. Nothing could surprise me."

I leaned forward and knocked on the fake wood on the dash. "You haven't seen me behind the wheel yet."

"So you're finally driving?"

"Not yet. I'm not ready, but Beau's been teaching me and thinks I'm ready for the interstate."

Cooper nodded slowly. "So, you and this Beau Ryan. Are you . . . a couple?"

I shook my head more forcefully than necessary. "No. Absolutely not. He has a girlfriend, Samantha—Sam. We just work together."

He looked at me and I realized I was still shaking my head and made myself stop.

"Is there . . . anyone else?"

I thought of Michael. "No and yes. It's a long story—I'll tell you later. But no, I'm not in a relationship with anyone."

The GPS told him to take exit four onto Franklin Avenue, and he flipped on his blinker. Despite the Louisiana license plate on his rental car, the use of his signal confirmed his identity as a nonlocal. As someone who was currently learning how to drive and was studying the state driver's manual very closely, I'd been surprised to find that despite what I saw on the roads every day, the use of turn signals was not, in fact, optional.

As he decelerated on the exit ramp, he said, "Do you still play backgammon? I think you have yet to beat me."

"I don't think that's right," I said, even though I knew it was. "But I'm willing to pull out my board and challenge you again. I don't think I've played since you left Charleston."

"Ouch. And here I was thinking we had succeeded in skirting that particular subject."

"Sorry. Trust me—I didn't bring up your leaving Charleston on purpose. I was hoping we could just, you know, forget about all that."

He stopped the car at the end of the ramp and put his blinker on. "I'm not sure there's anything I want to forget about Charleston except having to say good-bye. I was hoping that maybe we could just start over?"

I looked at him.

"You know. As friends."

I wondered if I was the only girl who'd heard that same line twice in as many days from two different guys.

Cooper pulled out onto Franklin Avenue, thankfully concentrating on driving, so he couldn't see my face. Not that I'd expected anything else, but to be firmly placed in the "friend corner" hurt.

I smiled. "Yeah. I'd like that."

We drove the remaining few blocks to the hotel, and pulled into its gated parking lot in silence.

CHAPTER 15

An hour later, Melanie, Jolene, Sarah, and I were piling into Bubba, eager to get our sightseeing started. Jack, JJ, and Cooper were headed into the Quarter to check out Bourbon Street while it was still light out and relatively safe for an impressionable twelve-year-old boy. Melanie had given Jack explicit instructions to spend no more than twenty minutes on Bourbon before heading over to the relative peace and quiet of Royal Street. My dad was on orders from my grandmother Amelia to check out the antiques shops, especially the Past Is Never Past, and introduce himself to Mimi and Christopher.

I sat in the backseat with Sarah. "So, how do you like the hotel? I toured the rooms when I made your reservations, and if I could afford it I'd be staying there. It used to be an active parish church with a Catholic school and convent, but they were all abandoned a few decades ago. Luckily, a forward-thinking local preservationist decided to renovate and repurpose it into a luxury hotel."

"It's stunning," Melanie said. "All of the fabrics and furnishings are gorgeous, and I love how there are no two guest rooms alike. We're in the schoolhouse building, and JJ is excited about the bunk room adjacent to ours. Sarah has her own room across the hall, but . . ."

I met Melanie's gaze in the visor mirror.

"Maybe JJ wouldn't mind if you took the other bunk in his room?" I suggested.

"Or I could just stay with you and Jolene, since I'm going to be moving in with you when Mom and Dad leave anyway." Sarah looked at me hopefully.

I knew what happened when Melanie and her sister, Jayne, were together. If they hadn't prepared themselves mentally to shield unwanted intrusions from lost spirits, they became a beacon to the wandering undead searching for someone who would listen. Melanie's go-to defense was ABBA music. I didn't know what Jayne used, but I assumed it was more subtle, as I'd never heard her break out in song in the middle of a museum or street or any of the spots I'd been with Melanie when she'd encountered a wayward spirit.

It made me wonder if the beacon of light that Sarah and Melanie together might be shining in an undoubtedly haunted location might be overwhelming for my little sister.

"It's fine with me," Jolene announced from the driver's seat. "That will give us more time together to do girlie stuff. Speaking of which, do you have your own Barbie head at home?"

Sarah gave me a questioning look, and I gave a quick shake of my head.

"No. I don't think so," Sarah said.

"Well, no matter. Having you at the apartment will be so much fun!"

I sent Sarah a sympathetic look and was surprised to see my sister leaning forward with excitement. "Could you show me how to curl my hair like yours? Mom says I'm too young for makeup, even though I'm practically a teenager, but if you show me how to do my eye makeup I'll already know how when it's time."

I sat back in my seat, realizing I wasn't part of the conversation.

We found street parking on Rampart Street, near Our Lady of Guadalupe Church. As we climbed out of the car, Sarah asked, "Why are we here?"

I sent a warning glance to Jolene so she wouldn't mention her quest to petition the saints for their intervention in her love life. "It's the oldest church in the city. Actually, St. Louis Cathedral is older, but it's been rebuilt at least once. This church building is original."

Jolene pulled down the car's visor and began reapplying her lipstick. "There are two statues I thought would be interesting. The first is an unusual one with a bit of a legend attached to it. His name is Saint Expedite. The legend has it that the statue arrived in a crate and the good nuns had no idea who he was. He's dressed as a Roman soldier and he's, like, a thousand years old, but he doesn't have a shield or a sword, and on the crate was just the word 'expedite.' So they named him Saint Expedite, and people come to see him to ask for a quick response to their prayers."

"Are you serious?" Melanie asked.

"As a dead person." Jolene pulled her compact out of her purse and dabbed at her nose while we all watched. "The other saint—and he's quite famous around the world—is Saint Jude. He's the patron saint of hopeless causes." Jolene smiled at us in the mirror before snapping the visor shut with authority despite the duct tape wrapped around it to keep it in place. "So the church is basically a one-stop shop for those desperate for intervention but needing it in a hurry." She opened her door and stepped out of the car.

Melanie stood on the sidewalk, her eyebrows pressed together as she looked up at the white stucco church. "Is there . . . anything else about it? Besides the saints?"

Sarah spotted the historical marker in the neutral ground and pointed it out to her mother. "It says it was built in 1826 as a funeral chapel for the victims of yellow fever." Their eyes met before they both looked at me.

"I'm sorry. I wasn't aware—really. Jolene just mentioned it was historic, and I thought it would be interesting to see something that was quintessential New Orleans." I crossed my arms and turned to Jolene. "I had no idea about . . . the yellow fever thing."

Jolene's face fell. "I'm so sorry. I wasn't thinking. Maybe y'all could wait here while I pop in for a few minutes? Since we're already here."

Melanie reached for Sarah's hand. "We'll be fine. For a little bit. Right, Sarah?"

My sister nodded, even managing a smile for Jolene.

Jolene beamed. "Thank you. I promise I'll be fast. I've already typed up and folded my requests for intercession, and it shouldn't take long to pin them on the wall and light a candle."

It was Melanie's turn to beam. "Nothing wrong with being organized, right, girls?"

She was looking at Sarah and me, and as if on cue we rolled our eyes in unison.

We slid off our sunglasses as we entered the church, and we were quickly enfolded in the dim serenity found in places of worship. The hushed voices of other visitors buzzed like sacred chanting amid the pale walls and jewel-toned windows. The scents of flowers and candle wax flooded the lofty space, huddling in the pews alongside the praying faithful. Statues and plaques of varying sizes filled most of the walls; at the far end was a simple altar with two angel statues standing at each side as guardians.

"Which one should I go to first?" Jolene whispered.

"Probably Saint Jude. Let him know what you're asking for, and then head over to Saint Expedite to ask him to hurry it up."

"Isn't that a bit blasphemous?" Jolene asked, her eyes round with worry.

"Not intentionally. Besides, you're not Catholic—remember? I'm sure that means you get a special dispensation or something."

"Good point," she said, smiling again. "I'll hurry."

As she walked over to Saint Jude's shrine, I left Melanie and Sarah near the door where we'd entered and I began walking around the perimeter of the building, admiring the architecture and the obvious care the church received.

I wasn't sure when I became aware of humming, the song "Dancing Queen" painfully familiar. I followed the sound to Melanie to ask her if she was ready to leave, and I saw that she was looking at Sarah. My sister stood in the alcove with Saint Expedite, facing the side wall full of flickering candles in glass jars in a kaleidoscope of colors. Her lips were moving so that the casual observer would assume she was praying. As I approached, she turned to me, a curious expression on her face.

"Who is Adele?"

I sucked in my breath, not sure if I'd heard her correctly. "Who?"

"Adele. Like the singer. Except she's not." She tilted her head, listening to someone I couldn't see. "She says you know who she is."

"Beau's mother," I said.

Sarah nodded, then tilted her head again, her forehead creased. After a moment, she said, "She's hard to understand. It's like . . ." She stopped, shook her head as if unable to come up with the correct word.

"Like she's underwater?" I asked.

Her face brightened. "That's exactly it!" Sarah's smile faded and she closed her eyes. "She says . . ." She frowned, shook her head. "I can't . . ." She stopped. "I think she just said something about Louis."

"Louis? Like the cathedral? Or the king?"

She shook her head, allowing her chin to sink near her chest. "No. It's—" Her head jerked up, her eyes wide, and she stared directly at me. "It's like a small city, with little white buildings. And crosses. Lots of crosses."

Melanie joined us, her expression one of concern. "Let's go outside, Sarah. You're looking a bit green."

Sarah shook her head. "No. I'm fine. She's gone now." She bit her lip, her blue eyes brighter than usual. "I don't think she was supposed to be here. I think she followed us because she knew she could talk to Mom or me, and that took up a lot of her energy."

"Did she frighten you?" Melanie asked, putting her arm around Sarah.

"No. She was just . . . a mom, you know? Except her skin was really white, and her lips blue. That's how I knew she wasn't alive anymore. She looked so sad, and I really want to help her. We need to find out what this Louis is."

"I think I know," said Jolene as she approached. "Did she give you a number?"

Sarah thought for a moment. "I don't think so. She kept holding up her index finger, but she went away before I could ask if that meant anything."

"No need. I think she means St. Louis Cemetery Number One. Maybe that's where the Ryan family crypt is and she wants to show us where she would like to be buried? Assuming her body is ever found," Jolene said, her voice hopeful.

I was already texting Beau. For once his response came right away. "He says their crypt is in Metairie Cemetery."

"Maybe she was just suggesting it as an interesting place to see on your visit."

We all looked at Jolene with blank expressions.

"Or not," Jolene said. "Although it is a good suggestion." She pointed down Rampart Street. "It's about two blocks that way, on Basin Street. We've got a couple of hours before we have to meet the guys, so we've got time. We could leave the car here and walk it."

We all looked at Melanie's heels. Even Jolene was wearing sensible, yet fashionable, flats.

"I'll be fine," Melanie insisted. "The weather is beautiful, and these sidewalks aren't as bad as others I've seen." She adjusted her silk scarf into the collar of her chic navy knit jacket, and I thought about mentioning that she looked like her mother, but I wasn't sure if she'd take it as the compliment it was intended to be.

"Maybe you and Sarah would want to wait outside the gates?" I asked.

Melanie pulled out an earbuds case. "I've got every song ABBA ever recorded, so I can listen and sing along if I get bothered. Although I have discovered that cemeteries aren't as haunted as people might like to think. Most of the time spirits prefer to hang out in familiar places, and most people don't hang out in cemeteries when they're still living."

"Unless there's a family mausoleum and they visit their family members a lot," Sarah added.

"Supposedly St. Louis Number One is one of the most haunted cemeteries in the country," Jolene pointed out. "But that could just be a rumor to encourage tourism, right?"

"Sure," I said. Turning to my sister, I said, "What about you, Sarah? Are you okay to go in? Or are you going to start singing ABBA, too?"

She looked horrified. "If you ever catch me doing that, please just slap me. I give you permission. But no. I can manage."

"Are you sure, Sarah?" Melanie asked. "I'll be happy to wait outside with you. We can listen to my playlist while we wait."

Sarah's eyes widened in fear, either from the thought of spending time listening to Melanie's playlist or because of the prospect of visiting a cemetery that might or might not be haunted. It was a toss-up. "Nope. I'm good. I've heard a lot about New Orleans's aboveground cemeteries, and I've been dying to see one in person." She laughed at her own joke, but her laugh sounded hollow. "Like you said, cemeteries aren't the most haunted places around. How bad could it be?"

Sarah began walking in the direction of the cemetery. "She's just like you at that age," Melanie said, her expression a mix of exasperation and admiration. "Not willing to listen to anybody, and needing to make up her own mind about everything. I think I'm too old now to go through this again."

For Melanie to admit to feeling her age meant she was serious. I slid my arm through hers. "Just give it another twelve or thirteen years and she'll be back to normal." Pulling her with me, I said, "Come on—let's take that tour. Like Sarah said, it can't be that bad, right?"

"Right," she said, her tone saying otherwise. "I only wish your father were here."

"Why?"

"So I could yell at him for giving me two daughters who are just like him."

CHAPTER 16

Jolene lifted her phone and began tapping the screen. "St. Louis Cemetery Number One is the first in the archdiocese to require guided admission, and the tours are usually sold out way in advance, but my first cousin twice removed on my mama's side works for New Orleans and Company—the renamed visitors bureau." Her fingers kept tapping as she talked, a talent unique to Jolene but not surprising.

She continued. "I've mentioned Suellen to you before, haven't I? Suellen Larue is named after my grandmama's mama. She was the one who was born with these huge earlobes, which, mercifully, she grew into. Thank goodness, or she'd still be called Dumbo, and she's a grown woman. Anyway, she can get us in for a tour last minute. I can't wait for you to meet her. She is a spitfire, let me tell you. She and her husband, Dale, have six kids, all boys. Can you imagine? They kept trying for a girl, but after the sixth boy she told Dale to either get himself snipped or she was going to tie it in a knot."

Sarah snorted, and I took the opportunity to interrupt when Jolene drew a breath. "Any luck? With the tickets?"

Jolene looked down at her phone. "We're in! The next tour starts in five minutes, so we can make it if we hurry." We began walking quickly, following Jolene's bright red head.

"Why would Beau's mom want us to check out the cemetery?" Melanie asked.

"Maybe she's a fan of Nicolas Cage?" Jolene said.

"What?" Sarah said. "I didn't know he was dead."

"He's not," Jolene said. "But he went ahead and built a nine-foot tomb in the shape of a pyramid for when it's his time. The locals weren't too happy at the intrusion from an outsider. If I were in one of the neighboring tombs, that would give me a reason to haunt the cemetery."

"Who else is buried there?" Sarah asked.

"I know one name," I said, having only recently learned it from Jorge, when he told me that was where I needed to go to get rid of the gris-gris bags that were piling up on my front porch. "The supposed tomb of voodoo priestess Marie Laveau."

Sarah screwed up her face. "Why would Adele want us to go there?"

"There are over one hundred thousand people buried here, sweetie," Jolene said. "Adele's focus could have been any of the tombs. And if she wasn't more specific, I say we just follow the tour guide and see if we find anything of interest."

I watched as Sarah and Melanie once again shared a glance, and for the first time since the birth of the twins, I felt a twinge of jealousy. Not because I was no longer an only child, but because what Melanie and Sarah shared wasn't something I could ever be a part of. I shook off the feeling like an ill-fitting coat, ashamed that the thought had crossed my mind, even if it had been just that once.

We met our tour guide and a small group of other visitors at the cemetery gate on Basin Street. When the guide asked us where everyone was from, I had to think for a moment before answering. "New Orleans," I said, testing it out for the first time since moving there and buying my house. It felt oddly satisfying, as if I'd finally answered the question I'd been asking myself for a long time.

The guide, Mary, had a great sense of humor and was very passionate about her job and the cemetery, creating a light atmosphere despite my constant worry about Melanie and Sarah. Melanie wore her earbuds and was humming softly to herself as she pretended to listen to the guide. Sarah's lips were pressed together tightly, her face stoic as we walked down the first narrow aisle, which was flanked by decaying tombs nestled neatly between pristine marble mausoleums and rusted iron fencing. Flaky orange spikes and fleur-de-lis topped metal gates with broken hinges and missing rails, while the tombs were watched over by crumbling angels and cherubim and other statuary. I found the benign desecration oddly appropriate for a cemetery in New Orleans, a city known for its sinners as much as its saints, the lines separating good and evil sometimes blurred.

As we passed the various monuments, all set out in rows like houses in a neighborhood complete with street names and signs, it became clear why the aboveground cemeteries were called "Cities of the Dead."

Next to a wall of what Mary referred to as "oven tombs"—appropriately, since the rounded brick fronts stacked one on top of another strongly resembled bread ovens—we stopped at a family mausoleum with over a dozen names inscribed on the stone plaque on the front, the first interment in 1855.

"It's not very big. How do all those coffins fit into that single tomb?" a member of our group asked.

Mary smiled excitedly, as if she'd been waiting all morning for this question. "They don't," she explained. "We're here in October, when the temperatures are much lower than in the heat of summer. The temperatures inside these tombs in the hotter months can reach one hundred fifty to two hundred degrees, assisting Mother Nature in a faster decaying process. The rule is that after a body is interred, they wait for one year and a day before reopening the tomb. At that point only bones are left. A cemetery worker will then take a pole and push the remains to the back of the tomb, making it ready for the next family member. This is where the expression 'I wouldn't touch that with a ten-foot pole' comes from."

There were murmurs of appreciation from the group and a bobbing nod from Melanie. I could hear the faint melody of "SOS" coming from her earbuds. I slid a glance toward Sarah, noticing her tightly clenched hands, and her lips that were now almost white from being pressed together.

I nudged her. "You okay?" I whispered.

She nodded without looking at me, her gaze focusing on the wall of tombs.

Mary continued. "Sometimes, like in the great yellow fever epidemics of 1878 and 1905, there were too many members of the same family dying, so they had to resort to temporary tombs until the year and a day had passed, and then the remains would be interred in the family vault."

"People bled from their eyes." Sarah's voice rang out clearly. "And vomited blood. Some of them weren't dead yet when they were put in the tombs."

Everyone turned to look at Sarah. Mary's smile slipped. "That's right. You've been studying your New Orleans history! More than forty-one thousand people died of yellow fever during the great epidemics between 1817 and 1905. Entire families were wiped out. You can imagine the rush the city was in to inter victims. At that time, the going belief was that the bodies of the infected could continue to spread disease, so time was of the essence." She smiled uncomfortably at Sarah. "So, yes, sometimes mistakes were made." On a cheerier note she added, "And from that comes another familiar saying, 'saved by the bell.' People were so fearful of being accidentally buried alive that there began a new practice where people would be buried with bells that they could ring for attention if they woke up inside a tomb."

Everyone, except for Sarah, smiled and nodded. Melanie noticed and unclenched Sarah's hands and placed one of them in her own. Melanie popped out one of her earbuds. "We can leave now. Or I can let you use one of these. It's up to you."

Sarah shook her head, her chin jutting forward stubbornly, just as I'd noticed our dad doing during an argument. I did the same thing, as had been pointed out once or twice. "I'm fine." She indicated the group, which had moved on. "Let's catch up." She dropped Melanie's hand and walked forward to join the group.

We continued to follow Mary, listening to the interesting histories of the tombs and the families who resided within them, as well as stories about the larger monuments of the fraternal and military societies within the city. We were standing near one of these, a monument for firefighters with an old-fashioned fire truck carved into the front, when I realized that Sarah wasn't with us.

I poked Jolene in the arm, and when she shook her head after I'd asked if she'd seen where Sarah had gone, I told her to stay with Melanie and said that I would go find my sister. When Mary wasn't looking, I ducked behind a tomb and began walking, calling Sarah's name while looking in the spaces between structures.

I found her standing outside the freshly painted iron gate of a well-tended family tomb, the two large urns standing guard at the sealed door filled with fresh flowers. A large stone lion, its mouth open in mid-growl, perched at the ready atop the mausoleum, the muscles and sinews of his legs and chest taut and primed, ready to pounce on an intruder.

Sensing my presence, Sarah spoke without looking at me. "I guess this family doesn't believe in angels for protection."

I started to laugh, relieved that Sarah was acting normal, but then I saw the family name etched into the marble. BROUSSARD.

"Why are you here?" I asked.

"She brought me here."

"Adele?"

Sarah shook her head. "No. The little girl. She took my hand and brought me."

"What little girl?" I asked, looking around.

Sarah gave me a half grin. "Not the kind you can see."

I nodded, feeling for the second time that day the small flash of unwanted and unexpected jealousy. "Who is she? Or was, I mean."

"I don't know. I've been looking at all these names on the front, trying to figure it out. There are lots of family members here, including extended members, like in-laws, I'm guessing, because of the different last names. I think there are over thirty names here, but I can't get close enough to read them."

I pulled out my phone to take pictures, but the battery, which had been fully charged when I'd entered the cemetery, was now dead. "Here," Sarah said, handing me her phone. Moving quickly before the battery drained, I snapped pictures of the tomb, including all the names, the flowers, and the menacing lion perched on top, its stone eyes narrowed as it appeared to focus on us.

"Do you recognize any of the names?" Sarah asked.

"Some. Jeanne Broussard was the woman who was murdered in my house by her own father, Antoine. And I see her uncle Frank is interred here, too. The fact that they've all ended up together would be enough of a reason for Jeanne to be haunting the cemetery, I guess."

Sarah shook her head. "Maybe, but it would be weird for her to appear to me as a little girl."

"Sarah! Nola!"

We both turned to see Melanie tottering in her high heels toward us over the dirt and gravel of the cemetery street. Her appearance surprised me, as I'd assumed she was too absorbed in her personal ABBA concert to notice that we were missing.

She came to stand next to us and looked up at the tomb for less than three seconds. "We've got to go. We shouldn't be here." Melanie grabbed an arm of each of us and began dragging us away. I wanted to stop and ask why, but when I noticed the matching expressions she and Sarah wore, I closed my mouth.

Mary sent us a disapproving glance as we rejoined the group. "Remember, everyone, that we need to stay in a group. This is for your own safety." She continued the tour, but of the four of us, only Jolene appeared to be listening.

When we were finally outside the cemetery gates, Melanie took hold of Sarah's hands and began chafing them between her own.

"They're ice-cold, Sarah." She took out a pair of warm leather gloves from her purse. "Here, put these on."

My sister did as she was told, but the color of her face remained almost corpselike. "Did you see it?" Her voice cracked, prompting Melanie to pull out a small bottle of water and hand it to her.

"I did," Melanie said.

Jolene and I shared a look. "What didn't we see?" I asked.

Melanie put an arm around Sarah and pulled her close. "It was . . . a man. At least, I think it was." She looked at Sarah, who slowly nodded. "It was hard to tell because it was just a shadow, but it . . ." She shuddered. "It didn't move like a normal shadow."

My blood froze and crackled. "Sort of like an inkblot?"

Melanie looked at me with surprise. "Yes. Which is why I pulled you two away. It was pure evil. And all of its menace seemed to be directed at us. I didn't want it following us."

My expression caused her to loosen her grip on Sarah and look at me closely. "What is it, Nola?"

"I think it's too late for that."

CHAPTER 17

Cooper held my car door open as I stepped out onto Prytania Street in front of the Ryans' house. My family was with Jolene in Bubba, and they slid up to the curb behind us, the thump and scrape of Bubba's bumper as familiar now as Jolene's greeting of "Hey, y'all."

Following our day of sightseeing, Mimi had invited us all over for supper so she could meet Melanie and Jack and my siblings before all but Sarah had to leave on Sunday. As the ultimate hostess, she'd extended the invitation to both Cooper and Jaxson. At some point, Jolene had found the time to bake a batch of her famous brownies and wrap them in a cute basket with a huge orange and black gingham bow. JJ, his infatuation with Jolene not a secret to anyone, offered to carry the basket into the house, and Jolene graciously accepted. In view of the age difference and Jolene's devotion to Jaxson, I hoped Jolene would let him down carefully.

As we waited for everyone to exit the car, Sarah, Melanie, and I stood looking up at the house, the exterior spotlights creating creeping shadows from the limbs and leaves of the magnolia trees.

"Isn't it beautiful?" I asked.

"Assuming you like old houses, I guess you could call it beautiful," Melanie said.

"So it's not just 'a pile of old lumber'?" I asked with a grin, repeating a phrase she used just about every time her historic home needed yet another expensive repair.

Her gaze drifted to the cupola perched at the top of the house. "It's very old. Not my favorite thing when it comes to houses." She huddled in her coat.

Jack noticed and stood next to her, wrapping his arm around her waist, pulling her close. To the gathering group, he explained, "She equates all old houses with money pits, and often refers to them as nothing a can of gasoline and a match can't fix. She looks so cute when she's trying to hide her true feelings when working with clients who are bound and determined to own one. The tip of her nose turns red, just like a clown's. A very cute clown," he added, tweaking her nose gently. "It does the same thing when I put something in a drawer the wrong way. Right, Mellie?"

She sent him a withering glance, although she couldn't completely hide the twitching at one side of her mouth. "Can we go in? I'm starving."

"Everyone, stick your hands in your pockets," JJ commanded with mock alarm. "When Mom gets hungry, nothing is safe."

"Very funny," she said, moving forward as Jack opened the gate with the hourglass and held it for all of us to pass through.

As everyone walked toward the front steps, I turned back to find Sarah still by the gate, looking up at the house. "Are you okay?"

She gave me a stoic nod. "I think so. There is definitely . . . something here."

"Oh, yeah. For sure. Even I feel it."

I caught sight of the red rubber band around my wrist. I slid it off and handed it to her. "Here. Wear this—I've got a stack more at home. Snap it against your skin whenever you need to remind yourself that fear can't win. Because you're stronger than it is."

Sarah placed it on her slender wrist, then held it up to see it in the light from the porch. "Thanks," she said, giving it a few plucks with her index finger. "Where did you get it?"

"I got it from Beau. He has one, too. He gave it to me when he started teaching me how to drive."

She raised her eyebrows.

"No," I said in answer to her unspoken question. "We are not a couple. He has a girlfriend, Sam, who you'll also meet. She and I are . . . friends."

"Uh-huh," Sarah said, sounding wholly unconvinced.

Melanie joined us. "Everything all right?"

She was looking at both of us, but I knew her concern was for Sarah.

"Yeah," Sarah said, nodding. "All good." She held up her arm to show Melanie the rubber band. "Nola gave this to me." Snapping it against her wrist, she said, "I just need to do that to remind myself that I'm bigger than my fear."

Melanie reached out and took Sarah's hand, then mine. "My girls," she said proudly. "Always remember that we're stronger together."

The front door opened. After one last nervous glance at the house, Sarah followed Melanie and me to the door.

Mimi stood between Beau and Sunny, greeting us warmly with hugs and handshakes. Jaxson and Christopher appeared to help with coats and take drink orders, and I almost laughed at Jaxson's expression when he met my dad, mostly because it reminded me of the way that JJ looked at Jolene.

As we crossed the foyer, I watched as both Sarah and Melanie glanced behind them at the portrait of Charles Ryan before continuing into the parlor. When I introduced Cooper and Beau, it was like watching two prizefighters sizing each other up. They were the same height and had similar builds, and even though Beau wore his hair longer and shaggier, and had opted for jeans and sneakers instead of khakis and loafers like Cooper, it was clear even to the casual observer that they had a lot in common, namely having been raised by

Southern mamas. After their excessively long handshake, which seemed to be a contest to see who could squeeze harder, they both entered the parlor to pull out chairs for the women before bringing them their requested drinks.

JJ stood in the middle of the parlor, sniffing the air. "I smell garlic, cayenne, paprika, and . . ."

"Oregano," Mimi finished with a smile. "That's Cajun seasoning I'm using in my jambalaya. I wanted to share something quintessentially New Orleans with you. I've already made this for Nola and Jolene, but they promised me that they could eat it again. Are you a budding chef?"

"Yes, ma'am. That's why we have to leave Sunday. I've got a junior cooking contest in Savannah starting Monday."

"How marvelous. If you like, I can take you back into the kitchen before supper and you can help me plate the food and bring it in."

JJ grinned, looking even more like our father than usual.

Sunny sat on the sofa holding Mambo the black cat, allowing Sarah to gently stroke his sleek fur, the fat tail undulating back and forth like a cobra as the cat purred in delight.

"You must be wearing catnip or something," Christopher announced. "Because that cat doesn't like anyone except for Sunny."

Sarah shrugged. "Dogs and cats seem to love me, which is a good thing since I love them, too. I'm actually thinking about becoming a veterinarian."

"That's a great idea," I said, thinking about how much easier her life would be if she didn't have to deal with humans—either the living or the dead kind.

"Mambo tolerates me," Jolene said, reaching into her purse. "But he'll love me forever when he sees what I made him." She pulled out a purple, green, and gold bow tie attached to a small cat collar. "Isn't this the cutest? I made one for Mardi, too, so they can wear them when they're together."

Sunny's eyes widened in alarm. "I wouldn't if I were you. He's not declawed."

As if to prove the point, Mambo let out a hiss, stopping Jolene's approach. Placing the bow tie carefully on a side table, she said, "I'll let you try later."

"I've never seen a cat so exclusively attached to one person," Beau said. "Since the day that cat waltzed in here, Sunny has been the only person he will allow to handle him."

"And he wasn't a kitten when we adopted him," Mimi added. "He knew how to use a litter box, so he clearly belonged to someone and had been around other people. It's just a little insulting, because I'm the one who feeds him and wouldn't mind even a rub against the legs in thanks. Instead, I just get hisses, and Sunny gets all the love."

"I understand how you feel," Jack said, earning him a gentle slap on the arm from Melanie. "But how strange. Even for a cat." He studied Mambo with a thoughtful expression.

"Thinking of something for your next book?" Jaxson asked.

"Who knows?" Jack said, studying the cat for another moment before turning his attention to Jaxson. "Everything is fodder for a writer."

"Well," Melanie said, "since we're giving out gifts, I've got something for Beau and Jolene, to thank them for all their help with Nola's house. I wanted to give them as birthday gifts, but Nola kept on forgetting to tell me the dates, so I figured now was as good a time as any. I also brought suspenders for Thibaut, so promise you won't ruin the surprise."

"No, ma'am," Jolene said as Melanie handed two beautifully wrapped boxes to Jolene and Beau and sat back to watch them open their presents.

"It's—" Beau began as he ripped through the wrapping paper on his.

"A label maker," Jolene said with undisguised joy. "I've always wanted one, but Mama said that I didn't need one more thing meant for organizing. She was wrong, of course. I'm just going to go to town with it in my kitchen, that's for sure. When Nola empties the silverware from the dish drain, she always puts the oyster forks where the demitasse spoons are supposed to go, and this should be a big help."

"Huge," I said, my eye roll halted by Mimi and JJ announcing dinner.

Dinner was enjoyable and relatively uneventful except for Jack's constantly having to remind JJ to eat instead of staring up at the orgy painted on the ceiling. I was seated in between Jolene and Cooper, Jaxson seated on the other side of Jolene. Jack sat on Jaxson's left side, meaning that Jaxson spent the entire meal talking to my dad. Unfortunately for Jolene, Jack didn't seem to mind being monopolized by Jaxson, their conversation evolving from books, to history, to politics, and then to books about history and politics.

Cooper had held out my chair, then waited to sit until all the women had been seated. Melanie saw me noticing and raised her eyebrows. She had always been a fan of Cooper's, and even my dad had come around to accepting his presence in our house. But then Cooper had left for California, breaking my heart, only to periodically reopen the wound every time he came home to Charleston to visit his family. Every time I saw him, I was reminded of why I'd fallen so hard for him, why every smile, touch, and hair cowlick squeezed my heart each and every time, making him very hard to forget.

"You seem to have found your tribe," he said, placing his napkin on his lap.

"I have. Mimi Ryan has practically adopted me, and Jolene is like a force of nature and the kind of friend it normally takes a lifetime to find. It feels good to be here."

"Well, you look good. Great, actually. I think New Orleans suits you."

"That's because it's not July and I haven't just finished sanding spindles on a staircase without air-conditioning. Come back then and let me know if you still feel the same."

He threw back his head and laughed, and my heart sighed. I felt someone looking at me from across the table and turned to see Beau wearing a frown, Sam thankfully absorbed in conversation with Melanie so that she didn't see.

"Oh, Nola. I've missed you. A lot. I still think about you. How we worked so well together to help your dad with clues needed to solve more mysteries than I can remember. We just sort of . . . clicked, didn't we?"

I nodded, taking my time sipping from my water glass. "Yeah. We did. It was . . . hard to see you leave. But I was young and impressionable, so I got over it."

"Did you?" he asked softly.

I turned to meet his eyes, his smile gone. "Sure." A corner of my mouth lifted as I remembered my schoolgirl crush on my best friend's older brother. After Cooper moved away, I'd told everyone—including myself—that I was over him. That it had been just a crush.

"That's a shame." He kept his gaze on me. "I was given a choice of locations for my new job, and I picked New Orleans mostly because I knew you were here. Because I never really got over you."

He turned to accept the bread basket from Jolene, who then asked him about "his people," whom, being from the South, Cooper knew to mean his family. That began a conversation about siblings and parents and SEC football rivalries. Jolene had season tickets for LSU, and she headed to Baton Rouge almost every Saturday when there was a home game and had the television on broadcasting the game in every room when there wasn't. LSU-themed muffins, cookies, and doughnuts began appearing, and I'd learned every word to the LSU fight song because I'd heard it so often. She and her mother had settled on their tailgate menus way back in January, and they had their purple and gold dresses neatly pressed and waiting in their closets before the very first kickoff of the season.

"That's right," Jolene was saying. "Every Saturday. Sundays are for Jesus, but Saturdays are the real holy day."

"Amen," Jack said, making everyone laugh. Although a staunch USC Gamecocks fan, he understood that any SEC team loyalty was a sacred thing and should be respected. And, as he had to remind

Melanie every time he bought a new *GO COCKS* pillow or any other type of team home décor, allowed.

I slathered butter on my corn bread, still thinking about what Cooper had said, and was unable to stop smiling until I caught Melanie looking into the parlor behind me, her gaze moving as if she was watching someone walk across the room. I looked away and asked JJ about his chances of winning the upcoming cooking competition. His answer was interspersed with snippets of Mimi's conversation with Melanie about a fund-raiser she would be hosting for the cathedral at the end of the month.

The hubbub of conversation was punctuated with the occasional loud voice or laughter, reminding me of home, and I found myself nostalgic for my life in Charleston, and missing my family before they were even gone. My gaze drifted up to the ceiling, and I caught myself smiling at its absurdity and the pure New Orleansness of it, wondering how something could be so garish and stunningly beautiful at the same time.

I realized then that I was where I was meant to be right now, in a place that wasn't perfect, showed its imperfections with pride, and was deeply loved and admired despite the cratered streets and broken windows. This city was now my twin, my home. And it was my calling now to make us both strong and resilient, and not too proud to show our spots of flaking paint, because they showed where we'd been. If only the restless spirits currently living in my Creole cottage would agree and leave me alone to accomplish my mission.

After dinner, we returned to the parlor to enjoy coffee and plates of homemade pralines and macaroons. I skipped the coffee, not worried about hurting Mimi's feelings since she was preoccupied fielding JJ's questions about how she'd made the pralines. When Christopher brought the desserts around, I filled my plate just to make sure I got some, since JJ had grown a hollow leg, according to Jolene. My brother ate more food at one sitting than I could manage in a week, and yet he remained skinny as a reed.

Melanie reached for my plate. "Oh, Nola doesn't eat refined—"

I grabbed my plate with both hands. "Don't touch. Living with the Pillsbury Doughboy's minion has crossed me over to the dark side."

"I heard that," Jolene said while holding her own plate containing a single praline. "Just let me know if you'd like me to stop."

"Well, if she does," Jaxson announced, "I'll happily sacrifice myself to be the beneficiary of Jolene's talents in the kitchen."

He squeezed her shoulder as if she were a small child or family relation. Watching Jolene's smile slip, I turned to Jaxson. "You should join us tomorrow morning at the apartment. Jolene's been baking and freezing all week, so I'm sure there will be enough food for an army. And since you helped with the decorations it's only fair. I'm sure my dad won't mind signing your collection of Jack Trenholm books. Right, Dad?"

"Absolutely," my dad said, sending a thumbs-up. "Just don't tell me that you're my biggest fan, or I'll get a restraining order. I usually only do that to anyone who shows interest in dating my daughters, but I sometimes have to make an exception for unruly fans."

Sarah's face flamed. *"Daaaad!"*

I joined in the laughter, even though I was equally as mortified as my sister. Especially because I wasn't completely convinced that Jack was joking.

Sarah sat in the seat beside me, either because she wanted my company or because it was the farthest seat away from Beau and Melanie and she wanted to dim their combined beacon. Beau frequently plucked at the band on his wrist, while Melanie's foot tapped to the beat of a song in her head that was undoubtedly of Swedish origin.

Sarah stared down at her untouched plate, her fingers silently pulling at her own rubber band. As if sensing me looking, she said, "There's a man standing behind Beau. He's holding a pipe."

"Is he the man in the portrait in the hall?"

She gave a quick glance into the foyer before turning back to her plate and nodding.

"That's Beau and Sunny's grandfather Charles."

"He's nice."

"I know. He saved my life when I was pushed over a stair railing in my house. He caught me. We thought that Beau had sent him into the light, but I guess he's back. We can't figure out why. Maybe you—"

"No," she said, cutting me off. "He said only Beau can help. But Beau isn't listening."

As if hearing his name, Beau looked over at us and caught my gaze before quickly looking away just as the unmistakable scent of pipe smoke drifted through the room.

CHAPTER 18

Sam excused herself and left the room, and when she didn't come back right away, I peered out into the foyer. She stood at the bottom of the stairs near the portrait of Charles Ryan and out of sight of the other occupants of the parlor. She caught me looking and eagerly motioned for me to join her.

"Any news?" She kept her voice low. "I expected to hear something from you after your dinner with Michael last night."

"Sorry," I said. "I got home late last night and I was with my family all day. The dinner was pretty uneventful. Except he asked me to spend next weekend with him and his aunt and uncle at their beach house in Pass Christian. He says they want to apologize to me for what happened, and then have me hear their side of the story. He wants me to act as a sort of ambassador to broker a truce with the Ryans."

"You got to admit—he's got balls. Or his family has him by the short hairs and he doesn't know how to wiggle out of it. And you've definitely got to say yes to next weekend. Beau is already planning to talk with Jaxson about the best way to launch legal action, so he's not waiting."

"Don't worry about Jaxson," I said. "He already knows what's going on, and he's setting up a meeting with his uncle Bernie. I just need Mimi to keep Beau busy."

"She is—she's given him a list of about ten condemned properties to go see and evaluate, each with a detailed ten-page report that she came up with all on her own. Who knew Mimi could be so crafty? And at the end of the day, he's got me to help him forget about anything else." Sam raised her eyebrows and smiled suggestively, making me feel a bit sick in the stomach.

"Great," I said with a forced smile. "Jolene's already said yes, but I'm hoping to also bring Sarah with us. I need to make sure it's okay with Melanie. Safety in numbers."

As if conjured, Sarah and JJ emerged from the parlor together. "Where's the bathroom?" JJ asked.

Sam pointed to the hallway leading off the foyer toward the back of the house. "Down there, and on your left—"

Before she finished, JJ had taken off in a sprint.

"JJ!" Sarah shouted. "Girls first! I'm telling Mom!"

"If you don't want to wait for him—"

"Ew. I'm not using a bathroom right after him. I didn't bring my gas mask."

I resisted rolling my eyes. "As I was saying, you can use the bathroom upstairs," I said. "Fourth door on the right."

Sam gnawed on her thumbnail as we watched Sarah until she'd disappeared at the top of the stairs. "Make sure that Beau knows. So that he thinks you're working to dig up information to share with him. Which, technically, you are. Except for the share-with-him part."

"I'll just shoot him a text when we're on our way. Otherwise he'll spend all week pestering me about it."

"On the way where?" Jolene asked, passing JJ on her way to the parlor.

"To Michael's beach house. But we're not telling Beau yet, remember?"

With her fingers Jolene made a movement mimicking zipping up her lips and throwing away the key. "Got it."

"Whose beach house?" Sunny asked, joining us in the foyer.

"The Sabatiers'," I said. "Michael invited me to the family beach house next weekend."

"Really?" she said, frowning. "That should be interesting. Awkward but interesting. I'd love to be a fly on the wall."

I couldn't help but wonder at her lack of enthusiasm. "Awkward or not, I'm hoping to gather some kind of incriminating evidence of their involvement in your abduction. That's a good thing."

"You should probably wear a wire," Sam said, her face lit with excitement. "We could ask Jaxson if it's legal to do that, but that could really be all we need—sort of a one and done. We just give the recording to Beau and he takes it to the police and we're done!"

"Not really," Sunny said. "Not to be Debbie Downer or anything, but apart from the dubious legality of it, do we even know how to get one and how it works? Besides, what if it gets discovered while she's there? Then what? At worst, Nola could be in real danger. At best, all doors are shut and we have no way of getting inside their family circle again. I don't think we should risk it."

"They might even press charges and Nola would have to spend time in the pokey," Jolene said.

We all looked at her. Finally, Sam said, "Nobody calls it that, Jolene. It's jail. And no, we wouldn't want to risk that." Turning to me, she said, "Maybe you can just do a little snooping in drawers, and if you get caught say you got lost."

"It's just like a Nancy Drew mystery!" Jolene said.

Sunny continued to frown. "I think it's best that you just listen to what they have to say and not do any snooping. What if you got caught? You wouldn't have a car to just leave when you wanted to."

"I'll drive," Jolene said. "That way you'll be able to leave whenever you want. I'm sure Michael will insist on picking us up, so just tell him that I'm driving because we need to bring Sarah back early on Sunday for her flight and don't want him to have to cut his own weekend short."

"You're a genius, Jolene," Sam said, looking surprised. But only because she didn't live with Jolene and didn't understand that there was a huge and complicated brain behind the cotton candy exterior.

"I don't know," Sunny said slowly. "The Sabatiers could feel as if you're ganging up on them and not be forthcoming. I personally think Nola should go alone. Nothing will happen to her since everyone will know where she is, and she can make sure the Sabatiers know it."

Jolene looked at Sunny with slightly narrowed eyes as if wondering at her reluctance to jump on board with what was clearly an excellent plan. "Actually," Jolene said, "I think it makes sense for the three of us to go together. I could be the distraction while Nola and Sarah do the sleuthing, just like Nancy, Bess, and George in the series! Although Nancy was a redhead like me, so we might want to rethink our roles, because—"

"Thanks, Jolene. We'll figure it out. And thanks for offering to drive."

"You're welcome. Bubba and I are always happy to help." She elbowed me gently. "Maybe we can ask Cooper to be on alert to swoop in if we need assistance. I don't think he'd mind rescuing you, Nola. I wouldn't mind if he did, either. He's sexier than socks on a rooster."

"I'm not sure what that means, Jolene, but if it means he's hot, then, yes, I've noticed it, too." As much as I wished Jolene would forget about the soon-to-be-engaged Jaxson, I wasn't quite enthusiastic about her focusing her attention on Cooper.

"So, are you and Cooper . . . ?" Sam said.

I gave my head an emphatic shake. "No. We dated briefly, a million years ago in Charleston. His sister, Alston, is one of my best friends."

"Was it a good breakup?"

"Is there such a thing? But no. He was my first heartbreak, and it took me a long time to get over him. I think we're ready to be friends again."

"Friends. Right. And now he's moved to New Orleans, where you're living. Isn't that nice?" Sam said. From her gleeful tone, I expected her to be rubbing her hands together like the Grinch on Christmas Day. "I'm just glad because now I can stop worrying about you and Beau. I will admit to sometimes feeling pangs of jealousy at the amount of time you two spend together."

"Beau and me? What?" My voice was so high, I was surprised it didn't squeak.

"It's not that I don't trust him—or you. It's just that he's pretty amazing, and we're really happy. So much so that I'm kind of thinking about a future together."

I didn't respond until I realized that both Jolene and Sam were waiting for me to say something. "That's great," I said. "No need to worry about me at all. I'm not actually looking for a romantic relationship right now. All my time and energy need to be focused on creating a safe haven for me here, restoring my house, and doing my real job—the one I get paid to do."

"And learning to drive," Jolene added helpfully.

"Thanks for reminding me," I said, my sarcasm flying right over her flaming red hair. "We should get back," I said. "Has Sarah come down yet?"

"Not yet," Sam said.

"Maybe she got lost?" Jolene suggested.

"In this house, anything's possible. I'll go check on her." Sam put her foot on the bottom step just as Mambo ran up to us and began purring at Sunny's feet.

Forgetting Mambo's proclivities, I reached down, only to be rewarded with a hiss.

"Thanks, Nola," Sunny said, picking up the now-docile cat. "I've got it. He needs to go outside, and I'm the only one he trusts to open the door." She took the cat down the hallway toward the kitchen.

"I'll go with you," I said to Sam. I needed to make sure that Sarah hadn't encountered any remnants of Mimi's artifact storeroom. Even though it had been converted into Sunny's bedroom, I wouldn't have been surprised if there had been a lingering spirit or two from the detritus of other people's misfortunes left to capture Sarah's attention.

"I think I'll go back to the party," Jolene said. "Jaxson and I need to talk about what we're going to film next for the YouTube channel. Your daddy would probably like a break from answering all of Jaxson's questions, too. I don't think he's left his side all evening." She winked before heading back to the parlor.

Upstairs, Sam and I took turns peeking into each bedroom, finding them all empty. Sam pushed open the bathroom door and peered inside.

"Anything?" I asked.

Sam shook her head. "No Sarah. But there's definitely . . . something. I'm not usually attuned to that sort of vibe, which means whatever it is must be pretty strong."

"Me, neither," I said. "But I feel it, too." I remembered sensing something up in the attic of a house on Queen Street where Melanie, Jayne, and Beau were battling it out with a spirit desperate to hold on to her secrets. I couldn't see or hear anything, but the sudden drop in air pressure inside the room had been like that of a hurricane preparing to hit. The atmosphere in the upper hallway now was heavy, and when I looked at Sam, I could tell that she was thinking the same thing.

"We need to find her," I said. "Now."

"This way," Sam said, leading me to a slightly ajar door at the end of the hallway. She pulled it fully open, allowing me to see a flight of uncarpeted stairs leading upward. "This is where Beau and I record our podcast episodes. He keeps relics—"

Not waiting for her to say more, I brushed past her to race up the stairs. I stopped at the top, waiting for my eyes to acclimate to the dim light shed by a small desk lamp. This was the round cupola room at the top of the house, the walls made of windows. Now, on an October night, the outside darkness penetrated through the glass, with only the sharp wedge of light from the desk lamp softening the utter blackness.

An oval table jutted out from one of the walls, a chair at each of the longer sides and at one end. Three headsets sat atop a pile of cords nestled between two laptops and desktop microphone stands. Each stand held a microphone facing an empty seat, the atmosphere in the room like that of an interrupted conversation.

A hand touched my arm, and I screamed, jumping back so that the edge of the table dug into my hip, wobbling the microphones. I slapped my hand over my mouth to stop the sound as soon as I realized that it was Sam. She was attempting to draw my attention to the other side of the room, where Sarah stood in shadow, holding a familiar jewelry box.

I let out a relieved breath as I moved to stand beside my sister. "That was Sunny's when she was a little girl." I felt Sam join me. "It plays 'The Blue Danube.'"

"I know," Sarah said, her voice almost normal. "She told me."

"Sunny told you?" I asked.

Sarah shook her head. "No. The woman in the water."

"Adele," I said.

"Adele? Beau's mother?" Sam asked.

Sarah nodded. "I think she drowned. It's why she sounds like she's talking underwater."

Sam blinked a few times before turning to me. "Does that mean . . . ?"

"She's like Melanie," I said. "And Beau. Except she's not in denial about it. Just trying to find a way to live with it."

"Wow. I didn't know. That could be very . . . helpful," Sam said. "What else did she say?"

Sarah smoothed her hand over the closed top of the box. "I can't understand her very well when she talks to me, but she wanted to show me this, so I followed her up here."

"Is she still here?" Sam asked. I could hear the hopefulness in her voice.

"No. She left. As soon as I picked up the box. Like she'd already said what she needed to say."

I took the box, unlatching the top before twisting the small knob on the bottom. The little ballerina with her net skirt twirled as the creaking old music wheel spun inside, nearly obliterating the soft strains of Johann Strauss's famous waltz.

"She didn't show you anything else?" Sam asked.

"No. Just this. And then she . . . went away."

I looked around the room at the assortment of objects resting on the deep windowsills, and I suppressed a shudder at the cluster of Frozen Charlotte dolls. It was almost as if Beau had placed them there for the sole purpose of tormenting me.

The music stopped and I gave the box a gentle shake, and it appeared to be as solid as it had been the last time I'd held it. I put it back on a windowsill, noticing a scattering of hairbrushes and children's toys in the space next to it. Turning to Sam, I asked, "Why are these here? I thought Mimi's collection had all been sent to the shop on Royal Street."

"It was. But sometimes Beau brings so-called psychics here for interviews, and he uses various objects to test them."

"I see," I said, although I didn't. It seemed to me that Beau wasted more time denying his abilities than using them for good. But that was an easy thing for me to say. The spirits that haunted me weren't the dead kind.

"We should get back," Sam said. "Before Beau notices we're gone and finds us up here. He considers this his inner sanctum and doesn't allow just anybody in here." She began herding us toward the stairs before I could point out that Sarah and I were hardly "just anybody."

Sarah walked in front of us. Sam stopped me at the landing and waited until my sister had disappeared into the parlor before speaking to me. "Let me know if you need help convincing her to spend her last day of fall break with the Sabatiers."

"Why?"

"Because she's our secret weapon. I have no idea if there are any lingering spirits at their beach house, but if there are, they might have something to tell Sarah."

"She might not want to go if I tell her we're using her as bait."

"Just don't tell her."

I sent Sam a withering glare. "You don't have sisters, do you?"

She shook her head.

"I figured. I once found a snake in my bed because I ate all the Kit Kat bars from Sarah's Halloween candy. I didn't even eat processed sugar back then, but I couldn't resist. I thought she'd blame it on Melanie, but I wasn't smart enough to hide the empty wrappers."

"A snake? But she looks so sweet."

"Yes, well, looks can be deceiving. It was a harmless garter snake, and she'd had JJ do it for her, but still. I don't want to make her mad."

"Well, then. You should ask her. Just don't let her say no."

"Right. That would be as effective as me telling you to stop biting your fingernails."

"Funny," she said. "Just keep me posted, okay? I'm really excited about this new development. This might be a lot easier than I'd hoped."

Sam waltzed down the rest of the stairs humming "The Blue Danube." I followed slowly behind her, feeling on the back of my neck a sting from the portrait's eyes following me as I entered the parlor. Everyone had already stood, preparing to leave and saying their good-byes as the telltale scent of pipe tobacco followed them to the door.

CHAPTER 19

When Jolene and Cooper had dropped off my family at the Hotel Peter & Paul the night before, I'd handed them each an itinerary for the following day. It had been met with various facial expressions and exclamations, but Melanie had immediately shushed them and told me how proud she was.

"I made the fonts pretty and designed the borders," Jolene said as she pointed out the red beans, Mardi Gras beads, and crawfish dancing around the edges of the page. "But Nola did all the hard work of organizing and getting tickets."

"Why is there a pair of red Dorothy shoes at the bottom? I thought Dorothy was from Kansas," Sarah said.

"That's right," Jolene said. "But there's always a spot for Dorothy's shoes, don't you think?" Before anybody had a chance to think, I hurriedly said good night to everyone, then climbed into Bubba.

When we opened the apartment door a muffled bark came from upstairs, causing Sarah to break into a run. She loved Porgy and Bess, but still missed General Lee and was thrilled that Mardi looked just like him. She said it felt a little bit like having him back and sent me daily texts to remind me to send photos of Mardi. This fueled Jolene's creativity and inspired her to dress Mardi in a new outfit every day. Jolene and Sarah were delighted. Mardi and I barely tolerated it.

"Mardi!" she shouted, running up the steps.

"He's in the bathroom," I said. We'd had to resort to putting him there when we left, because otherwise he'd drag everything he could find to the front door, including his water bowl, which meant a massive shove was required to open the door, and then cleanup was necessary. In the bathroom, we left a soft bed, toys, comfy towels, and a water bowl to keep him contained yet happy.

Sarah had reached the dining room when she stopped suddenly, letting out a shattering scream. I pulled out my phone to dial 9-1-1 while Jolene quickly flipped on the lights.

I started laughing. The disembodied Barbie doll head, dressed in all her Mardi Gras finery, sat in the middle of the table like some barbaric sacrifice, but with perfect makeup.

"What *is* that?" Sarah demanded, slowly approaching the table.

"It's just a Barbie head," Jolene said. "For two smart women with an excellent education, I must say that there was an important part left out of your schooling."

"I think it's the surprise element," I explained. "Maybe next time you should give a warning."

"If there is a next time," Jolene said, sounding as if she'd just been accused of wearing white before Easter or after Labor Day.

Sarah rushed to the bathroom to open the door and was completely bowled over by the gray and white fur ball that was Mardi. She lay on the floor where he'd knocked her, and she giggled as he left doggie kisses all over her face, head, and neck. I picked him up to give her a chance to breathe, but she immediately stood and asked me to hand him to her. She cradled him in her arms so that all four of his paws were in the air, just like she'd once held General Lee, and I watched as he rested his head against her shoulder while casually licking the underside of her chin.

"I think he likes you," I said.

"Good. Because I like him, too." She placed a kiss on his nose, and I thought that Mardi might swoon with pleasure. She caught sight of the princess phone on the desk. "What's that?"

"You're kidding, right? I know you've never used one, but surely you've seen one."

She thought for a moment before nodding. "Actually, I think I have. My grade went on a field trip to DC and visited the Smithsonian's National Museum of American History, and they had some. Right next to the typewriters."

Despite being only twenty-six years old, I suddenly felt very, very old.

"Does it work?"

Before I could stop her, she picked up the receiver and held it to her ear. "Hello?"

I watched her face go from mild amusement to curiosity, and then to something that looked a lot like fright. She pulled the receiver away from her ear, and I grabbed it before slamming it down on the base.

She stared at it a long time before raising her eyes to meet mine. "I'm pretty sure that was her—the woman in the water. I couldn't understand what she was saying." Sarah shuddered and took a step backward.

I quickly picked up the phone and shoved it into one of the bottom drawers of the desk before slamming it shut. "We'll leave it in here and we can just forget about it. Why don't we get ready for bed?"

She stared dubiously at the drawer. "It doesn't ring, does it?"

"How could it?" Jolene asked. "It's not plugged in."

I felt Sarah looking at me but avoided meeting her eyes. "Come on," I said. "Let me show you where everything is. And if you hurry, Jolene will pop us some popcorn and we can watch an episode of *Wives with Knives.*"

"As fun as that sounds, I'm pretty tired. I don't even know if I can manage washing my face and brushing my teeth before I fall asleep."

Jolene looked horrified. "You should never go to bed without your nighttime skin care regimen. My great-granny was one hundred three when she died and didn't look a day over seventy lying in that coffin. Some say it's because my grandmama is not only a great funeral director, but she is also an amazing beautician and can do wonders with hair and makeup. But my great-granny looked good anyway because she took such good care of her skin since she was a girl. She claimed her secret was Merle Norman—they used to have a shop at the mall before it closed—but I know she also wasn't a stranger to that Botox needle, if you know what I mean. Her best friend's granddaughter's nephew was a dermatologist, and he—"

Sarah yawned, practically swaying on her feet.

"Thanks, Jolene," I said. "We get the point. We can finish this conversation tomorrow, after Sarah's had some sleep."

Sarah sent me a grateful smile. Communicating with spirits exhausted her. She'd once explained it to me as how the muscles of an athlete must feel after a triathlon—pushed to their limit and needing rest to recuperate. Melanie's mother, Ginny, was the same way, sometimes confining herself to her bed for an entire day after an episode. Surprisingly, it didn't affect Melanie at all. But then again, maybe not so surprising because Melanie had been called many things, but never normal.

Jolene had already placed an inflated air mattress in the back bedroom, and that's where Sarah settled in to sleep, with Mardi spooning against her. I took a picture and sent it to Melanie and Jack to let them know she was fine.

I heard Jolene pulling dishes from the cabinets in preparation for breakfast the following morning, and I joined her in the kitchen to ask if she needed help. As usual, she thanked me but declined my offer. The kitchen was her domain, and I was happy to relinquish all claims. I had yet to figure out when she slept, as I always went to bed before her, and no matter what time I woke up, she was always already dressed, with hair and makeup fully done, my coffee in my mug, and breakfast already started. For Christmas I was going to ask for hidden cameras to discover her secret, although a little part of me thought that might be the same as sneaking downstairs on Christmas

Eve to spy on Santa Claus. My childhood hadn't allowed me to have that particular fantasy, which meant that I wanted this one to last as long as possible.

As I left the kitchen, Jolene handed me a stack of plates to put on the desk on my way to my room, as the desk would be used as a buffet. I carefully moved aside the confetti and streamers for the plates and then, before leaving, opened the bottom drawer just to make sure that the phone was still in there.

I fell asleep going over my conversation with Cooper, feeling the stupid smile on my face as I drifted off. Which was why I was surprised to have been dreaming about Beau when I was abruptly awakened in the middle of the night by a wet nose on my left cheek and someone's finger poking me in my right arm.

"Nola?" Sarah whispered. "Are you awake?"

"Yes. I had to wake up because someone poked me in the arm."

"Can we sleep with you?"

Mardi had curled up in his spot at the foot of the bed and was already snoring. "Do I have a choice?"

She didn't move.

I scooted over to the other side of the bed and held open the covers before patting the mattress. "Come on in. Was the air mattress not comfortable? Jolene hand made the quilt and the mattress pad, so you might not want to tell her."

I felt her shake her head. "No. It wasn't that. It was . . ."

I was silent, waiting for her to finish, my toes curling with dread. I could see the outline of her face from the outside light creeping between the blinds.

"I kept hearing this rustling sound from a pile of pillows—you know, those monogrammed ones?"

"Yeah. Go on."

"I thought you might have mice. Or even roaches. JJ said the ones here are even bigger than the ones at home."

"Could be," I said, my toes curling even tighter. "Was it roaches?"

She shook her head again. "No. It was Adele."

"Did she say anything?"

"Not at first. She gave me something."

I sat up. "What?"

"Something fell on me, but I knew it was from her. It was a ribbon. Like the kind I used to wear in my hair. It was short and wide, and felt like satin. I don't know what color it is because I was too afraid to turn on the flashlight on my phone."

"It's yellow," I said. "It used to be Sunny's, when she was little. It fell out of her hair when she was kidnapped."

Sarah was silent for a moment. "Maybe her mother just wanted to thank you for trying to help find her when she was still lost."

"Maybe," I said, recalling Adele's appearance at the church. I couldn't understand how it might be related to the ribbon. Not that it had to be. It's just that during the years living with Melanie and watching her help the living and the dead, there was always a reason.

Sarah sat against the headboard, drawing up her knees and wrapping her arms around them, mimicking me.

"What did she say?" I asked.

"I'm not exactly sure. But she kept showing me a book. Not like a textbook or like a book that Dad writes. More like . . ." She thought for a moment. "More like the kind of book Grandma Amelia keeps at the antiques store. To keep track of her customers and what they bought."

"A clientele book."

"I guess. It's black and wider than it's long. And has a bunch of metal rings to hold the pages."

"Yeah. I know exactly what you're talking about. Did she say anything about it?"

"She tried, but it came out really garbled. She kept motioning for me to open it. Like she wanted me to take a good look at it."

"I guess it's a good thing that it's not in the back room anymore, or she might have dropped that on you, too."

"I don't think she would have. She seems nice. But I didn't want to stick around, so I left and didn't look back."

"It's all right. I know what book she's talking about, and I even know where it is. I just don't know what it is she wants us to see. Jolene and I have gone through it so many times and we haven't found anything of interest."

Sarah slid down until her head was on the pillow, and she was silent for so long that I thought she'd gone to sleep. But then she said, "I saw something else."

"What?"

"She was crying. I know it because even though it was dark in the room, there was this light around her, you know? And I could see her face, and her hair, and everything was dripping with water. But I know those were tears in her eyes—not just water, you know? I could see the difference, and I think it was important to her that I notice."

Her breath fell into a soft rhythm, so I slid down on my own pillow in an attempt to fall back asleep. I had just closed my eyes when slow, tired words fell from her mouth. "She said something else, too. I'm not sure if she said it out loud or if she just put the words in my head. But I'm pretty sure she needed me to tell you."

"What?" I asked, wide-awake now.

"She said to stop hiding the phone."

When I awoke the following morning both Mardi and Sarah were gone, but the unmistakable scent of brewed coffee filled my room along with the clang of pans and dishes coming from the kitchen.

I stumbled out of my bedroom door and was met by Sarah holding up my steaming cup of coffee. I mumbled my thanks before shuffling toward the dining table. I was confused at the absence of chairs, so Sarah took my arm and gently led me to one of the chairs that had been moved to the perimeter of the room.

"Smiley face pancakes are coming right up!" Jolene called cheerfully from the kitchen.

I blinked in response and took a sip of coffee.

"Is she always like this in the morning?" Sarah whispered.

I nodded, my eyes now open enough to take in Sarah's outfit. I recognized the blue sweater as one of my hand-me-downs, and a gold cashmere sweater had been knotted around her shoulders. It matched the gold Mardi Gras beads draped around her neck and the two large gold balls that hung from her pierced ears.

"You look very festive," I said.

"Jolene let me borrow some of her stuff. And look." She turned around so I could see her beautiful thick hair twisted into a perfect French braid and tied at the bottom with an enormous bow that would have looked at home on a Mardi Gras float.

"Gorgeous," I said. "But isn't the bow a bit . . . big?"

Jolene appeared from the kitchen carrying on a stand a tray with my breakfast neatly displayed on top, including a folded napkin tucked into an empty juice glass. "The bigger the bow, the more your mama loves you. Since we'll be out and about today, I thought Melanie would appreciate it."

"I'm sure she will." I placed my napkin on my lap and looked at my pancakes. They appeared different than usual beneath the whipped cream and syrup smiley face I was used to, but my foggy brain couldn't figure out how.

"I'll get the orange juice," Sarah said, disappearing into the kitchen before returning with a full pitcher of juice and filling my glass. "I told Jolene to use whole wheat flour for the pancakes. It's a lot healthier and tastes just as good."

"If you like eating cardboard," I said, noticing that the usual fat slab of butter had been reduced in size.

"You sound just like Mom!" Sarah chortled. "That's why Jolene and I decided you need to eat something now, before everyone else gets here, since we know how hangry you get when you haven't been fed. Mom's like that, too."

I stared at her in horror, realizing she was right on both counts.

The doorbell rang, and Jolene froze, taking in my wild hair and baggy sleep shirt and lack of makeup. "If it's Cooper or Beau or any other male who isn't related to you, let's throw a blanket over her and decorate it with streamers and confetti." Jolene quickly opened the door-camera app on her phone—one of the security measures Jaxson and Beau had helped install after the break-in during which the only defense Jolene had was a Barbie doll head. It had worked inasmuch as it had made the intruder run, but everyone agreed that a more aggressive would-be robber might not be as accommodating.

"It's Sunny," she said. "I wonder what she's doing here so early." She looked pointedly at Sarah.

"I know, I know. I'm the door greeter." Jolene disappeared back into the kitchen as Sarah leaned in and whispered, "She said if I'd do it cheerfully each time, she'd let me keep some of the makeup she's going to show me how to use. Just don't tell Dad."

"Dad? What about Mom?"

Walking toward the door, she called over her shoulder, "I don't think Mom's the one I need to worry about."

I had almost finished my pancakes—not as bad as cardboard but definitely not as good as buttermilk—when Sarah and Sunny came up the stairs, Sunny carrying a gift bag with paw-printed tissue paper exploding over the top. Jolene whisked away my tray and refilled my coffee so I could speak coherently.

"Good morning," I said, noticing how Sunny barely reached Sarah's chin, and noting the stark contrast between her blond locks and Sarah's almost-black hair. Sunny wore her hair pulled back in a sleek ponytail, her darker roots showing around the hairline. Not as dark as Sarah's, but definitely not blond. I recalled what Jolene had said about Sunny's bad dye job and hoped that my roommate would take her in hand and show her the right way to choose a shade. Not that I'd noticed or even cared, but I liked Sunny, and didn't want her to be at a disadvantage as she navigated her new world. I could relate to how hard that was.

Noticing my state of undress, Sunny said, "Don't worry—I took the streetcar and came alone. The rest will be here later. I thought you could use some help." She turned toward the table, noticing the decorations for the first time, and gave a high-pitched yelp.

"It's okay. We had the same reaction. It's not real." Turning to Sarah, I said, "When you greet people at the door, make sure you warn them."

"I heard that," Jolene said, carrying in a tray of homemade pralines and placing them on the coffee table. She spotted Mardi licking his lips and changed course to place the tray on top of an empty plant stand.

Sunny squatted, and Mardi ran toward her and nuzzled his face in her chest.

"He really likes you," Sarah said, dropping down next to them.

"He likes everybody," I said ungraciously.

"Ignore her," Sarah said without looking up as she scratched Mardi behind his floppy ears, his eyes narrowing with pleasure at the attention. "She's grumpy in the morning and hasn't had her second cup of coffee."

They both ignored my grunt.

Sunny reached for the bag. "I brought him a gift." She held the bag open for Mardi to sniff inside. After an intense olfactory inspection, Mardi stuck his head inside and pulled out a small gray plush Eeyore, a pink bow at the end of its tail. Mardi held it in his mouth, giving it several satisfactory squeaks.

"What an adorable ass!" Jolene exclaimed from the dining room, where she was placing a large oval tray of sliced pieces of king cake.

We both looked at her.

"It's Eeyore," I said. "From Winnie-the-Pooh."

She stared at us blankly.

Sarah stood. "Have you never heard of Winnie-the-Pooh?"

"Who?" Jolene asked, her eyebrows pressed together in question.

I looked at her closely to see if she might be joking, but she seemed serious. "How can you be the queen of all knowledge concerning *The Wizard of Oz* but not know about Winnie-the-Pooh?"

She turned to artfully arrange the pieces of cake on the plate and shrugged. "I have no idea. But whatever it is, it's adorable. And Mardi looks so cute with that ass in his mouth."

Jolene returned to the kitchen as Sunny, Sarah, and I exchanged looks behind her back.

Mardi ran to the door and pawed at the glass, the toy still in his mouth. "I'll take him out," Sarah said, grabbing his leash off the hat rack by the door. She reached down to take the toy, and he let out a low growl. "I guess he really likes it," she said, opening the door and leading Mardi down the stairs.

I turned to Sunny. "You can ask Jolene if she wants help, but she'll probably say no. You might as well make yourself comfortable and flip on the TV until she thinks of something you can do that won't interfere with her prep work. I'm going to go get ready."

"Sounds like a plan. Is there another TV I should watch so I won't be in her way? I haven't seen the rest of the apartment, so I'm not sure of the layout."

"You're welcome to walk around and take a tour, but that's the only TV. My bedroom and Jolene's bedroom are on either side of the bathroom. The front room is basically junk storage for now, until Jolene figures out how she'd like to transform it. It's where we stored the old Maison Blanche door for a while before Beau threw it into the swamp. The hatboxes were here, too, until we sold most of the contents to a secondhand store. So basically, it's where we keep our suitcases and Rubbermaid boxes full of Jolene's hoarded seasonal decorations."

"What about the rest of the old clothes and hatboxes? Mimi said there were other things found in the closet."

I decided to be deliberately vague with my answer, unsure if Beau wanted Sunny to know that he hadn't destroyed everything as he'd told Mimi he had. "I think Jolene donated the empty hatboxes and anything the vintage store didn't want. There was a Mr. Bingle doll in pristine condition, and it's still here. I put it in the back room because I couldn't think of a better place."

Sunny nodded. "When I was here before and I came in through the back door, I saw a back room with a wall full of casement windows. Is that the same room?"

"That's sort of my office-slash–music room. It's also big enough for a blow-up mattress. Sarah's staying back there all week, so I guess you can also call it our guest room. I'd hoped the light from the windows would creatively inspire me with my music."

"Has it?"

"Not yet. I'm still getting settled into my new life."

Sunny smiled, reminding me of one of the framed photos Mimi kept in her house of a very young Beau with his parents and sister before the abduction and Hurricane Katrina. Sunny's white-blond hair blew around her pixie-like face, her trademark smile shining out from the frame. It must have been hard for her family to forget that smile or why she'd been nicknamed Sunny.

"Don't worry—you've got time. Mimi tells me that when I was little I could pick out any song on the piano, but I can't even imagine doing that now. I guess I've got time, too. As soon as I settle in."

"Well," I said. "I guess we can settle in together."

"Especially since we'll be working together fixing up that house on Esplanade. I know that Beau sort of sprang that on you, and I hope it's okay. I'm a quick study, and I've always been interested in old houses and how to fix them up. And I promise I won't get in your way."

"Thanks," I said. "It will be a learning experience for both of us." I headed toward the bathroom so I could shower and dress but stopped halfway. "Quick question for you, Sunny. Do you ever feel your mother's presence? Or see any evidence that she's been near?"

She looked at me, her face blank. "Like what?"

"Well, I'm not what anybody would call psychic, but I can sense cold spots and certain . . . atmospheres, depending on how strong a spirit is. I know you said that you didn't think you'd inherited any of your family's psychic gifts, but I was just wondering if maybe you had a more heightened sense than the rest of us normal people."

"No. At least not that I know of." She shrugged. "Maybe I have and I didn't recognize it and my adoptive parents just sort of brushed it off. Because it's not something people would expect."

I nodded. "Have you noticed puddles where there shouldn't be any? Or wet footprints that just appear?"

She shook her head. "Definitely not—and I hope it never happens. I'd probably be so scared, I'd faint."

"Yeah. Me, too."

"Why? Does that happen to Beau?"

I nodded. "We're pretty sure it's your mom. She's trying to tell him something, but he doesn't want to listen. I was wondering if she might be trying to talk to you, too."

"Nope—nothing. Beau got all the psychic genes in the family, and I got the short body." She grinned. "But I can't help but wonder why our mother keeps trying to talk with him. Maybe he just needs to force her to go to the light so they both can move on, because there's no reason anymore for her to be hanging around."

I was surprised by her harshness. She sounded almost bitter, but maybe I did, too, when talking about my mother, Bonnie. Regardless of the reason for a mother's disappearance, a child's understanding of it can be either softened or sharpened by memories. I fought almost every day with my own recollections of the mother I'd loved and hated. "Don't you want to hear what she has to say?"

She crossed her arms. "Not really. Our family was destroyed, and it's time to rebuild what we lost. I just think that Beau should be focusing on finding our dad instead. He might still be alive. Otherwise, wouldn't Beau have seen him, too?"

"You might think. But I have no idea how this works." I was about to mention Sarah, and how she was still trying to figure out her unique gift, but it wasn't for me to share. Instead, I said, "Maybe we should be grateful that we're not the ones being awakened in the middle of the night with a ghost needing to tell us something."

"Well, then," Sunny said. "I guess we should be grateful." She tucked a loose strand of hair behind her ear, flashing the fleur-de-lis tattoo on her wrist.

"I like your tattoo," I said.

She lifted her arm to look at it, as if to make sure she knew what

I was talking about, although from what I could tell, it was her only tattoo. "Thanks. I like it, too. It reminds me of where I was always meant to be."

I smiled and headed to the bathroom, feeling a wistful pang of jealousy at knowing the answer could be summed up in a small symbol marked in permanent ink on the skin.

CHAPTER 20

Despite Jack and Melanie's insistence on a nap after the massive quantities of food we'd just consumed at Jolene's New Orleans–themed feast, I helpfully pointed to the itinerary. Everyone had forgotten to bring the ones I'd handed out the previous night, but I'd fortunately printed extras.

"As you can see," I said, indicating the third item on the list, "we have to be at the swamp tour dock by twelve thirty. Which means we have exactly forty-five minutes to tour my house before jumping into our cars."

"But the hotel is so close," Jack insisted. "Mellie and I could use a little time in bed."

"Ew," JJ and Sarah said in unison.

"I'm sure he meant sleeping," I said. "It's an hour's drive, so you can nap in the car on the way."

"Unless you're driving," JJ said. "Then all the screams will keep them awake."

"Very funny. And no. I'm not driving. Beau and Sam said they'd meet us here with Beau's truck and he's volunteered to drive." I didn't mention how they were supposed to have joined us at breakfast; I preferred not to think about what they might have been doing instead. Beau had at least had the courtesy to text me to let me know they'd meet us at my cottage.

When we arrived—ten minutes later than I'd allotted per our itinerary—Beau and Sam had already arrived. I also spotted Jorge's and Thibaut's trucks at the curb, indicating that they were inside. They usually didn't work on Saturdays but instead used the time to film content for the YouTube channel. I found it incredible that Thibaut, a man who didn't even own a cell phone, had become a social media star. He never watched his performances, and he said he didn't even know what social media was, but he enjoyed doing it. That was apparently his rule for everything he did in life. If he didn't enjoy it, then he didn't do it.

As if conjured, Thibaut and Jorge appeared on the porch with handfuls of tennis balls, making me glad we hadn't brought Mardi, who would be going wild. They began one of their juggling routines, facing each other while juggling the balls, then turning around and walking in opposite directions without dropping a single ball. I'd seen the routine with small tools before, and I was glad they had stuck with soft, round objects for this particular show. JJ was watching them with a contemplative look, as if he were imagining rolling pins and whisks in place of tennis balls.

We applauded, and they bowed before opening the front door and motioning for us to follow them inside. "Please know this is a work in progress," I announced as I stepped up onto the porch. "There was a lot more work involved than I had originally anticipated when I bought the house. I have a full-time job to pay for the renovations, but that keeps me from spending all day here."

My parents hugged me from each side, planting kisses on my cheeks. "Nola," Jack said, "we couldn't be more proud of you. You've accomplished so much." I knew he was referring to more than just the house, and it made me blink my eyes.

"Even without knowing how to drive or owning a car!" JJ blurted out. He'd met Trevor during our dad's visit to the Past Is Never Past the previous day, and Trevor had shown him where I was hiding my bike from my parents. I needed to remember to be nice to JJ, since he now knew my secret.

"I'm pretty resourceful," I said, giving him the eye-dagger look I'd learned from Melanie. "Shall we go in?"

Melanie and Sarah exchanged looks before moving to the back of the group. I asked Jolene to show everyone around while I went back outside to check on them. Melanie was already adjusting her earbuds in her ears, and Sarah wore the same grim look of determination she'd worn the day before at the church and cemetery. As I approached she held up her hand, showing three rubber bands on her wrist.

"Three?" I asked.

"In case two of them break. Jolene gave me the extra ones. She said your house has a lot of memories in it. I translated that to mean it's haunted and that I should be prepared."

I looked at Melanie, who paused her humming of "Mamma Mia" to speak. "And my lips are sealed. Unless you've changed your mind about needing my help."

I shook my head. "Nope. I can handle it." I wasn't completely sure of this since the incident in the upstairs closet, but I wasn't yet ready to admit defeat.

Cooper came up on the porch to stand next to me. "Melanie showed me pictures of what it looked like when you bought it. You've done an incredible job."

"Thanks," I said, his compliment making my cheeks flush. "I didn't do it all on my own, though. Thibaut and Jorge are true craftsmen, and Thibaut is as patient as Job in teaching me new skills so I can do things myself. It's taking longer that way, but I think it's worth it." I glanced up to find Beau wearing a speculative expression.

"And Beau," I added. "He's helped a lot, too, with resources and advice. Not to mention loaning me Jolene to do the decorative stuff and the social media. She's the one who's made the YouTube channel a huge hit."

"Jolene is . . ."

I waited for him to fill in the blank.

"Amazing," he finished. "At first glance it's easy to think she's purely decorative, especially after she opens her mouth. But I think beneath that red hair is the mind of a genius."

"You're not wrong. And I'm glad you said something nice. You had me worried there for a minute. Jolene is one of the most wonderful human beings I've ever known, and if you'd said something bad about her, I don't think we could be friends."

He raised his eyebrows at the word "friends."

"Nola mentioned that you might want to look at our new property on Esplanade." Beau's voice boomed from behind my shoulder, cutting short my conversation with Cooper.

"Yes," Cooper said. "I'd love to take a look. It's incredible what putting in a lot of heart and soul can do for a home. Seeing what Nola's done here is really inspiring."

"Thank you," I said, leading them inside the house. My phone buzzed, and I glanced down to see Michael's name. I had only just unblocked his number, and seeing his name filled me with more conflicting emotions than I could list. I looked up to see Beau and Cooper watching me. I was fairly sure they'd both seen Michael's name. "I'll call him back," I said, shoving my phone into my back pocket.

"Nola has quite the social life," Beau said.

"Ignore him," I said to Cooper. "I'll explain more later." I looked behind him and spotted Melanie and Sarah approaching the stairs. "I'll let you two talk." Without waiting for a response, I began walking toward the bottom of the staircase.

"I don't think you want to go up there." I leaned casually against the newel post from which I had painstakingly stripped fourteen coats of paint and varnish.

Melanie popped out an earbud, the tinny sound of a beat leaking out. "I don't think we should go up there."

Sarah rolled her eyes. "Good idea. I heard JJ say something about collecting a few flying roaches to breed with the ones from home.

You might want to go find him before he ignites a biological disaster on a national level."

With an alarmed expression, Melanie headed off in the direction of the kitchen, speaking to no one in particular. "Someone please remind me again why I had children."

I turned back to the familiar sound of a rubber band being snapped against skin as Sarah looked toward the top of the stairs and the closed closet door. "Mom said you didn't want her letting you know if she saw anything in your house."

"Yes."

Sarah frowned, her gaze focused on the closet door, her finger playing with the rubber bands. *Snap snap snap.* "Do you want me to tell you what I see?"

My automatic response of no tumbled to the tip of my tongue, but it sat there, suspended. Maybe asking my little sister for help wasn't the same as relying on my parents. Maybe if I'd asked Melanie what she'd seen the first time she'd visited my house, a lot of turmoil could have been avoided. Not that I would ever admit it, at least out loud. My newfound sense of independence was still too fragile, liable to shatter from the slightest crack. I needed to at least give the impression that I was fine and doing everything on my own.

"All right," I said. "But don't tell Mom or Dad."

She sent me a look that reminded me so much of Jack when I'd tell him that it was the other drivers on the road who were the problem that I laughed out loud, but I quickly sobered when Sarah returned her gaze to the top of the stairs and an almost imperceptible shudder rippled through her. "I see two men." She tilted her head, a tentative smile playing at her lips. "One of them is smoking a pipe. He says you've met before."

"That's Beau's grandfather Charles. Can you ask him why he's still here?"

Sarah moved to the first step, then stopped, a deep frown forming on her face. "He says that you and Beau still need him."

I'd expected that answer, but to have it spoken out loud hollowed out a small pit of fear in my stomach. "Can he tell you why?"

Her gaze shifted, traveling slowly across the upper hall as if following something I couldn't see. "It's the other man. He's . . . evil." She turned to look at me, her pupils dilated, her blue eyes almost black. "He says there's unfinished business." Another shudder went through her as her hand flew to the banister, then gripped it tightly. "He wants to hurt Beau. And you."

I sucked in a breath. "I think it's Antoine Broussard—the man who killed his own daughter in this house and got away with it. Can you ask him if I'm right?"

Sarah gave a violent shake of her head, her gaze returning to the top of the stairs. "No. He's not the type of spirit I should interact with. Grandma Sarah calls spirits like him 'soul stealers.'"

I remembered the feeling I had while locked in the closet, the bleak sense of dread and hopelessness and unending fear. A lot like Jeanne must have experienced when her father choked the life from her on the exact steps upon which we were currently standing.

Jolene approached with her tour group consisting of Jack, Jaxson, Cooper, Sam, and Sunny. Sunny's blond ponytail now sported an oversized purple ribbon, tied with Jolene's signature perfect bow. "If you think the kitchen is amazing, just wait until you see what they've done upstairs." Jolene winked at me as they approached. "Pay special attention to the floor tile in the upstairs bathroom. I've never been to Italy—yet—but I don't think those Romans could do a better mosaic."

Sarah and I stepped back to allow them to pass, watching as each one rubbed their arms as they passed the closet door.

"Are they okay up there?" I asked.

"Charles is up there. As long as he's there it's okay. But I get the feeling that he doesn't want to be here anymore, and that he's only staying to protect you and Beau. That Antoine guy has got to go."

"I know. I've already had a bad experience."

"Maybe Beau can help? I wish I could do more, but I know just from standing here that I'm not strong enough. Yet. I'm only here a week, and I don't think that will be long enough." Her eyes traveled to the closet door, and we both watched as it slowly opened.

I took Sarah's arm and pulled her away from the stairs and into the kitchen. "Are you still on board with coming with Jolene and me to Michael's beach house? Like I said, I have no idea what to expect, but Michael and his family are all related to Antoine Broussard."

"At least we have an escape hatch, since Jolene's driving, and we can leave if things get a little crazy."

"Yes—and I'll make sure people know where we are."

"In case we go missing?"

"That's not going to happen, Sarah. I just thought it would be in our best interest if people knew where we were—for any reason."

"Like if King Kong suddenly appeared to destroy New Orleans and we needed saving?"

"Has anyone ever told you that you think too much like Dad?"

She grinned up at me. "Mom does all the time."

"Okay, everyone," Melanie announced from the middle of the living room, "according to Nola's schedule, it's time for us to leave if we're going to make it to the swamp tour in time. Everybody outside!"

I was the last to leave, Thibaut and Jorge having already left after their show, and I went around the house turning off lights and making sure the doors and windows were locked. As I reached the front door, I noticed a large purple ribbon on the floor, strands of blond hair stuck in the knot. Figuring it was Sunny's hair bow, I shoved it into my jeans pocket since I needed both hands to close and lock the door.

It took almost fifteen minutes to situate everyone in the available vehicles to drive us all to Ponchatoula for the swamp tour. Sam said it was ridiculous for Cooper to drive, since there was room in the backseat of Beau's truck for Cooper and me. Sunny would sit up front between her brother and Sam. Jolene, Melanie, and Jaxson would ride in Bubba's front seat, and JJ and Sarah would ride in the back. That left Jack, who instead of riding with Melanie chose the middle of the backseat in Beau's truck. When I strongly suggested that he might be more comfortable in Jolene's car, he just smiled and said he was looking forward to spending the time catching up with Cooper.

"It's not like I'm going to get pregnant sitting next to him," I hissed.

"I have three kids, Nola. I know what backseats can do to a levelheaded male."

"You do know that I'm an adult, right? Not to mention that there will be three other people in the front seat."

"Just saying," he said with that infuriating grin that Melanie found so inexplicably attractive. Which just went to show that love truly was blind.

I realized that Sarah was still standing on the sidewalk, looking at the house. I called out to her, "Come on, Sarah. Let's go. I'm riding in Beau's truck, so you don't have to sit on the hump."

She didn't appear to have heard me, so I moved closer. "We're ready to leave."

Sarah bit her lip but kept her gaze focused on the house. "Is Thibaut's wife dead?"

I would have been surprised to hear that question from anyone but her. "Yes." I didn't elaborate.

"She loves him. She wants him to know that."

"Okay. I'll tell him. I think that will help him."

She nodded. "He doesn't look it, but he's very sad. He misses her."

When she didn't say any more, I took a step toward the car.

"He didn't kill her." Sarah was looking at me now, her expression earnest.

I paused. "Is that what his wife said?"

"Yes." Her gaze traveled back to the door through which Thibaut and Jorge had disappeared.

"Did she say who did?"

After a long moment, Sarah faced me. "No. She didn't want to talk about when she was killed. Just that she loved her husband."

I walked her back to Bubba and held the door open while she slid next to JJ in the backseat. Before I could close the door, she asked, "Is this the same swamp where Beau dumped the Maison Blanche door?"

"Yeah—why?"

"Great," Sarah said. "I read that it's haunted."

"Just old rumors to draw tourists," Jolene said. "There was supposedly an old voodoo queen named Julia Brown who cursed the area, and on the day she was buried the great hurricane of 1915 swept in and destroyed three towns around the swamp, killing just about everybody in its path, so naturally people thought she was responsible. Which is silly because no woman I know would cause a hurricane if there wasn't a man involved, and Julia was a widow."

Sarah leaned into the front seat. "You know that doesn't make sense, right?"

Jolene grinned. "Of course. I was just trying to take your mind off the idea that the swamp might be haunted."

Sarah sat back in her seat. "That's not what I'm worried about."

Melanie turned around to look at Sarah. "What is it, sweetie?"

"I'm worried about that door floating back to the surface, and what else it might be bringing up with it."

CHAPTER 21

My dad and I sat at our table in the lush courtyard at the Elysian Bar inside the Hotel Peter & Paul nursing our seltzer waters with lime, feeling too full from dinner to get up and go to bed or, in my case, hunt down Jolene for a ride home. She'd excused herself to powder her nose at least twenty minutes before but hadn't yet returned. Everyone else had gone to their room to pack, and I was grateful that I didn't have to do any lifting or bending, as I didn't think my stomach would comply.

For dinner, I had gorged myself on crab-and-ricotta gnocchi and then the rosemary panna cotta for dessert. I hadn't wanted the whole piece, but only Melanie and I wanted something sweet to finish our meal, and neither of us believed in sharing food. Especially dessert. I was left with no alternative but to eat the entire thing.

For about the fifth time since we'd sat down I squeezed into the palm of my hand a dollop of the hand sanitizer that Melanie had left on the table, and I scrubbed my hands together.

"Aren't you done eating?" my dad asked.

"I am, but I keep remembering I spent all afternoon in a swamp and actually touched a baby alligator. I don't think my hands will ever feel clean again."

"That reminds me. I should probably check JJ's suitcase before we leave to make sure he hasn't packed any swamp creatures to bring home."

"He wouldn't really, right?" I asked.

Jack responded with raised eyebrows before leaning forward and squeezing my hand. "I know we won't get another chance to talk before we leave in the morning, but I wanted to tell you again how very proud I am of you. And not just where you are right now, but where you've been. You amaze Mellie and me with every success, because we know what it's cost you."

I stirred the ice in my drained glass. "Yeah, well, I think you mean what it's cost you. You paid for my tuition—remember?"

He laughed. "Hard to forget. It gave me an incentive to sell my next book, that's for sure." He tugged on the two silver bracelets I wore, each with a four-leaf clover charm. They had been separate gifts for high school graduation from both of my parents, and I never took them off but kept them as a reminder that I was loved and cherished even at those times when I failed to love myself.

I leaned over and kissed Jack on his cheek, and he put his arm around me and squeezed. Sitting back in his chair, he said, "Is there anything you want to talk about while I'm here and we're alone?"

"Besides my disappointment that we didn't see that door bobbing up and down in the swamp today?"

"Why disappointment? I thought you'd be glad to put that behind you."

"Oh, I am." I'd decided not to tell my parents my plan of revenge involving Michael or about my upcoming visit to his family's beach house. With Sarah. There were some things that were best shared after the fact. "It's just that it would be nice to know where it is, just in case psychic evidence is ever allowed in a court of law. It would be a slam-dunk case for sure."

"I wouldn't hold your breath on that one," he said, and drained the last of his water. "But I admire your enthusiasm." He put his glass down with a small thunk. "And you're okay with Sarah staying for the entire week?"

"I wouldn't have said yes if I minded. It's not like she's a baby or needs a lot of hand-holding. Plus, we'll have Jolene."

Jack grinned. "Can't wait to hear all the new phrases Sarah will pick up. I'll probably have to call you to translate."

"Text me. You know that anyone younger than thirty only texts."

"Yeah, well, feel free to call me anytime. I miss hearing your voice."

I blinked hard. "Same," I said.

"But you would call me if there was something important you needed to tell me, right?" He was looking at me closely and I had to resist the need to squirm in my chair.

"Of course. I'm an adult, but you're still my dad."

"And everything is all right with you?"

"Yes," I said. "Of course. Why are you asking?"

He leaned back in his chair, thrumming his fingers on the armrests, his eyes narrowed. "I'm a writer, which means I'm pretty observant. I noticed how you and Beau seem to have a mutual do-not-touch zone, and not because you don't *want* to touch but because you probably shouldn't. And I'm pretty sure Sam isn't oblivious to it."

I started to object, but my dad kept speaking as if I hadn't said anything. "I also find it interesting how Sunny is trying so hard to fit in. She listens closely to every conversation, and when she asks a question, it's usually something about how she was as a child, or about Mimi and her psychometry. And what other psychic abilities have been passed down. It's as if she's taking a crash course in her own family history."

"To be fair, Dad, she is. She thought she was Donna Mathieson from Edina, Minnesota, just a few months ago. I'd probably be doing the same thing."

"Sure. I get that. But I did find it a little odd that when she was asked about her life before, she kept her answers short, making it clear it wasn't something she liked to talk about."

"I don't blame her. Her adoptive parents were recently killed, so there's a lot of sadness connected with those memories in addition to the turmoil of being thrown into a new life. I remember what it was like being plucked from one life and thrust into a completely new and unfamiliar one. It was sort of a safety mechanism not to think about my past."

He patted my hand resting on the table, and we were silent for a moment as we both remembered the woman who'd given birth to me and saddled me with the nickname I still proudly used, and the circumstances that had brought me to Charleston.

"I understand. But from what she told you, she had a happy childhood. You didn't, yet you brought your love of music with you to your new home, and eventually shared your memories with us—even the not-so-good ones. In retrospect, I could tell it was your way of laying it all out on the table so that if we were going to reject you, we'd do it sooner instead of later."

I frowned. "What—so you're a shrink now?"

"Nah. Just a writer. I get paid to analyze people. Most of them are already dead, so I have to read between the lines in their letters and historical accounts. That's always where I find the most interesting stuff."

I rolled my eyes, just to remind us both of old times. "What else did your eagle eyes notice?"

"You and Sarah having a dramatic moment at the bottom of the stairs." He looked at me expectantly. When I didn't say anything, he said, "Is there anything you need to tell me?"

"About what?"

He let out a heavy sigh. "As you keep reminding me, you're an adult. I love you and trust you, which is why I agreed to let Sarah stay with you for the week. I'm sure you wouldn't put her in harm's way."

"Why would you think I would?"

"I didn't say you would. I'm just curious about something Mimi told me the other night at dinner."

"Really?" I kept my voice relaxed.

"She pulled me aside to say she was grateful for your help in her 'little project'—she didn't elaborate, since she probably assumes you told us—and that she would make sure that you were safe."

I leaned back in my chair with studied casualness. "Oh, that. She and Beau have decided to start a new project flipping unsellable old houses. They want me to be a part of it, sharing my expertise in historic preservation."

He nodded slowly, his overly observant gaze making me want to squirm again. "And why would that cause her to reassure me that you would be kept safe?"

"Oh, you know. Lots of sharp tools and rotting wood. That sort of thing."

"Uh-huh. Well, all I can say is that I'm glad Cooper is here now. Beau, too, although I think Sam keeps him occupied enough to divide his attention."

"Are you saying that you've asked Cooper to report back to you? Don't deny that you asked Beau when I first moved here. I can take care of myself."

"I know. You've proven that. But I'm your father, so I'm allowed to worry. But no, I haven't asked Cooper anything. I just feel better knowing that he's here in case you need any muscle."

"That's very misogynistic of you, Dad. What about Jolene? She might be small, but she's fierce. And resourceful. You should see what she can do with a Barbie head."

"Yeah, I heard." We both looked up as Cooper entered the courtyard from the open doors leading into the bar area. My dad stood and shook Cooper's hand. "I should be going on up to pack. Hopefully I'll get there in time, before Mellie decides to do it for me. I don't think she brought her labeling gun, but just in case, I should hurry. Those labels are hard to get off toiletry items."

Cooper laughed, but he quickly sobered when he saw he was the only one laughing. "You're joking, right?"

My dad and I responded with blank stares.

I stood and glanced behind Cooper. "Have you seen Jolene and Sarah?"

"Jolene remembered that she has an early morning tomorrow and asked if I would drive you home. Sarah said she was tired and went with her."

"That's ridiculous. This is your hotel. Why don't I just take an Uber?"

"Not a good idea," they said in unison, which won Cooper an appreciative look from Jack.

"Fine," I said, gathering my backpack and tossing my phone inside. "Totally unnecessary, but thanks."

As Cooper and I passed by Jack, he said, "By the way, Nola. That was a great conversation deflection. Don't make me regret not drilling you a little harder."

"Drills—right! That's another sharp tool we use during renovations. I'll order extra safety glasses so you don't have to worry."

"I think I'm beginning to see why Mellie says we're just alike."

I gave him another peck on the cheek, then followed Cooper to the parking lot.

"What was that all about?" Cooper asked as he pulled the car out onto the street.

"Dad was saying how glad he is that you're here now."

He turned his head, his half grin lit by passing streetlamps. "Yeah? And what about you?"

I faced the road, my lips turning up in a smile. "I'm glad, too." Leaning forward, I said, "Hey, we're about to pass my house. Slow down so you can check out what the neighbors across the street have done with their Halloween yard decorations. You know I love Charleston, but no city beats New Orleans in terms of holiday celebrations. I haven't been here for Mardi Gras, but I can only imagine."

The vast majority of houses on my street sported some sort of lighting display and impressive pumpkin carvings and nice assortments of skeletons climbing trees and walls, but Ernest and Bob's house glowed like a lighthouse in the middle of a darkened sea. Fat old-fashioned orange Christmas tree bulbs striped the roof, wrapped around the chimney, and boldly outlined the corners of the house and the roofline. But the pièce de résistance was the pair of waving skeletons dressed in tuxedos along with the short, plump dog skeleton dressed in a silk lounging robe and wearing a tiara. They stood in front of the two coffins containing Christmas trees, their limbs gloriously filled with all things Halloween and a sprinkling of black and orange twinkling lights.

Cooper stopped in the middle of the street, lowered his window to get a better look, and laughed. "Amazing. I lived in California and even I can't say I've ever seen anything like it. Can't wait to meet them."

His casual comment filled me with a comfortable warmth at the thought of him becoming familiar enough to meet my neighbors. "Me, too. Ernest and Bob are great, and their dog, Belle, is her own character. Mardi's in love with her, but she hasn't yet acknowledged that they're meant to be together."

He laughed again, then turned his head to say something, but stopped as his gaze focused on something behind me. "I think there's something going on at your house, or is that part of your Halloween décor?"

I turned, following his gaze. My house was bathed in the orange glow from across the street, spotlighting the previously locked windows across the front of my house now slamming open and shut in a random rhythm only a demon could recognize. Various tools and paint cans lay strewn across the lawn, and a dark, viscous liquid appeared to be leaking from the sill of the upstairs hall window, dripping slowly down the newly painted siding.

I couldn't speak, could only sit and watch the spectacle from Cooper's car.

"Should I call the police?" Cooper asked.

"Do you really think that will help?"

He leaned closer to get a better look. "No. But I'm fresh out of other ideas."

I glanced down the street, amazed that no one had come out of their houses to look. I had to hope that my neighbors thought the spectacle was my contribution to the street's holiday décor. My street was hosting a friendly Halloween decorating contest, so it would be logical that they would simply assume I was in it to win it.

"Me, too," I said.

We sat in stunned silence for a solid minute before Cooper spoke again. "Should we call Melanie?"

"No. I don't want to worry her."

"Yeah, but won't she know what to do?"

"Probably. But so will Beau." I pulled out my phone to text him, but hesitated. He and Sam had left following dinner, walking hand in hand toward Beau's truck. I looked at the time on my screen. "It's almost eleven o'clock."

"Nola, in case you hadn't noticed, your house is going berserk and there's something that looks a lot like blood dripping out of one of the windows. If Beau can help, you need to text him."

I reluctantly began to tap on my screen. Need help asap at cottage. I hit the Send button, then began typing again. The house is bleeding

I'd barely touched the Send arrow before Beau responded. OMW

Cooper and I exited the car and stood in the street, then watched as one by one the windows slammed shut and stayed closed. By the time Beau's truck roared into the street and stopped at the curb, whatever had been dripping from the window had stopped, the long tongues of liquid sucked up from the wall and swallowed under the sill. All that remained to confirm that we hadn't imagined everything was the debris scattered in the grass, one of my spreadsheets stuck in the oleander shrub at the corner of the porch.

Despite everything, I still felt relief that Beau had come alone. I wanted to think it was because he and Sam hadn't been together when I'd texted him. After greeting us and allowing me to explain what had just happened, he moved toward the porch. He stopped when he saw we weren't following.

"I need the key, Nola."

"Sorry," I said, fishing it out of my backpack. "I wasn't sure you'd want to go inside."

"I'm good at a lot of things, Nola, but figuring something out by osmosis isn't one of them. Otherwise you'd be driving by now."

Cooper coughed and I gave him what I hoped was a stinging glare. "Whatever," I said, stomping up onto the porch and sticking the key in the lock. The knob turned easily, and nothing pressed against the door as I pushed it open.

"I think whoever it was is gone," I said.

Beau stepped into the room and flipped on a light switch. I made a move to follow, but Beau said, "Stay there until I give you the all clear. In the meantime, you can start picking up stuff from the yard. Keep the door open so you can hear me shout if I need you."

I watched Beau pause at the bottom of the staircase and look up. I saw that the closet door was partially open, filling me with panic. "Don't go in the closet."

"Trust me, Nola. I have zero desire to go in there right now." His index finger began strumming the rubber band on his wrist. With a burst of energy, he ran up the stairs, taking them two at a time, then disappeared in the upstairs hallway.

Cooper and I began gathering the bits and pieces that had been strewn by unseen hands or just blown out of the windows, and we stacked them by group on the porch. After about ten minutes we had a collection of tape measures, screwdrivers, and boxes of nails, miraculously intact. In another pile we had all the spreadsheets that I'd left tacked to the wall, and in a third pile, a dozen rolls of soggy toilet paper whose origins I didn't want to know.

"Is this yours?" Cooper stood from behind the oleander bush, holding up a yellow hair ribbon.

"Let me see." He handed it to me, and I held it up in the light from the porch so I could see it better. The satin between my fingers had long ago lost its stiff newness, myriad creases and wrinkles pressed into it like the papery skin of an old woman. It was still knotted in the middle, stray blond hairs captured where I imagined the ribbon had slid from a ponytail unnoticed. Or had been forcibly pulled.

"It's not exactly mine, but I'm pretty sure I know who it belongs to." I smoothed one of the ends between my fingers. The night had turned chilly, and a cold breeze blew through the yard, rattling the papers and making the wind chimes sing. But tonight the chimes had taken on a deeper tone, like the chanting of monks. I examined the ribbon, hoping I'd find something different than the ribbon from the hatbox. Something to prove that my suspicions were wrong. "If it's the same one, I have no idea how it got here. The last time I saw it, it was in my apartment."

"And you're sure it's the same?"

I nodded. "It would be pure coincidence that an identical yellow ribbon would be found in my yard."

"Except there's no such thing as coincidence," we said in unison. Despite the confusion with which my brain was grappling, a half smile formed on my lips as I recalled the times Cooper and I had heard my dad say that as we stood in the kitchen or sat at our dining table at the house on Tradd Street, trying to work through the clues of a mystery. He'd been the Ned to my Nancy Drew, and the memory swept through me, wrapping me in its comforting warmth.

Beau stepped out onto the porch. "Do you want the good news first or the bad news?"

"Does it matter?" I was too mentally exhausted at this point to care one way or the other.

"Fine. I'll give you the good news first. The house is clear. Nothing is broken, and there's no blood or any other substance in the upstairs hallway, or anywhere else that I can see. Whatever *visitors* were here are gone. Or, more likely, are taking a rest. Which brings me to the bad news."

"Can you wait to tell me tomorrow? I'd like to get some sleep tonight."

"I could. But knowing you, you won't be able to sleep because I didn't tell you, and then you'll end up texting me and waking me up to find out and then we're both not sleeping. So let me tell you now."

I was freezing, but I wasn't about to suggest going inside to talk. As if reading my mind, Cooper settled his jacket over my shoulders. It still carried his body heat and I snuggled into it, enjoying the warmth and the faint yet familiar smell of him.

"Fine. Go ahead, then."

"So, the bad news is that it takes a lot of energy to make something move—much more for multiple objects simultaneously. It takes even more to manifest the image of something leaking from a window or dripping down a wall. The only reason why it stopped is that the entity simply ran out of energy."

"Why is that bad news?" Cooper asked, his Citadel education dictating his need for a clear and concise answer to a situation that was neither.

"Because," Beau said, his gaze moving to me, "that means that this is a very powerful spirit. Stronger than anything I've ever personally encountered."

"Great," I said. "So how am I supposed to get rid of it?"

Beau scratched the back of his head. "Good question. First off, we have to make sure we know who it is, which I think we do, but I'm not going to say his name out loud because I'm not interested in conjuring him right now, regardless of how weak he might be feeling. And then we need to figure out why he's suddenly here, which may or may not be related to why my grandfather's back. Otherwise . . ."

"Otherwise?" Cooper prompted.

"Otherwise, I'll have to figure out a way to confront it directly."

"You could ask your mother," I said softly, watching my breath rise in a puff of steam. "She wants to help."

As if I hadn't said anything, he moved back toward the front door.

"I'll turn off all the lights and check the windows. You wait here so you can lock the door behind me."

"I'm coming, too," Cooper said. "I'll do the upstairs."

They both went inside and I stood in the yard, watching as the windows went dark one by one, tracing their progress through the house. When they finally emerged, I locked the door and we moved to the street.

I realized I still clutched the yellow ribbon, and I held it up to show Beau. "Cooper found this behind the oleander bush."

Beau took it, his eyes widening with recognition. "Where did it come from and how did it get there?"

"Good questions. I think it might be the one I found in the hatbox and that I thought was safely hidden in my apartment. Your mother handed it to Sarah last night."

His eyes flicked to mine as he gave the ribbon back to me. "You should hide it with the other stuff from the hatbox. Not that hiding anything seems to matter."

I smoothed the fabric between my fingers. "More important than how it got here is why."

Beau rubbed his face with both hands. "We're too tired to think about any of it now."

He glanced behind us, toward the two vehicles at the curb. "Are you on your way home?"

"Yeah. Cooper said he'd drive me."

"Why don't I drive you, since Cooper's hotel is so close? Your apartment is a lot closer for me."

"I'm happy to do it," Cooper said, his voice neutral.

I could feel them both watching me, waiting for an answer that felt a lot weightier than it should have. And a decision that I shouldn't be so conflicted about.

Avoiding looking at Beau, I said, "If Cooper doesn't mind, I'll ride with him. We've got a lot of catching up to do. And I'm sure Sam's waiting for you."

Beau sent me an odd look, then headed toward his truck. "We'll talk tomorrow. We need to discuss plans for the Esplanade house." He indicated my cottage. "And what that was all about. Hopefully you can dig up some stuff next weekend."

After saying our good-byes, Cooper opened the passenger-side door of his car and I slid inside, the leather seats cold beneath me.

"Next weekend?" Cooper asked after he'd sat behind the wheel and started the engine.

"Yeah. About that. Drive slow. I've got a lot to tell you."

"Can't wait," he said, with no sarcasm and with the enthusiasm for problem-solving I remembered. And had loved.

As Cooper began to drive, I nestled into the seat, not looking back at the house that had chosen me, afraid of what I might see.

CHAPTER 22

"Can't we take the streetcar?" Sarah asked for the third time since we'd pulled out of the driveway. The first time had been after Jolene had shot across the streetcar tracks on St. Charles Avenue, and the second was when evasive action had had to be taken at the appearance of a giant pothole that could possibly be access to Australia.

"Would you prefer that I drive?"

"No, thanks. I think Mom and Dad would prefer me to return home in one piece. But I *am* supposed to be playing tourist, and it's hard to see anything when I'm too afraid to open my eyes."

"If you would bother to look at your itinerary and the map I provided, you would see that we're headed to St. Louis Cathedral. We have a private tour that starts at ten o'clock. Mimi arranged it for us, so I thought it would be nice if we arrived on time. If I thought you'd want to get out of bed two hours earlier to allow us the extra time to take the streetcar and then walk all the way from Canal Street, I would have suggested it."

Sarah pressed her head back against the seat with a heavy sigh. "I probably could have gotten up earlier if you hadn't stepped on me and woken me up in the middle of the night. Whatever it was you were doing, I'm sure it could have waited until morning."

"I'm sorry—I didn't mean to step on you. I was looking for something in the monogrammed-pillow pile and didn't see you."

I felt both Jolene and Sarah waiting for me to explain. Instead, I pulled out my copy of the itinerary. "Since it's another beautiful fall day, I thought we'd walk around a bit before we head to Muriel's for lunch to meet Jaxson and his uncle Bernie. But that means we can't dawdle at the cathedral."

Jolene grinned at my unintentional use of one of her words. Her expressions and sayings were like tiny viruses spread between people living in close quarters. It was bound to happen.

"Muriel's, uh, has some well-known memories, but Uncle Bernie selected it. Since he's doing us a favor, I didn't want to argue."

Sarah leaned forward, her arms resting on the seat back. "You mean it's haunted."

"*Supposedly* haunted."

"Don't worry," she said. "I came prepared."

I turned to look at Sarah. She had taken off her coat and was touching a navy-, green-, and gold-jeweled brooch in the shape of a peacock pinned to her soft pink cardigan. I recalled seeing the brooch in Melanie's jewelry box many times. "That belonged to Grandma Sarah."

"It did. Mom said I could have it."

"Oh." I sat back in my seat, quelling the small thread of envy looping around my stomach until I remembered Sarah telling me that she spoke with Grandma Sarah as a coping device when spirits were near.

"I've got the rubber bands, too, so I'm good to go. I read that New Orleans is more haunted than Charleston, so I figured I'd better be ready."

"Well, whatever your reasons, I think it's wonderful to see a girl your age wearing vintage jewelry. It makes you unique, which is the highest form of compliment I could give a person." Jolene gently touched her own set of pearls.

"Anyway," I said, "if we stick to the schedule, we'll have time to head across the square to Café du Monde and get beignets."

"That's why I wore pink," Jolene said. "It hides powdered sugar a lot better than navy blue."

I looked down at the navy sweater Jolene had strongly suggested I wear instead of the T-shirt JJ had given me for my birthday. She said it was because black wasn't my color, but I think it had to do mostly with the words printed on the front: *WHAT HAPPENS IN THE FIELD STAYS IN THE FIELD.* Jolene made it clear that the problem wasn't just the suggestive nature of the wording, but mostly that no grown woman should be wearing any sort of printed T-shirt except while playing a sport or painting. And, she'd added, even then, pearls would be an appropriate accessory.

"Do they do to-go boxes?" Sarah asked. "I thought I could take some beignets back home for Mom. You know how much she loves doughnuts."

Melanie's doughnut obsession was legendary, but I realized that Sarah's question probably had a lot to do with missing our mother. We'd said good-bye to Jack, Melanie, and JJ earlier that morning, both Melanie and Jack separately pressing wads of cash into my hand. Dad said his was to cover entertainment costs for my sister and that I should bill him for the rest, and Melanie said hers was for just-in-case necessities (which I took to mean coffee and doughnuts) and to give what was left over to Trevor's computer fund.

Although I knew Sarah was excited to be spending the week with me, I was well aware of the constant tug on the heart from the ties of home and family. As I'd discovered, it was always comforting to know they were there, but it took Herculean strength to move in the opposite direction.

"Good idea," I said. "Let's plan to come back before you leave so we can make sure they're fresh."

We found parking in a garage and walked the short distance to Jackson Square and the iconic Spanish-style stucco cathedral with its triple steeples towering above the neighboring Cabildo and Presbytère buildings. Despite the cathedral's being the most recognizable landmark in my new city, I had yet to visit it. For obvious reasons, I rarely ventured into the heart of the French Quarter, with its high density of bars, although to visit a historic church seemed a valid excuse for a preservationist. Especially a church of such historic significance, one that had been destroyed and rebuilt multiple times. It's what old buildings and I had in common.

As we walked across the flagstones toward the front gate, Sarah's pace slowed. "Is something wrong?" I asked, noticing her index and middle fingers plucking at one of the bands on her wrist.

She pressed her lips together, remaining silent as a tour group filed through the door ahead of us. I glanced at my phone. Ten minutes after ten o'clock. Meaning we'd need to hurry to keep on schedule. But I knew that I couldn't rush Sarah any more than I could tell her to just ignore whoever was trying to speak to her.

"How old is this place?" she asked.

"Seriously? Have you not even read the notes I attached to your itinerary?"

She gave me a blank stare and I shook my head. "I should make you look it up, but it's too late. The short answer is that the original church on the site was built in 1727, then destroyed by fire in 1788. Since then, it's undergone various restorations and additions."

By the grim look on her face, I knew I hadn't answered the question she'd intended to ask. "So, is anyone buried here?" *Snap snap snap.*

The door had opened again and a familiar woman, dressed in the same matronly, conservative outfit she'd been wearing when I'd first met her at the Past Is Never Past, looked at me with recognition. "What a nice surprise," she said. "When I heard Mrs. Ryan had set up a small tour group, I didn't expect to see you."

"Mrs. Wenzel," I said, recalling her name only because I'd seen her; her sister, Honey; and their bird, Zeus, twice in the same day—not something easily forgotten. "It's good to see you again. I've brought my friend Jolene and my sister, Sarah."

They greeted one another, while Sarah shifted uncomfortably.

Addressing Sarah, Mrs. Wenzel said, "In answer to your question, since 1721 there have been numerous people laid to rest beneath the cathedral, all but two graves unmarked, and most of them unknown."

Sarah nodded in acknowledgment, her gaze focused behind Mrs. Wenzel. "Did any of those people wear long dark robes when they were alive?"

The older woman frowned. "Many were clergy, yes. But not all. Why do you ask?"

"Oh, no reason." Sarah turned to me, her smile more of a grimace.

"You still want to go on the tour?" I asked.

She patted the pin on her sweater. "I'm good."

"Will Mrs. Ryan be joining us?" Mrs. Wenzel asked.

"I'm afraid not."

"Oh." Her face fell. "This is a disappointment. I was hoping that she'd be with you. It's why I volunteered to give the tour. I'm a docent, but I usually don't give tours—just answer questions."

"Yes, well, we do appreciate it." I looked beyond her to give her the hint that we were ready to get started.

Instead of moving, she said, "I hope you will tell Mrs. Ryan how much you've enjoyed the tour."

I didn't point out that we had yet to take the tour, instead just smiled and nodded and took a step closer to the door, making room for yet another group to go ahead of us.

She continued. "Honey and I are hoping for invitations to her fund-raiser party. My sister and I have only been volunteering at the cathedral for a few months, but I think that should count, don't you?"

I vaguely remembered Mimi talking at dinner about a fund-raiser that she would be hosting at her house to benefit the cathedral. There had also been mention of costumes, making me think it was a Halloween party.

When she still hadn't moved, I thought if I feigned interest she might actually then give us the promised tour. "It's a Halloween costume party, right?"

Mrs. Wenzel looked offended. "Of *course* not. It's a Catholic institution. The party is scheduled for November first."

She looked at me as if I should know what that meant. I took the safe route, deciding that remaining silent was probably better than admitting I wasn't Catholic.

"Then it must be for All Saints' Day," Jolene said, her voice appropriately reverent and earning her an appreciative smile from Mrs. Wenzel.

"Yes, that's right. I believe the costumes you were referring to should be saint related."

"Ah. Like, dress as your favorite saint," I said, for which I received a tight-lipped look from our guide.

Jolene looped her arm through Mrs. Wenzel's, leading her—finally—through the door. "I can't wait to hear all about this beautiful church. I understand that Pope John Paul II stood right here, under this very same roof?"

That earned her a wide smile from the older woman. "That is correct. In 1987, the pontiff graced us with a visit." She detached her arm from Jolene's. "If you would please follow me, we can begin our tour."

"How did you know that about the feast day?" I whispered to Jolene as we followed our host into the vestibule.

"My best friend in sixth grade was Mary Lou Bianca, one of the Delta I-talians. She taught me everything I know about Catholic feast days. She even did a diorama presentation with clay figures about them for her history project. I think she got an A. Or maybe it was a B, but the teacher raised her grade for effort. I mean, all those halos she'd made from clay. And they all had little eyes and noses and hair." She frowned. "Wait, where was I?"

Feeling the weight of Mrs. Wenzel's disapproving stare, I held my finger to my lips. Finally taking the hint, Jolene dutifully directed all her attention to our guide and was thankfully silent for the rest of the tour. The only sound besides hushed voices and the steady tromp of feet on the black and white marble tiles was the constant *snap snap snap* from Sarah, who stayed close to me.

"The Cathedral-Basilica of Saint Louis King of France is the official name, but the structure that we are currently standing inside is most commonly known as St. Louis Cathedral, the oldest Catholic cathedral in continual use in the United States. It is the third church to have stood on this site since 1727." I only half listened to Mrs. Wenzel discussing the long and storied past of the cathedral and its relevance and importance to the city and people of New Orleans, my attention drawn toward the soaring ceilings and the filtered light flooding through the stained glass windows.

During my pursuit of my graduate degree, I'd studied many historic buildings in all stages of existence, from hopeless to monuments of careful preservation. My favorite structures had always been sacred spaces, whether they be the tiny praise houses on the barrier islands surrounding Charleston, or the grand churches like St. Michael's, with its Tiffany windows, on Broad Street. A sense of peace saturated these places, a welcome respite from whatever internal battles I was facing. Even now, surrounded by tour groups and worshippers alike, I felt my blood slow, and a lightness edged out the heavy sense of anxiety over the entities in my house, and about my impending visit to the Sabatiers' beach house.

"If you will look at the central nave ceiling," Mrs. Wenzel was saying, and the three of us dutifully tilted back our heads, "you will notice that its infrastructure is deteriorating in places. Much of the plaster key is damaged. It is one of the vitally urgent repairs for which our current capital campaign is raising funds." She smiled. "Mrs. Ryan's fund-raising event should be a huge help for the ceiling repairs and other much-needed work."

We continued to follow our guide as she talked about the history of the building and the people buried beneath our feet, about the stunning stained glass windows, the sculptures, and the architecture.

She began to warm to me as I spoke with knowledge about old buildings and the importance of preservation, a topic that was apparently very dear to both of us.

We had reached the end of the tour and were standing by the main entrance when another tour group entered and I recognized the guide from Love Cocktail Challenge in City Park I'd gone to with Michael. It was the night when I'd discovered his betrayal and had attempted to erase all memories of it, but Patricia Casey (T'ish to her friends) had stuck with me. It could have been her thick New Orleans accent, which was a perplexing mix of Southern and Brooklyn, or it could have been the unique spelling of her name. Either way, I'd found her memorable, which was why I recognized her and called out a greeting.

"Nola!" she said, herding her small group inside to stand behind one of the pews. "So good to see you again." She glanced over at Mrs. Wenzel and her smile dimmed. She reached inside her fanny pack and pulled out a business card. "Please call if you need a tour. I'm happy to do private tours of neighborhoods and specific sites. I do cemetery tours, too."

"Hashtag nope," Sarah said quietly behind me.

I took the card and put it in my jeans pocket. "Thanks, T'ish. Will do."

She winked, then began herding her group into the cathedral as I turned back to Mrs. Wenzel. "I hope to see you and your sister at Mrs. Ryan's party," she said, her voice warmer than when we'd started, due to our bonding over foundational cracks and re-leading stained glass seams.

I wasn't sure if either one of us would be on the invite list, so I only smiled and nodded.

In a lowered voice, Mrs. Wenzel added, "I would appreciate an introduction to Mrs. Ryan. I'm sure she knows who I am, but we've never actually met. I've been trying to speak with her regarding . . . an important topic, and I was hoping that if perhaps we had a more personal connection, she might make time for Honey and me in her busy schedule."

"Is this about your brother and his family?" At her look of chagrin, I said, "There are a lot of families in your situation who need . . . help from Mrs. Ryan."

She nodded. "We've heard that Mrs. Ryan has a special gift. It's not something we have ever considered, but we are desperate and willing to try anything." With a stiff smile, she added, "Saints wouldn't be saints without miracles, so we know they happen."

"Of course," I said. "I hope I have the opportunity to introduce you at the party."

As we were saying our good-byes, a movement glimpsed from the corner of my eye caught my attention. A bright blue feather drifted in the air above Mrs. Wenzel, its distinct color bringing all three of us to look at it. Sarah reached out and snatched it from the air, then held it out on her open palm to see it better.

She stroked it gently with her finger. "It's from a bird."

We all looked up at the ceiling as if expecting to see one flying above us. I thought of Mrs. Wenzel's caged parrotlet, Zeus, with its azure feathers and its odd fascination with Beau.

With her sensibly short and unpolished nails our guide plucked the feather from Sarah's hand. "How odd. I do believe that belongs to Zeus. It must have been stuck to my jacket."

"Must have been," I agreed, as Sarah and I nodded vigorously.

We said another quick good-bye and exited the church. We didn't speak until we'd reached the park gates surrounding the statue of Andrew Jackson.

"I don't think that feather could have come from her coat," Jolene said.

"I'm pretty sure it didn't," I said. Feeling Sarah's gaze on me, I said, "I'll explain later." I looked at my watch. "We should head over to Muriel's. I don't want to be late. We can do Café du Monde afterward."

Jolene was looking with interest at the various vendors set up on the flagstones between the park and the cathedral. The eclectic group included landscape and portrait artists in different mediums, as well as mimes, palm readers, magicians, tarot readers, and everything in between. Somewhere in the back of my closet I had a chalk portrait I'd had done when I'd moved to New Orleans the first time, for my freshman year at Tulane. The artist was actually quite good and had delivered an accurate representation of what I'd looked like at the time—young, hopeful, and incredibly naïve. I no longer recognized that girl—which was why I'd relegated the portrait to the back of my closet—yet I still couldn't make myself throw it away.

Jolene paused to watch a man with a long purple braid painting a watercolor of the cathedral. I stopped, too, amazed at how a brush dipped into paint could replicate on paper an exact image of a church steeple. My artistic talents extended only to stick figures with hair and eyes.

"We should get our tarot cards read," Jolene suggested. "I think we have time."

"No," Sarah and I said in unison.

"Melanie considers tarot cards to be in the same category as a Ouija board," I explained. "Meaning they could invite unwelcome visitors."

"Well, that's a shame," Jolene said, drawing out her lipstick and mirror from her purse. "I guess I can come back another time."

"Because you want to know if Jaxson is going to propose to Carly or not?"

"How did you guess?"

"Because a person doesn't have to be psychic to guess the obvious."

We returned to watching the man painting, until I became aware of someone staring at us. I turned my head and noticed a woman seated in a folding chair near a black iron fence, in front of a small table draped with a black satin cloth. Sparkling glitter had been sprinkled liberally over it and a crystal globe—the same kind every Disney witch used to see the future—that sat in the middle of the table. The woman wore a black cape with a hood almost covering her long black hair streaked with gray. Her craggy face showed years of hard living and bad choices (she was what Jolene labeled a person who obviously didn't use sunscreen), but her large and almost black deep-set eyes were clear and steady, her penetrating gaze on me like a guided X-ray.

Sarah joined me in watching the psychic, whose attention was now directed past us. I shifted my gaze but saw only the steady stream of tourists walking around on the flagstones in front of the church.

"What about having our palms read?" Jolene suggested, heading toward the woman with the crystal ball.

"No," I said. Only a strangled sound emerged from Sarah.

"Why . . . ?" Jolene began, then stopped as she and I saw what Sarah was looking at. On the gray flagstones, a single set of wet footprints, perfectly formed and so fresh that droplets from the ends of the toes glinted in the sunlight. I'd seen them before, but always with Beau. And they were always together, as if left by a stationary person who'd been listening so intently that they hadn't moved. But these were different, each print separated by about two feet, the impressions from the balls of the feet heavier than the heels and facing the opposite direction from where we'd been standing. As if the person were running away.

CHAPTER 23

Sarah and I were silent on the short walk to Muriel's, only half listening to Jolene talk about her various theories about the footprints. If they were Adele's—and that was one assumption we all agreed on—maybe she was just letting us know that if we didn't hurry we'd be late for lunch. Or maybe that we were running out of time to stay one step ahead of Beau, because Jaxson had let us know that Beau had started calling Uncle Bernie for help. Or maybe Adele had been a runner when she'd been alive, which meant that she probably still enjoyed exercising in the afterlife.

This last made Sarah and me look at each other, but we were spared the need to comment because Jolene had already started on another tangent about one of her grandmother's clients, who'd placed a Matchbox car replica of his beloved 1969 cherry red Mustang in his coffin as a compromise instead of actually burying him inside the vehicle. The man's daughter had kept the car, but she never drove it because she said it was haunted by her dad and could prove it with pictures of the shadowy figure that she swore was her dad sitting behind the wheel, and with a radio that never played anything except an oldies station.

This last part I listened to, curious as to where the Mustang was now, the seed of an idea sitting uneasily in my head.

By the time we reached the restaurant, Jolene had announced that she'd talked all her lipstick off and we had to pull to the side of the sidewalk so she could reapply. Then she reached into her large purse and pulled out a pair of heels and changed into them so quickly that it was clear she'd done it many times before.

"Y'all ready?" she said, implying that we probably weren't but she would be happy to wait. "I've got six different shades of lipstick in my purse." She looked at us like a waiter tempting diners with a dessert menu.

"I'd like to—" Sarah began.

"We're good," I said, giving Sarah the same look I knew Dad would if he saw her wearing lipstick in one of Jolene's bright shades.

"I'm almost thirteen," she protested.

"You will always be a little girl to our parents. I'll let you work that out with them and leave me out of it."

Sarah let out an exaggerated sigh, then followed us into the restaurant.

I immediately loved the ambience of the fully renovated grand mansion, with its dark red walls, tall windows, and equally tall French doors, and its eclectic collection of hanging plates and wall art.

The *snap snap* from behind me told me that Sarah didn't find the atmosphere as relaxing as I did. She caught me watching her and said, "I'm fine. I did some Googling on the history of the building, so I'm prepared."

We were greeted by a hostess who led us to our table by a window in the main dining room, where Uncle Bernie and Jaxson were already waiting. Jaxson stood while Bernie struggled with his cane, and I rushed over and placed a hand on his shoulder while Jolene gave him a kiss on his cheek and told him to remain seated.

He grinned up at us. "If I'd known that all I needed was to grow old and crippled to get all this female attention, I would have done it long ago."

We laughed as Jaxson held out our chairs for us to sit and the hostess gave us our menus. "I hope this is okay," Jaxson said, indicating the dining room. "They have a much cozier indoor courtyard bar and the séance room, but—"

"But that would be a hard no from both of us," I said, indicating Sarah.

We chatted and looked at our menus, all of us ordering water except for Uncle Bernie, who asked for a bourbon on the rocks. "Another perk of growing old," he said. "I can pretend that I'm too deaf to hear people telling me I shouldn't drink bourbon at lunch."

"Maybe when I'm ninety I'll be allowed to wear lipstick," Sarah muttered.

"Assuming Dad doesn't come back to tell you that you shouldn't."

She looked at me over her menu. "That's not funny."

Our waitress came to take our order, and Jolene ordered the salad. Uncle Bernie leaned across the table and whispered loudly enough to be heard across the room, "Don't worry. I'm paying. You can get whatever you want." He winked at me, bringing to mind the last time we'd eaten together, when I'd been thinking I'd have to wash dishes to cover the bill. He'd unexpectedly and generously paid, saying my company was enough payment.

Jolene smiled at him. "Thank you, Bernie, but I'm fine with a salad. We're headed to Café du Monde for some beignets when we're done, so I have to save up my calories."

"I don't know why," Jaxson said, cutting into a bread roll. "You look pretty perfect the way you are."

I imagined I could hear the fireworks going off inside Jolene's head even though she just smiled and murmured her thanks.

"I'll have the shrimp and goat cheese crepes. And a cup of the gumbo to start." I studied the waitress closely. Before the bill was presented I was prepared to waylay her.

"Who are you and what have you done with my sister?" Sarah said, feigning shock.

"They didn't have cardboard on the menu, so I had to order something else."

Bernie chuckled. "I need to make a point to hang around younger folks more often. I feel like I've been bathed in the fountain of youth."

Jaxson excused himself to take a call. I spotted a battered black leather briefcase that sat on the floor behind Jaxson's vacated chair. Bernie saw me looking at it and patted my hand on the table. "Don't worry. We'll get to it. As my beautiful bride always reminds me, business can wait."

"I was hoping she'd come with you today, since we missed meeting her last time."

He took a sip of his bourbon and nodded. "She would have loved to meet y'all, too, but she hates to go out. Always insists she can make a better meal for half the price." He leaned forward and in a conspiratorial whisper said, "She's probably right, but there's something to be said for food being brought to the table for you and someone else being responsible for the cleanup."

"Unless you live with someone who prefers to do all of it even though your offers to help are sincere." I eyed Jolene.

"If I thought you knew how to boil an egg or the difference between sterling and stainless, I'd be happier than a tick on a fat dog. We all have our talents, and that's just not yours, bless your heart." She winked to take the sting out of her last words.

Jaxson returned, his expression not exactly grim but definitely not giving off happy vibes. "Everything all right?" I asked.

"Yeah. That was Carly. She was supposed to meet me after lunch to check out the exhibit on the history of Mardi Gras at the Presbytère, but she says something's come up at work and she needs to deal with it. I bought the tickets weeks ago."

"Well, as Bernie's wife says, business can wait."

Jaxson looked at me oddly while Bernie stared down at his plate.

"I mean, I believe in working hard, but everybody needs a break now and then."

"You should tell that to Mom and Dad," Sarah said. "They make me do my homework the second I come home. They're ruthless."

I sent my sister a side-glance. "Jolene has been dying to see the exhibit. Sarah and I have plans for after lunch, but maybe you could bring Jolene. I can call an Uber when Sarah and I are ready to head home."

Jaxson turned to Jolene. "Would that be all right with you?"

"I'd hate for your tickets to go to waste, and I have been wanting to see the exhibit." She smiled sweetly at me. "Only if Nola really doesn't mind taking an Uber. Or I could give you Bubba's keys and Jaxson could bring me home."

"Please, no," Sarah shouted before I could say anything.

"She means to say that I only have my permit and I can't drive by myself yet. Although if I could, I might take the opportunity to drop my sister off in the middle of the Causeway and tell her to find her own way back."

"Uber it is," Jaxson said, grinning broadly. "And Uncle Bernie's poker buddy Frank is supposed to pick up Uncle Bernie after lunch, so he's all set."

"Is Frank a younger friend?" I asked cautiously.

Bernie slapped his hands on the table, making the silverware rattle, and laughed loudly enough that people at neighboring tables craned their necks to see. "Frank's my age, and can barely see over the steering wheel, but he's got a big car, so people know to stay out of his way."

"Jolene says the same thing," Sarah said, reaching over to high-five Bernie's upheld palm.

Our food came, and with it another round of waters and a bourbon on the rocks for Bernie. My crepes were heavenly, and I had fully intended to take home half of my meal, but it was so good I couldn't stop eating. I would just sit at Café du Monde and not eat any beignets myself, ignoring Melanie's voice in my head telling me that there's always room for one more doughnut.

Bernie ordered two desserts, but I didn't panic over the bill this time, as I thought about the two wads of cash from my parents. Assuming anyone took cash anymore. As Bernie dug into his flourless chocolate cake, Jaxson opened up the tattered briefcase and pulled out Jeanne Broussard's clientele book and handed it to me.

I took it, then looked over at Sarah, who was watching us with large, interested eyes.

"Why don't you and Jolene head on over to Café du Monde now? I can meet you there when I'm finished talking to Uncle Bernie."

"That's a great idea," Jaxson said, already standing. "I'll go, too. Text me when you're done, and I'll come get him and bring him outside to wait with him until Frank arrives. If that's all right with everyone?"

We all agreed, Jolene a little more enthusiastically than everyone else.

When they had left, I turned to Uncle Bernie. "So, did you find anything?"

My excitement dimmed at Bernie's expression. "I used every bit of my training and knowledge as a detective to search for anything that might be a clue as to why this book was so important that someone had to keep it hidden. I even got some help from some of my poker buddies—don't panic; I didn't tell them why—to look up every single person in that entire book."

He took another bite of his cake, and I waited impatiently for him to finish chewing and then take another sip of his drink. He was already shaking his head before he put the glass back on the table. "The addresses were a big help, since they could be cross-referenced with marriage and birth records and obituaries. Unfortunately, the people we could find had long since passed or were too old to remember anything. My buddy Frank is really into that genealogy thing, and he and his lady friend at the library spent hours trying to find any connection between the Broussards and the people in the book. There was absolutely nothing. Nothing."

He sat back in his chair and thrummed his large fingers on the edge of the table. "I hope it's all right, but I did make copies of the pages so we could keep looking. Because there's a reason why Beau's daddy hid that book. It's important. I'm sticking by the ABC rules of a good detective and won't rest until we've exhausted every lead."

I shoved the clientele book down into my backpack, pushing down my disappointment at the same time. "What are the ABC rules?"

He tapped his forehead. "Assume nothing; believe nothing; challenge and check everything. We haven't found an answer, so we're not done investigating."

"Well, I appreciate it. Let me know when your next poker game is, and I'll supply the doughnuts."

Uncle Bernie laughed, the buttons on his shirt threatening to pop open. "I get it—cops and doughnuts. Just to let you know that some stereotypes exist for a reason"—he leaned forward—"I'll coordinate with Jaxson. I can't turn down a doughnut."

I texted Jaxson to let him know we were done, then excused myself from the table, taking my backpack with me. I turned in the direction of the restroom, then quickly diverted from my path as I spotted our server heading toward another table with a pitcher of water.

"Excuse me," I said, digging into my backpack to extract the money. "I'm at the far table in the corner, with the older gentleman. I'd like to go ahead and settle our bill now, please." My fingers found one of the wads of money at the bottom and I drew it out to show the waitress.

She looked at the money and then back at me and frowned. "I'm sorry, but I can't take that."

My stomach clenched, and I was afraid I'd have to give up half of my crepes after all. "I have a credit card, but it's maxed out until my next paycheck, so if you could wait to actually charge it . . ."

"I mean that I can't take it because the older gentleman at your table gave me his card when he walked in, so it's already taken care of."

I returned to the table to see Uncle Bernie grinning up at me. "You have to get up pretty early to get one step ahead of me. I may be old, but my mind's still nimble. Just don't tell the wife, but I think it's the bourbon. It worked for Winston Churchill." He raised his glass and drained it.

"Well, next time it's my treat, okay? You're doing all of this work for me, and I'd like a way to repay you."

"No repayment necessary. I appreciate the chance to be in an active investigation again—although unofficially. I should be thanking you." He slid a wrapped piece of Dove chocolate across the table. "I always carry something sweet with me for emergencies. I thought you could use one since you're not getting a beignet."

I didn't hesitate and picked it up. "Aw, that is so nice. Thank you." I stood to put it in my back pocket for later, and my fingers quickly discovered the pocket wasn't empty. I pulled out two crumpled ribbons, one yellow and the other purple. Uncle Bernie's detective eyes looked at them with interest.

"The purple one fell out of Sunny's ponytail a few days ago. The yellow one . . . well, I'm pretty sure this is one of the ribbons Sunny wore when she was kidnapped. Mimi has one, and I thought I had the other hidden in my apartment. And I know it was there, because my sister found it and I made sure I put it back. But when I checked after I found this one, it wasn't there."

"So you think it was stolen?" he asked, no doubt recalling the previous break-in, thwarted by Jolene and Barbie.

"Um, sort of."

"Sort of?" I imagined he was probably going over his ABC checklist. *Believe nothing.* I took a deep breath, deciding to test his ingrained training. "I think there may have been something paranormal at work."

"I see." He held out his hand and I gave him the ribbons. *Challenge and check everything.* He placed both ribbons on the table, then pulled out a pair of reading glasses from his pocket and leaned closer. Examining the knotted parts closely, he said, "There's blond hair stuck in both of them."

"I know. The purple one I know for sure is Sunny's, since I saw it in her ponytail right before I picked it up, and the yellow one would have her hair, too, assuming it was one of the ones that fell out onto the street when she was kidnapped."

He looked at me over the rims of his glasses. "Assume nothing."

"Okay," I said slowly. "Do you want me to compare it to the one Mimi has?"

"Not yet. Right now, would you mind if I borrowed them? Given how much the yellow one has been handled, we probably won't find anything, but there might be some latent prints or DNA not belonging to Sunny or any of her family members. I can pull some strings with the crime lab. New Orleans keeps them pretty busy, but there's always a favor to be called in. I hold on to them like gold coins—only to be used for special occasions."

"That would be great," I said, reaching for the purple one.

Bernie stopped me. "Let me take that one, too. Since you and Sunny handled them both, I can exclude your DNA from the yellow one so that any additional ones will be easier to pinpoint."

"That makes sense," I said.

He pulled a handkerchief from his shirt pocket and carefully wrapped up the two ribbons without touching them. "Don't get your hopes up, Nola. It's a long shot to begin with, and New Orleans crime keeps the lab hopping as it is, and they might not be able to squeeze it in. Not only is this a very old case, but it's no longer considered cold since the missing child has been found."

"I know. But justice hasn't been served. Even if the people who were responsible are dead and won't see any jail time, it just seems right that their names be written down somewhere to show they were bad people."

He carefully replaced his glasses in his shirt pocket. "And I'd agree—if we were dealing with any other family. I long ago realized that sometimes just knowing the truth has to be enough."

"But that's not really fair."

Bernie leaned forward and patted my hand. "Life is rarely fair, Nola. Take the advice of an old man who's seen a lot. Sometimes we have to choose what's worth the fight."

"Then what do we do with the rest?" I asked.

"We let it go."

"I hope I'm not interrupting." Jaxson stood next to the table. "I know I was supposed to wait outside, Nola, but Frank is already here. Should I tell him you need a few more minutes, Uncle Bernie?"

The old man squeezed my hand before sitting back. He picked the wrapped ribbons up from the table and put them in an inside jacket pocket. "Nola and I were just finishing up. She's sending me off on a new assignment now, so I'll let you know when we need to meet again."

Jaxson and I helped Bernie stand, then walked with him to the door. I waved to Frank in the driver's seat of a car that looked to be about the same vintage and size as Bubba while Jaxson assisted Bernie into the passenger seat. I stepped back as the car pulled away smoothly, without hitting anything, allowing myself to let out a sigh of relief. As it rumbled slowly down the street, I thought about what Uncle Bernie had said about the unfairness of life, making choices, and letting go. It was a lot to unpack, and the only thing I knew for sure was that making choices was usually about deciding between a rock and a hard place and moving forward with a sledgehammer while hoping for the best.

Jaxson and I met up with Jolene and Sarah outside Café du Monde, Sarah clutching a bag of beignets she'd ordered for me. Jaxson and Jolene waited until our Uber arrived to take us uptown. I resisted the impulse to tear open the beignet bag and get powdered sugar all over the inside of the car. There were lots of ways to receive a bad rating from your Uber driver, and I was pretty sure that was one.

"Would it be all right if I looked at the book?" Sarah asked.

"The clientele book? Sure—if you think you could help. We've pretty much exhausted our resources, so maybe a new perspective is what we need." I turned to look at her. "What made you ask?"

She didn't meet my eyes. "There was an old lady—well, not old old, but like Gigi and Grandpa. Like that. She had curly gray hair and wore an apron. She was standing behind Bernie the whole time, with her hand on his shoulder. She said I should take a look, that there was something there that nobody else could see."

"Did she tell you her name? I know the restaurant is haunted, but she doesn't sound like any of the ghosts I read about."

Sarah shook her head. "No. But she knew Bernie. Maybe his mom?"

"Maybe." My phone beeped with a text. When I saw it was from Michael, I responded with Call u back ltr? and dropped the phone into my backpack. I didn't need Sarah overhearing anything that might get repeated to our parents. Or anything that might make her question my motives, making me second-guess them all over again.

"What's it like to have three hot guys interested in you? I haven't met Michael, but Jolene said that despite his 'low-down cheating ways' he's 'hotter than fish oil,' so I guessed that meant he was smoking hot. And I'm asking in all seriousness as your little sister who's looking for advice, and not being judgy in any way. Not that Dad will let me date until I'm at least thirty, but I figure it's not too early to get some pointers."

It took me a moment to come up with an answer that would make sense to both of us. "First of all, I don't have three guys interested in me. Michael is, well, not a viable candidate, for reasons I've already explained."

"Basically, because he was paid to date you," Sarah said matter-of-factly.

I frowned. "Thanks for putting it in those terms, but basically, yes. And I just saw Cooper for the first time in years, so we really don't have a relationship right now. That could change, but for now, we're just friends."

"Uh-huh," she said, sounding a lot like Jack when he was listening to my explanation as to why I was coming home after curfew. "What about Beau?"

"Well, he's . . ." I stopped, still unable to define our relationship. Or forget the unforgettable kiss we'd shared on the couch in my living room. "He's in a serious relationship with Samantha. Besides . . ." I shrugged as if that should explain all the other plausible reasons why Beau wasn't interested in me.

"Besides?" she prompted, reminding me of Melanie when I'd tried to explain to her why steel-cut oatmeal was a better breakfast option than doughnuts.

"We're incompatible." I turned to face her, eager to change the focus of our conversation. "Why are you asking? Is there a boy you're interested in?"

She shook her head. "No. Just something Adele said to me before she ran away."

Despite the warm coziness of the heated backseat and my sweater, an icy chill swept through me. "Adele?"

Sarah nodded. "There were two things, actually. One was just a name. Does the name Buddy ring a bell?"

"That's Beau's dad. Did you see him, too?"

"No. Adele wanted me to notice that he wasn't with her, but that's not what she wanted to talk about—something about choices. I don't think it was *about* you specifically, just something she wanted you to know. And she kept saying Beau's name, like she needed him to know, too. I don't know why she won't tell him herself."

"Because he won't talk to her. He's still angry with her for leaving him. But I can tell him. Do you remember exactly what she said?"

Sarah sucked in her lips, a way of concentrating for her since she was a baby listening to conversations nobody else could hear. "Something about choosing what's worth the fight."

"And letting the rest go," I finished for her.

She turned her head in surprise. "That's spooky."

I nodded in agreement as the full body chills began, and we rode the rest of the way back to my apartment in a silence interrupted only by the soft sounds of the local jazz station, WWOZ, playing on the radio, and by the jolting thump and squeal of the car as its driver attempted to swerve around potholes and dipped into others that were either too big or too unexpected to avoid.

CHAPTER 24

Jolene dropped me off at the Ryans' house on Prytania on her way to take Sarah to the Past Is Never Past. Not a big fan of antiques, for obvious reasons, Sarah was there mostly to meet Trevor when he showed up after school and to walk through the Quarter with Jolene. I strongly advised them both to avoid Bourbon Street. Thank goodness it was fall and the eau de Bourbon stew wasn't as strong as in the summer months, but there were still things on Bourbon Street that I warned Sarah would scar her for life. Granted, it was a weekday afternoon, but still. Not only cockroaches mated out in the open if given the opportunity.

Sunny ran down the walkway to greet us. "So happy to see y'all," she said, then winked at Jolene. "Did you hear how easily I slipped in that 'y'all'?"

"I did," Jolene said. "I'd say you're hovering right below the Mason-Dixon Line, which is better than last week."

"Where was I last week?"

"Maine," Jolene said with a straight face, making Sunny laugh.

She laughed easily despite the last few traumatic months, which was a relief given her childhood nickname. But right now, with the sun glinting off her golden hair (which was still the wrong shade, according to Jolene), all she needed to do was add a yellow ribbon to look exactly the way one could imagine the grown-up version of Sunny should look.

Sunny opened the hourglass gate for me, and surprised me with a hello hug. Turning back to the car, she said, "Don't y'all want to come in for a bit? Mimi and I were in the back garden, and I was helping her get it ready for the big party. I bought us matching monogrammed gardening gloves, but Mimi has a huge collection in her gardening shed that y'all can borrow. She taught me how to make sweet tea, and there's a fresh pitcher in the fridge if all y'all would like some."

Jolene grinned. "Your correct usage of 'all y'all' is very impressive, Sunny. Sounds a lot more like me than Mimi, but I figure you already know that and can slide into her accent, too. That's a talent, by the way. I guess my own accent is too strong to disguise. My high school French teacher gave me a passing grade halfway through the semester just so that I'd stop coming to class and butchering the language. She said there hadn't been that kind of a French slaughter since Waterloo."

"Isn't that an ABBA song?" Sarah asked.

"And you're one of the few people under fifty who knows that," Jolene said. She turned back to Sunny. "We would love to join you, but Sarah and I have plans. Hopefully we can come back before Sarah leaves on Sunday."

Sunny moved closer to the car. "Have you come up with a plan for your beach house visit?"

"Not yet," I said. "I'm guessing that's why Beau wanted to see me today. To be honest, I'm not really sure what he hopes I'll discover. I mean, I doubt I'll find Antoine Broussard's journal lying out in the open where he admits that he killed his daughter, or even Jeanne Broussard's diary saying she was being molested by her uncle. If they ever existed, I'm sure they've long since been destroyed. I don't think there's even a slim chance of that murder ever being solved."

"And you know what?" Sunny said. "I'm fine with that. I'm back and Mimi is happy. *I'm* happy, even though I've just been through some of the worst months of my life. I think at some point Beau is going to have to realize that things are good right now, and there's no need to stir the pot."

"At this point, I think if I can just convince Beau that I'm working hard to find answers, and Mimi keeps him occupied with this 'murder house flip' idea, maybe he'll lose interest. The only thing I can think of that might help is reaching out to Michael's biological parents—wherever they are."

"Why would you want to do that?" Sunny had raised her voice, making the three of us turn toward her. Even Sarah looked up from her phone. Sunny grimaced. "I'm sorry—didn't mean to shout. It's only that I just finished saying how happy and settled everyone is right now. I don't understand why you'd want to rock the boat by contacting Michael's parents. It seems to me they left for a good reason and have stayed away for the same reason. Can't we just let them be?"

"I'm sorry. I am. And I do understand. But don't you want to know if they're connected to your kidnapping? Even if they aren't, they might know who is. At the very least, I need to ask so that I can tell Beau I've exhausted that line of questioning. Then we can all move on. Do you think you can live with that?"

Sunny was silent for a long moment, making us all shift uncomfortably. Then her face transformed from distressed concern to relaxed understanding. "Yes. Of course. Don't stress yourself. Just go to the beach house and have fun. Sam and I can help you figure out what to tell Beau later."

"Now, that's a plan I can live with." I stepped back from the car. "Tell Trevor I said hello and that I'm still waiting for that fanny pack I said to be on the lookout for."

"You do not need a fanny pack, regardless of what the Instagram influencers are saying," Jolene said. "They are tackier than white shoes with dark stockings. You just need to carry a pocketbook like a normal person."

I started to respond, but she was already rolling up her window. She and Sarah waved as Bubba squealed away from the curb and drove away.

Sunny linked her arm through mine to show that we were still friends. "She's right, you know. Unless you're ninety years old, you don't need a fanny pack. Tell me what you need it for and maybe I can make it for you. My mom taught me how to sew, and I made most of the costumes for all the high school productions. I really wanted to be on stage, but I never quite made the cut, so I was the star of the costume department instead." She laughed her bubbly laugh, contagious enough that I laughed, too.

We stopped on the front porch. "I'm wanting something like my backpack but smaller. Something I can wear with dresses when I'm not wearing jeans, so that I have a place for my phone and keys."

"You mean like a purse?"

"Yeah. Sort of. But I don't want to be fussing with where to put it, so I want something I can strap around my waist and forget about."

"I'm actually with Jolene on this one. They do make purses called crossbodies, you know. They're smaller and you just wear them across your body." She was speaking slowly to me, the way elementary school teachers spoke to their charges.

"I know. But the ones I've seen are so . . . purselike. I wanted something soft and slouchy that would blend into whatever I was wearing. Like a fanny pack."

She opened the front door and ushered me in. "I have an idea of something, but it's going to be a surprise. And it won't be a fanny pack."

I followed her inside. As she closed the door, she said, "Is there a date with Cooper I need to know about? I work best with a deadline."

My cheeks flushed. "He's new in town and I'm happy to show him around. He'd like to take a look at the house on Esplanade, too, so I figured I could show him. Just to be clear, I'm not interested in a relationship right now. He's an old friend, and I might want to wear a dress now and again, like when my jeans are being washed. Jolene has a closetful of purses, but I'd like something that's more me."

"Got it. I'll get to work right away. Although, by the way Cooper kept looking at you when we were on the swamp tour, I'm not sure if he's planning to remain long in the friend zone. And you should make up your mind soon. I don't know how patient he is, but looking like that, I don't think he'll stay single for long. That man is finer than a frog's hair split four ways."

She'd said that with such a perfect imitation of Jolene's voice that it made me laugh out loud. "Wow. You're amazing."

"Like I said before, I'm a quick study when it comes to imitating people. Probably comes from hanging around backstage for all those high school productions." She let out her bubbly laugh again, and it kept me smiling until we'd reached the kitchen.

Beau sat at the table beneath the large picture window overlooking the vibrant garden. Just like in Charleston, flowers and foliage alike burst forth with a new palette of fall colors. I peered out the window, trying to see what was being planted now that I considered myself an amateur gardener working on her green thumb.

Melanie's father, an avid gardener, had given me my own trowel as soon as I'd arrived in Charleston, and I had knelt next to him in the dirt, reluctantly at first, for many hours as we made holes in the earth to plant seeds and bury roots. I learned how to coax dormant plants to rise and grow, and how every living thing in the garden had a purpose and a cycle. Most of the time spent had been in silence, our bond forming through the scents of green growing things and through the unspoken connection we had to each other and to the house on Tradd Street. He'd never asked me to call him Grandpa, but when I did, it wasn't a surprise to either of us.

A deck of cards sat on the table, along with three individual cards placed facedown.

"What are you playing?" I asked.

"Not a game, really," Sunny said. "We're trying to see if I have any psychic abilities, so Beau's testing me on guessing the cards."

"Any luck?" I asked.

Sunny grimaced. "Nope. Nada. I was hoping that maybe all the psychic genes hadn't bypassed me completely. Or maybe Beau just hogged them all before I came along."

Beau squeezed her around the shoulders, then used his knuckles to rub the top of her head. "But you got all the looks."

"And the brains," I added.

They both laughed as Sunny tried to jump high enough to give her brother a noogie and failed miserably.

Mimi entered the kitchen, and her face broke out into a wide grin as she spotted her grandchildren. She looked years younger, her eyes brighter and her face more relaxed than I'd seen since we'd met. It had been as if she'd worn her grief like a sheet of cellophane that muted her features. The sudden reappearance of her granddaughter had ripped it away, allowing us to see the grandmother she had planned to be before Sunny had been taken and her son and daughter-in-law had been lost in the storm.

"Children, settle down or take it outside." Her smile took away any sting that her words might have held if the children in question were, well, children.

"Sorry, Mimi," Sunny said, and planted a kiss on the older woman's cheek. "Beau started it."

"I'm not sure that's how I remember it," I said.

"Well, regardless," Mimi said, trying to sound stern. "I lost my helper, and I need her back to help me move a bag of mulch."

"I'm on it!" Sunny said, opening the door and motioning Mimi ahead of her. She hesitated briefly before following Mimi outside.

Beau turned to me. "I thought we could go up into the studio room so we could talk in private."

I thought of the Frozen Charlotte dolls staring at me from the wall shelves. "How about a snake pit? Or a mime convention?"

His lips quirked. "If only I knew where to find one."

"What about your grandfather's library?"

"No. Absolutely not." His abruptness startled me.

"He's not there, you know, if that's what you're worried about. He seems to have made my house his permanent residence."

Beau opened the refrigerator and took out a pitcher of iced tea. "It's not that. Mimi doesn't allow anyone to go in there, not even Lorda. Mimi does all the dusting and vacuuming. She hasn't moved a thing since he died." He held the pitcher up to me. "Sweet tea?"

I shook my head. "Blech. Just water for me, please."

"Blasphemy," he said as he reached into a cabinet for two glasses. "Does Jolene know you don't like sweet tea? We might have to ask Jaxson's brother the priest to say a mass for you."

"Very funny. And yes, she knows. She has a plan to convert me." He handed me an empty glass. "Back to your grandfather. Do you think you can suggest to him that he return to wherever it was we sent him?"

He glanced out the kitchen window to where Mimi and Sunny stood next to an empty flower bed. "You might not want me to. Not yet. Let's talk about this upstairs."

"Fine." I bent down so I could fill my glass from the large bottle dispenser ubiquitous in New Orleans homes. When I'd straightened, I started to walk out of the kitchen the way we'd entered. I was almost at the stairs when I realized that Beau wasn't behind me. I retraced my steps, but Beau wasn't in the kitchen, and I would have seen him if he'd walked by me. The only other way out of the kitchen was out the back door. More than a little annoyed, I walked past the banquette and into the adjacent morning room that contained three walls of windows but no doors.

I stuck my head around the corner. "Beau?"

I was already headed back toward the kitchen when I heard him call my name from behind me. I startled, my hand flying to my throat as I spun around. "Where did you come from?"

"The hidden stairs behind the wall." His face was serious, but his eyes made it clear he was messing with me.

"Of course," I said. "The hidden stairs. Because according to Nancy Drew and Scooby-Doo, all old houses have at least one set."

"Something like that." Beau slid his finger along the thick chair rail on the wall without windows until I heard a *click*. A small portion of paneling popped open, revealing a set of worn wooden steps, faded dips in the middle of each stair where over a century of feet had landed.

"Servants' stairs," I said, an educated guess based on the hundreds of historic houses I'd studied during the pursuit of my master's in preservation.

"Good guess," he said. "But I bet you've never seen a set like this. They were altered at some point since the steps don't lead to any living area anymore, and the hidden door was added. Which probably sounds strange to you until you actually see it for yourself."

Intrigued, I followed him up the narrow stairwell with plastered walls until it reached a landing with one door in front of us and one to the left. The only light came from the open door behind us. Beau rested his hand on the knob of the door in front. "Be prepared to be amazed."

"I've heard that before," I said.

"Yeah, but this time it's for real." He held the door open and waited. Just as I reached him, he said, "Watch where you step." I turned my head to where our noses were almost touching in the small space, and I could see his eyes laughing.

I stepped through the narrow door and immediately felt the chill of an unheated attic. A wide footpath of unstained wallboards crossed over the studs and ended on the far side of the attic. There were no handrails, which reminded me of pictures I'd seen of workers on high-rise scaffolding, their legs dangling into the abyss below.

Beau stepped through the doorway and moved to stand next to me. "Hold on to me, and then look down."

My instinctive response to Beau telling me what to do meant that I immediately looked over the edge of the wooden path. The disorientation hit me right away as my eyes attempted to adjust to what seemed like a fun-house mirror on the floor. I knew my feet were on the ground, but my mind didn't agree, thinking instead that I was riding a wave on a surfboard. I started swaying, tilting more and more to one side despite my matter-of-fact mind insisting that I needed to stand up straight or I'd fall. Yet my body kept tilting, one foot letting go of the walkway and then the next sending me toppling over the edge.

CHAPTER 25

Beau's strong hands grabbed my arms from behind, immediately pulling me back onto solid ground. At least physically. "You might want to get your hearing checked, Nola. I told you to hold on to me before looking down."

I gave a quick nod, too shaken to say anything.

"I'll keep holding on to you, but when you're ready, look again. I think you'll find it interesting."

I took a couple of deep breaths before looking over the edge again, and then a few more as I registered what I was seeing. The floor beneath us was only about a foot away. It also wasn't actually a floor. "It's . . ." I began, unsure how to explain what I thought I was seeing.

"You're looking at the reverse side of the dining room ceiling mural. It appears to be painted on the ceiling, but it's just canvas that's been ingeniously installed to look like paint on plaster. In daylight, and at night when the lights are on, you can see straight through to the people eating below. And the acoustics are so good you can hear people whispering to their tablemates.

"When Mimi had her dinner parties when I was a little boy, I'd sneak up here after I was supposed to be in bed and I'd spy on her and her guests to see when dessert was served. That always meant that it was time to sneak down the secret stairs and into the kitchen, where Lorda would make a plate for me with extra dessert."

"Why is this even here?"

"I would bet that the idea came from my grandfather's brother, who had the mural painted. My great-uncle had a lot of questionable friends and business associates, including Antoine Broussard. When I discovered this space as a kid and told Mimi, she wasn't surprised. Spying on guests was exactly the kind of thing people would have expected my great-uncle to do. What I don't know is if my grandfather ever knew it was here."

I thought of the all-seeing eyes in the hall portrait, and the failed attempt to send him into the light. "My guess is that he did. From what I know of him, he doesn't seem to be the type of person who would miss much."

"Let's go," he said, gently placing me in front of him. "I'm going to keep my hands on you to guide you until you're safely out of the door. Please notice that I didn't pose that as a question."

Even though I was grateful for the steadying pressure of his hands, I still looked back at him so that he could see my frown. As soon as we were out on the landing, he dropped his hands and turned toward the second door.

"I'll go first. Just in case there are critters. Dead or alive. I haven't been this way in a while, so there's a good chance there's something here that shouldn't be."

I wondered if he might not have been referring to the nonliving invaders, but I didn't want to ask in case he told me.

Beau opened the door and revealed another set of steps. He began climbing them, and I followed him up to another dark room like the one we'd just left, with exposed rafters and beams, except this flooring covered the entire space, negating the need for a walkway.

"We're in the attic space above the upstairs hallway, in case you're wondering," Beau said, reading my mind. "And no, there aren't any peepholes into the rooms below. None that I know of, anyway." When he looked back, he was grinning, which meant he was joking. I hoped.

I followed him to the other end of the attic, to what appeared to be a wooden ramp with boards nailed horizontally every two feet.

"Careful," Beau said. "This is above the sloped ceiling at the end of the hallway. Whoever put this here couldn't figure out how to put in another set of stairs, so he did this instead. Pretty smart, I think. Just make sure you grip the boards with your feet so you don't slip."

He indicated a finished plaster wall facing the end of the ramp without any space in between. I leaned in to see, from the other side of the wall, a faint light outlining a door.

Beau gently pushed on the wall at the center of the door's outline. I heard a very soft *click* as that portion of the wall gently swung out toward us. He stepped inside and I followed him into the attic recording studio. I turned just as Beau shut the wall panel, leaving no evidence of its existence.

"I feel like we're definitely in a Nancy Drew novel," I said.

"Except the ghosts are real." He wasn't smiling as he pulled out Sam's desk chair for me, then sat down in his own. "I thought we should talk before this weekend."

"I'm not going to blurt out my questions about Sunny's kidnapping, if that's what you're worried about. I'll be a lot more subtle. I'll keep my eyes and ears open, and ask questions when appropriate."

"Well, then," Beau said, leaning back in his chair. "It seems like you've already given this some thought."

"Of course I have. Every single minute I'm with Michael is a lie, and I'd rather not make the process last longer than necessary."

"Why? You still have feelings for him?"

"Whether I do or not, I don't like lying to him. Or anyone. It makes me feel . . . dirty. Dishonest. I've been accused of lots of things, but neither one of those, nor am I wanting to start."

"Fair point. I just need to make sure I know where we stand. So if you do turn up anything, I can trust that you will tell me. Everything."

I kept my eyes on him, remembering to keep my breathing steady—my dad had told me that uneven breathing was a big "tell" when determining whether someone was lying. I couldn't tell Beau about my deal with Sunny and Sam, or that any withholding of facts would not be due to any residual feelings I might or might not have for Michael.

"Of course," I said. "I don't have any loyalty to Michael." At least that part was true. Eager to change topics, I asked, "Have you ever visited the Broussard mausoleum?"

"Do you really think I'd voluntarily visit a cemetery?"

"That's what I figured. But when we were playing tourists the other day at St. Louis Number One, Sarah was led to the Broussard tomb."

"Who led her?"

"Initially your mother. Adele appeared to Sarah when we were visiting the Our Lady of Guadalupe Church and told her to go to St. Louis Number One. While we were there, a young girl brought Sarah right to the Broussard mausoleum."

"Who was the little girl?"

"We don't know. She wasn't there when I found Sarah. But whoever she was, she wanted us to see it. The mausoleum is where Jeanne's remains are mixed with those of her murderer and her molester. I'd haunt whoever would listen if I were her, so I'm not going to blame her for sticking around, even if it was at my house. I'm glad she's found peace and I hope she stays there. Because whatever is there now scares me."

"It's Antoine Broussard. I'm sure of it."

"Me, too. I'd like to know why he's suddenly appeared."

Beau looked at me with worried eyes and an expression I'd never seen on his face before. I leaned toward him, careful to keep any accusation from my voice. "You're afraid to face him, aren't you? Because he's much stronger than Jeanne and your grandfather."

Beau banged his hands on the desk and stood. "Of course I am.

I'm petrified. I have no idea what I'm doing, and if I open another door and can't close it, then we're all in trouble. Especially . . ."

"Especially what?" The words he'd spoken to his mother on the phone that night in my apartment reverberated in my mind. *She's dangerous. I can't afford to lose my focus. I can't ever let that happen again.* I stepped back, sucking in my breath. "It was me, wasn't it? We let him through when we sent Jeanne and your grandfather into the light."

He didn't answer because he didn't need to.

"So that day at Mardi's gotcha party, when you said we made a great team, you were lying?"

"No. I believed it then. I thought everything had gone as planned. And then . . ."

"And then Antoine made his presence known in my house, and I'm scared to be there alone. We're going to have to do something."

He looked at me in the dim light as if daring me to say what we were both thinking. "You need to ask your mother for help. You were a little boy when she disappeared. Maybe it's time you looked at your relationship with her from a new perspective. Maybe find a way to forgive her for something she might not even know she did."

He started shaking his head, but I cut him off before he could speak. "Sarah saw Adele again after our lunch at Muriel's. She wants to help you." I closed my eyes briefly, trying to remember what Sarah had told me. I had the sense that it was important that I get it exactly right. "She said you need to decide what's worth the fight. And let the rest go."

He stared at me without speaking, his body unmoving. Only the steady rise and fall of his chest told me that he hadn't turned to stone.

"Have you heard that before?" I asked.

His head bent forward in a slow nod before he raised his eyes to meet mine. "My mother. She says it every time I'm stupid enough to answer the phone."

"Do you know what she means?"

"No. And I'm not interested in knowing. She chose to leave me, and I choose to figure things out on my own."

I found myself on the verge of laughing, and struggling to hold it in.

He looked at me with irritation. "What's so funny?"

"You. You're starting to sound just like me."

"That's not funny, Nola. It's downright alarming. And wrong. I'm fine with accepting help. Just not from her."

I sobered. "What if we have no other options? What if she's the only one who *can* help?"

He looked at me as if I'd just suggested going on a bank robbing spree. Naked. "There must be another way. Like exposing the Sabatier family secrets."

"And if that doesn't work?"

"We'll cross that bridge when we come to it."

I wanted to point out how illogical his reasoning was, that once we reached that bridge it might be too late, but it was clear he didn't want to discuss it anymore.

"One last thing," I said. "You might want to talk to Sunny before we get any deeper into this. She isn't on board with punishing whoever was responsible for her kidnapping. She's happy now and wants to move forward, and she believes your need for justice is irrelevant. She wishes you'd just let it rest. Don't forget that she was the victim, Beau. She should have a say."

"We were all victims. I lost my sister, my parents lost their daughter, and my grandparents lost their granddaughter. And that's all I'm going to say on the subject." He didn't raise his voice, but his words were clipped and hard-edged, letting me know that our discussion was over.

Beau pulled from a desk drawer a square plastic box with a round screen in the middle and placed it on the desk. "Please make sure that your phone is always charged and on. Sometimes cell coverage can be spotty in coastal areas, so I'm letting you borrow my Wi-Fi hot spot so you will at least have e-mail access. Just put 'SOS' in the header and I'll call nine-one-one and head your way ASAP."

"Do you really think I'll need that?"

"No. If I thought you'd be in real danger, I wouldn't ask you to go. I just like to be prepared. I guess I got that from my dad."

The mention of his father reminded me of something else Sarah had said. "When Adele was talking to Sarah, she made it clear she wanted Sarah to notice that your father wasn't with her. Do you know what she meant?"

Beau shrugged, and his studied nonchalance left me unsettled. "My dad chose to remain behind instead of coming with me when the storm hit. He made his choice, and I'm now making my own. If he's out there somewhere, he knows where to find me."

His voice didn't sound as hard as his words. "What if he can't?"

Beau stood, picking up the hot spot and handing it to me. "That subject is closed. Let's focus on the weekend. Once we're on the other side of that, we'll see where we stand. Either way, my parents won't be part of it, all right?"

I took the hot spot without saying anything, figuring that now wasn't the time to tell him that he was being stubborn and shortsighted. The same things he'd called me more than once in our long history.

I headed toward the hidden door, but Beau called me back. "Let's go the other way. I don't want to take the chance of anyone seeing us coming out of the panel in the kitchen. I'd prefer that not everyone know it's there."

"But surely Lorda and Mimi know about it."

"Yeah, but that's it. Unless my grandfather or great-uncle told anyone, and anyone they told is probably long dead."

"What about Sunny?"

He thought for a moment, then shook his head. "Not yet. Hasn't come up, I guess. It's a great way to scare the crap out of someone in the dining room, or just pop up downstairs after someone saw you go upstairs using the front staircase. I think I'll find the right opportunity to let Sunny know about it."

He gave me a seductive grin that I wanted to tell him should be reserved for Sam, but it was too late. I turned away and headed for the door, thinking about choices and regrets, and all the ways we live our lives attempting to ensure that one doesn't result in the other.

CHAPTER 26

When I returned to the apartment that evening, I found Sarah lying on the sofa, wrapped up in one of Jolene's robes, with a thick green goo spread over her face, her toes separated by cotton balls and all nails painted a bright pink. Jolene's Bluetooth speaker played gentle spa music in the background as a lavender-scented candle burned on top of the coffee table. The scents of garlic and tomato sauce billowed from the kitchen in an interesting collision of smells that wasn't as horrible as it should have been.

Sarah raised her hand in greeting, then pointed at her face. "Can't talk."

I nodded in understanding, having been the subject of more than one of Jolene's mask concoctions that dried to cement so that any mouth movement was impossible. I wasn't exactly sure what she put in them, and I was too afraid to ask. She'd make lemon bars or brownies as a treat if I didn't complain.

Looking for Mardi, I started to ask Sarah where he was before my question was answered by Jolene walking in from the kitchen, followed by Cooper holding Mardi. My dog ignored me as he slathered kisses on Cooper's jaw.

"I hope you don't mind," Cooper said. "Jolene texted me and said she was making some of her famous spaghetti and meatballs, so what's a guy supposed to do?"

I laughed, embarrassed at how happy I was to see him, and my dog, and my dog with Cooper.

"And he gets two servings of lemon meringue for dessert because he helped me find Mardi's ass," Jolene said as she emerged from the kitchen. "Mardi hid it between the oven and the cabinet, and I somehow missed it." She held up the Eeyore toy while Sarah did her best not to crack her mask.

Cooper managed to keep a straight face as he handed me Mardi, who quickly delivered a kiss to my nose. "You can just call him Eeyore, you know," I said as Jolene disappeared back into the kitchen and I followed her.

Jolene looked up from where she was stirring a large pot simmering on the stove. "But not everyone knows what that is. Everyone knows what an ass is, and since Mardi is always hiding his, we all know what to look for."

"Actually," I said, "I don't think that's right. . . ."

"Can I take this off now?" Sarah yelled out from the living room. "My nose already fell off."

Jolene and I moved to the kitchen doorway. "Go ahead," Jolene said. "Use warm water and a rag and soak it until the mask is soft. You don't want to take off the outer layers of your skin, all right?"

Sarah gave me a wide-eyed look of panic as she headed toward the bathroom. I set Mardi down and faced Cooper. "Why don't you ditch your jacket and take a seat and I'll get you something to drink? I can't wait to hear about your new job. What would you like?"

"I'll take a be— I mean, water is fine."

"Beer is fine, Cooper. Really. That's all behind me. All we have is Faubourg—is that all right?"

"Sounds great, thanks. I figure I should start drinking what the locals drink, right?"

"Exactly." I returned to the kitchen to pull out a bottle and a pilsner glass. I normally wouldn't have thought about using a glass, but Jolene was watching, so I carefully poured the beer, then grabbed a cocktail napkin. I stopped in the middle of the living room and watched Cooper high-fiving with Mardi.

"Wow—did you just teach him that?" I asked as I handed him his glass.

"No. I held up my hand like I used to do with my dog, and Mardi tapped it with his paw. When I said, 'Other paw,' he tapped it with the other. His previous owner must have taught him."

I sat down next to Cooper, bending down to scratch beneath Mardi's ears. "I wonder what else he knows. We tried to find his owner, but no one ever claimed him. Chances are, if his old owner did happen to see him on the street, they wouldn't recognize Mardi with his newly discovered flair for fashion."

Cooper laughed. "And who's responsible for that—you or Jolene?"

"You seriously have to ask?"

His face sobered. "I haven't seen you in a while, so I wasn't sure if you'd changed your position on pet clothing."

I settled back into the couch. "For the record, I haven't. But Jolene gets up before I do, and the damage is already done before I've had my first cup of coffee."

Cooper slid back, too, crossing a foot over his knee and stretching one arm along the back of the couch behind my head. "I hope you don't mind me surprising you like this. Jolene made it sound like the invitation came from you, too."

"You're always welcome here, Cooper." I met his eyes and felt my cheeks flush. "I mean, I promised my parents that I'd help you get settled so you'll feel more at home. I was thinking we should set up a time for you to look at the house on Esplanade soon. And if you decide you're interested in purchasing it after the renovation, JR Properties has a lot of rentals you can look at until it's ready. Or I can help you find a brand-new condo or town house or apartment if you decide that crumbling plaster and old pipes aren't your thing. I know the neighborhoods pretty well now, and I've learned a thing or two from Melanie about real estate."

He smiled, looking so much like the Citadel cadet who'd been my first love that my chest hurt. It took me a moment to find my breath again.

"Let's start with the Esplanade house, and we can go from there."

"Sounds like a plan. I'll check with Beau and set up a time that works for you."

"I'll let you know. I'm traveling for the rest of this week, but I'll be back late Friday. I had the option of traveling Saturday morning, but I wanted to be here just in case you needed me. Since you told me about Michael, I'll be honest and tell you that the thought of you joining him and his aunt and uncle at their beach house is more than a little concerning."

My heart constricted. "You're very sweet to think of me. But Jolene and Sarah will be with me. Power in numbers, right?" I gave him a weak grin.

"Yeah. But just in case, please make sure you have my number on speed dial and that you have a strong cell and Wi-Fi signal. I'll stay up all night to make sure you're all right."

I tried not to hear the echo of Beau's words. "Thank you. I don't think there's any danger, but it's nice to know that someone's looking out for me."

"That's what friends are for." He smiled at me, but it definitely wasn't the usual kind of smile between friends, and I felt a warm flush bloom in my chest. "Not to mention that I'm pretty sure your mom and dad would develop unique forms of torture for me if anything happened to you."

I sat back. "I don't need your protection, Cooper. I'm pretty good at taking care of myself."

"I know. It's one of the things I've always loved about you. But even Wonder Woman needs her magical bracelets from time to time."

"Are you calling yourself a bracelet?" I asked, leaning forward slightly.

"Get a room," a clean-faced Sarah said as she joined us in the living room and plopped herself down on a chair. "There are children present."

As if we'd just been caught doing something inappropriate in front of a child, we both sat back. "We were just talking," I said.

Sarah looked at me over her phone and rolled her eyes. "Have you seen the pictures from the cemetery yet? I sent them all to you."

"No. I don't think I got them." I moved to the edge of my seat. "Why?"

She sighed heavily. "Well, I sent them. I'll resend them all later, but right now you need to see this one." She began scrolling through her photos. "It's one where I'm standing in front of the mausoleum but looking at you. I think I was answering your question about the little girl who brought me there." She handed me her phone.

"A little girl?" Cooper slid closer to me on the sofa and leaned over to get a better look.

"She's not in the picture," Sarah said, "but there's definitely a large white orb right next to me. I think that's her."

I zoomed in on the picture, the figure in the close-up looking less like an amorphous white blob and more like the hazy outline of a little girl with a large bow in her hair. I flicked left and right to the pictures before and after that one to see if it could be a speck of dirt or dust on the lens, but that one picture was the only one with the orb.

"Wow," I said. "That's creepy enough to be on one of those 'caught on film' paranormal TV shows."

"Welcome to my world," Sarah said.

"I should send it to Beau. See what he thinks. He might have a better idea of who the little girl is."

My sister smiled smugly. "Already did. You're slowing down in your old age, Nola. You have to be pretty fast to keep up with the younger generation."

Cooper laughed loudly until I turned to glare at him, and even then he continued to chuckle.

"I don't know what you're laughing about, Cooper. You're older than I am."

He responded with a raised eyebrow and a crooked grin that made him look just like the boy I'd once known and loved what seemed like a million years ago.

My phone buzzed with a text. I looked at it, expecting it to be from Beau, but was surprised to see Michael's name on the screen. "I need to respond. Excuse me for a second."

I stood in the hallway outside the bathroom and looked at the screen.

Are you free Friday? He ended the sentence with a bicycle emoji.

Sure. When?

8am Audubon Pk bring ur wheels The bicycle emoji was followed by a thumbs-up emoji.

See you then. I followed that with a smiley emoji. It felt weird using emojis with anyone besides my siblings and Melanie—my brother and sister because they were the age when they considered emojis cute, and Melanie because she had a hard time reading texts without her glasses, so emojis were a useful shorthand.

Cooper was speaking when I walked back into the room. "I don't know how it works, but even to me, that sounds strange."

"What sounds strange?" I asked, settling myself back onto the couch next to him.

"Sarah was just telling me about how Thibaut's wife spoke to her and wanted Sarah to tell Thibaut that his wife loved him."

"Outside of a dead person speaking and a woman declaring her love for the man who supposedly killed her, what sounds strange?"

Cooper smiled while he pretended to think. "Good point. But we were actually talking about Adele, and how she appears to Beau a lot."

"And calls him on an unplugged landline phone that Adele has asked me to stop hiding," I added. Cooper didn't even raise his eyebrows, which reminded me of yet another reason why I liked him so much. He knew my history and my family, so there was never any need for explanations.

Sarah said, "So, I told him about Thibaut's wife, which made me think of Sunny and her adoptive mom and dad. They died in a car crash, right?"

I nodded. "Right around the time Sunny discovered who she really was."

My gaze met Cooper's, and I knew we were both thinking of the same word: "coincidence."

"I know, it does seem like perfect timing or whatever you want to call it, but Beau and Mimi verified that everything she told us was true. Sadly. The good news is that her parents didn't seem to be in on the illegal parts of the adoption. They brought Sunny into their family in good faith."

Sarah had screwed up her mouth to one side, an expression I'd seen a thousand times on Jack as he sifted through clues in his head. "What is it?" I asked.

"Well, I'm not an expert at this—not like Mom and Aunt Jayne, anyway—but I was just thinking it was kind of weird that her mom and dad haven't come to me to pass on a message to Sunny."

"Maybe because they're new at the being-dead part and they're not exactly sure what to do, either?"

Sarah scrunched up her face. "You think? Could be. I haven't seen a rule book anywhere that explains it, so who knows?"

"They could just need more time to learn the ropes of the afterlife," Cooper suggested. "Although I've always hoped that after we die we can just rest and relax, nothing more strenuous than floating on clouds."

"I think you've seen too many Renaissance paintings," I said, elbowing him.

"Oof." Cooper exaggeratedly rubbed his arm. "Maybe your likeness to Wonder Woman isn't just rumor."

The sound of gagging came from across the room, where Sarah

was pretending to throw up. "Is that supposed to be flirting? I'm only twelve and even I think that's lame."

"It might not be all that strange," I said, ignoring her. "Sunny is happy and back with her family. Her adoptive parents can rest in peace now. It's not like every person who dies comes back to haunt the living. There's usually a reason."

"True," Sarah said. "Like Adele and Beau. I'm not really sure what's going on, or why she dragged me to the Broussard mausoleum, but there's definitely some unfinished business there. It's too bad he won't talk to her. Maybe that's all he needs to do so she can rest."

"Could be," I said. "I really thought she'd head for the light as soon as Sunny came back. Which brings me to another question: Why isn't she leaving footprints around Sunny, too?"

Cooper leaned back, stretching out his long legs and crossing them at the ankles. "What about Thibaut's wife? Nola said that his dead wife spoke to you just that once, right? She wanted him to know that she forgave him. If there were a rule book, that could fall under the heading of 'unfinished business.'"

"Yeah," Sarah said. "Except she didn't say anything about forgiveness. She just wanted him to know that she loved him."

"That's so heartbreakingly beautiful," I said.

"A love that transcends death," Cooper added.

"Like a Hallmark movie," we said in unison, making us both laugh.

Sarah stood. "Before I lose my appetite, I'm going to go back through the clientele book and look for clues that Uncle Bernie and his friends might have missed. I talked to Dad, and he and I agreed that of all the things Beau's dad hid away in the closet, that's the one item that isn't obviously a clue, you know? It's not a hair ribbon or tie clasp or film negative. So there has to be something hidden in the clientele book. I guess I'll just have to keep looking until I find it. Maybe we should talk about my hourly rate first."

"How about room and board?"

Before she could respond, Jolene called from the kitchen, "Sarah, sweetie? Could you please come slice lemons for the iced tea?"

My little sister let out a big sigh. "Do I have to do everything around here?" She began dragging her feet with each step until she reached the kitchen.

I stared after her, frowning. "Jolene never asks for help in the kitchen. That is strictly her domain."

Cooper draped his arm around me. "Maybe she wants us to have some quiet time together."

"Hmm," I muttered, not really listening, my gaze drifting to the telephone on the desk. I wasn't surprised that it was no longer in the drawer where I'd put it.

Cooper sat up. "What are you thinking?"

I faced him, silently staring until his last words sank in. "I'm thinking about unfinished business, and making sure final messages are passed along. I've discovered that a person doesn't have to be psychic to get a phone call from a dead person. Maybe it's easier to understand it if there's a psychic connection, but it's not impossible if there's not."

"So you're wondering why no one has called Sunny."

I nodded. "I think that's what's bothering me. I mean, Adele is around, and Sunny's adoptive parents were taken suddenly. You'd think at least one of them would have a final word for their beloved daughter, right? And this phone is very active."

"But, as Sarah said, there isn't a rule book. How spirits behave is probably as unpredictable as how they acted in life." Cooper stood and walked over to where the phone sat on the corner of the desk, the unplugged cord dangling over the side. He picked up the receiver and held it to his ear before hanging it up again. "No dial tone. No surprise there."

He had almost reached me before the phone rang, the sound glaringly loud in the quiet apartment, the second ring accompanied by a bark from Mardi. Sarah ran out of the kitchen. "Is that the phone?"

I was surprised that she knew what it was until I remembered that Melanie kept a landline phone in her bedroom and Sarah had undoubtedly heard it dozens of times. "It is, but I wouldn't . . ."

Ignoring me, Sarah answered the phone. Her head jerked in my direction, her eyes wide. I moved toward her, hearing the vile breathing on the other end of the line as every hair on my body tingled with electricity.

"Sarah?"

Her eyes rolled back in her head, two white marbles staring back at me. A dark, shimmering mist exploded from the receiver and my sister screamed, the sound like that of a trapped wild animal. The handset slipped to the floor as a hundred different voices shrieked from the phone in various bouts of agony.

Cooper quickly grabbed the receiver from the floor and slammed it into the cradle. All was silent except for the myriad echoing screams that wouldn't completely go away.

I gathered a sobbing Sarah into my arms and looked up as Jolene reappeared in the kitchen doorway.

"From all that caterwauling in here I'm guessing that either Alabama just lost to Auburn or you've dialed into a portal to hell. Either way, I hope it's given y'all an appetite, because I've got a mess of spaghetti that's enough to feed an army, and the only excuse I'm accepting for refusing to eat is if your jaw's wired shut or you've gone on ahead and died on me. There's no wallowing on my watch, and you're going to need your strength to tackle whatever on God's green earth that was." She jutted her chin in the direction of the phone. "So come on and get it before they call back."

CHAPTER 27

I pedaled down Broadway toward Audubon Park, watching out for carelessly flung-open doors of cars parked against the curb and for vehicles on the road swerving around potholes without their drivers looking first.

My utilitarian bike with the floral basket hooked on the handlebars looked out of place among the ten-speed racers ridden by the coeds zipping past me on their way to class, but when Sam had asked me if I'd like to borrow hers, I'd declined. I'd wanted the comfort of the familiar, regardless of how it might look to strangers. Or Michael. The hardest part had been getting the bike to my uptown apartment. Beau had happily volunteered to put it in his truck, but then had made me drive. All I could say about the journey from the Marigny to Broadway was that my hands still felt stiff from gripping the steering wheel, and there were at least three dog walkers and two joggers who would have nightmares for days.

I met Michael at the fountain near the St. Charles Avenue entrance. I was glad for the barrier of the bikes; otherwise he might have expected a kiss on the cheek or at least a hug. Regardless of any residual attraction I felt for him, I wanted to dodge any comparisons to

Judas and had promised myself to avoid physical contact with Michael. As if that might exonerate me later. I didn't examine my thoughts too closely; I was afraid they might not stand up to scrutiny. Instead, I pushed them to the back of my mind to consider later. I knew that was a Melanie thing to do, but there were some things, like preparing spreadsheets and organizing drawers, that were absorbed like a type of latent hereditary skill by living for any length of time with someone like my stepmother.

"Good morning," Michael said. The early sun made his dark hair gleam, and when he smiled, I could have sworn his teeth sparkled. "You look as beautiful as ever."

He had to have been lying, because Jolene had let me wear my ancient sweats with the holes in the knees and elbows and hadn't even insisted that I brush my hair before I pulled it back in a plaid Ashley Hall scrunchie I'd worn in high school. She'd allowed me to get as far as the landing before catching up to me with a tube of lipstick.

Knowing I could either waste time arguing with her or just give in right away—since either way, she'd win—I allowed her to put lipstick on my mouth. Despite what Michael might say, I knew a swath of bright pink on my lips wasn't enough to transform me.

"Thank you," I said, not bothering to hide my sarcasm.

He smiled even more brightly. "That's what I love about you, Nola. Your honesty. For the record, I do think you'd be beautiful bald and wearing a potato sack. But the lipstick is a nice touch." He lifted his foot onto a pedal. "You ready? Let's take it easy so we can talk."

I focused on my own foot placement while I grappled with the punch to my stomach at the word "honesty." Forcing a smile, I began pedaling, following him toward the bike path.

Despite the cooler temps and partly sunny sky, the park wasn't crowded, allowing us to pedal next to each other at a leisurely pace. "We're looking forward to your visit to the beach house. My aunt and uncle left today to make sure everything is ready."

"I'm looking forward to it, too. And I appreciate them allowing my entourage to come with me."

"I get it. Your sister is only here for a short time. Don't worry—she'll have fun. There's so much to do there. Or nothing at all. Lots of great reading nooks and hammocks. Too cool to water-ski, but the beach is nice to walk on. You know, I'm more than happy to drive you and Sarah myself. There really isn't a need for Jolene to come just to drive you."

"It's too late. I can't rescind the invitation, or it will hurt her feelings. Unless you want to do it."

"*Noooo.* I'd rather not get on her bad side. I've seen what she can do with a Barbie head." He grinned, and I found myself grinning back.

We rode around a group of oblivious pedestrians in the bike lane. I had a precarious moment swerving around fresh goose poop before returning to Michael's side.

"I like your basket," a little girl from the group called out. I chose to wave instead of being insulted that only a five-year-old might find my basket attractive.

"So," Michael began, "besides my aunt and uncle wanting to explain their side of the story about the whole misunderstanding . . ."

"Misunderstanding? You mean having you pose as a romantic interest and break into my house to find evidence that could be used against them in a kidnapping? That misunderstanding?"

"Not in so many words, but yes. Obviously, there's a lot that needs to be discussed about that . . . whole mess. They just want to be able to tell you their side and hopefully earn your understanding and forgiveness."

"And if they don't?"

He leaned back, sitting straight up in his bike seat. "At least they tried. And maybe I'll understand a little more about their motivations. I know you don't believe me, but I was in the dark as much as you were."

"Until you ran away to your house in the North Carolina mountains, where there wasn't any cell coverage. Very manly of you, by the way."

"I'm not proud of that." He slowed his bike and I did the same, following him as he dismounted and walked his bike across the grass to a park bench facing the lagoon. We leaned our bikes against one of the weeping willows and sat down on the bench, keeping more than a hand's width apart.

"I know it's hard for you to believe," he continued, "but maybe when you meet my aunt and uncle you'll understand how hard it has always been for me to go against them in any way. My parents abandoned Felicity and me when we were very young, but old enough to know that we'd been rejected. Our aunt and uncle raised us as if we were their own, giving us the love and attention that our parents seemed unable or unwilling to give. I owe them my loyalty. Which is why I have never questioned anything they've ever asked, knowing that every request comes from love and respect. And family."

He leaned his elbows on his legs, clasping his hands between them. "You need to understand that my aunt, Angelina, and my father, Marco, were raised in the same household that included their grandfather Antoine. As you can probably guess, he commanded complete allegiance and devotion from every family member and his employees."

"How? By fear and intimidation?" I thought of the dark shadow in my house and the unholy voices coming from the phone in my apartment. "Did he make people who crossed him disappear?"

Michael looked at me sharply. I met his gaze full on until he dropped his own to stare at his hands. "I don't know for sure. He died when I was eight years old. Old enough to understand that he demanded my respect, but not old enough to know what would happen to others if he felt disrespected."

"Your parents knew. Your father was his only grandson. That must have been a tough burden. But your aunt and uncle knew him and chose to stay."

"I didn't think you'd understand, but I had to try to explain."

Instead of arguing, I stared out at the pond as a snowy egret stood still, serenely watching its reflection in the water.

"By the way, congrats to Beau for snatching up that shotgun on Esplanade."

I knitted my brows together. "How did you know about that?"

He shrugged. "My uncle told me. He keeps an eye on real estate, and other things that might interest him, tidbits he might find useful."

"That he might 'find useful,'" I repeated.

He had the decency to look embarrassed. "I realize now how bad that sounds. But don't worry. The Sabatier Group isn't interested in that house. I don't know if you've been inside, but it's a complete dump. The missing man's sisters are acquaintances of my aunt's. That's how we knew it was being sold."

"Yeah, well, you definitely wouldn't want it after you learned how haunted it is." I wasn't sure why I'd added that. Maybe because of a defense mechanism, so his uncle wouldn't renew his interest.

He reached over and took my hand. "The reason I'm telling you all of this is to give you some insight on why we are the way we are. My uncle doesn't want to come across as a bully, but his business training came from Antoine Broussard."

I slid my hand from his. "Did that training include kidnapping?"

He frowned. "There's no proof of that. Any evidence that Mimi Ryan thought she had is either circumstantial or simply baseless. A blurry film negative of a black car with an indistinct license plate means nothing. My family agrees with you on this point: What happened to Sunny was horrendous. And we are beyond grateful that she has returned to you as a happy and well-adjusted young woman. We applaud Beau's efforts to find her kidnappers, but he should be looking elsewhere."

"Michael. Either you're lying or you've been brainwashed. Don't you remember standing in my house in the middle of the night and telling me about a phone conversation you overheard your uncle having with someone? He quoted Leviticus. 'Broken bone for broken bone, eye for eye, tooth for tooth.' That was when you realized that Sunny's kidnapping and Jeanne's murder were related. Remember?"

He was shaking his head. "No. I mean, I remember saying that. I asked him about it, and he was having a conversation with someone about Antoine. Apparently, that's something my great-grandfather would say. I misunderstood a lot, and I know how it must look to you, but it's the truth. It's why I want you to meet my aunt and uncle. They're good people, Nola. They wouldn't be involved in a kidnapping."

I stood, ready to walk away and forget the reason why I was with Michael in the first place. "Then why did your uncle want you to break into my house and steal anything in connection with Jeanne's murder? And don't tell me that your uncle has no idea what Mimi can do with a piece of evidence. She doesn't keep her psychometry a secret."

Michael stood to face me. "It's clear that you were raised by a stepmother who can communicate with the dead. And a father who writes bestselling true-crime books. It's no wonder that you see zebras when there are only horses. You have an incredible imagination. It's one of the things that first attracted me to you."

"You didn't answer my question about why your uncle wanted you to break into my house."

Michael rubbed his palms against his pants. "You'll be happy to know that I asked him after you found out that Jeanne was my great-aunt."

"When you ran away to North Carolina."

"Right. When I ran away. Because I was confused and needed answers that only my uncle could provide."

"And?" I prompted.

"He said he didn't know why, only that on his deathbed Antoine told Uncle Robert to always be on the lookout for anything that might be related to Jeanne's murder, because it might reflect badly on the family. Not because it would imply any guilt. He understood that after his death others might try to drag his reputation through the mud in retaliation for his success. Which is exactly what is happening now with the Ryans trying to dig up anything they can find."

"And your uncle did as he was told. Without question."

"It's how he was taught. Uncle Robert married my aunt when he was nineteen and started working for my great-grandfather and my grandfather Carl. Eventually, my dad, Marco, joined the business. Because Antoine only had his one surviving daughter, Marguerite, he groomed his son-in-law and grandson to take over one day. His way of doing business is ingrained in them. And after my parents bolted, and when my grandfather was dying from cancer, my uncle Robert took over as Antoine's heir apparent and right-hand man.

"He inherited the company when Antoine died and now it bears his name, although everyone knows that Antoine Broussard was behind all of it. It's why my uncle is respected in New Orleans. It's why he strictly adheres to Antoine's way of doing things."

I hadn't taken another step toward my bike, but I hadn't returned to the bench, either. "Even now that Antoine is dead, you and your uncle both do things without question because they're what your great-grandfather would have done."

"How do you think great dynasties are built, Nola? Look at the Kennedys. The Medicis. Even the British royal family. They survived because of loyalty and purpose."

"I think you need to find better comparisons, Michael, if you plan to use your argument elsewhere. It's hard to overlook illegal activities, poisoning, and beheading."

He gave an exasperated sigh. "I meant within reason, of course. I was just trying to make you understand what would make a person agree to do something without asking why. Do you see now?"

I wanted to walk away right then. Whether what Michael was telling me was true or not, and whether or not he and his uncle were simply carrying out the orders of a man who had died—supposedly—decades before, the Broussard-Hebert-Sabatier family weren't the kind of people who would want to hear the truth. Or face the consequences if it were publicly revealed. Mimi was right. Revealing it would be suicide. Or deeply and permanently regretted. I couldn't help but wonder if this was the choice Adele kept trying to tell Beau about, a mother's warning from beyond the grave to protect her son.

Yet the stubbornness in me rebelled against an entire family claiming innocence for a murder and kidnapping simply because they were doing what they'd been brought up to do. I could still adhere to the original plan and not tell Beau anything that I might discover. But that didn't mean I had to stop looking.

I moved back to the bench and sat down. I watched a blue heron sweep down from a tree on Bird Island in the middle of the lagoon, and skitter across the water's surface before rising again with a tiny fish flapping in its beak. "Yes. I do see. I'm not sure I agree with it, but I do get it." I forced myself to smile with understanding. Apparently Sunny wasn't the only one with acting skills.

He sat down again, this time close enough that our legs touched, and smiled with relief. "I knew you would. And I'm so glad we had this conversation before you met them. They truly are wonderful people, and I didn't want you going in thinking they were monsters."

I continued to smile. "Of course not."

Michael turned to face me. "There's another reason why I asked you here today."

I raised my eyebrows to show casual interest and to disguise the alarm bells ringing out in my head.

"It's about the fund-raiser party Mimi is throwing for the cathedral. In the past my aunt and uncle avoided many of the charities and committees that Mimi Ryan is involved with, due to the misunderstandings between the families. But Aunt Angelina wants to change that. She and Uncle Robert recently made a sizable donation to the fund for the renovation of the cathedral, so they should have received an invitation by now but they haven't. They were hoping that if I asked you, you might be able to talk with Mimi. They really are eager to extend an olive branch, and what better way than through a mutual love for the cathedral?"

"What better way?" I repeated, wondering how I'd be able to talk Mimi into sending an invitation to the people she suspected of attempting to ruin her life.

"So you'll talk to her?"

"Of course. I mean, your aunt and uncle are inviting me to spend the weekend at their beach house. That's certainly a good opening, right?"

"Right!" he said, standing, then reaching for my hands to pull me up. "I'm so relieved we're on the same page. I'm not sure if most people would be as sympathetic as you are. You're really one in a million." Without warning, he placed a hand on either side of my face and pulled me toward him. I just managed to turn my head in time for him to place a kiss on my cheek.

"We're just friends, remember?" I said, pulling back.

"Sorry. I got carried away. We *are* friends. But I'd be lying if I said I'm not hoping that you might give me the chance to become more. In time, of course."

I just smiled, unable to find a suitable response that didn't involve throwing up, then headed for our bikes. We finished riding around the oval path in tandem since more bicyclists had descended on the park, making the lanes crowded with both bikes and pedestrians. I felt relief not having to make any more conversation with Michael, his words still tumbling around my brain and refusing to settle into any conventional slots where I could make sense of them.

CHAPTER 28

After exiting the park, we crossed St. Charles Avenue and I pointed my bike toward Broadway to head home. "Do you want something to drink? My house is right here," he said, indicating the arched entranceway over Audubon Place.

As much as I was dying to see the inside of the Sabatiers' mansion on the famed street, I needed time to absorb everything I'd just heard and then find a way to convince Mimi to invite the Sabatiers to her party, if only to show Michael that I was acting in good faith.

I was just forming a plan in my head when I heard a familiar voice behind me.

"Nola!"

I turned to see Sunny wearing a yellow sweatshirt and pants in the same hue, her blond hair piled on top of her head in a high ponytail held in place with a yellow ribbon. It appeared she'd just come from beneath the arched gates of Audubon Place. "What are you doing here?" I asked.

"Good morning to you, too," she said with her customary wide smile. "I actually stopped by the apartment looking for you, and Jolene told me you were here. I figured it was such a beautiful day that I could take a walk in the park on the off chance I'd bump into you." She looked over my shoulder to where Michael stood with his bike.

"Oh," I said, realizing the awkwardness of the situation. "This is"—I turned to Michael, his face a shade paler than it had been—"Michael Hebert."

Sunny's smile faded. "I didn't . . ." She stopped and chewed on her bottom lip. Then, as suddenly as it had disappeared, her smile reappeared and she shot out her hand. "I'm Sunny Ryan."

Michael hesitated for a moment before taking her hand in his and shaking it. He didn't speak at first, just held her hand while avoiding looking into her eyes. "It's, um, nice to finally meet you."

She let her hand slip from his. Still smiling, she said, "Likewise. I figured we'd have to meet at some point, so I'm glad that's over."

"Me, too," he said, finally meeting her eyes. "I know there's a lot of ill will between our families for reasons you doubtless already know and that Nola can explain, but I'm hoping this is the beginning of our two families reconciling. Your grandfather and my great-grandfather were once friends. Hopefully, we can rekindle that connection. Once all the misunderstandings are explained."

I glanced over at Sunny to get her reaction to the word "misunderstandings," and I saw her nodding in comprehension. "I agree," she said. "Without any solid proof, I'm not going to point fingers at anyone. It would be a dream come true for all of us to put that unpleasantness behind us."

Michael smiled. "It's reassuring to hear you say that. Nola and I were just discussing the same thing. As a matter of fact, I was soliciting her help in asking Mimi to invite my aunt and uncle to her upcoming fund-raiser. They haven't received their invitations, so now that I know we're on the same page, maybe you can expedite their request."

"Absolutely." Sunny clasped her hands in front of her. "I can't think of a better way to bring our families together. Don't you agree, Nola?"

She turned to me, her face open and honest. "Sure," I said, not convinced at all. "Mimi loves her grandchildren more than anything. I'm sure if you and Beau both asked, she'd agree."

"Yay." Sunny clapped lightly. "It's about time we moved on, don't you think? Without any real evidence and with only conjecture about wrongdoing, I don't see why our families can't be friends again."

Michael nodded. "That's exactly what Nola and I have been talking about. And I'm excited that she'll be meeting my aunt and uncle this weekend to see how very kind and wonderful they are."

Sunny laughed; it was high-pitched, like a young girl's giggle. "Like a kind of ambassador, since Nola's not related to either family. It's perfect!"

"Right. Perfect," I repeated. I stepped back to avoid a good-bye hug or kiss from Michael. "I've got to get back—lots of work to do so I can be gone all weekend."

"And you gave Jolene the address?"

"Yes. And we know to use Google Maps instead of Waze so we don't end up in the Gulf."

Michael laughed. "Yep. Pass Christian is only a little more than an hour from here, so if you leave by ten you'll be there by lunch. Aunt Angelina is a great cook and loves to entertain, so you don't want to miss a meal."

"We're looking forward to it. I'll text you with our ETA when we leave."

We said our good-byes, and I watched as he got back on his bike and rode through the entrance to Audubon Place, waving to the guard.

"He's so hot," Sunny said as we walked away, with me pushing my bike. "It's obvious that he's really into you, but if that doesn't work out, just let me know."

I peered closely at her. "Is this your way to keep your friends close and your enemies closer?"

Sunny looked at me with genuine surprise. "I really don't consider Michael and his family enemies." She stopped in the middle of the sidewalk, causing me to stop, too. "There are so many open questions and so little proof that I'm seriously finding it hard to believe that this whole thing has gone on as long as it has. I mean, think about it, Nola. Why would a family with their kind of wealth and position steal a child for an illegal adoption?"

"You don't watch a lot of true-crime shows, do you? Otherwise you'd know that there are motives other than money for kidnapping. Like revenge. It wasn't a coincidence that you were taken from your family at the same time Charles threatened Antoine with exposing the truth about his daughter's death. Sounds very much like an eye for an eye, which—interesting fact—was one of Antoine's mottoes."

"Have you considered that the Ryans might have it wrong? That it really is a coincidence?"

"There are no such things as—"

She cut me off. "I know. And I would usually agree. But the more I think about it, the more ridiculous it seems that a man as rich and powerful as Antoine Broussard would wait so long before exacting his revenge. It doesn't make sense. Especially since the entire scenario is based on the supposed witness account of Antoine killing his own daughter that Mimi says a *door* told her. As much as I love Mimi, the whole account and connections seem more than improbable."

"Then why had Antoine been looking for the door and any other evidence that might be related to Jeanne's murder if he didn't know the truth?"

"But that's just it, don't you see? First Mimi's best friend is murdered, and then four decades later her granddaughter is abducted. The trauma of it all probably messed with her brain a little bit. That happens a lot in cases like this. It's the brain's way of making sense of a difficult situation."

"So what you're saying is that Mimi made it all up. To try to explain two tragedies four decades apart."

Sunny gave me a sympathetic smile and even reached out to touch my arm. "We both know and love Mimi, and it's hard to reconcile any sort of mental confusion with someone who is otherwise so strong and smart. But it happens."

We started walking again. "Have you ever seen Mimi read an object?"

"A couple of times. At the shop. Why?"

"What did you think?"

She shrugged narrow shoulders. "Well, if I were desperate and needed to believe that someone could channel my loved one's last moments by simply touching an object, I would definitely see the random observations as more specific than they actually are. Like fortune tellers. They make a guess and wait for the reaction before making the next guess."

"Are you saying that Mimi is a liar?"

"Not at all," Sunny said, looking insulted. "I'm just saying that if she believes in what she's doing, and the person receiving the reading believes, it's a match made in fantasy heaven. And what harm is done if Mimi can offer some kind of peace? I mean, even Beau doesn't believe it's real. I was listening to his archived podcasts the other day and I heard the one about psychometry. He debunked it right there on his show."

Sunny stopped walking and I looked around, surprised that we'd already reached my apartment. I faced her again. "But how do you explain your kidnapping?"

"Well, I think it was simply a crime of convenience. Someone was driving by the house and spotted me alone in the driveway and saw an opportunity."

"But it was a crime against you and your family. Don't you want whoever was responsible punished?"

"Why? It was so long ago. I just want to live my life now. To move forward and not be forced to recall any of the awfulness that happened so long ago that I don't even remember it. All I know is that I was raised by a loving mother and father and given a wonderful life. And now I have my real family back and I just want to be left alone to be a family again."

I shook my head, feeling momentarily suspended, undecided as to which side of the fence I should fall on. "Unfortunately, I understand your position. But I also understand Beau's. And even Mimi's, which seems to be firmly planted between the two." I blinked, trying to clear my head. "I'm going to spend the weekend with the Sabatiers and get to know them, and you will ask Mimi to invite them to her fund-raiser. Beyond that, I don't have a clue. I hope Sam does, because I'm fresh out of ideas."

Sunny helped me carry my bike through the door and lean it against the wall at the bottom of the stairs. "And don't forget, if you discover anything—which I doubt you will—it needs to be shared with Sam and me and not Beau. Just make sure you practice first in a mirror before you lie to him. You have a pretty glaring 'tell' when you lie. Most people probably wouldn't notice. But Beau would. He notices everything about you."

I narrowed my eyes. "What do you mean?"

She stared at me with the look Melanie gave JJ when he told her he'd already brushed his teeth.

Ignoring it, I said, "I wasn't aware that I was a habitual liar."

"You're not. But even when you're just skirting around the truth, I know."

Crossing my arms, I said, "Okay. What's my 'tell'?"

"You put your fingers on your throat. To others it looks like you're thinking, but I've learned that you're thinking of a more palatable way to phrase something. Like the other day when we were all at your house and Thibaut asked if you'd minded that he'd finished fixing the plaster in the upstairs bedrooms and you said no."

My eyes widened. "Oh. Wow. That's amazing."

She grinned. "Thank you. Because I was a backstage costume person throughout my high school career, I learned a lot about acting just by watching. Like I've said, I'm a quick study."

"Impressive," I said, heading up the stairs. I paused halfway up, remembering something. "You said you were looking for me—was there anything you needed?"

"Yeah. Two things, actually. Sarah mentioned that she was going through the clientele book again. Now, personally, I think nothing's turned up yet because there isn't anything there. But until we start working on the Esplanade house, I have some free time, so I wanted to offer my help, even if it's just to disprove the theory that my dad hid all those items in your house. I highly doubt that they hold some clue to either mystery, but I'm happy to look."

I continued up the stairs, Sunny right behind me. "All right," I said. "Sarah's pretty possessive, so I'm not sure if she's ready to relinquish it yet, but you're welcome to ask. What's the second thing?"

"I'm missing a purple hair ribbon, and I was wondering if you'd seen it. I think I lost it when your parents were visiting and you were showing them your house. It's not valuable or anything—it's just that it perfectly matches a cute sweaterdress I bought and I'm not sure if I could find another."

"Oh, yeah. I picked it up and shoved it in my pocket. I—" I made the mistake of opening the door at the top of the stairs and was immediately attacked by a gray and white ball of fur carrying a stuffed Eeyore in his mouth. He quickly dropped the toy to assault my face with a pink tongue.

Jolene came out of her bedroom, dressed for work, the familiar scent of perfume and hair spray wafting around her. Seeing Eeyore, she said, "I was looking for that all morning and finally found it under Nola's bed—along with all the dirty laundry she hides there. Mardi does love that toy, Sunny, but I swear, I spend half my days looking for it." She looked at her watch and sighed. "And now I've got to go tell Beau I'm late because I couldn't find Mardi's ass."

Jolene said good-bye and stepped past us, closing the door behind her. Sunny looked at me with her laughing blue eyes. "She does know what she's saying, right?"

I shrugged. "Who knows? I've tried to tell her, but it didn't stick."

With one last scratch behind Mardi's ears, Sunny stood. "I'll go find Sarah and see if she wants any help."

"Good luck," I said from my prone position, where Mardi had trapped me and was now butting my hand so that I'd pet him.

I eventually stood and went to my bedroom, then knelt next to my bed so I could pull out the jeans I'd been wearing all week that might need washing. I found them beneath a long-sleeved shirt and sweater and turned out all the pockets. Frowning, I stared down at the cotton pocket linings that now resembled protruding tongues. I took their rudeness personally, sitting back on my heels to think.

My legs had gone numb from sitting in that position by the time I recalled giving the ribbon to Uncle Bernie, along with the yellow one Cooper and I had found in the yard. I wasn't old enough for memory-loss issues, and I chalked my lapse up to the fact that I had had an extremely busy week and it was a miracle I remembered my own name.

I shoved the jeans back under the bed and stood to go tell Sunny that I didn't have the purple ribbon. I'd made it to my door when my phone buzzed. I smiled when I saw that the text was from my dad. Wherever he was in the world, and even if he was on deadline, he called at least once a week. He said it was to hear my voice, but I had a feeling that he knew I needed to hear his just as much.

Good time to talk?

Like Melanie, Jack preferred to use the phone to talk instead of texting. But unlike my stepmother, he would actually text first to make sure it was a good time for me to chat instead of just calling out of the blue. He also was a proficient texter and could actually make it through an entire sentence with just one or two glaring typos.

I sent a thumbs-up emoji followed by Ive got work but have 10 mins? Only takes 5 to get ready.

I laughed out loud at his response, and not just because of the content. Dont let jolene hear you say tit out loud.

I returned to my bed and flopped down on top of it before selecting my dad's number in my favorites list. By the time I hung up, I'd forgotten all about the ribbon, and Uncle Bernie, and the fact that everyone who evaded the truth, including me, had a tell.

CHAPTER 29

Sarah and I watched as Jaxson struggled down the narrow stairs with Jolene's two large suitcases and a garment bag. Jolene walked in front of him carrying a smaller case that she clutched to her chest possessively, not trusting anyone else to touch it.

"Is that jewelry?" Sarah asked.

"Even more valuable, sweetie. It's my makeup and hair products."

Sarah glanced at me to see if she should laugh, and I shook my head.

Jaxson had volunteered—without coercion, supposedly—to dog-sit Mardi and keep an eye on the apartment while we were gone. Jolene had put fresh sheets on her bed and dragged Mardi's pallet onto the floor in her room even though Jaxson had insisted he'd just sleep on the couch since it was only one night. Carly was at a friend's bachelorette weekend in Bermuda, so he was free to binge-watch whatever he wanted on TV and eat the refrigeratorful of meals and snacks that Jolene had made ahead of time.

Jolene popped open Bubba's massive trunk to allow Jaxson to place her suitcases inside. "I thought you were just going for two days," Jaxson said with a straight face. "Not a three-week cruise."

"A girl has to be prepared for all weather—you know how unpredictable it can be on the coast this time of year. And I never know what kind of swimsuit to bring, depending on what sort of activities I will be participating in and if it's warm enough. Plus, if mealtimes are formal or casual or both, I need to make sure I'm prepared."

"Of course." Jaxson reached for the two small duffel bags Sarah and I carried, and he gently tucked them in between Jolene's baggage.

"Where's the rest of your things?" Jolene asked.

"It's only one night," I said.

"I really hate to say this again, but bless your heart, Nola. And Sarah? Well, I'm here to help." She looked us up and down, stopping at Sarah's sneakers. "What size shoe do you wear?"

"A six. Sometimes a six and a half."

"That should work. And I love your sweater and skirt."

"Thanks. My mom bought me the whole outfit so I'd have something to wear in New Orleans besides my school uniform."

"I figured your mama had something to do with it." Jolene smiled until she turned to me, taking in my fleece jacket thrown over a white long-sleeved T-shirt.

"They're clean," I pointed out. "And I'm wearing the pants you made me buy when we went shopping. Besides, I don't need to impress anyone."

"Remember, Nola. We don't dress nicely to impress people. We try to look good on the outside so we feel good on the inside. It's about respecting others and yourself so that others see the most confident and dignified you that you can be. Right now, you're dressed like you're going to a dogfight. In the dark. And those Birkenstocks should be thrown on a bonfire. Wherever did you get those?"

"Our family friend Dr. Wallen-Arasi gave them to me as a grad school graduation gift. She said they would be like walking in her shoes—literally. And they're super comfortable. Really, Jolene—they're fine. Besides, I don't have time to change. We're already running late."

"Nola Trenholm," she said. "Have I taught you nothing? As I've said before—it is always better to arrive late than ugly. Now, march yourself upstairs and let's rethink your outfit. And I'll grab the tin of brownies I made to take with us while we're at it. I'm giving them to Sarah to hold. Otherwise they'll be mostly gone by the time we get there."

She gave me a warning look before taking my elbow in a surprisingly strong grip and leading me up the stairs.

We pulled out of the driveway a good forty-five minutes later than planned, with Jaxson holding up Mardi and waving his paw while Jolene reminded Jaxson where she kept the dog's wardrobe so he'd be comfortable with any weather changes.

As promised, I texted our ETA to Michael, receiving a quick Can't wait! in response. I hadn't even put down my phone before another text binged. I didn't recognize the number other than the 504 New Orleans area code.

Champagne is chilling! followed by an emoji of two champagne flutes and a bottle.

Another text from the same number appeared right below the first. This is Angelina btw followed by a smiley face emoji.

"Doesn't she know that you don't drink?"

I turned to see my sister leaning over the front seat, reading my texts. "Sarah—put your seat belt on!"

"It is. It's only a lap belt. Just chill, Nola. I can tighten it. But then you have to answer my question."

"Actually, I don't—"

"They must not," Jolene interrupted. "But they know you're coming, so I'm sure they have lots of tea and lemonade and Co-cola. I also packed some sparkling vitamin water that looks like champagne just in case Nola wants to get fancy."

"As long as I can wear my Birkenstocks. I put them in my backpack when you weren't looking."

"I know. That's why I took them out and replaced them with a cute pair of ankle boots that will look darling on you." She gave me a warm smile that made it impossible to be angry with her.

Instead of arguing over what staticky station to play on the car's AM radio, I suggested using my phone to listen to a recent episode of Beau and Sam's podcast. Sarah objected at first, until I promised her that the podcast was meant to be more informative than scary. With the promise that we'd turn it off if she felt frightened, we began listening. "You might even find it more interesting since you've met the cohosts. I think you'll enjoy their dynamics—very much good cop / bad cop."

At the mention of Sam and Beau, Jolene slid a glance toward me, which I chose to ignore, and I would never have admitted that for the first ten minutes I couldn't focus on the subject being discussed, as I was too tuned in to how natural their repartee was, and how well versed they were in each other's opinions and feelings.

But then the term "shadow people" caught my attention, drawing me into what Sam was saying. *The Choctaw called them "soul eaters," but every civilization since the beginning of time has had some mention of these dark beings, referring to them as ghosts or a collection of negative energy.*

Or as I like to call them, Beau said, *figments of active imaginations where people are in a dark room and see a coat hanging on the back of a door, or a pile of blankets on a bed, and think it's some paranormal being.*

"Do you hear that?" Sarah asked, her voice tight.

I turned to look at her, pressing herself against the backseat, her eyes wide. "Hear what?" I asked.

"The whispering on the radio. In the background."

I raised the volume on my phone and held it up between Jolene and me and listened closely. Beau was still speaking. *And then a so-called psychic will be called in to get rid of this supposed dark energy, charge a small fortune for removing the coat or pile of blankets, and the poor guy really thinks the psychic has done something. Just another example of . . .*

Sarah slapped her hands over her ears, and I lowered the volume. "What are you hearing?" I asked.

"It sounds like a crowd of people speaking all at the same time, but I can't understand what they're saying. But I don't think it's . . . nice. I think they're talking about us."

Memories of the phone call with the strange screaming and the unsettling photo of the shadow figure in the closet and the horrifying moments I'd spent trapped inside shook me with tremors. I hit Stop on my iPhone, silencing Sam and Beau and whatever it was that Sarah had heard.

"Let's play I spy," Jolene suggested.

I figured it was better than listening to my teeth chatter or traumatizing Sarah, so I agreed. I caught sight of the side-view mirror, with my sister's pale reflection, and said, "I spy with my little eye something that begins with M."

"Mascara!" Jolene called out.

"How can you see mascara?" I asked. "You're the only one wearing any."

"Well, that's a problem that can be fixed. I've got a tube in my purse right there at your feet, so go ahead and help yourself."

"In a moving car? I'll poke my eye out."

Jolene sighed. "We can pull over before we get there and I can fix that. And you need some color on your lips, too."

I looked back at Sarah, expecting to see her making a face at me, but instead she was staring out her window, lost in her own thoughts.

"You okay, Sarah-belle?" I said, using the name I'd called her when she was a toddler because even as a baby she'd been so ladylike, never putting her fingers into food and always sitting straight backed in her high chair. She'd been the complete opposite of JJ, who considered building blocks projectiles, and whatever was on his plate wall decoration.

She turned her head, her brows knitted. "Is there anything in the house that I should . . . worry about?"

"There shouldn't be," I said. "From what Michael told me, Antoine Broussard's father bought the four and a half Gulf-front acres back in the early nineteen hundreds and built a small beach cottage. The good news—for you, anyway—is that Katrina completely destroyed the house, so anything of that original house, and any connection to Antoine, is long gone. That's why I thought it would be okay to bring you."

She offered me a slight smile. "So what's there now?"

"I looked it up online, and let's just say that the new house would definitely not be considered a cottage in today's terms. It was built in 2008 by Robert and Angelina, and the architecture has old-plantation-house throwbacks. Michael says that he and his sister, Felicity, spent very happy summers there growing up, so there should be lots of good vibes. Even though Felicity never returned to New Orleans permanently after she was sent up north to boarding school, she'd go to the beach house during school breaks and holidays."

Sarah continued to frown. "Did they put anything from the old house in the new one?"

I felt a tingle on the back of my neck. "I don't think so. Hurricane Katrina washed most of Pass Christian and other Gulf Coast towns completely off the map, so I don't think there would have been anything left. Why?"

She sent me one of her "duh" looks. "For the same reason Mom and I avoid museums and antiques shops. And why Mimi has a roomful of personal effects from crime scenes. Residual energy."

"Well, then. Like Michael said, the house is new, and has lots of happy family memories. You just need to sit back and relax."

"While you dig for dirt," Sarah added.

"Basically."

"And what's my role?" Jolene asked.

"I need you to be a distraction so they won't notice what I'm up to."

She wrinkled her nose. "Should I have brought my twirling baton and karaoke machine?"

I grinned. "No. Just be yourself."

CHAPTER 30

As we drove down Highway 90, the scars of Katrina were still visible all these years later in the new roofs, porches, and entire sections of older homes alongside new construction, and in the younger trees that dotted the median where Jolene said hundred-year-old oaks had once stood. For an old-house hugger, it hurt to see the evidence of what Mother Nature could do to human lives and all the history contained in old buildings. It was also reassuring to see evidence of resilience in a town rebuilding itself from utter devastation.

As we pulled into the circular driveway, I recognized the three-story Greek Revival–style house I'd seen online. Brick pavers led to the white-columned second-story main entrance—a wise choice in a flood-prone area—with wide white stairs leading to the massive double doors on the covered porch. Three dormers sat in perfect symmetry on the hipped roof, a round cupola crowning the house at its pinnacle. The first-floor porch was held up by sturdy brick columns and furnished with a wrought iron table and chairs and an upholstered bed swing suspended from ropes and swinging in the breeze as an advertisement for the perfect location for an afternoon nap.

The front door opened as we climbed out of the car, and Michael appeared at the top of the steps. He ran down to greet us as a middle-aged couple, presumably his aunt and uncle, walked out onto the porch and waved.

"Perfect timing!" he said. "I just mixed the mimosas, including two virgin ones so no one is left out."

"Thank you," I said, staying far enough away that he wouldn't greet me with a hug.

Jolene unlocked the trunk and Michael looked inside, doing his best to hide his surprise at how much we'd brought. "We have an elevator on the first floor, so I'll bring these in. Y'all go on ahead upstairs. My aunt and uncle are excited to meet you."

He looked dubiously into the trunk. "Does all this go inside?"

Jolene and Michael greeted each other with neutral smiles, as if acknowledging an unspoken truce. Jolene moved to stand next to him. She leaned over and unzipped one of the two large Vera Bradley bags she'd thrown in at the last minute "just in case," and she pulled out a pair of roller skates and a set of extra-large heat rollers. She hesitated a moment, then zipped the bag closed, but not before I'd seen the Barbie head.

"I never know what to bring," she said. "So I just bring everything."

I smothered a smile as Michael gathered up as much of the baggage as he could. "I'll make two trips. See you upstairs."

Jolene, Sarah, and I headed toward the steps. "Everything good?" I asked Sarah.

"So far. It's a pretty house, and I like that it's so near the water."

"It's a bit like tempting fate, but I get it."

"Just like living in Charleston," she said. "I guess it's the price to pay for living in paradise."

Jolene put her arm around Sarah's shoulders. "And here I was thinking Nola was the smart sister."

We were still laughing—and panting from the long climb—when we reached the couple waiting for us at the top. A petite and very attractive dark-haired woman, who shared more than a passing resemblance with Michael, stepped forward and embraced me warmly.

"I'm Angelina Sabatier, and you must be Nola. We've heard so much about you, I feel as if I already know you."

"Likewise," I said, keeping my voice even. I was in uncertain territory here, and I needed not only to be on the alert but also to try to be fair-minded. It was the only way to ferret out the truth. Yet as I looked into the friendly and warm face of Angelina Sabatier, it seemed ridiculous that I had people waiting by their phones for an SOS from me.

She turned to the tall, slender man beside her. His salt-and-pepper hair was cut military short, and his hazel eyes smiled with the rest of his face as he offered his hand in greeting. He didn't seem nervous, or evil, or anything other than like a family man hosting a weekend house party. Or maybe Sunny wasn't the only actor. "It is such a pleasure to finally meet you. We are so pleased that you all could spend part of your weekend with us."

I introduced them both to Jolene and Sarah, then followed them inside. As expected, the house was expansive, with towering ceilings and elegant furnishings. I didn't have time to inspect anything closely as we were led through the house onto an enormous screened-in porch that covered the entire rear portion of the second story. A table had been set with six place settings in the russet shades of autumn leaves, along with a stunning centerpiece of fall vegetables and pinecones. Despite it being midday, candles in small hurricane lamps lined the center of the table. Four tall heat lamps encircled the table, and an outdoor fireplace blazed beneath a wooden block mantel.

"I was hoping the weather would be a little more cooperative for waterskiing, but I'm afraid it's too chilly," Angelina said.

"No worries. There is still plenty to do, including swimming in the pool, since it's heated," Robert said as he pushed in my chair before moving to Jolene's. "Or hanging out in the basement, where there is a theater, a popcorn machine, and just about every game ever invented. We just want everyone to relax and have a good time while we all get to know each other."

As Michael began pouring mimosas, Angelina picked up a silver pitcher and began filling my and Sarah's glasses. "It's made with Perrier instead of champagne," she said. "After Mardi Gras each year, I can't stand the taste of alcohol for at least a month, so I'm an expert on all sorts of mocktails. And sugar-free, carb-free—"

"And taste-free," Robert added with a laugh.

"—foods," Angelina finished with a grin. "I tell myself each year that I'm not going to go overboard, but then there's all the parties and festivities, and I can't seem to help myself. That's what Carnival season's all about, isn't it? Indulgence before penance." Her face became serious. "It's actually a lot like life."

There was an awkward silence before Michael said, "I'll help you bring out the food." He headed inside through the French doors, with his aunt following behind.

We had an amazing brunch of biscuit and pancetta casserole, French toast with praline syrup, and deviled eggs, followed by ciambella Romagnola-Italian breakfast cake, which, despite protestations from Angelina that it was incredibly easy to make, I told her was the best thing I'd ever tasted. Even Jolene agreed. While I was wishing that I had worn my much stretchier jeans instead of the wool pants, Jolene cornered Angelina to discuss recipes, and Sarah asked Michael what sorts of classic arcade games might be in the basement and how good he was on each of them. Robert asked me about my job and what projects I was working on, and we commiserated about the constant battle against the termites that thrived in New Orleans.

It felt odd to be discussing such mundane subjects with someone I'd always equated with evil. I had to remind myself that Robert Sabatier had married into the Broussard family and that his genetic makeup was not shared with Antoine Broussard. That still left a lot of questions, but I couldn't believe that Robert would do something like mastermind the kidnapping of a small child.

The whirring of cicadas from the oak trees that dotted the property sent a wave of homesickness through me. It's not that I never heard the croak and whine of the large insects in my new home, but the wall of sound from all the trees here reminded me too much of sitting in the garden on Tradd Street and listening to the insects' love songs in the side garden's ancient oak, from which a swing had hung since long before I had joined the family. Under its sheltering arms countless family photos had been taken, starting with photos of Jack and Melanie's wedding, the songs of the cicadas inseparable from my memory of long summer days and posing with my growing family.

The morning turned into afternoon, the languid conversations reminding me of my own family eating and talking around the dinner table, and I had to blink a few times to remind myself that I was with Michael and his aunt and uncle, the same people the Ryans suspected of either having knowledge of or being directly involved in the kidnapping of Sunny and the murder of Angelina's aunt Jeanne.

I got up to use the bathroom twice, and both times half-heartedly peeked into other rooms. I even opened a drawer in a hallway chest—it was empty. Despite my initial intentions, I knew any kind of snooping would yield nothing. And if I were caught, my embarrassment would be terminal.

When the mimosa pitchers ran empty, and I was sure the button on my pants would pop and take out someone's eye, Angelina stood and began clearing the table. "Nola, would you please help me put the food away? And Michael, if you would please show Jolene and Sarah the basement . . . Maybe choose a movie and make some popcorn? I'm looking at the clouds outside, and I think we're in for a storm."

He didn't protest, which made me think that this had all been prearranged and there was something Angelina needed to talk to me about. Alone. Robert excused himself to go check the score of the Kentucky–Ole Miss game, with a promise that he'd be back to help.

Angelina and I made small talk as we loaded the dishwasher and stored leftovers in matching Tupperware containers. Angelina asked me to sit down at the kitchen table to take a rest, and she gave me a tall glass of ice water while she wiped down the counter. We chatted about my parents and their visit, and about whether I planned to be home for the Christmas holidays, since it would be the first year I would be living on my own in another city.

I had begun to relax, believing that our visit really was about getting to know one another without the background of hints and allegations. I took a sip of my water as Angelina joined me at the table. She took a deep breath and smiled softly.

"It has been lovely meeting you, Nola. As well as Jolene and your sister. You are everything Michael told us—smart, beautiful, and funny. And you love your family. I feel like we're friends already, and I hope you aren't a stranger once we get back to New Orleans."

"Oh. I, um—thank you. And likewise." Robert still hadn't reappeared, and I was beginning to think that he wouldn't.

I took a long sip from my glass. "What year was the original house built on this property? I've always been fascinated by the history of buildings. Even those that no longer exist."

"Me, too," Angelina said. "Nineteen oh five. It survived several major storms, including Hurricane Camille in 1969, but was no match for Katrina. We were one of the fortunate families with good insurance and the funds to rebuild better and stronger." She stood to refill my glass, then joined me again at the table.

"Robert and I are very aware of our blessings, which is why we make it a priority to support not only many of the economic recovery organizations in the Gulf Coast and New Orleans but also many of the preservation groups throughout Mississippi and New Orleans. I'm sure you agree that our collective history is held inside older buildings and we cannot let them be destroyed. Once they are gone, they are gone forever."

Her words mimicked ones I had said many times over the years, making me like Angelina even more. Which might have been her intention. "So, was the original house built by Antoine and his wife, Paulette?"

Angelina turned her head slightly, as if the name alone had acted as a slap.

"Excuse me." Sarah had silently appeared, her footsteps cushioned by the carpeted stairs leading down to the first floor. "Michael is on a Mario Brothers streak and he sent me upstairs to get us something to drink."

Angelina stood and opened the refrigerator. "Is sweet tea all right?"

Sarah nodded vigorously, having inherited Melanie's love for all things sugary.

When she'd gone, Angelina sat down again, and part of me hoped she'd take up the conversation where we'd left it, because I didn't think I could bring it up again.

"So, where were we? Right. You were asking me about the original house. My grandmother Paulette Mouton was given the property as a wedding gift when she married my grandfather. A small cottage was here, and it stayed rather humble for the first years of their marriage. Gradually, it was added onto, and things like electricity and indoor plumbing were added as my grandfather's businesses became more successful."

"Your grandfather Antoine Broussard?"

Her face stilled, her previously animated eyes now shadowed and quiet. Almost in a whisper, she said, "We don't speak his name out loud."

I recalled the dark spirit that had trapped me in my upstairs closet, and I shivered. "Have you . . . felt his presence? Since his death?"

She gave a sideways glance as if to make sure no one was near, then gave one short nod. "It's best not to get his attention. It won't . . . end well. Trust me. My miscarriages . . ." She shook her head quickly. "Just trust me."

I searched her eyes, waiting for her to say more, but instead she smiled and folded her hands on the table like a judge banging a gavel to signal the close of a case. "So," she said, her bright demeanor returning, "while I have been wanting to meet you for a while now, I need to admit that we had ulterior motives for bringing you here."

I sat up straighter.

"I understand that you have become close with Mimi Ryan and her son, Beau."

"Yes." I kept my voice neutral.

She smiled softly, as if she understood. "And I'm sure with this recent unpleasantness involving Michael, you're probably needing some explanation."

I raised my eyebrows. "By 'recent unpleasantness,' are you referring to the break-ins and attempted robberies at both my house and my apartment that could have ended in serious injury?"

She kept her face and voice calm, her gaze never wavering. "I was sorry to hear about that. If I had known beforehand, I wouldn't have allowed that to happen."

"So you admit that you know the reasons for the break-ins."

She held up her hand, palm out. "Not at the time. Unfortunately, I was kept in the dark. Otherwise I would have suggested another way." Angelina grabbed my hand and held it tightly. "I need you to understand my family. It wasn't for Robert or Michael to question. Only to act to protect our family's reputation." Angelina leaned forward, her expression earnest. "Despite that, I can tell you with all honesty that we had nothing to do with Sunny's abduction. I will swear on a Bible to that."

I pulled my hand away from her grasp but kept my eyes on hers. "Then please explain where you were when Sunny was taken. Give me a reason to believe you."

Angelina closed her eyes and took a deep breath before opening them again. "I'd just suffered my third miscarriage in June 2005. Both Robert and I were devastated. My grandfather was getting older, his mental capacity failing, and his son-in-law—my father, Carl—had recently died from lung cancer. The entire family business empire rested on Robert's shoulders, leaving him little time to grieve or to be with me so we could lean on each other."

"I'm so sorry." I'd expected to hear some sort of confession or explanation during my visit. But I hadn't expected this. Or the way her words pinched my heart.

"As you can probably imagine," Angelina continued, "Robert and I were preoccupied at the time of Sunny Ryan's abduction. I was already at our house in the North Carolina mountains, where I'd fled to nurse my bruised soul, and Robert joined me right before Katrina hit."

"And your brother Marco and his wife and children—did they go with you?"

Angelina shook her head. "No. Marco was very stubborn, as was my sister-in-law. If only one of them had been, we would have been able to convince them to come with us. But not with both of them digging in their heels at the thought of evacuating. They had stayed in New Orleans through every storm and hurricane threat since they could remember. They lived in a house on Napoleon in the Garden District, which is one of the areas on the highest ground in the city. They had a generator and lots of bottled water on hand and had stocked up on supplies, so they were prepared to survive. Just not prepared for what they witnessed."

"I can't imagine." I shook my head slowly. "The footage and photos I've seen are horrifying enough. To have observed it firsthand would have been inconceivable."

"I believe that's why they suddenly found religion and devoted their lives to mission work. They had seen too much horror and destruction during Katrina, and they were trying to atone for the sin of having survived."

I sat in silence, trying to reconcile what I was hearing with what I had previously been told.

Angelina continued. "I need you to understand that Robert and I had nothing to do with Sunny Ryan's abduction. We were more preoccupied with saving our lives, those of both our family members and our tenants in the rental properties we owned around the city. That's what Robert spent his time doing in the days before the hurricane, trying to convince people to evacuate."

"Was he successful?"

"Only partly. But he had to try. I finally convinced him that he had done what he could and to get out of town while he still could. So he did, and joined me in North Carolina, where we watched in horror as the levees broke and the streets flooded. It was made worse because we had no communication with Marco and his family, so we had no idea if they had survived until two weeks later, when Robert finally returned to New Orleans and found them barricaded in their house."

"Why haven't you told this to Mimi and Beau Ryan?"

"Because I can't." Her darkening eyes met mine. "I've tried—multiple times. But each time they demand some kind of reckoning for what my grandfather may or may not have done. As I've already told you, it's better not to have anything to do with him or say his name. Nothing good can come of it."

"Then why are you telling me?"

"Because Michael has told me about your stepmother, Melanie Trenholm, and how you're familiar with the paranormal world. Maybe not how it all works, but at least enough to believe the unbelievable, and to accept things that others might not."

"Okay . . ." I said slowly.

"Robert and I have decided that it's long past time that we mend fences with the Ryans. Our families were quite close at one time, working toward the betterment of our shared city through various charities and community projects. Out of our sorrow for the tragedy of the Ryans' daughter's abduction and their suspicions about us, we slowly dropped out of all shared interests and resigned our board positions. It was incredibly sad, but we knew it was necessary. I understood what the loss of a child felt like, and I didn't want to add to their grief."

"So why now?"

She smiled brightly. "Because it's time. And because you've given us an in. You're the perfect bridge to facilitate a reconciliation."

I almost laughed, remembering Beau telling me practically the same thing. Except instead of reconciliation, his motivation had been revenge.

"And how do you propose I do that?"

"Since you've now met us and know what sort of people we are and have heard our story, we are hoping that you could share it with the Ryans. So that they will feel willing to publicly welcome us back into society."

Sitting back in my chair, I smiled smugly. "Yeah, Michael mentioned it. You want me to ask Mimi to invite you to the cathedral building fund-raiser."

I respected Angelina even more when she didn't feign surprise. "Yes. We've already made a sizable donation to the cathedral, so technically we should be on the list. But it's in two weeks, and we still haven't received our invitation. I'm not naïve enough to believe it's an oversight."

I thought of everything I'd seen and heard since my arrival, not the least how Robert had attempted to evacuate his tenants. These were not the type of people I imagined kidnapping children. Or willingly hiding evidence from a decades-old murder. Other family members, probably. But not them. Angelina and Robert were the kind of people to take in their nephew and niece and raise them as if they were their own. Assuming everything they'd told me was true, I had to agree that it was time. *If* it was true. I'd learned long ago not to assume anything.

"What would you like me to do?" I asked.

"I need you to tell Mimi and Beau what I've just told you. That Robert and I had nothing to do with Sunny's abduction. They won't listen to me, but maybe they'll listen to you. We have become social pariahs in New Orleans, and it's time for that to change."

"I understand. All I can say right now is that I will try. Although you should know that I will do my due diligence and check out all the facts as you've shared them with me."

"Of course. I wouldn't expect anything less." She pressed her hands together, the fingertips turning white. "Please excuse me for repeating myself, but it's imperative that you understand."

I raised my eyebrows.

"When you speak with Mimi and Beau, no one can say my grandfather's name out loud. He's very dangerous. Even now." She gave me a knowing look. "If I knew how to get him to go away permanently, I would. Right now, I've learned that it's best we don't disturb him. Or he might come back with a vengeance."

I bit my lip at the memory of my house going berserk when no one was inside, and of the ominous shadow figure lurking in the upstairs hallway. I pushed back my chair and stood. "I can only promise that I'll try."

Angelina surprised me by embracing me in a warm hug. "I understand. I really do. I know that you will try."

I pulled away and nodded. "Of course I will. Your grandfather doesn't need to know anything about it," I said, smiling at Angelina despite recalling being locked in a closet while a phrase in my head repeated itself nonstop: *It's too late.*

CHAPTER 31

I was sitting up in bed with a book, reading the same sentence over and over as I replayed in my head the events of the day. I had expected the Sabatiers to be monsters, and not the kind, doting aunt and uncle Michael had said they were. I had to keep reminding myself that Angelina and her brother Marco were the murdered Jeanne Broussard's niece and nephew, the children of Jeanne's only sister, Marguerite, and her husband, Carl Hebert. And that Angelina was the granddaughter of Antoine Broussard. I had to keep reminding myself of that fact, that Michael's beloved aunt was a blood relative of an evil man whose influence was still felt even years after his death.

Either Angelina and Robert were brilliant actors, or they were just desperate to cover up two crimes that might or might not have directly involved them. Or maybe none of the above. What if they were as innocent as they claimed? Was it even possible for generations of a family to turn a blind eye to the actions of a beloved patriarch? Or to be so loyal that any request would be indiscriminately followed?

I wanted to believe that I was a better person. That my answer to all the above would be an automatic no. But I couldn't forget all the times I had lied for my mother, Bonnie, to keep her out of jail and away from trouble. To let her believe that she was a better mother than she was. And I thought of Jack and Melanie, and everything they had done for me and given to me, and how much I loved them and JJ and Sarah. I considered what I would and would not do to protect them, and I could suddenly and very clearly see how my answer could be yes.

Yet none of that seemed to matter now. Of all those reasonings I had tossed around like salad in my head before my conversation with Angelina, I hadn't even considered the one thing that now appeared to be the most obvious. If Angelina's palpable anxiety at the mere mention of Antoine's name was real, everything else made sense. I knew firsthand why she was petrified of stirring her long-dead relative. So was I. Fear was a powerful motivator.

I started at a quick tapping on my door, my book sliding off the tall bed.

"Who is it?"

"It's Sarah. Can I come in?"

I slipped from the bed and unlocked the door before pulling it open. The light from my bedside lamp lit her pale face and wide eyes. "Are you all right?"

She stepped inside the room, closing the door behind her and relocking it. "Yes. I just . . ." Sarah looked past me to the giant bed. "Do you think there's room for both of us in your bed?"

"Since Mardi's not here, yes. Otherwise you'd have to duke it out with him."

She took a running leap for the bed and buried herself under the covers so only her face on the pillow was visible.

I crawled in beside her. "What's wrong?"

"I'm not sure. I couldn't get to sleep, so I was just thinking."

"Me, too." I hesitated, not wanting to hear that she and I had been thinking in tandem. "You first."

"Well, one thing is just a random observation. The other thing is a little more . . . dark."

"Let's start with the random observation. So I can prepare."

"Good plan. So, remember how at home Mom and Dad have about a million photos of you, me, and JJ all over the house, and Mrs. Houlihan complains because it makes it hard to dust?"

"Go on."

"Well, did you notice how there are hardly any family photos here? Just a few of Michael on a boat or water-skiing, and a couple of Mr. and Mrs. Hebert, but there's only one photo of their daughter, and it's from when she was really little."

There was a quiet knock on the door, and when Sarah remained under the covers without moving, I slid from the bed with a heavy sigh and went to open it.

Jolene quickly stepped into the bedroom. "Can I come in? That crying baby is keeping me awake."

"What baby?" I asked.

Sarah sat up. "I heard it, too!"

They both looked at me. "I didn't hear anything, and I've been awake the whole time."

"That happens sometimes," Sarah explained. "You don't have to be psychic to hear stuff."

"Then why didn't I hear it?"

Sarah shrugged as she settled back onto her pillow, and Jolene made herself comfortable on the pretty floral chaise longue near the bed. "If I understood how this worked, I'd be a millionaire. Just go with it. Because when you think you've figured out how something works one time, it will be different the next. Guaranteed."

Jolene pulled the blanket from the back of the chaise and wrapped it around her. "I'm not one to eavesdrop, but I couldn't help but hear what you were talking about before I knocked—about the family pictures. I noticed it, too. But I did see that in the one photo of Felicity she has a huge bow in her hair. And you know—"

"The bigger the bow, the more your mama loves you," Sarah and I finished for her.

"Y'all sure catch on fast. I'm very proud of you."

"Thanks," I said. "Assuming it's true, she's loved by her

mother—whether her biological mother or the woman who raised her. I'm guessing it's the latter. I don't think any woman who loved her daughter would voluntarily surrender her to be raised by another family member to pursue a calling. I mean, why not bring your children with you?"

"Who knows?" The covers moved as I felt Sarah shrug. "Adults are weird."

I thought for a moment. "This is their beach house, not their main house, so I wouldn't expect the number of family photos here that they probably have at their New Orleans home. And Felicity has lived out of state since she was first sent to boarding school, and now she lives and works in New York City. It would make sense that there are more photos of Michael than Felicity. He's also older than she is, so he's been around longer and had more opportunities to have his picture taken."

Sarah was silent for a moment. "Yeah, that makes sense. Just like how Mom and Dad have a million more pictures of you than me and JJ."

"As it should be," I said smugly. "Since I'm the favorite child."

She elbowed me under the covers, catching me in my rib cage.

"What was the other thing you wanted to tell me?"

"Did you notice when you were talking with Mrs. Sabatier about the people who built the house, Paulette and An—"

I pressed my hand over her mouth. "Don't say that name out loud, okay? Angelina told me it's how to summon him. And I can tell you that I've met him up close and personal and it's not an experience that I am interested in repeating. Ever."

Sarah nodded, and I lifted my hand. "What about it?"

"The cicadas stopped singing." The room became eerily silent as Jolene and I looked at each other and then back at Sarah. "Actually, now that I think of it, all of the sound stopped. No birds or crickets. Nothing. But the cicadas had been the loudest, so that's what I noticed the most."

"Well, then," I said. "It looks like we should watch what we say until we leave. And when we get back, too. At least until I can figure out how to get rid of him who shall not be named."

"I can help," Sarah said, her voice wobbling just a little.

I smoothed the hair off her forehead like I'd done when she was a little girl. "No. Not this time, anyway. When you're older and more experienced, maybe. But not now."

She smiled with relief. "I won't tell Mom, either."

"Smart girl," I said, scratching her behind the ear as if she were Porgy or Bess and making her squirm away from my hand. "I guess it runs in the family."

Jolene glanced at the bedside clock. "My carriage is about to turn into a pumpkin, so I'm going to bed to get my beauty sleep." She paused at the door. "If I hear the baby crying again, would it be all right if I brought my pillow and blanket and slept on your floor?"

"Of course. Just leave the Barbie head in your room, okay? That's the last thing I want to see when I open my eyes in the morning."

As we prepared to leave the next day, Michael found me sitting alone by the pool in the backyard, watching leaves and pine needles drift into the water. He sat on the lounger next to me, leaning his forearms on his knees. His olive skin was still tanned from the summer, his dark hair glossy, with sun-lightened strands.

"Have you enjoyed yourself?" he asked.

"Very much. I really like your aunt and uncle."

"Me, too. They're good people. I'm glad you could see that. I'm hoping you can convince Beau and Mimi."

"All I can do is tell them what I think and share your aunt's story. Then it's up to them."

He nodded, looking away toward the pool. "That's a start." When he turned back to me, his face was contemplative. "Do you think now that we—you and me, that is—could be friends?"

I couldn't help but recall the moment when I'd first discovered his betrayal and he'd ghosted me with no explanation. That came later, only after I'd confronted him. It wasn't a feeling that I ever wanted to experience again. Or remember.

"Maybe. After some more time has passed, I think."

He took a deep breath and expelled it slowly. "That's fair. And honestly, more than I expected."

I nodded. "We can never be more than friends." I said it with a conviction I didn't quite feel.

He tried to smile, but it faltered. "I understand. I wish that weren't the case, and I'm not going to lie and say that it doesn't hurt. But I understand."

He stood, then leaned down to kiss me gently on the cheek, leaving me alone to watch the leaves fall soundlessly into the still pool.

When we returned to our apartment in the early afternoon, Cooper was waiting on the doorstep with Mardi. I felt a reassuring warmth at seeing the two of them together, and it was unclear which one I was happier to see.

"Carly called Jaxson and said she was going to be staying a couple of extra days because the resort was so nice, and she asked Jaxson if he'd join her. He called me figuring since I was new in town I wouldn't have any plans, and he was right." Cooper grinned. "But I was happy to do it. Mardi and I have become good buddies, haven't we?" He held up his hand and I watched as Mardi high-fived him.

Mardi was dressed in a hunter green sweater—one of his best colors, according to Jolene, who had "done his colors"—and it made me smile to imagine Cooper dressing the dog to make us happy. Well, Jolene at least. I just went along with it.

Jolene hid her disappointment at Jaxson's absence by scooping up Mardi and covering him with kisses before grabbing a bag and heading upstairs. We had barely finished bringing in all of our luggage from the car when Sunny arrived. She said she'd been shopping on Magazine Street when she'd received my text that we were on our way back, and she'd decided to stop by and discuss anything new we might have discovered.

I was surprised to see her so soon, since even Sam had said that to give me a chance to breathe she'd wait until the following day. I hadn't heard from Beau at all, making me wonder if he might be with Sam and too busy to text. Not that it was any of my business.

Sunny plopped herself down on the sofa while Mardi dug Eeyore out from behind the end table and brought it to her. Bending down to scratch him behind the ear, she said, "I can't believe he doesn't object to Mambo's cat hair all over me. And I know I must be covered in dander, because Mambo is like my shadow. He even sleeps on my pillow."

"Probably because Mardi is an equal opportunity attention seeker. If you pet him or scratch him behind the ear, he'll love you forever," Jolene said. "Just be glad he doesn't seem to have any Mississippi leg hound in him. My uncle Virgil once had a dog that even a piece of furniture wasn't safe from him humping the varnish off. Once, he—"

"Thanks, Jolene," I said, cutting her off. "We get the picture."

She disappeared into the kitchen to "whip us up something tasty" for supper after getting a count of how many were eating. Cooper was a yes, but Sunny declined, saying she already had plans.

"I've been dying to hear how the weekend was! I can't believe I agreed to radio silence while you were in Mississippi. It was torture worrying about you all and dying of curiosity all at the same time."

Cooper and I joined her in the living room, sitting down in the mismatched chairs. "It wasn't what we expected at all," I said. "In a nutshell, Angelina and Robert claim they had nothing to do with your kidnapping and weren't even around when it happened. I'm going to ask Christopher to verify that, but if it's true . . ." I shrugged. "And I really liked them. They're very nice people and have deliberately kept a low profile over the years in deference to Mimi's and Beau's grief. They have even tried to reach out to Mimi over the years to tell their side of the story, but Mimi hasn't been interested in hearing it, which is why they're in a stalemate."

Jolene entered the room to place a creatively displayed charcuterie board on the coffee table. "I liked them, too. But nice people can be criminals, too. John Wayne Gacy was a clown for children's parties, remember."

"Thanks for that, Jolene," I called out to her departing back. Turning to Sunny and Cooper, I said, "I didn't get serial killer vibes from them at all."

"Well, that makes this easy," Sunny said, her excitement making her face glow. "No more need to hide stuff from Beau or try to dig up dirt on the Sabatiers. Do you want to tell Beau, or should I?"

"Hang on," Cooper said. "What about what Michael did to you, Nola? Did they plead innocent about that, too?"

"No, actually. They admitted to being responsible, which made me like them even more. But their reasoning—which I will discuss later, when I'm not so hungry and can explain better—made sense to me. Not that it makes it any less warped, but there you have it."

"So Michael's off the hook, too?" Cooper asked.

"Not quite. I'm not sure what he did to me is forgivable."

"I'm glad to hear you say that." He smiled, and I felt that warmth in my chest again.

"But we're done, right?" Sunny asked. "Chapter closed?"

Cooper was still looking at me. "Maybe not. I think there's something else that's bothering Nola."

I looked at him with appreciation. He'd always been accurate when reading me, one of the reasons why when we were together we never talked a lot. We didn't need to. "Yeah. Just a loose end, really. But it's there kinda like a hangnail, you know? It's not that big of a deal until you accidentally touch it."

"What is it?" Sunny asked, her elation somewhat diminished.

Sarah had emerged from her room, where she'd been repacking for the flight home that evening, and joined the conversation. "The crying baby, right?"

I nodded, then turned to Cooper. "I didn't hear it, but Sarah and Jolene did."

"I tried to find out where it was coming from, but every time I entered a room, the sound moved. And we were too far away from the next house for it to have been coming from there."

"Maybe it's from one of Mrs. Sabatier's miscarriages?" I asked.

Sarah screwed up her face, thinking. "It's possible, I guess. Except I'm pretty sure it was just one baby."

"It seems to me," Sunny said, "that the baby might be connected to the property and not the Sabatiers. Didn't you say they didn't own it until nineteen hundred and something? I'm sure other houses have stood there. It probably has nothing to do with this." She pulled out her phone. "I can call Beau now if you like."

"Hang on," I said. "I'd like to tell him myself. And we need to talk about the other problem, and how to get rid of it."

"Do you mean . . . ?"

"Don't," Sarah and I shouted together. "Angelina Sabatier said it's best not to say his name out loud."

"Why?"

Cooper surprised me by responding, "Because he might be listening. It's better not to summon a spirit unless you know what to do with it."

I smiled my thanks, happy to know that he remembered the idiosyncrasies of our time together in Charleston involving true crime and restless spirits. His presence felt like having the best parts of my growing-up years sitting in my living room.

"And Beau does know what to do with it," I said. "So let me talk with him first. I'm going to ask him to convince Mimi to invite the Sabatiers to the fund-raiser. I think you should do it together so it's two against one. She'll find it hard to say no. Meanwhile, I'll talk with Christopher about doing some digging. I've already texted Sam with an update. She said she's going to go to the chapel of Our Lady of Guadalupe and light a candle to ask for this feud to be over. She must be desperate, because she's not even Catholic."

Sunny nodded enthusiastically. "Sounds like a plan. And I can help Christopher. I've been shadowing him at the shop to learn about the antiques business, so I see him every day."

"Sure. Hopefully, if there's anything to find, we'll know before the party—good or bad."

"Which reminds me," Sarah said. "Sunny, did you bring back Jeanne's clientele book? It's not in my room, and I want to give it one last look before I leave. I realized that I didn't look at it upside down. I know that's a long shot, but I'm willing to try anything at this point."

"Oh. Right. I think it's still in my car. I haven't had time to look at it yet. If you want, I'll give it the upside-down look and let you know if I find anything."

Sarah stood. "That's all right. I'd like to do it myself. It runs in the family." She looked pointedly in my direction. "If you want to toss me your car key, I'll be happy to get it."

"Sarah?" Jolene called from the kitchen. "Supper's almost ready. Could you please come set the table?"

Before she could sigh heavily or roll her eyes, I stood. "I'll help."

"Whatever." She looked back at Sunny, who hadn't moved.

"My feet are killing me from shopping," Sunny said. "Let me just rest them for a bit, and I'll get the book before I leave—just remind me."

"Fine," Sarah said before heading toward the kitchen with the steps of a condemned person on the way to the gallows.

Sunny excused herself to use the bathroom, leaving Cooper and me momentarily alone.

"I don't think I can thank you enough for, well, everything. For staying with Mardi, for one thing. And just for . . ." I shrugged, unable to fill in the missing words.

"For knowing you well enough that you don't need to explain anything."

"Yeah," I said, smiling up at him. "I'm glad you're here."

"Me, too."

We were standing close enough to each other that I could feel his warm breath on my face and see a small scar on his chin that I hadn't noticed before. I touched it with my finger, the familiar feel of his skin warming my blood.

"This is new. What happened?"

His gaze moved from my lips to my eyes, the flicker of a shadow passing through it. He looked stricken, like a man searching for breath after being unexpectedly punched in the chest.

"Nola!" Sarah's voice bellowed from the kitchen. "The table won't set itself!"

Cooper stepped back as Sunny returned and plopped down on the sofa, Mardi jumping up on her lap. "You'd better go. I've seen Sarah when she's angry, and it's not pretty."

His attempt at levity didn't fool me, but I went along with it. "If you're referring to her spectacular tantrums, she has fortunately grown out of them. You've been gone a long time."

His smile disappeared completely. "Yeah. I know."

"Nola!"

"Coming." I didn't move.

"You go on. We'll have time to talk later."

I hesitated, then headed toward the kitchen, fighting the impulse to look back. If there was one thing I'd learned so far, it was that there was nothing to be gained by looking back; its only purpose was to make you stumble because you weren't looking ahead.

CHAPTER 32

On Monday morning I awoke to the sound of the attic stairs being pulled down from the ceiling outside my bedroom door. I sat up, my breath creating white puffs in front of my face. Mardi and Eeyore lay curled on top of my feet, the only warm spot on my body.

"Jolene?" I called out. I didn't get up because I didn't want to disturb the dog.

My door opened to reveal my roommate already dressed, with perfect hair and makeup and holding a long-handled lighter. "Sorry—I was trying to be quiet, but I have to relight the pilot. Dangblasted cold snap snuck up on us last night and the dagblamed heat's gone out."

I'd never heard Jolene curse before—if that's what you could call it—but because she was a true Southerner, it made sense that the cold would bring out her worst. "Shouldn't we call someone?"

She raised a delicate eyebrow. "Sugar, I can gut a deer and bait my own fishing hook, among other life skills every woman should have, according to my daddy. I do not need help with a pilot light except for someone to hold my high heels so I can climb the ladder. But don't worry—stay where you are. If you'll keep Mardi away from my shoes, I'll just leave them on the floor."

As she began her climb, I reached for the sweater I'd worn the day before—it was conveniently on the floor next to my bed—and slipped it over my head. In typical Southern fashion, a day of hard winter was following a perfectly balmy autumn day that would more than likely be followed by a spike in the mercury. And hurricane season wasn't even over yet.

The sweater helped slow down the shivering, but my teeth had begun to chatter as I picked up my phone to read my texts, tucking a corner of the blanket around Mardi as he continued snoring.

I felt a stab of disappointment reading the first text, from Cooper, letting me know that he had to fly to New York for work and would be gone the entire week. I'd wanted to have the conversation we'd been about to start when I'd asked him about the scar on his chin. He'd said we'd talk about it later, but it seemed later would have to wait. I also realized that I'd miss him, and that I was already looking forward to seeing him when he returned. I told myself it wasn't because he reminded me of the young and naïve girl I'd once been, and a life I'd taken for granted. The Cooper Ravenel I was just beginning to know again was different, too, in ways I couldn't yet explain but didn't make him any less appealing. I found myself looking forward to getting to know him again.

The second text was from Sarah, with three full lines of a crying-face emoji and the words "I miss you." I had enjoyed our time together as much as I thought she had, and my eyes stung as I saw her nickname on my text screen: *Smatchen*. It had been one of the vocabulary words I'd learned in high school, and as a typical older sister I had immediately assigned the name to Sarah, even though technically it wasn't true—at least not all the time. And when JJ got his first phone, his name in my contact list became *Cuisinier*, one of my French vocabulary words, so that he wouldn't feel left out.

Her next text made it clear that she'd been buttering me up with the first.

Sorry accidentally packed book will give bk at 🦃

I knew that she was referring to the clientele book with the same certainty that it hadn't been an accident.

My thumbs were poised to reply when something hit the attic floor above. "Son of a bee sting!" Jolene shouted.

I dropped my phone on the bed, gently slid Mardi and Eeyore off of my feet, then ran to the bottom of the attic stairs. "Is everything all right? Do you need me to do anything? Like call an ambulance?"

"Could you please hand me my phone? It's on the desk."

I did as she asked, noticing as I did that the princess phone was perched in its usual corner. I stood on the third rung to hand Jolene's phone to her, then quickly stepped back down. "Aren't there roaches up there?"

"I'm sure there are. I just don't show them any fear, so they leave me alone."

I wasn't convinced that was how it worked, but I was too cold to argue. After tossing around the question of which to do first, I headed to the bathroom intent on taking a long steaming-hot shower to help me thaw, and then having my first cup of coffee. By then Jolene would have fixed the problem and our heat would come back on.

I turned the hot water on full blast and let it run while I brushed my teeth and undressed. Then I stepped in without checking the temperature first, too frozen to care, and with happy anticipation of almost-scalding water.

The feeling of thousands of icicles pricking my skin had the same effect as a gunshot at the start of a race. In my haste to exit the icy shower, I managed to pull not only the shower curtain but also the rod down with me, bringing both Mardi and Jolene into the bathroom.

"Are you all right?" Jolene asked, tossing me my towel.

"Better than the shower rod, at least." I stood, wrapping the towel around me.

"What were you doing? I told you the pilot light was out."

"I know. That's why I wanted to take a shower, to warm up."

She stared at me for a long moment. "This apartment has gas for everything—including water. If the pilot light is out, then everything is out. Including the water heater. Did you not know that?"

My teeth were chattering too hard to speak, so I just shook my head.

"Well, bless your heart. It's cold enough to freeze the balls off a pool table, and here you are naked as a jaybird. You go on and put you some clothes on, and I'll get your coffee while we still have electricity."

She met me with a full cup of steaming coffee when I emerged from my room. Mardi was already dressed in a navy blue argyle sweater, his tolerant expression very similar to the one I wore when I allowed Jolene to do my makeup.

"So, the good news is that the gas company can come today. The bad news is that the time window is between nine o'clock this morning and six o'clock tonight, so I won't be able to drive you to Abita Springs for your fieldwork. I'm so sorry, but I'm thinking you'd like hot water for your next shower. Maybe Cooper can take you?"

"No—he's in New York for the week. I guess I'll take an Uber. Abita Springs isn't *that* far."

"It's too far to take an Uber, Nola. Call Beau. I know he'd be happy to help."

"Maybe I should ask Sam."

"Don't be silly," Jolene said, pressing a number on her phone. "I need to tell him that I'm going to be able to work from home today so that he's free to take you. I'll be killing two birds with one stone."

"Whatever," I said, sounding too much like Sarah. "At least he has a working heater in his truck."

Beau was already around the corner, at a property on State Street, so I was able to get out the door without a complete makeover and had to submit only to a hair brushing, as well as a blue cashmere sweater thrown over my head, before escaping the apartment.

"Your lips match your sweater," Beau said as he held the passenger door open.

"Th-th-th-thanks," I said, tossing into his truck my backpack and the enormous puffer coat Jolene had let me borrow, before sliding into the seat and reaching for the temperature controls.

As Beau slid behind the steering wheel, he said, "You know you're always welcome to stay at the house on Prytania. We've got plenty of room. Jolene, too, of course."

My teeth were clenched together, making it difficult to respond. "I'll keep that in mind. Hopefully, this can be fixed in a day and we won't have to." I knew that I would prefer to sleep in a snowsuit and covered with blankets than spend a single night in a room in the same house with Beau. We had tried it before, which had resulted in our first and only kiss. Something both of us never talked about and chose to pretend had never happened.

"Would you like your heated seat turned on?"

"Is the sky blue?" I replied, annoyed that I hadn't already thought to ask.

Beau pressed a button, and after a few minutes I began to have feeling in my lower extremities and backside again. I leaned forward and looked up through the windshield. "It's not supposed to rain, but I don't like the looks of those clouds. If it does rain, the roads will become sheets of ice. It's a good thing we're in a truck, right? Because we've got four-wheel drive." I was proud to spout off my newly acquired knowledge like I'd always known it.

He sent me a sidelong glance with a familiar expression.

"Why are you looking at me like Jolene does when she says 'Bless your heart'?"

"Believe me, I was thinking it. Four-wheel drive means nothing on ice unless I attach ice skates to my tires. And no, those don't exist," he added, saving me from asking the question and embarrassing myself. "If the roads are icy, here in Louisiana the best thing to do is find a safe spot and wait until the sun comes out and makes the ice melt."

I whipped out my phone and checked the forecast. "According to the weather app, there's a sixty percent chance of rain, but it's not supposed to start until three o'clock." I checked the time. "It's nine thirty now, Abita Springs is about an hour away, and I should be done with what I need to do in about three hours—four hours tops. That would put us driving back before two o'clock and home before it starts to rain. I think we can do it, don't you?"

Beau peered down at his dashboard. "It's thirty-three degrees now, which means the ground is already pretty cold. Does it get any warmer?"

I looked at my phone. "No. It's actually going to get colder—but not until after sunset, which is . . ." I scrolled down the screen. "At six fifteen tonight. But we should be home well before that."

We'd stopped at a traffic light before the on-ramp to Interstate 10. "We should," Beau said. "But I should probably ask how important it is that you do this today. It might be worth waiting until next week, when the temp will probably be in the seventies again."

"The fieldwork was supposed to have been done last week, but I asked my boss if it could wait until today since Sarah was here, and he agreed—as long as it was done no later than today."

"Well, then," he said as the light turned green and we headed up the on-ramp. "We're going to Abita Springs. I've got a full tank of gas, and a cooler full of snacks, and a big umbrella. Mimi taught me that the more prepared you are for an emergency, the lower the chances of anything happening, so we should be good."

We slid into the middle lane in what was noticeably light traffic considering it was still technically rush hour. I glanced in the back-seat, feeling reassured by seeing the giant Yeti cooler.

"I'm surprised that you didn't ask Michael or Cooper to drive you before you asked me," Beau said.

"I would have asked Cooper, but he's in New York all week. And I did consider asking Michael, but since I'd planned on calling you today to go over the weekend with the Sabatiers while Jolene drove, this kills two birds with one stone."

"Wow. I'm flattered. I guess I should be happy just to have been nominated." The half of his face I could see was grinning, so I didn't feel the need to apologize.

I'd been hoping that Sam would have filled him in, so I'd know where to start. "Have you had a chance to talk with Sunny?"

"Oh, yes. She was practically gushing over what you'd told her about Michael and his aunt and uncle, about how nice they were and how they could prove that they weren't involved with her abduction. She also wants me to go with her to Mimi to beg her to send fundraiser invitations to Angelina and Robert Sabatier as an act of goodwill. I told her I needed to talk with you first, because she sounds like she's been either hit on the head or brainwashed."

"I know. And if I hadn't met them myself, I'd be agreeing. But I did, and their story is believable, and so are they. I've asked Christopher to do some digging to make sure. I know that Mimi had asked him in the past to help find Sunny, so I thought he would be the right person to ask. Regardless, I think they should come to the party. So that you and Mimi can come to your own conclusions."

He shook his head slowly. "So, you're like the Trojan horse—letting the enemy inside our city gates?"

"I'm impressed you know your Virgil. And here I thought you were just a simple redneck. But no—I'm letting you and your family decide. It seems logical that if Sunny wants them there, they should be given a chance. I'm going to leave it up to you, though. You asked me to use Michael to gain access to his family, and I have. I think my job is done."

"Tell me more to convince me, because I'm now thinking that whatever they did to Sunny they did to you, too."

I rolled my eyes. "Whatever. But you also need to know that they're as afraid of Michael's great-grandfather as we are."

"What do you mean?" He looked at me long enough that someone in the adjacent lane honked at him for drifting.

"They don't mention him by name at all because they're afraid of summoning him."

Beau's face remained rigid. "Have they seen him?"

"Not that I know of, although Sarah and Jolene experienced a few freaky things that could have been caused by his presence. But that's something I've been wondering about." I adjusted myself in my seat so I could face him. "The spirit whose name we aren't going to mention has been felt in more than one location—at the Sabatiers' beach house and my cottage, and I'm pretty sure the negative energy that Sarah and I experienced at the cemetery was from him. I should probably already know this, but aren't ghosts supposed to be stuck in just one place? It seems unfair that they should be allowed to wander."

He looked at me with the hint of a smile. "Unfair? That's one way to describe it. Sort of like why some people can communicate with them and others can't. Or why some spirits can find enough energy to show themselves and others remain hidden except when someone like Melanie or me shows up."

"Exactly. So . . . why?"

"I don't know."

I frowned. "You don't know?"

"That's right. I have no idea. There are some things that will always be a mystery. Like, why do some guys believe that women can't understand sports and think that a beer pong championship in college belongs on a résumé? Or why do I think about you every time I see a shade of blue on something that matches your eyes?" He shrugged. "There are just some things I can't explain. Just because I can see and talk to spirits doesn't give me a lot of understanding concerning their reasoning. The one thing I know for sure is that ghosts behave pretty much like they did in life, appearing in places where their influence was felt when they were living."

I struggled to listen to what he was saying, my mind replaying the part about my eyes. I forced myself to focus, hearing his last words.

". . . or a person they were closely connected with in life. Especially if there's unfinished business the deceased believes needs to be taken care of."

"Like your mother." The words came out of my mouth before I could think to call them back.

His jaw clenched. He was silent for a long time, the rhythm of the tires against the road the only sound in the truck. "A ghost doesn't need a roof or walls, Nola. A person can be just as haunted as a house."

His words stung. I knew that. I had always known. "Then maybe you need to speak with your mother. Ask her why she's here. Maybe all she wants is your forgiveness so she can move on."

As if I hadn't said anything at all, he said, "Michael's great-grandfather had such a powerful hold on his family, it would make sense that he would continue to try to control them even from the grave." He turned his head to look at me. "Or return to the scene of a crime to keep his involvement a secret by terrorizing anyone who would threaten exposure."

A shudder threaded its way through me as I recalled the shadow at the top of the stairs and being locked in the closet. "Great," I said. "An equal opportunity ghost. Sort of like an 'expect it when you least expect it' spirit."

"Pretty much. I didn't make the rules. By an accident of birth, I'm just forced to live with them."

We drove in silence for several miles before Beau reached forward and turned the radio on to the weather channel to give us both something to worry about besides an angry spirit seeking vengeance and controlling the living from the grave.

CHAPTER 33

After we made a quick stop at the Maple Street Bakery & Café in downtown Abita Springs to fortify ourselves with hot coffee, Beau drove us several miles west of town on a two-laned highway. The road ran through a tunnel of tall pines and other old-growth trees that hung over the roadway like nosy neighbors. We didn't pass another vehicle, either because it was generally a less-traveled road or because other people had the sense to stay at home as the temperature hovered just above freezing.

I was looking for an old farmstead that sat on more than one hundred acres of overgrown fields and would have continued to exist undisturbed if my company's client, a real-estate developer, hadn't decided that it would be the perfect spot for a new neighborhood. Despite my general dislike of developers, this one seemed to at least have a conscience, as he'd asked for a report on any viable historical properties that might still be standing and might be restored and incorporated into the new development.

The GPS coordinates had Beau turning onto a weed-choked drive through more trees, eventually stopping at a clearing. A once-grand Victorian farmhouse with a wraparound porch and a corner tower with a pointed turret sat in the middle of what might have once been a lovely vista over fields full of crops. Now desolation swept through the broken windows and missing front door like a quiet hurricane, the destruction taking years instead of minutes.

Beau studied the house, his face grim. "I'm not leaving you here and coming back to pick you up when you're done like we did last time. This is like the beginning of every horror movie I've ever seen."

"Just because it's old and abandoned doesn't make it creepy."

"Maybe not, but the old woman staring at us from the top turret window sure does."

As I followed his gaze, I became aware of the snapping on his wrist and of the first drops of rain hitting the windshield from the hovering dark clouds. "Fine. You can wait in the truck. I'll work fast, but I need to be thorough, so I can't race through it."

He surprised me by sliding out of the truck to join me next to the broken front steps. "It'll go faster if I help. Just show me what to do."

I grinned. "I've been waiting for years for you to say that to me."

"Funny," he said without smiling, his eyes scanning the leaden clouds. Fat plops of rain began pelting fallen leaves around us. "I thought you said it wasn't supposed to rain until after three o'clock."

I opened up my weather app again. "It now says ten percent chance, but the temperature is still thirty-three degrees and is supposed to stay there until sunset, when it will dip into the twenties. So we're good, right?"

"Assuming the temperature remains above freezing until we get home, we're good. Otherwise . . ."

"Otherwise what?"

"Let's cross that bridge when we get to it. Come on—let's get this done."

As soon as we entered the house, the clouds opened up, allowing water to cascade through holes in the ceilings and broken windows, leaving puddles on the well-worn heart pine floors. I checked the temperature again, just to be sure. "It's still thirty-three degrees."

Our eyes met. "It's your call," he said. "Just know that if you end up making the wrong one, I will never let you forget it. But I'll go along with whatever you decide."

I sighed. "We're already here. Let's get this done so we can leave." I threw him a measuring tape and a notepad with an attached pencil I'd pulled from my backpack. "You start with each room upstairs and begin measuring and documenting everything you see. And take pictures of everything, including door handles, crown moldings, and any plumbing fixtures. We need to be as accurate as possible."

We lost track of time as we worked inside the house, which seemed to be at least twenty degrees colder than outside. I had to keep stopping to thaw my fingers so I could type on my laptop and press the button on my camera.

I could hear Beau talking to someone upstairs, the words too muffled for me to understand, which was fine with me. Three hours later, as I was taking pictures and documenting the handmade tongue-and-groove cabinets in the kitchen, I heard Beau curse, and then the sound of his feet clattering down the steps.

"Have you looked outside?"

I rushed to the porch to see a newly white landscape, with a thin layer of snow dusting the weeds and rocks of the yard, like the house had been graced by a fairy godmother and dressed for an enchanting evening. Except it wasn't.

I looked at my weather app. "It's twenty-eight degrees and falling. I'm so sorry, Beau. I didn't mean—"

"Grab your stuff. We've got to go. Now."

I threw my laptop, notepads, and camera into my backpack and ran out toward the truck. I had made it about two feet when I slipped on a hidden rock and ended up on my back with the wind knocked out of me.

Beau's face appeared above me. "Are you all right?"

When I nodded, he unceremoniously hauled me to my feet and held on to my elbow until I was safely inside the truck. "This isn't good, is it?"

"Nope." He started the engine and I felt the welcome blast of the heater on my face. Taking out his phone, he said, "I'm going to check on road conditions on I-10 to figure out what to do next. Meanwhile, I want you to try a different weather app and let me know what the temperature is doing."

Still feeling winded from my fall, I just nodded and did as he asked. I groaned. "It's twenty-seven degrees now, and there's now a weather advisory indicating an expected accumulation of up to half an inch across the New Orleans metro area." If Beau were from the Northeast, or anywhere except the South, I would have had to explain to him that even a single snowflake could paralyze entire cities and clear out all grocery stores of bread and milk.

"Today is not our day to buy a lottery ticket. I-10 eastbound is completely shut down with a jackknifed tractor trailer, and they've shut down the Causeway because of icy conditions."

I pushed back the panic crawling up my throat. "Okay. Let's drive back to Abita Springs. These back roads are mostly dirt and gravel, so less slippery, right? Then we can get a couple of rooms in one of the inns I saw downtown."

He turned on the wipers and I watched the blades make fans on the windshield as they pushed back the snow. After putting the truck in gear, he said, "Let's just hope that everybody else had the sense to stay home. That will give me less of a chance of hitting someone."

"I'd offer to drive, but I don't think that would help the situation."

"Nope. But you do need to get your license. You can do it next week."

"I'm not—"

"I'm not asking. It's time." He began to inch the truck forward. "That doesn't mean you can't ask me to drive you. You'll probably miss my company."

"Can you just focus on driving, please? It's already getting hard to see." I sat as far forward as I could to help him navigate the road, whatever part of it was still visible in the dim light.

"I'm guessing Abita Springs doesn't have a snowplow."

Beau snorted as his hands gripped the steering wheel. "I don't think the entire state of Louisiana has a snowplow. Which is probably a good thing. People around here can't drive cars. Can't imagine what would happen if we put them behind a plow."

It took us more than an hour to retrace our route back to town and find our way to a hotel I remembered passing while looking for the café earlier that morning. It was a turn-of-the-century home that appeared to have been converted into an inn that I might have found more charming if it were warmer outside and I weren't feeling desperate. "Should we have called ahead for reservations?" I asked, looking around at the small but full parking lot.

"This isn't New Orleans during Mardi Gras, Nola. And nobody with half a brain would be out driving anywhere in this kind of weather." He sent me a pointed look. "Stay there and I'll come get you."

I slung my backpack over my shoulder and opened my door. The ground showed only a thin layer of snow, and the asphalt parking lot didn't look slippery. I stepped out onto the ground, and before I could tell Beau *Never mind—I can do this myself*, my feet had skidded out in front of me for the second time, landing me firmly on my backside.

"You okay?" Beau asked, his words of concern not completely hiding the twitching of his lips.

"Just fine, thanks. I wanted to admire the house from a different angle."

"Come on." He reached his hands toward me, and I took them, allowing him to pull me up. "Hang on to me until we're inside. And before you argue: I'm wearing work boots with a thick tread. You're wearing sneakers. If you want to be stubborn, fine. But I'm going to leave you out here to crawl on your hands and knees when you fall again."

I was pretty sure he was joking, but just in case he wasn't, I held tightly to his arm until we'd reached the covered porch.

Stepping into the quaint lobby, I was relieved to see that part of the renovations included central heat, and I could feel the tip of my nose beginning to thaw. An attractive middle-aged woman with big blond hair and glasses attached to a chain around her neck smiled at us from the check-in desk.

I smiled back. "Good afternoon. We need two rooms for one night, please."

"Do you have a reservation?"

I fought the impulse to turn and give Beau my "I told you so" look.

"No, we don't. This is sort of an emergency situation because of the weather. We were supposed to drive back to New Orleans."

"Can't do that," she said, shaking her head. "The Causeway's closed and I-10 looks like a hurricane evacuation. Ain't nobody going nowhere." She gave a hearty smoker's laugh, followed by a cough.

"Yes, we heard," Beau said. "That's why we need to stay overnight. It's supposed to be in the sixties tomorrow, so we can drive back then."

I began to worry when she didn't start tapping on the computer keyboard in front of her.

"Yes, well, I'm afraid that's going to be a problem. All of our rooms are full and have been booked for months."

"For months? Can you recommend another hotel nearby?" I asked. "Like, within walking distance?"

"Oh, sugar, I wish I could, but there's not an available room for, like, forty miles of Abita Springs. There's the annual Water Festival going on this weekend, and the Boudreaux family reunion is here all week. And you know those Boudreauxs! You could line 'em up from one end of the country to the other and they'd bump into the ocean on both sides."

"I guess we could sleep in the truck," Beau suggested. "I think we should have enough gas to last until morning. If not, I've got a blanket."

I wasn't sure if it was because of the cold, the idea of sleeping outside in a truck, or my very bruised backside, but I began to cry. Beau made it worse by putting his arms around me and pressing my head against his jacket, which smelled of him and reminded me of being home and warm.

"Don't cry," the woman said, which only made me cry harder. Beau's patting me on the back didn't help, either.

"Look," she said, her voice low. "I may be able to help you out."

I sniffled and turned to look at her.

"We have a small room in the attic. It's got a bathroom and it's clean. It used to be a maid's room, but now we just use it for emergencies, and I'm going to make the executive decision to call this an emergency."

"Oh, thank you so much," I said, my relief releasing more stupid tears.

"Don't thank me yet. The room is tiny, and it's got a pitched roof on account of it being in the attic, and there's only one bed." She looked at Beau's six-feet-plus stature. "And it's a twin. I'm not sure how you'll both fit in it, but it's yours if you want it."

"We'll take it," Beau said, sliding his credit card across the desk.

We walked up the three flights of the narrow and creaking staircase—a description I had once considered charming—before sticking in the room key with a burst of optimism that lasted until the door fully opened.

"She did say it was small," Beau said, eyeing the ceiling that would allow him to stand only in the middle of the room, and the lone twin bed covered with a handmade quilt and a single pillow shoved into a far corner against the wall.

I squeezed past him to peer into the en suite bathroom, hoping to see a bathtub that could be lined with blankets and used as a bed. A tiny shower stood in the corner, the bathroom itself barely big enough to also hold a toilet and sink.

I turned to find Beau behind me, obviously having had the same thought as me. "I could sleep in the truck," he offered. "I've done it before."

"Not in freezing cold weather. We can make this work." I looked down at the hardwood floor that didn't even have a rug. "We can take turns sleeping in the bed and use my backpack as a pillow on the floor."

He didn't look convinced. "I'll let you get settled and freshen up while I go back downstairs and ask about a place around here for dinner. I'm starving."

At the mention of food, my stomach began growling. "I'll meet you downstairs in ten minutes. I think I have a pair of dry socks in my backpack I need to change into, and then I'll be right down."

As soon as the door shut behind him, my phone binged with a text from Sarah.

Can I put lemon juice on last page of
clientele book? Dad says spies do

Very old school but I say yes

Gd bc I already did and saw hidden words.
Can I do whole page?

I sighed out loud. She was way too much like Melanie. What words did you see?

Dear Mother

Wow let me know the rest when u finish

👍 Also I'm resending all pics from cemetery note
shadow and orbs around names wet handprints too

The pictures were still downloading when she sent me a final text. Gotta go mom calling me to eat.

I stood staring at my phone as the photos slowly began to download, the hotel's Wi-Fi apparently powered by hamsters on a wheel.

I closed my phone, knowing that it would take much longer if I stared at each pixel, and I began to search through my backpack for anything resembling a toothbrush or toothpaste. I remembered laughing at both Melanie and Jolene as they told me that I should always have an emergency stash of toiletries and makeup with me just in case. In a pinch I figured I could use the edge of my notepaper to floss between my teeth, but that would have to be the extent of my nighttime routine.

A thump sounded on the door, and I took the one step to cross the room and answer it. Beau stood on the other side holding his cooler from the truck. I backed up to allow him inside and watched as he kept his head ducked as he set it down, filling the space between the bottom of the bed and the door.

"Restaurants all closed early because of the weather, so we're going to have to make do. I can't promise that my snacks are more nutritious than those in the vending machine in the lobby, but at least we'll have a variety. And now we have someplace other than the bed to sit."

While he set out our feast of bottled water, candy bars, and salty snacks on the tiny bedside table, I texted Jolene to let her know that I was okay but that Beau and I were snowed in for the night and expected to return the following morning. Her response was only a wink emoji.

As I bit into a Snickers bar, I asked, "You don't happen to have any toothpaste or a spare toothbrush with you, do you?"

"I could pretend to go check or just tell you right now that I know that I don't. And they don't have any downstairs, either. I already asked. At least there's soap and shampoo in the bathroom."

I nodded casually, as if this were a normal dinner on a normal night. But there was nothing normal about any of this, and I was almost preternaturally aware of the bed I sat upon and how very small it was. "Did you let Mimi and Sam know that you wouldn't be home tonight?"

"Yep. Mimi told me to stay warm and she'd see me tomorrow. Sam said I should sleep in the truck."

I groaned. "I am so sorry. This is all my fault. You gave me a choice, remember? And I obviously made the wrong one. Look, nobody's sleeping in your truck. I'll sleep on the floor, okay? I've got my backpack for a pillow, and Jolene's down coat will make the perfect blanket. I'll be fine."

"You're not sleeping on the floor, Nola. We're both adults. I think we can manage sharing a bed to sleep without any . . ." He waved his hand in the air.

"Hanky-panky?" I suggested, recalling the word my dad would use when warning me about my curfew and boys in general before I headed out on a date.

"That's one word for it, I guess, although I can't say I've ever heard it actually spoken out loud by anyone under fifty. But yes, exactly."

I glanced at my phone. "Sarah sent me the photos she took at the Broussard tomb. They're still downloading, but she said there are some interesting anomalies."

"Like what?"

"I'll let you see for yourself as soon as they finish downloading."

He shifted his gaze to the small lamp nailed to the wall behind the bed, the only source of light in the room. "I'll look at them tomorrow. I'm so tired that my eyes are crossing."

My phone binged with another text from Sarah.

Omg the lighter works!!! Started from bottom line
definitely from Jeanne more soon

"What's that about?" Beau asked. He'd moved to sit next to me while we were eating, the old mattress rolling us together so that our thighs touched.

"I, um—nothing. Nothing, really."

"Is she referring to Jeanne Broussard?"

I nodded while closing the screen on my phone. "She asked to look at the clientele book after Uncle Bernie said he and his friends couldn't find anything."

"Uncle Bernie had it? How did he get it and why didn't I know anything about it?"

"Yes, well, Sam and I—"

"Sam? You and Sam?"

I'd always been a terrible liar. Either I'd begin to spout gibberish or I'd blurt out the unblemished truth. From Beau's angry expression, I decided on the latter. He'd be upset either way, and the thing I'd learned about lies was that they always circled back around to kick you in the backside.

"Yes. She and I had breakfast to talk about things, and because we were worried about you. So we thought that maybe we could find some answers ourselves." I looked down at my lap, unable to bear the look of anger and disbelief rotating across his face like a beacon.

"Worried about what?" His words were pinched, as if forced between clenched teeth.

"You. That you would stick your neck out a little too far and get into real trouble. We thought that if I could find out anything important before you did, we could figure out the best way to handle it. . . ."

"You thought." He shook his head. "So the two of you have been going behind my back?"

"No. I mean, not exactly. I told you I went with Michael to his aunt and uncle's beach house, right?"

"Where you only got enough information to defend them. So, what's this about the clientele book and Uncle Bernie? And where was I when this was happening?"

"We—I mean I—thought that Bernie or his police friends could help decipher what might be hidden in the clientele book, but they couldn't find anything. And then Sarah took it home with her to see if she could give it a try. I mean, she took it without asking, but I figured what could be the harm, right?" I attempted a smile.

His expression remained stony.

I began to ramble, eager to get him interested in what we'd learned so he'd forget that he was angry. "So many people had looked at it, but I just had a feeling that something had to be there. We all agree that there's a reason why your father locked it up in the closet with the other evidence, right? But what evidence? So that's what Sarah was telling me—that someone, possibly Jeanne, wrote a note in lemon juice on the last page of the book. It's an old spy trick—I remember Dad telling us about it when researching one of his Cold War books."

"I know what that is," Beau said, his eyes still hard. "Go on."

I wiped my palms on my thighs, embarrassed to find them sweating. "Sarah thinks she's found a hidden message on the back page that starts with 'Dear Mother.' She's uncovering the rest right now and will let me know."

"And who were you going to tell, Nola? Sam? And leave me in the dark even though I have the most skin in this game?"

I wanted to grab his shoulders and shake him, but the look in his eyes made me stay at arm's length. "Actually, Sunny does, and she's all for reconciliation and letting things go."

His eyes narrowed, and I desperately needed to backtrack. "Our intention wasn't to keep you in the dark. Sam and I were just trying to protect you. . . ."

"Just don't," he said, retrieving his coat from where he'd dropped it on the floor and putting it on with short, jerky movements. "I'm going out for a walk in the snow. I need time to think."

I stood, the springs of the mattress squealing in protest. I was angry now, too. Even as a child arguing with my mother, whose versions of the truth made me more sad than upset, I found it wounding to have my words flung to the side as if they didn't matter. As if I didn't have the right to speak the hard truth. Even when I knew it was best to keep silent. Like now.

"You know, Beau, that if you would have just talked with Adele, all of this could have been avoided. You're so busy cooking up revenge plots and seeing betrayal where none exists that you refuse to ask for help from the most obvious source. Your mother wants to help you. She's been following you around for years, waiting. You just need to ask. But you're so damned stubborn that you can't see over your self-imposed prison wall."

My last words reverberated in the quiet attic as we stared at each other like two boxers in a ring. He raised his eyebrows, as if expecting an apology. But I couldn't say I was sorry when I knew I was right.

Without another word, Beau walked calmly out the door, slamming it hard behind him.

CHAPTER 34

I woke up sometime in the darkest part of the night, disoriented and confused by the arm around my waist and the gentle breathing on my cheek. I struggled to sit up, but the arm tightened, pulling me back as unintelligible words were whispered into my ear. As my eyes adjusted, I turned slightly to see Beau on his side, pressed against the wall, his head sharing the single pillow with me.

Now that I was fully awake, my mind replayed our argument over and over. After stewing in the room for several hours before going to bed, I admitted to myself that I should have apologized for the way I spoke to Beau about his stubborn refusal to communicate with Adele. But I wouldn't apologize for saying it when we both knew that I was right.

Warm lips pressed against my bare neck, sending chills all the way down my spine to my toes, giving me not-so-terrible flashbacks of the night he'd spent on my couch and sleepwalked through a conversation with his mother on the phone. And then shared a memorable kiss with me. All of which he seemed not to remember.

I tried to move away, but I was trapped by his arm, and the narrow bed didn't give me any room. "Beau?" I whispered.

His lips traveled up to my ear, my nerve endings erupting in a happy dance all over my body. "Beau—are you sleeping?"

"Mmmmm." He rolled over so that half of his body was on top of mine, his head nestling between my head and shoulder.

"Wake up." I gave him a gentle shove on the shoulder, telling myself that I didn't want a repeat of the night he'd spent in my apartment, even though my body argued with my conscience.

"Nola." The word was drawn out and slurred, but I knew he'd said my name.

I stiffened. "Okay, Beau. You need to wake up. I'm not Sam."

"Shhhhhh." His lips blew the sound into my ear, the effect rippling through my body.

Without warning, he lifted up on his elbows, his eyes dark shadows hiding in the planes of his face as he hovered over me. And then he was kissing me, and I was kissing him back because it seemed the most natural thing to do. My hands had nowhere to go but to his head, to thread through his hair and pull him closer, our bodies and mouths fitting together as if they'd been molded from the same clay.

Beau's phone jangled with an old-fashioned ringtone, jolting us both. He lifted his face and grabbed the phone from the bedside table, the screen flashing in front of me long enough that I could see Sam's name and the small square of her head. Beau glanced at it, then flung it across the room. I winced as I heard it slam to the floor.

Neither of us moved as it rang three more times. The room fell quiet except for our breathing, and the air held a sense of expectation. Beau looked down at me, his eyes hidden in shadow. Unreadable. Without speaking, he placed his head down next to me on the pillow, and I waited until his breathing resumed the steady pulse of sleep.

I slid out from under him, then grappled in the dark for my backpack. Then I lay down in the middle of the floor using the backpack as my pillow before pulling Jolene's coat over me. I listened to Beau's breathing until I eventually fell back asleep, still tasting his lips on mine.

~

When I awoke the following morning, Beau was already showered and dressed and sitting on the corner of the bed tapping on his phone. I thought about the phone call from Sam and wondered what she'd wanted in the middle of the night. Testing the waters, I said, "Good morning."

He grunted and didn't look up from his phone. That meant that either he did remember our kiss and was angry with himself, or he was remembering our argument and was angry with me. Or maybe—I hoped—like the first time it had happened, he didn't recall the kiss at all. I just needed to know for sure so I would know how to proceed.

After I retreated into the bathroom, I turned on the shower before quickly texting Sam.

> Have you heard from Beau? Heads up he knows. Want you to be prepared.

I hit Send and, while the water ran, waited a full five minutes for her to respond. Maybe she and Beau had talked earlier and she already knew and didn't think she needed to respond. She still hadn't texted by the time I got out of the shower, the steam on the mirror fortunately hiding my reflection.

I stepped back into the room, having second thoughts about the mirror. Aware of what my hair usually looked like in the morning, I attempted to comb through it with my fingers. I doubted my success when Beau finally glanced at me, his eyes wandering to the top of my head before they dropped back to his phone.

"Hurry up and get ready to go. I want to get on the road."

The skin around my mouth and chin felt raw from his beard stubble, an unwelcome reminder of the previous night. I knew my reddened face would be as obvious as Rudolph's nose to even the most casual observer, and for the first time in my life I wished I had a makeup bag in my backpack. I kept my face turned away from Beau and was happy, at least for now, that he had no interest in looking at me. As I stood and gathered my things from the floor, my phone binged with a text from Sarah. Even though I felt Beau's impatient gaze on me, I opened it.

See pic!!!!! This was followed by an exploding-head emoji.

I opened the photo to see a handwritten page from what looked like the back of Jeanne's clientele book, each cramped cursive letter rounded over the next as if for protection. I imagined the writer clutching the cotton swab—or whatever instrument she'd used to dip into the lemon juice—close to the end. The characters themselves were the color of burnt paper. Which, I realized, was what happened when a fire source was held close to a letter written in invisible lemon-juice ink to make the writing visible. There was a singed hole on the far right of the second paragraph, and I could only hope that Sarah had parental supervision while experimenting with fire and paper. Knowing her, and her similarities to Melanie, I somehow doubted it.

I looked at Beau with excitement. "It's from Sarah. She found something in Jeanne's clientele book!"

He didn't acknowledge that he'd heard me, still focusing on his phone. "I'll read it out loud, then, okay?" When he didn't respond, I said, "The letter starts with the date January 16, 1964, the year Jeanne was murdered. And it's signed by her." Beau finally lifted his eyes but remained silent. Assuming he wanted to hear the rest, I continued to read:

Dear Mother,

My diary isn't safe—Father goes through it and thinks I don't know. I hope you remember Marguerite and me playing Nancy Drew and writing secret messages and that makes you search where Father wouldn't. If I die you will look for a reason and I pray you look here. I'm pregnant by Frank.

Can't call him Uncle because of what he did. Father knows and wants me to accuse Dr. Ryan. I won't and Father is angry. You and I know what he is capable of and I am afraid. Not of what he will do but that he and Frank will get away with it. Whatever happens, I love you.

Jeanne

I looked up to find Beau still watching me, his face unreadable.

My triumphant smile faded. "This is the proof you've been looking for! It not only exonerates your grandfather, but it points to the two guilty parties. I thought you'd be a little more excited. This is big," I added, as if he needed reminding that one of the two huge questions haunting his family for decades had finally been answered.

He didn't smile, or dial Mimi's number to tell her, or jump up and down—all the things I'd imagined we'd both do if we ever made this kind of discovery.

Instead, his voice was flat when he finally spoke. "So, tell me, Nola. Would you only be showing Sam instead of sharing it with me if I didn't already know about your little agreement? Was that the deal? To curate all information so that decisions would be made on my behalf without my knowledge?"

I couldn't breathe, his accusation sucking the air out of my lungs. I didn't respond because we both knew the answer. Instead, I cleared my throat. "I'm going to e-mail this as an attachment to both you and Sam, all right? I'll let the two of you work out what you want to do. I expect you'll want to tell Mimi, too."

He rubbed his hands through his hair, and my mind wandered to how soft his hair was beneath my fingers and against my neck. His words jerked me back to reality. "This has nothing to do with you anymore, Nola. Do you understand? I don't want you involved. I'll handle it from here."

I knew I should keep my mouth shut, but it wasn't in my nature to allow myself to be dismissed without having a final word. "Fine,"

I said. "Just don't forget that it was you who asked for my help to begin with, and I agreed against my better judgment. And before you get angry with Sam, remember that she was just trying to protect you, because for some unknown and completely incomprehensible reason she has feelings for you."

He stared at me in silence for a long moment, then stood. "It's time to leave. I'll be waiting outside in my truck."

When I crossed the lobby, the same receptionist from the night before looked up from her book, saw my chin, and winked. Mortified, I ducked my head, gave her a quick wave, and headed toward the door.

The truck was already warm, and my seat heater had been turned on, which at least meant that he didn't completely hate me. Or maybe his upbringing and ingrained good manners couldn't be forgotten.

As he pulled out of the parking lot, the tires turning the snow beneath us to a watery slush, I sent a quick text to Jolene to let her know we were on our way back. She responded with a thumbs-up emoji and another wink emoji. I quickly turned off my screen so Beau wouldn't see.

"How are the roads?" I asked.

"Fine."

I knew I was wading into dangerous territory, but I had to know. "Do you want to discuss last night?"

"No. There's nothing to discuss. I want my mother to go away, and she won't as long as she thinks I need her. And I don't."

I wanted to point out the obvious, that if he found out what she wanted he could send her to the light. But the subject wasn't up for discussion, so I said nothing, feeling more than a little relieved that he didn't seem to remember anything past the time he went to sleep or why he found me sleeping on the floor in the morning.

We drove in complete silence, the lack of sound as unnerving as a crowd blowing vuvuzelas at a soccer match. In an attempt to lessen the tension, I flipped on the satellite radio and scrolled down to the eighties station to play our old "name that tune" game.

"Don't look at the screen," I said. "That would be cheating."

He didn't even turn to acknowledge that I'd said anything.

At the intro to the next song, I blurted, "'Steppin' Out' by Joe Jackson!"

Beau continued driving without a word as I waited for the next song. The first notes of the intro had barely played before I shouted, "'Tarzan Boy' by Baltimora!"

After three more songs, including two with me shouting out glaring and deliberate mistakes, and Beau's continued disinterest, I gave up and flipped off the music. I turned on my phone and checked my photo album, annoyed that Sarah's photos from the cemetery still hadn't completely downloaded.

I checked my texts, answering a few from work and one from Alston in Charleston asking when she and Lindsey could come visit, and then put my phone away. I spent the rest of the ride staring out the window until I passed out with exhaustion from a restless night, my dream one with a pervading sense of dread mixed with a longing for something just out of reach.

The following week was spent working on my cottage, replacing termite-ridden baseboards and patching the existing floors to hide places where we'd moved walls upstairs. I never went alone, making sure that Thibaut and Jorge were there, and then leaving when they did. I didn't make the mistake of mentioning Antoine's name, but his presence was a palpable one, felt most strongly on the stairs where he'd murdered his daughter and in the upstairs hallway outside the closet where the clientele book had been hidden.

The discovery of Jeanne's secret letter had been anticlimactic. Not because we already knew the truth, thanks to Mimi's ability to read the Maison Blanche door, but because I hadn't been allowed to be a part of telling Mimi that we had proof. Nor had I been able to discuss with Beau why Antoine was still haunting my house even after the incriminating evidence had been found. It seemed that the more answers we discovered, the more questions we had. And the more questions I couldn't ask.

Sarah's photos from the cemetery had finally downloaded, and I'd forwarded them all to Beau without even looking at them first, because he'd made it clear that he didn't want me involved anymore. He hadn't responded, and I told myself I was okay with it.

I'd been hoping to hear from Beau about starting work on the Esplanade property, or at least to get an answer about when I could show it to Cooper, but there had been no word from him since he'd unceremoniously dropped me off in the driveway of my apartment and driven away with only a curt "Good-bye."

I was home early on a Tuesday afternoon because Thibaut and Jorge had begun the process of sealing the wooden floors and needed them to dry overnight. I'd gone as far as opening the front door, just to peer inside to check on their progress, but I was met with a foul smell that had nothing to do with the wood stain, and with a heavy feeling that drew my attention up the stairs to a large black shadow masquerading as a water spot on the upstairs ceiling. I'd slammed the door and locked it, then headed home to my apartment.

Beau's absence from my life meant that I had a lot more free time on my hands than I was used to. Cooper and I were supposed to meet for dinner, but he'd texted me to say that he was swamped at work and had asked to move our dinner plans to the following night. By the time I'd fed Mardi and taken him outside for a walk and played fetch with Eeyore, it was only five o'clock.

I changed into my sweats and seriously contemplated using one of Jolene's face masks, but when I looked at her vanity, I was too confused by the vast array of tubes and bottles. I briefly considered heading into the kitchen and surprising Jolene with dinner for a change, but I realized that I was in over my head as soon as I stepped into her domain and was faced with a fridge full of food I didn't recognize and an array of *Wizard of Oz* kitchen gadgets I wasn't sure how to use. Instead, I headed toward the couch, flipped on the Investigation Discovery channel, and opened up the pizza delivery app on my phone.

Ten minutes later, the doorbell rang and I raced downstairs without looking at the door camera, assuming it was my pizza. Instead, Sunny Ryan stood on the doorstep, wearing her customary yellow and her bright smile, and holding a dressmaker's mannequin.

"Is Jolene here yet? I'm a little early."

"Not yet, but I'm sure she's on her way. You and your friend can come on up and wait. I think I ordered more pizza than we need, so you're welcome to stay for dinner, too."

"Thanks," she said, moving past me with the plastic torso. "Molly and I will be happy to accept."

"Molly?"

"Molly Mannequin," Sunny said as she continued up the stairs, the torso tucked under an arm. "Jolene said she'd help me make my costume for the fund-raiser."

I closed the door and ran up the stairs behind her, then had to wait for her to greet Mardi and play fetch a few times before I could ask the questions burning in the back of my throat. "Jolene's going?"

Sunny plopped down on the couch. "Uh-huh. I just told her today. Mimi wants her there because she's always a fun addition to any party. I told her she could invite a date, but she said she'd probably be going solo."

"Oh," I said, trying not to sound hurt. "I haven't talked with Beau, so I don't know what's going on, but what did Mimi say about inviting the Sabatiers?"

"She's all for it. Beau was still on the fence, but I was totally all in, so she agreed."

I found her nonchalance about the ordeal of her childhood surprising, but then again, she'd been a toddler and then raised in a happy home. I told myself that there was no reason she'd want to hang on to a trauma that she didn't feel was part of her life.

"I really think it's a step in the right direction," Sunny continued. "I'm super excited about meeting them."

"I'm glad." And I was. I was just surprised at my disappointment at being excluded. I felt as if I'd just planned a fabulous two-week vacation but was being left behind on the dock when the ship set sail. Maybe I could convince Jolene to bring me as her date.

"And now that Jeanne's secret letter is out in the open, we can close that chapter, too," Sunny said. "I can't tell you how happy I am that all that messy business is behind us. It's the one thing that's been dragging on my happiness since I came back, you know? I'd like to just enjoy being with my family now."

"I totally get it." And I did. But nobody seemed to want to address the literal black shadow on the wall. It was still there, lurking, and nobody seemed interested in acknowledging its presence or initiating moves to get rid of it.

Sunny slid to the edge of the couch. "Do you still have the clientele book and any of the stuff in the hatboxes that you didn't already get rid of?"

I had to think for a moment. "I guess I do—I haven't taken anything out of it. And Sarah sent back the book after she discovered the hidden letter. I brought it over to Christopher to give to Mimi." At her raised eyebrows, I added, "Beau isn't speaking to me right now, so I didn't want to run into him at the house."

"Ah, well, that explains it. I figured something was up since I hadn't seen you. If it were up to me, I'd destroy all of it. So that whole situation is erased. If you want, I could take it back to Beau and let him deal with it."

I considered saying yes but quickly changed my mind. "Before we do that, let me double-check with Beau. I'll have to wait until he's willing to speak with me again, but I don't want to do anything without his permission. Been there, done that. I don't think there's any rush, so let's just leave it all here for now."

Wanting to change the conversation, I said, "So, I'm assuming Beau is going to the fund-raiser with Sam? I haven't spoken with either one of them since the night Beau and I were stranded in Abita Springs, so I have no idea what's going on at the house on Prytania."

"Yeah, they're definitely going—Sam's so excited about their costumes and has asked Jolene and me to make them. I know there was that little disagreement about Sam and you working together, but Beau and Sam have apparently made up, since his bed at home hasn't been slept in since he returned from Abita Springs." She waggled her eyebrows, making me feel a little sick. "They're coming dressed as Saints Timothy and Maura—a young Egyptian couple who were only married for twenty-six days before being crucified facing each other and spent one third of their marriage dying together."

"How romantic."

"I know, right? The best part is that so many of these early AD saints' costumes are basically just draped fabric, so Jolene and I can whip them up pretty quickly. Except I'm going as Joan of Arc, so that will be a little more complicated, since I'll need a sword. Jolene says she saw a pair of lace-up boots in the window of one of those sex shops on Bourbon Street that I might want to get to complete my outfit."

"Great idea," I said. "Are you going solo?"

Her cheeks flushed. "No," she said slowly.

"Anyone I know?"

She looked up at me with a timid smile and nodded. "Michael Hebert."

"Michael Hebert," I repeated.

"Yeah, Michael. I know, right? It was sort of out of the blue when he called and asked me right after his family received their invitations. It was a surprise, but a nice one, since we'd only met that once—outside Audubon Place." Her smile was quickly absorbed by an expression of concern. "I hope you're not mad."

"Mad? Why would I be mad? It's not like Michael and I are a couple or anything. We're sort of trying to start over as friends, but that's it. I honestly don't care. I'm just . . . surprised."

"Good," she said, her sunny smile returning. "Oh, and Mimi wanted me to let you know that you're invited, too. She'd assumed that you would know that you were welcome, but she put an invitation in the mail just in case. It comes with a plus-one, so you can invite Cooper. Beau invited Jaxson, who's bringing Carly. It will be so much fun!"

"Yeah. So much fun."

"I'm thinking I could get dressed here so Michael will have a reason to come pick me up like a real date, since the party's at my house and my costume will already be here. Oh, and before I forget, did you ever find my purple hair ribbon?"

I'd forgotten all about it. I knew exactly where it was, but I couldn't tell her that I'd given it to Uncle Bernie. "No—I'm sorry. I promise to keep looking."

"Thanks." She stood and hefted the mannequin—Molly—and headed toward the back of the apartment. "Jolene said to put her in that back room and she'll make it the sewing room. You and Cooper will have to come up with a costume idea pretty soon. Just remember that Saint Timothy and Saint Maura are already taken."

"Maybe I can go as Drew Brees," I said as she walked away.

The doorbell rang, announcing our pizza delivery, and as I headed toward the stairs, the muffled sound of the phone ringing from the desk began. I hesitated only a moment before taking the stairs down to the door, knowing that whoever it was on the phone, I wasn't supposed to answer it.

CHAPTER 35

If you'd just let me wear the football helmet, you wouldn't have to fuss with my hair," I said to Jolene's reflection in the mirror as she held a Costco-sized can of Aqua Net over my teased and sprayed hair.

"Oh, hush your fuss. If you'd just listened to me, you could have gone as a Saints cheerleader and had a much cuter outfit." She held a hand over my eyes as she let loose with the spray can again.

"Cheerleaders aren't really considered Saints," I said, waving the thick aerosol fog away from my face. "But Drew Brees is considered an actual saint for the 2010 Super Bowl victory, so this was obviously a better choice."

She hit the spray one more time.

I turned my head to see her better, eyeing her white-veiled head and flowing chiffon robes, the large crucifix hanging around her neck. "I only hope that nobody is offended by your choice of costume."

"People say I'm very motherly, so it makes sense. Plus, I'm single, just like Mary."

"I hope your date is okay with it." I'd done the one thing I'd always sworn I wouldn't do and set up a friend on a blind date. Connor

Black, the brother of Meghan Black, the graduate student assistant to Sophie Wallen-Arasi in Charleston, was now living in New Orleans as a project manager for a major building supply company. It had actually been Melanie who'd given me his phone number, so if it went horribly wrong, I could always blame her.

"Sunny, your turn!" I looked toward the closed door leading from Jolene's bedroom to the back room that for the last two weeks had been surrendered to Molly Mannequin and so many bolts of fabric that I'd lost count. Jolene had produced a sewing machine that she evidently kept under her bed, and I'd hear the clacking of the needle way into the wee hours of the night. She was even making Mimi's costume—Mother Teresa, of course—which explained the full-sized poster of the canonized nun in what had once been my guitar room.

Sunny did most of the finishing handwork on all the costumes Jolene made, something she was very good at and enjoyed, since it reminded her of all the backstage theater costume work she'd done in her previous life. I'd watched her work several times, her needle expertly diving into all kinds of materials, creating beautifully embroidered flowers on a long vest, or hand-stitched wounds in the shapes of sharp stones on ragged cloth, depending on the saint, and I'd been impressed by her economy of movement. Her expertise was impressive, considering it had never been more than her hobby. The same thing could be said about Jolene, except that she never did anything casually.

Something crashed to the ground on the other side of the door, quickly followed by Sunny's calling out, "Sorry—I'll clean it up later!" Then the door opened, and Sunny walked through it carrying a plastic sword and wearing a metallic tunic and leggings that had come from an S and M shop in the Quarter and had then been softened with fringe and embellishments by both Jolene and Sunny. The tall boots had been wrapped in foil to look like armor, disguising their origins until I saw the stiletto heels.

"Looks great." I walked around her, admiring the stitched flames on the bottom of the tunic recalling Joan's sad end on a fiery stake.

"Thanks—but not as great as Cooper will look in those tight football pants," she said, winking at me.

"Sadly, he's going as Sean Payton."

Sunny stared blankly at me.

"Y'all are pathetic," Jolene said. "I had to explain to Nola, too. Sean Payton was the Saints' coach in 2010 when they beat the Indianapolis Colts in the Super Bowl. I personally don't think anyone should be allowed to even live in New Orleans without knowing that important fact. It's as important around here as knowing that Christmas is December twenty-fifth. Or when hunting season starts."

I let that sink in before I turned to Sunny. "Trust me, I wouldn't mind seeing Cooper in those pants, either, but he didn't have a lot of time to come up with a costume, and all he needed was a black sweatshirt and visor with the Saints logo and a headset to dress as Coach Payton. Done and done."

Sunny replaced me at Jolene's vanity. "You know," I said, "I don't think Joan of Arc wore makeup when she was leading her troops against the English."

"How would you know?" Jolene asked. "You weren't there, so I say it's open to interpretation."

Sunny's laughter burbled out of her like shiny bubbles, a sound I'd come to love and would try to coax from her whenever we were together. I even found myself anticipating working with her once Beau gave us the go-ahead on the Esplanade house.

"Are you nervous about meeting the Sabatiers for the first time tonight?" I asked Sunny.

"A little. I'd hoped to have met them before tonight, but Beau wouldn't let me until Christopher had a chance to make sure everything Angelina told you was fact. Which makes tonight even more special, since we can officially let go of the past." She beamed at us in the mirror over the vanity.

Jolene began pinning back Sunny's hair before starting the makeup process. Sunny closed her eyes as Jolene began smearing something she called primer on Sunny's face. "I guess we'll just have to wait and find out. I'll go sit on the couch so we don't miss the doorbell."

"Hang on," Jolene said. She grabbed a tube of lipstick off the dressing table and tossed it at me. "Don't forget your color."

I caught it, then left the room. After realizing that my pants didn't have pockets, I stuck it in my bra. Jolene had let me borrow an evening bag, but it didn't work with my costume, so I was making do without it.

I had just plopped down on the couch when the landline phone began to ring. I jumped up, headed down the stairs, closed the front door behind me, and sat on the steps to wait.

In typical Louisiana fashion, the temperatures were back up to the high sixties and lower seventies by the night of Mimi's cathedral fund-raiser, dubbed All Saints No Haints. Mimi admitted to having had help with the name from Sunny.

Michael arrived at the apartment first, and seeing him again after our beach weekend was just as awkward as I'd expected. We'd parted amicably, but I'd expected at least a text if we really were friends. Granted, I hadn't texted him either, so maybe we were in the wait-and-see phase.

He wore a Franciscan habit and worn brown sandals that I recalled seeing him wear at the beach house, and a stuffed bird was perched on each of his shoulders. He kissed my cheek in greeting. "I would say that you look beautiful, but the football jersey is distracting me."

I turned so he could read the name BREES on the back. He laughed out loud. "Ah, *that* saint. I wish I'd thought of that before Jolene suggested Saint Francis." His smile faded as I turned back around to face him. "Are you okay? I mean, with me taking Sunny?"

I waved my hand. "Why shouldn't I be? We're still working on being friends, remember?"

"Yeah. I just—well, I wanted to be sure. No hurt feelings, right?"

"No hurt feelings," I said, giving him a thumbs-up like I was on a tarmac guiding planes.

A red Ford pickup truck slid into a parking spot in front of the house and a young dark-haired man wearing another Saints uniform stepped out.

Connor Black greeted us with a wide, easy smile as I introduced myself. I saw the strong resemblance to his sister, Meghan—but without the pearls and Kate Spade. Turning around, I showed him the back of my jersey and he laughed. "Oh, man—I thought I was being so creative dressing like Drew Brees. I guess great minds think alike."

"At this rate, we'll probably see the entire team roster at the party," Michael said. "It's so much easier than coming up with an actual saint and an appropriate costume." He shook Connor's hand and introduced himself.

I checked the time on my phone. "I'm still waiting for my date, so why don't y'all go on upstairs? Jolene left snacks and libations on the kitchen table, so help yourself. I'll shoot Sunny and Jolene a text to let them know you're coming up. They should be done by now." I thought for a moment, recalling that I was talking about Jolene, then amended my statement. "Or within the half hour."

As soon as they left, my phone binged with two texts, one after the other. The first was from Cooper, telling me that he was running late but he was on his way. The second was from Sarah.

Did u look at pics yet?

I hadn't, and since Beau was clearly not interested in discussing them with me, I'd deleted them from my phone.

No why?

Three dots appeared, and then a single photo came in as a text attachment.

I was bored in science class and looked at pics instead and thought this might b important

I clicked on the picture to expand it. I see it what am I looking for?

My phone rang, and I heard Sarah's voice. "I can't believe that I'm saying this, but it's easier to talk IRL than text. Look at the photo again."

I put her on speaker so I could open my screen to the photo. "Okay, got it."

"See the names in the second column on the stone slab?"

I used my fingers to expand the photo, zeroing in. I saw Jeanne's name and dates, and below them the names of her father and uncle, Antoine and Frank. Her mother, Paulette, sat right beneath them. Just looking at their names carved in marble sent a shiver through me. "What are you wanting me to look at?"

She sighed in my ear, as if I had bricks instead of brains, and I wondered if I'd been that insufferable when I was twelve. "Keep looking under Jeanne's family. You'll see a list of three names of children who died close to or on their birth dates. See them?"

"Sadly, yeah." Each name had the last name of Sabatier and every date was in the nineteen nineties and early two thousands. "Mrs. Sabatier said that she'd had three miscarriages, so those must be her babies."

"Yes. And those were the last members of the family to die, right? Because every name is in chronological order, starting with the top name on the far-left column, with some old guy named Pierre Riviere Broussard who died in 1835 at the age of ninety-eight."

Sunny, Jolene, Connor, and Michael came out of the door, looking like a ragtag band led by a Franciscan monk. I told Sarah to hang on while I stood. "You all can go on ahead. Cooper's on his way, and I don't want to make everyone late."

"I really should get there as soon as possible," Sunny said, her face lacking its usual animation, her skin drawn and pale in the porch light, "since I'm a member of the host family. I need to be there to help Mimi greet her guests."

"No problem. Like I said, Cooper's on his way, and I'm happy to wait for him. You go on and we'll see you there."

I watched as Connor pulled out a small step from his backseat to assist Jolene into the front passenger seat before sliding in beside her. Michael and Sunny got into Michael's black Mercedes, the same one he'd used to pick me up for our dates. I waved and gave them a wide smile so they'd know I didn't care.

As soon as they'd left, I sat down on the steps again to finish my conversation with Sarah. "Sorry. Okay, where were we?"

She gave me another exaggerated sigh and I pictured it being accompanied by rolling eyes. "Sorry to interrupt your social life. So, look at the last name in the first column. It's out of place there because the dates are out of order. It's almost like it was an afterthought. Or maybe whoever asked for it to be put there didn't want anyone to notice."

Enlarging the photo again, I scanned down the first column, stopping when I came to the bottom. F. JEANNE BROUSSARD. 2003–2005. "Should I recognize the name?"

"I don't know. Do you?"

"No. I mean, I recognize the middle and last names, but the years are different, and there's a first initial."

"Yeah, well, remember I said I saw wet handprints? They look like they're making parentheses around that one name."

I squinted to see what appeared to be dark parentheses on either side of the final name in the left column. I squeezed my fingers closer to put the picture back in perspective, and with a sickening nausea rising in my throat I knew that those weren't random marks on the stone.

"I see them." My voice sounded thick. "Adele's?"

"I think so, since she's the one who told us to go to the cemetery."

"But you said it was a little girl who brought you to the Broussard mausoleum, right?"

"Uh-huh."

"What did the little girl look like?"

"She was little—like Button." Button was Aunt Jayne's youngest, who'd just turned three years old and was named after Jayne's paternal aunt, from whom she'd inherited her house on South Battery. "She had really blond hair, and it was in a ponytail with a big yellow ribbon."

"It was yellow? You're sure?"

"Pretty sure. It matched her dress; I do remember that."

I listened to myself breathe in and then out, trying to make sense of what Sarah had just told me.

"Nola? You still there?"

Cooper's car turned into the driveway. "Yeah. Thanks. I need to go."

"Wait—that's it?"

"I'll call you tomorrow." I hit End and closed the screen.

Cooper walked toward me, carrying a small duffel. "I'm so sorry I'm late. . . ."

I ran to him and threw my arms around him for no other reason than that I was happy to see him, and because if there was anyone who could understand what I was grappling with—besides Beau—it was Cooper.

"What's wrong?" he asked, holding me at arm's length and looking closely at my face.

"Nothing—I mean, I'm fine. It's just . . . I need to work out some stuff I just learned, and I need someone to talk it out with."

"Sure. I have to go inside and change into my costume anyway, so come on. We can do that thing your dad does with a large piece of poster paper and markers and begin to connect the dots. If you think Jolene won't mind it hanging on the wall."

"As long as you don't mind her monogramming it and giving it a decorative frame, we should be okay." He followed me through the door and up the stairs. After greeting an excited Mardi, Cooper went into the bathroom to change, and I went in search of poster paper.

The back room's original purpose, with its two walls of windows, was supposed to be as an office area, but mostly it was for me to rediscover my love for writing music and playing guitar. It had instead become more of a multipurpose space serving as a guest room, craft room, sewing room, and general catchall.

I stifled an inward groan after flipping on the lights and seeing the tall pile of pillows, books, and magazines that had apparently toppled over, the obvious source of the crashing sound made as Sunny was getting changed. When she'd made the promise to clean it up later, by "later" she'd obviously meant "by someone else."

Using my sneaker-clad foot to clear a path, I made my way toward the back corner of the room, where Jolene kept her carefully organized art supplies. I'd gone only halfway when I stopped at the sight of Jeanne's hatbox lying on its side, its lid resting on the desk.

I picked up the hatbox, knowing it would be empty before I'd even looked inside.

I felt Cooper enter the room behind me. "Everything okay?"

"No. It's not." Dropping the hatbox on the desk, I grabbed his hand and began leading him to the door. "How fast can you drive?"

"As fast as you need me to."

I grabbed my house key to be tucked into my bra next to the lipstick and led us down the stairs, ignoring the muffled ring of the phone until I'd locked the door behind us.

CHAPTER 36

I was already texting Beau before Cooper had shut my car door. I used the one word "URGENT" to get his attention, followed by a text to let him know that I was on my way and needed to speak with him ASAP. I stared at my phone, waiting for a response, but the screen remained blank. After a minute I called him, and hung up when the call went to voice mail.

I considered texting Sam, to tell her that I needed to speak with Beau, but having no idea what had transpired between them, I didn't. Instead, I sent Beau another text with "CALL ME" in all caps.

"You might want to leave a voice mail," Cooper suggested as we waited for the light at Broadway and St. Charles.

"I know you're older than me," I said, "but nobody leaves voice mail anymore."

"Exactly. Which makes voice mails stand out."

"I disagree. I mean, I can't tell you the last time I checked my voice mail. Because I guarantee there's not a single one. Even spammers don't leave them anymore, because they know it's a waste of time." To prove my point, I opened my phone app. A red circle hovered over the voice mail icon, a number 3 inside it. I clicked on the icon and saw three voice mail messages waiting to be listened to. They were all from Uncle Bernie, and the date stamps told me they had all been sent four days before.

With a sidelong glance at Cooper to see if he was giving me the "I told you so" look—he wasn't—I pressed the arrow button to play the first message, then held the phone to my ear.

Hello, dear. This is Uncle Bernie. I'm afraid that I don't have any exciting news for you about the two ribbons you gave me to test for DNA. We were able to extract DNA from the roots of some of the hair found in the yellow ribbon, and it matched the previous samples on file from Sunny Ryan. No surprise there. And the purple ribbon you gave me to use as a representative sample didn't match the DNA from the yellow ribbon, which means they didn't come from the same person. Not quite sure what to make of it, but me and my buddies have plenty of theories. Call me so we can discuss over a nice brunch.

And, because Bernie was of a certain generation, he recited his phone number, which was clearly printed on my screen. Not that there was anything else I needed to know. Because I was pretty sure I already knew everything.

"Can you go any faster? I'll fill you in while you drive, but the sooner we get there, the better."

I held on tightly to the door handle as Cooper sped over potholes on our way to the house on Prytania.

The house was lit from every window, the luminaries set along the walkway, front steps, and porch like runway lights leading the saintly partygoers to heaven. A valet service had been hired for the evening, and an attendant dressed like Saint Peter stood guard at the hourglass gate—Jolene's idea.

After checking off our names on the guest list, Saint Peter handed Cooper's car key to a valet and let us pass.

The front doors and the tall windows in the front parlor had been flung wide open to the mild night air, with guests milling about the foyer and onto the porch, where black-tie servers brought out food and beverages on silver trays.

We'd made it only up the front steps before Christopher appeared, dressed as the famed Saints coach. Despite the urgency, I had to laugh. Cooper grinned as he shook Christopher's hand. "How many of us Coach Paytons are here?"

"Only four or so right now. But there's about twelve Virgin Marys, and even more Mother Teresas. There's a couple of Pope John Paul IIs, but they had to take off their miters because they were afraid of hitting the Baccarat chandeliers." He looked over at me. "And we have more than enough Drew Breeses to fill an entire roster."

"I'll try to be more creative next time." I looked past him into the throng of people in the double parlors where the raffle items were on display. "Have you seen Beau or Sam?"

"No. And Mimi's upset that Beau wasn't here to greet their guests. We're assuming they're together, but neither one of them is answering their phone."

I tried very hard not to think about the implications. "It's really important that I talk to him as soon as possible."

I thanked him, and then Cooper and I moved inside through the parlors and toward the dining room. My eyes scanned the crowd, but I didn't see anybody I recognized except for Sunny and Michael, who stood in a corner chatting with Angelina and Robert Sabatier. And Mimi. Like the majority of guests, the Sabatiers wore vague costumes that could have been any number of saints. Angelina turned first and smiled, followed by Robert and Mimi. I smiled back but allowed the smile to fade as I faced Sunny. She still wore the pinched expression I'd seen back at the apartment, but her eyes now had a wary look, like that of a mouse sensing the presence of a cat.

We didn't join them, but instead moved through to the adjoining parlor, where I spotted Jolene and Connor chatting with another Mary and yet another Sean Payton and two older women dressed as Saints cheerleaders, with noticeably longer skirts than the actual cheerleaders. It took me a moment to recognize Mrs. Wenzel and her sister, Honey. We waved but kept moving toward the dining room, where platters of food overflowed onto the two matching English mahogany and satinwood buffets. The extravagant excess made me look up at Bacchus and his orgy in the mural on the ceiling.

"Do you think anyone here has noticed this?" Cooper asked, his head tilted back.

"Kind of hard to miss. Most everybody knows it's here, so it shouldn't be a surprise." Lowering my voice, I said, "If you see Sunny approaching, let me know. I need to talk with Beau before I know what to say to her."

"Got it." He selected two plates from the end of the table and handed one to me. "Put some food on your plate so you don't look like you're on a mission."

I had put only a spoonful of shrimp and grits on my plate when I heard my name being called. "Nola!"

I turned to find Carly and Jaxson standing in the doorway. She wore a tight-fitting red-sequined strapless evening gown with matching red lipstick that I'm sure rubbed off on my cheek when she leaned down from her stiletto heels to kiss me hello while Cooper and Jaxson shook hands.

While Carly introduced herself to Cooper, Jaxson leaned close to my ear. "Have you talked to Beau yet?"

I shook my head. "No, and I really need to. Have you seen him?"

"Not yet, but we need to talk. When Uncle Bernie didn't hear back from you, he called me, and I called Beau, but I haven't heard from him since. Have you listened to your voice mail yet?"

"I just did tonight. So Beau knows about the DNA on the hair ribbons?"

"Yeah. But I haven't been able to reach him again, so I'm not sure what sort of conclusions he's made. Obviously not the same one we have, since Sunny is still here."

"Did he mention anything about the cemetery photos I sent him?"

"Just briefly—something about how the truth has been right

there, out in the open, all this time. I asked him what he meant, but he said he had to go. And that's the last I heard."

Our eyes met. Jaxson lowered his voice. "I'd really like to talk to Beau and figure out what's going on."

"Me, too. He isn't here, and that alone tells me something is wrong."

"Or he's preparing for battle."

A thread of panic wove its way through me as I recalled the last battle Beau and I had faced, in my cottage, and how I'd almost died except for unseen hands breaking my fall.

"Why are you dressed as a man?" Carly said, interrupting my thoughts. If it had been anyone else, I would have been grateful.

"Why are you dressed as a hooker?" The panic I'd felt earlier made me speak without thinking.

Carly surprised me by laughing. "No—I'm Mary Magdalene!" she said proudly. "Aren't I clever?"

"That's one word for it," I said. "And unique. You certainly won't see yourself in duplicate tonight."

We turned to Jaxson, who wore a priest's cassock with a white collar, black pants, and shoes. "Nice costume," Cooper said. "Very authentic."

"Because it is," Jaxson said. "I borrowed it from my brother the priest."

"Better known as 'Father What-a-waste' because he's so hot," Carly said, knocking back something pink and bubbly in a martini glass.

Jaxson kept smiling. "I'm Saint John Neumann, just in case you were wondering."

"I was, actually," Cooper said. "I thought it was either him or possibly Saint Francis Xavier, since both have schools named after them in New Orleans."

I looked at Cooper, impressed. "How did you know that?"

He shrugged with a smile. "What can I say? I'm a nerd. I remember that you once said it's one of the things you liked about me.

Anyway, I did some studying up since I'm probably the only non-Catholic here."

"Besides Jolene and me," I corrected.

"Jolene!" Carly shrieked, waving wildly. Grabbing Jaxson's arm, she pulled him away to go say hello. I stayed where I was, not wanting to witness the carnage.

"Sunny and Michael are headed this way," Cooper said quietly.

I kept my focus on the table, spearing a piece of ham to place on my plate. "Keep them here for a bit, okay?"

"Got it."

I stepped around the edge of the table and walked toward the swinging door on the opposite side of the room, quickly moving through it without looking back.

The kitchen bustled with the waitstaff and caterers, and after a few disinterested glances in my direction, I continued through the room to the banquette table, pretending to look out to the back garden, where more luminaries and twinkling lights lit the shadowed garden.

When I was sure no one was looking, I left my plate on the table and walked around the corner and into the morning room. I slid my finger along the chair rail like I'd seen Beau do until I found a soft depression in the wood, and I pressed.

The hidden panel in the wall popped open a crack and I hurried through it, pulling it closed behind me. I took out my phone—too big to fit in my bra—which I had cleverly concealed in the waistband of my pants, held in place by something Jolene called a pasty, something she'd once sworn by in her beauty pageant days and always kept on hand.

I flipped on my flashlight and shone it up the dark staircase. An icy wind wafted down the steps, blowing my hair and misting my face with damp. "Beau?" My voice came out in a strangled burst, not loud enough to be heard by anyone. Aiming the light in front of me, I began to slowly climb the stairs. The temperature dropped with each step, my teeth chattering by the time I reached the top.

I looked at the two closed doors, trying to decide behind which one I might find Beau. I wasn't even sure how I knew he was up there. It was just a feeling. If there was anything I'd learned from Melanie, it was to always pay attention to my instincts. They were the closest thing most people had to a sixth sense. I knew Beau was nearby. But so was the source of the icy breeze whistling through the rafters of the old house despite the still night outside.

My hand gravitated to the door on the left. I turned the knob and went through it to the attic hallway I remembered from when I was there before. Beau sat in the middle of the walkway, leaning against a brick chimney, a camping lantern and crystal tumbler beside him, a thin layer of amber at the bottom of the glass. The distant hum of voices from downstairs formed a steady backdrop to the *snap snap* of his plucking at the rubber band on his wrist.

He looked at me, his face expressionless. "Well, if it isn't Nancy Drew. I'm surprised it took you this long to find me."

I stopped walking. "And I'm surprised that I even bothered. You've been ignoring my phone calls and texts. You're allowed to be mad at me, but you're not allowed to just walk away without telling me why. I thought we were friends."

"Friends?" He smiled. "Is that what we are?"

I didn't say anything. He was wading into dangerous territory, and I hadn't worn my boots.

"Friends don't conspire against me behind my back."

I reached for the feeling of anger, and clung to it like it was a life raft. "We weren't conspiring—we were trying to protect you, you idiot. Something your grandmother fully supported. Not to mention that I was doing the exact same thing you'd already asked me to do. You're welcome, by the way."

"For what? Bringing Antoine Broussard back?"

The lantern flickered and my phone shut down, the battery dead. "Don't," I whispered, knowing I was already too late. His presence oozed between us like oily fingers tracing the ridges of my spine, making my blood still. Fear and anger vibrated inside me and my breath shook in my chest. "What about Sam? Why can you forgive her but not me?"

He looked away, shadows obscuring his face. "My relationship with Sam is far less complicated than my relationship with you."

I stared at him, knowing this wasn't the time or the place to untangle what he'd just said. Instead, I took a deep breath. "What are you doing here?"

"Good question. Waiting. But mostly I've been thinking. About my family, about the Broussards and the Sabatiers. About hair ribbons and DNA that doesn't match when it should. And about a strange inscription on a tomb for a little girl who would have been the same age as my sister—who, by the way, is not the person downstairs who calls herself Sunny. But I'm sure you've already figured that out." He raised his glass to me. "And I've also been doing a lot of thinking about Miss Nola Trenholm. The most aggravating person I've ever known but can't stop thinking about. She's like a tick, burrowing under my skin and poisoning my blood."

Tension emanated from him like a wave, washing over me like an icy plunge. I wanted to leave. I *needed* to leave. The atmosphere in the attic had become thicker, filling my lungs, choking me. But whatever that unnameable thing was between Beau and me had rooted my feet. Even the things he'd said about me couldn't make me leave. I had the bizarre thought that he needed me.

"Do you know who that woman is?"

"No."

"And the little girl who is buried in the Broussard tomb—is she connected to Sunny's disappearance?"

He took a sip from his glass, then leaned his head against the chimney. "Of course. 'Broken bone for broken bone, eye for eye, tooth for tooth.' Isn't that Antoine Broussard's motto?"

I stepped forward. "Stop saying his name!"

He laughed, the sound hollow and echoing off the bare rafters. "Doesn't matter. He's already here. Remember what I said? About how a spirit doesn't need a house to haunt?" A white cloud formed in front of his face when he spoke, his voice shaky from the cold.

The bitter wind blew harder, swirling with small invisible

cyclones all around us, carrying with it the stench of rot. But somewhere behind it, lighter than air, the scent of pipe smoke drifted past us. It took me a moment to find my voice. "Are you drunk?"

"No. Just scared. Pardon my French, but the shit's about to hit the fan." He put down his glass. "You need to go now."

The sound of people's voices downstairs grew louder, carrying across from the attic space above the mural toward us through the closed door. "What's going on?"

Beau stood, picking up the lantern. "Sam's here. She had to go to the airport to pick up a special guest, and from the sounds below, I think they've both just arrived. I told her to guide the crowd into the dining room so I could see what's going on. To determine if Antoine will go quietly."

"And if he won't?"

"Then I stay up here and wait for him. Because he will be looking for me. And this." He leaned into the shadows and retrieved Jeanne's clientele book, the leather on the cover muting the reflected light. "Even in life he was never the kind of person to forgive. He'll want to punish whoever is responsible for revealing all his dirty secrets. Which, because you so stubbornly refuse to listen, includes you." He stepped in front of me, guiding us back down the walkway toward the landing.

"You can destroy the book. And everything else, so there's nothing left to prove anything. Although I'm pretty sure Sunny's already disposed of what was in the hatbox."

"It's too late for that." He indicated the stairs. "You really need to go now. For your own safety."

"But what about yours?"

He shook his head angrily. "Don't you see? Your very presence dilutes my focus. How do you think he got in?"

"I'm sorry. I didn't know."

"But now you do. So leave. Leave now, before things get dangerous. I'm hanging on to the hope that once everyone downstairs hears the truth, and he's got nothing else to hide, he'll go away."

"And if he doesn't?"

He blinked slowly. "Then I'll have to convince him to leave."

I drew back, understanding. "That's why you have the book—to bring him to you."

"Go, Nola. Please. Just this once, would you please do as I'm asking?"

Ignoring him, I said, "You're not alone. Your grandfather is here to help. I smell his pipe."

"I know. I saw him."

"And you could ask your mother. She wants to help you." I held my breath until my chest hurt.

Beau shook his head. "No. I don't need her. I never have. And now she can go, too. Because we've finally found my sister."

He opened the door leading to the attic space above the dining room mural, the cacophony of sound loud enough for me to pick out individual voices.

Facing me once more, he said, "Go. Now." Then he walked through the door and closed it behind him.

I stood on the darkened landing for several moments, the faint light from around the secret door at the bottom of the steps the only guide down the narrow stairwell. The pungent aroma of pipe smoke wrapped around me like a hug, giving me a jolt of courage. With a deep breath, I faced the door Beau had just closed. Then I put my hand on the doorknob and turned it.

CHAPTER 37

Beau lay on his stomach on the suspended walkway, looking over the edge to the scene in the brightly lit dining room below. He jerked his head toward me and made an angry shooing motion with his hand as if I were an irritating fly.

In response, I closed the door behind me with a slam. Beau put his finger over his lips, although from the sound below it was doubtful we could be heard. I moved toward him, carefully holding on to the railing, remembering not to look down, and lowered myself beside him.

"You're a terrible listener," he said quietly.

"So are you," I whispered back.

He shook his head, then returned his gaze to the room below, and I did the same, scooting over to find my own vantage point. The acoustics were perfect, but the visuals less so, with only snapshots of various people moving or stopping directly below me, depending on the opaqueness of various paint colors in the mural. I shifted my body to the right so that I was now directly above the middle of the room, able to get at least a partial glimpse of people standing on the periphery.

I spotted Sam first, standing alone and holding off a roomful of bystanders. In front of her stood a sobbing Angelina Sabatier, her arm around a petite blond-haired young woman. For a moment, I thought it was Sunny—or the Sunny I knew—but Sunny was glaringly absent from the crowd below. Christopher stood beside Mimi, his arms loose at his side as if he was prepared to catch her. Michael pulled out a dining chair and sat with his head in his hands while Robert stood behind him, clenching his hands on the back of the chair and wearing the white-lipped expression of a man facing a firing squad.

"Felicity," I whispered. "Sam brought Felicity." I looked from Felicity to Angelina. I could almost hear the pieces clicking into place. "The F initial on the tombstone—it stands for Felicity, doesn't it?"

Beau turned steady eyes on me. "Yeah. And the last name should be Hebert, not Broussard. Not that having the right name on the tomb would have helped us, since we never bothered to look."

"And Mimi? Does she know?"

"Christopher gave her a note from me fifteen minutes ago."

I looked down again, watching as Robert tried to lay a comforting hand on his wife's shoulder and she angrily brushed it off, stepping back with Felicity cradled against her. "So if Michael's real sister died, then . . ." I looked at Beau.

"An eye for an eye, a tooth for a tooth—remember? If Antoine blamed my grandfather for making him kill his own daughter—as crazy as that sounds to sane people—it makes sense that he would exact revenge by taking away my sister."

"And when the real Felicity died, it was the perfect opportunity to take one child and replace her with another. But what about Felicity and Michael's parents? They would have to be complicit, right?"

"Oh, yeah. Didn't you wonder why they became missionaries and moved to another continent? Their guilt forced them to leave their children in the care of their father's sister and her husband, two bereft and grieving parents who'd suffered too many losses and would find it almost impossible to say no, or to ask too many questions about a little girl with the same name as the niece they knew had died."

The reek of moist soil and decay wafted past my nostrils, making me gag. Beau coughed, but kept his attention focused below. Robert had moved to the middle of the group, his hand raised, the crowd behind him now silenced except for the occasional sobs from Felicity and Angelina. Mimi was strangely silent, her attention fixated on Felicity as if she were seeing a ghost.

Robert started to speak, his voice too thick and heavy for him to be understood. I strained forward, noticing the bald circle at the crown of his head. He coughed, and a man dressed as Saint Joseph with a baby carrier on his back emerged from the group to hand him a glass of water. "I am sorry," Robert announced. "I know any apologies are grossly inadequate, but to those I have wronged, I am heartily sorry." He looked at his wife, who turned her face as she continued to cradle a sobbing Felicity against her chest. His own face turned toward Mimi. "And I will not feed the rumor mill by going through all the painful details of a crime you will undoubtedly be reading about for years."

His voice had been rising as he spoke, the bare emotion distracting me from the attic air that had become icy and the cloying stench that made me think of death and decay, of a stale old mausoleum.

"My wife, Michael, and Felicity are blameless. My wife's brother and his wife I also hold blameless, their actions born of grief and desperation over the loss of a child. They are still doing penance with lives of servitude and forced separation from their family and the children they adored. I alone will answer for all the sins and ills of this family."

He clenched his hands into fists and pounded one on the dining table, causing the china and crystal to tremble alarmingly. "But I will share the blame with Antoine Broussard, whose evil nature still exists, along with his sins, sins that are well-known but carefully buried beneath layers of threats and fear. But the time has finally come for his true nature to be revealed to the very people whose acceptance and reverence he craved."

The cover of Jeanne's clientele book slammed open on the walkway between Beau and me, the sound drowned out by Robert, whose words were now being shouted as he walked in a small circle, like a man uncertain of where he should turn.

"He and he alone planted the seeds for this unconscionable crime. He told me how I could make my despondent wife the mother she desperately wanted to be. When he told me it would involve abducting an innocent child from her loving family, I refused. He countered by threatening the life of my beloved Angelina."

The frigid air surrounding us pulsed in and out like a rancid breath as my own throat tightened in fear. Pages from the book began tearing loose and flying through the air.

"He's not going to leave peacefully, is he?" My voice shook with cold and dread.

"Leave now. While you still can." Beau was looking at me, the tips of his eyelashes frosted with ice.

I spoke through chattering teeth. "Only if you come with me."

A strong wind rushed through the attic as Robert's raised voice echoed from the room below. "And I curse Antoine Broussard. May he rot in hell for all eternity!"

The walkway beneath us began to tremble, and the people in the dining room turned their gazes upward in unison. It took me a moment to realize that they weren't looking at us but at the giant chandelier that was now swaying drunkenly above the table, the plaster ceiling groaning and crackling like an old man after a long sleep.

"Don't you just love old houses?" Jolene exclaimed from her spot near the foot of the table as she stretched out her arms and began funneling guests toward the doorway. "You'd think all the settling would be over by now, and then—the chandelier starts shifting. The one thing that's as sure as your grandma forgetting her teeth on the bathroom sink is their unpredictability."

Christopher stepped forward to take Mimi's arm, then spoke to the crowd with a friendly yet commanding voice. "Let's all go outside to the back garden, where we will enjoy this beautiful evening and announce the winners of the raffles."

Loud chatter erupted as several people quickly moved toward the nearest exit. Christopher and Mimi led the way, while Jaxson and Cooper and several other guests helped guide the group out of the dining room, and a saint I couldn't name but who carried a shepherd's crook led the last stragglers out through the kitchen.

Only Robert remained, his gaze focused on the ceiling and the wildly swaying chandelier, as flecks of painted plaster dusted both him and the table, sprinkles of white seasoning the leftover food.

Beau struggled to a stand; his legs bent like a surfer's to keep his balance as the wind buffeted us. "Go, Nola. Please. I need to draw him up here, and I can't be responsible for what happens next. Or who might come through with him."

I shook my head, my eyes tearing from the force of the wind.

"Then hold on tight," he shouted. He grabbed the now-empty clientele book and held it in the air. "Antoine Broussard, you son of a bitch, it's time to meet your maker and face the justice you deserve."

The house shuddered, causing Beau's feet to shift. I stifled a scream as he struggled to regain his balance. "Come on and face me, you coward. You hid behind threats and money to ensure you and your family maintained a good and respectable reputation. But it's all over now, you bastard! Everyone knows what you've done. There's nowhere to hide. And you know what? You're not wanted here. It's time to leave."

The wind ripped the clientele book from his hand, then hurled it across the attic at the window, shattering the glass. I pressed my forehead against the floor, covering my face as shards flew into the spiraling squall, cutting any exposed skin. Peering up at Beau, I saw he had on his forehead a red gash that was dripping sideways because of the strength of the wind.

I remembered one of the things Melanie had told me about dealing with spirits was that you shouldn't goad them, because it made them angry and unpredictable. Unless, I thought as I peered down into the dining room and saw the chandelier now swaying gently, it was important to draw a spirit close so they could be dealt with and eradicated. Just like the Ghostbusters but without a proton pack.

The wind picked up strength, rushing at us from the rafters. I stayed flat, barely able to lift my head to see Beau dropping into a squat, his hands gripping the floor. "You were the one who ruined your family, Antoine. Not Robert. Not me. It was you, you sick bastard."

I opened my mouth to tell him to stop, but the words clogged my throat as Beau's head jerked backward before his body was flung down the length of the walkway. He lay unmoving, with his head facing me, his eyes closed, and blood trickling from his nose. I screamed his name and began crawling toward him, digging in the toes of my sneakers to move me forward.

Something that felt like a foot stepped hard on my back, pressing me against the ground, forcing the air from my lungs and making it impossible for me to move. I watched as Beau's foot slipped toward the edge of the walkway, pushed by unseen hands.

I tried to scream his name again, but I couldn't breathe, the pressure on my back crushing my lungs. Tiny spots of light danced around my peripheral vision. I watched in paralyzed horror as Beau's other foot slid to the edge. "Adele," I managed to choke out. "Please. Beau . . . needs . . . you." The dancing lights behind my eyelids grew bigger, obscuring my vision until I could no longer force my eyes to stay open.

I awoke to the smell of pipe smoke drifting past my face, and I sat up with a start, noticing that the pressure on my back had gone. The temperature in the attic was just as low, but the wind had diminished to a strong breeze. I saw the wet footprints first, my gaze following them to the spot where Beau had been before I'd passed out.

Beyond that point, water spots tinged with pink marked Beau's path to the far wall, where he now stood with both hands gripping the hand railings. Blood dripped down his face, and a flash of white appeared as I approached. "Thank God you're alive. Because if you weren't I'd kill you with my bare hands for scaring me like that."

My own smile wobbled. "Sorry."

The house groaned, the wind picking up again but at a greatly diminished force, like an injured dragon saving its energy for one last attack.

Beau wiped blood from his forehead with the back of his wrist. "Just leave, Nola. Please leave. He's still here."

"So is your grandfather. And your mother."

"I know. They're the reason we're not dead." He looked up toward the roof. "Jeanne is here, too. To forgive him. He just needs to ask."

I looked toward the door leading to safety, then back at Beau. The tobacco smoke was stronger now, and I could hear the slow tread of wet feet against wood coming up from behind us. "Good—so there's five against one. I like those kinds of odds." I swallowed. "I'm not leaving until this is done."

He gritted his teeth. "You're a slow learner, aren't you?" Then, throwing back his head, he shouted up to the rafters. "Killing another person isn't going to make things easier for you, Antoine. You will need to admit your sins if you ever want to find peace. You are no longer needed here in the place you loved in life but made miserable for so many others, including your own family. Including your daughter, Jeanne."

The breeze billowed drunkenly, blowing away the pipe smoke and replacing it with the putrid stench of rot and dead things. I fought the urge to vomit, knowing that his energy would feed on any show of fear or weakness.

Beau's head dropped as his chest rose and fell and his hands, which gripped the railing, turned white as he fought for consciousness. He lifted his head and rested it against the wall behind him. "Of all your sins, killing your own daughter is the most unforgivable. We all know what you did—what your brother did. You chose to protect a rapist over the life of your own daughter."

Beau's legs flipped out from under him, landing him on his back. I heard the crack of his head as it hit the wood. I pushed past my paralyzing fear and crawled toward him, touching his foot. "Beau?"

He held up his hand, either to show me that he was okay or to command me to leave—or both—then slowly pulled himself up, bracing himself against the rail.

His chest rose and fell as he struggled to catch his breath. He was losing this battle, and Antoine knew it. The wind and the reek of decay intensified, and I could only hope that this show of force was hiding a dying energy, and that Beau had a reserve hidden somewhere in his stubborn body.

"Jeanne forgives you, Antoine. She *forgives* you. You don't have to release your guilt and self-loathing on the world anymore. The world has left you behind, and your daughter is showing you the path toward a better place. She's offering you peace."

The wind skittered with rotating bursts of energy and stillness, as if we were on a sailboat heading toward the doldrums. With his last reserve, Beau pulled his head back and shouted, "Go. Now. Follow Jeanne into the light. Find the forgiveness and penance you seek. It is all waiting for you on the other side."

A doorway of brilliant light opened near the ceiling, and a young woman with a bouffant hairdo stood in the center of it, with rays of luminosity spilling from behind and around her. I recognized Jeanne, with the same dazzling smile from the old black-and-white photo I'd seen, as she extended both hands toward her father.

The wind stopped abruptly as the rancid stench was overtaken by the sweet and earthy scent of pipe tobacco. The bulb in the camping light flickered twice before shutting off, the glow from the dining room and the ethereal door casting everything in a diffuse radiance. The house rumbled softly, as if settling in for sleep, as a dark shadow crept out from a high corner of the attic before morphing into the familiar shape of a man with thick white hair.

Jeanne smiled at her father and opened her arms in welcome. With only a brief hesitation, Antoine Broussard walked into his daughter's arms and into the light until all that was left of it was a tiny glowing pinprick that shone brightly for several seconds before extinguishing itself.

I turned to Beau, my shout of excitement dying in my throat as I watched his knees buckle and his body slide to the walkway, to be positioned half on and half off, with his legs dangling over the edge.

Lurching forward, I grabbed his forearms just as gravity pulled the lower half of his body over the side. His hands loosely gripped my arms, weak with exhaustion. I felt him slipping from my grasp, my hands now holding on to his wrists. I wasn't sure how much longer I could keep my hold on him.

"Beau—wake up! You need to hang on."

He only groaned, his eyes slowly drifting open before closing again.

"Help!" I screamed as a last resort, hoping someone in the kitchen or outside could hear me. Or one of the two spirits I knew had been there but had apparently depleted their own energy. I wasn't going to let go. I couldn't.

The door at the end of the walkway slammed open, followed by heavy footsteps. "Keep holding on to him," Cooper said calmly. "I'm going to step around you and pull him up by his belt. I'll let you know when you can let go."

Cooper knelt beside me, reached over with one hand, and tightly gripped Beau's belt before doing the same with the other. After adjusting his balance, he said, "Situate yourself so you can use your upper body. Give it all you've got but pull gently. If you do it too fast, he's liable to slip. Ready?"

I nodded, and very carefully, inch by inch, we gradually managed to pull Beau to safety. We placed him faceup on the walkway, with Cooper on one end and me at Beau's feet. I took Beau's wrist, almost crying when I felt the thready beat of his pulse. Cooper was already on his phone calling 9-1-1.

The entire time we waited for the ambulance, I kept my hand on Beau's wrist, relaxing only once I heard the police sirens. It was then that I took a good look at Cooper, questioning his sudden appearance. "Thank you, by the way. But how did you know where to find us? Did you hear me scream?"

"No. It was a woman who came to me outside, in the garden, and led me to the hidden stairs. She told me I needed to hurry because you were in trouble."

I stared at him. "A woman? Do you know who it was?"

"She didn't say her name, but she was very persuasive and told me I needed to hurry whenever I asked her any questions."

I thought for a moment. "Had you seen her earlier, at the party?"

He shook his head. "No. And she wasn't really dressed up, either. But there was one thing that was kind of weird."

"Weird?" I asked. "In what way?"

"Her hair was dripping wet."

CHAPTER 38

Three weeks later, I was on the front porch of my cottage, scraping the remnants of peeling paint from the porch floor. After much discussion between Jolene, me, and Thibaut and Jorge (although I'm still not clear why they had a say), and an open contest on our YouTube channel that garnered thousands of entries, we'd chosen the historically accurate colors of pewter for the outside walls and mist gray for the trim, shutters, and porch floor.

The Marigny fell inside a "full control" district of the Historic Districts Landmarks Commission. Any exterior changes to my house had to pass their approval, but not exterior paint, as was evidenced by my neighbors' eclectic choice of colors that resembled a child's crayon box. Still, since I was a certified old-house hugger, it would never occur to me to draw outside the lines for the exterior paint shades. Yet I had reserved the front door for a bit of artistic license and had chosen Charleston green for it. When I'd told Melanie, she'd sent me a brass palmetto tree door knocker to hang in the middle.

The renovation was nowhere near completed, nor were we at the stage to paint the exterior (we were still working on rehabbing all the windows), but I felt as if I'd made a huge step forward by choosing my home's new look. When the door was painted and my new door knocker attached, I would finally be able to feel at home in this place that reminded me so much of where I'd come from, of who I'd been and who I was meant to be. It was a nice hybrid, one that now felt as comfortable to me as a worn pair of jeans.

Jolene opened the front door holding a notepad and pen. "I'm working on the guest list for the house-blessing party. I know it won't be until January, but with the holidays coming up I don't want to get too distracted. I've already got twenty-eight so far, including you, me, and Cooper, and I'd like to invite Connor Black. Do you think any of the neighbors will come?"

I looked across the street to where Ernest and Bob had changed their Christmas trees to a Thanksgiving theme, with strings of lit turkeys and a large cutout of their dog, Belle, wearing a Pilgrim costume.

"It's possible," I said. "With Antoine Broussard gone, the house feels almost normal, and no more weird light shows." I still winced when I said his name, unable to forget the events of the night of the fund-raiser. "And no more pipe smoke either, which means no more calls from the neighbors across the street about the dangers of smoking. People might actually come."

"But will they RSVP? That's a real problem these days. It's like they were raised in a barn or something."

I sat back on my heels. "I can't imagine."

"And I hope you don't mind, but I've already asked Jaxson's brother for his available dates in January so we can narrow it down. Unless you'd prefer another priest for the house blessing."

"No—he's perfect. Not that we've met, but he's Jaxson's brother. Besides, he's the only priest I know about. We'll have to invite Carly, you know."

She kept smiling. "I know. Jaxson's planning on giving her the ring over Christmas, so they'll be engaged by then."

"But if they're not, we don't have to invite her."

"I'm going to pretend I didn't hear you say that," she said, writing something in her notebook.

We looked up at the sound of an approaching vehicle and watched as Beau parked his truck at the curb. I hadn't seen him since the night he'd been taken from his house in an ambulance, but I hadn't needed to. He seemed to play a starring role in my dreams each night.

"Are you supposed to be driving?" I called out.

"Nope. But neither are most of the people out on the road, so I figured I'd fit right in."

He held something wrapped in tissue paper, and when he stepped up on the porch he gave it to me. Then he sat down in one of the rocking chairs that Jolene kept dragging up on the porch even when I'd told her they were in the way. She had informed me that no house was a home without rocking chairs on the front porch, a battle she easily won.

Beau was breathing heavily, as if the effort of walking from his truck had exhausted him. I supposed two weeks in a hospital with a fractured skull along with a scattering of broken ribs would do that to a person.

"Go ahead and open it," he said, indicating the package.

I put down the scraping knife, then pulled back the tissue, revealing a rectangular dark blue denim pouch with a long, narrow leather neck strap. A pocket, just the size for a house key, had been carefully stitched onto the front, along with the embroidered outline of my house in pale blue thread.

I looked at Beau with surprise. "It's from Sunny, isn't it? She said she was going to make one for me. I was thinking it was just part of her act."

He examined it with narrowed eyes. "What is it?"

"A phone pouch. I needed one for times I didn't want to bring my backpack."

"And so you don't keep losing your phone in the house," Jolene piped up. "Much better than that Velcro contraption you rigged up to stick on your sweatshirt, if you ask me."

I wanted to point out that I hadn't, but the smell of something baking in the kitchen made me hold my tongue.

Beau grinned, then grimaced as he shifted his weight in the chair. "She left it in her room with a note for me to give the package to you."

My eyes stung, not just from the thoughtfulness but also for a lost and lonely girl willing to risk everything for the role of beloved daughter she'd always wanted to play. I reached inside the pouch and was surprised when my fingers touched a piece of paper. I drew out an entire lined notebook page written in round, childish print, the top ripped as if yanked out in a hurry.

After reading through to the second paragraph, I looked up at Beau. "I think you need to hear this." I cleared my throat and began to read:

Dear Nola,

Thanks for being a friend. I wish we'd had more time together because I think we could have become really good friends. I also want to say that I'm sorry. I know that's a piss-poor thing to say about something so awful, but I'm an actress, not a writer. Still, you get the sentiment.

One last thing. I've always been a believer in psychics. And like Beau says, there are good ones and bad ones. I had a reading from a good one right after I'd decided to come to New Orleans. She knew I was going on a big trip and I'd meet lots of new people—lame, right? But she said some other stuff that she couldn't have just guessed at, and then gave me a message for a new friend I'd meet in my new city and said that I'd figure out who it was once I met them. I think she meant you.

She said the message was from a young mother who had crossed over a while ago. Her voice was garbled, like she was talking underwater, but she wanted you to know that she's with Bonnie and they are watching over you because your demons aren't done chasing you.

I'm hoping that means something to you and you'll know what to do with it.

I am sorry for everything. I wanted you to know that the short months I spent in New Orleans were the happiest of my life.

Peace out,
Sunny/Paige

I folded the note back up and tucked it inside the pouch. "Bonnie was my mother."

"I know. It's nice to know they're together, don't you think?"

"Yeah. But what about that thing about the demons? I hope she wasn't referring to my drinking issues, because I'm over those. Maybe there are newer demons I haven't yet met."

"That's one way to look at it." His face was serious, making me nervous.

Eager to switch topics, I asked, "Do we even know where Sunny—or Paige, I guess—is now?" I'd purposefully thrown myself back into my work and house renovation, unwilling to face the entire impact of all the revelations yet.

"She disappeared—with the cat, Mambo. Mimi said she thinks the cat was Sunny's before, and she couldn't live without him so managed to plant him as a stray so they could be together."

"Well, she can't be too bad of a person, right?" Jolene said. "I mean, she gave Mardi his ass, and it's his favorite toy. Anyone who's attached to an animal like that can't be all bad."

"That might not be completely true," I said. "Didn't Hitler have a dog?"

Jolene blew out a puff of air. "Whatever. Still, I didn't like what Sunny did, but I did like her. Just so y'all know, if they call me to be a character witness, I'll stand up for her. Mardi wouldn't lie to us, right? And he took to her right away, like a pig to mud."

"But where did she come from?" I asked. "She had everything

right—down to the color of her hair and her sunny disposition. It's like she'd been studying for the part her whole life."

Beau nodded. "She probably had. During Robert Sabatier's interrogation, he said Sunny—whose real name is Paige Mukowski, and she's from Cleveland—answered his online ad for an actress looking for a long-term role. She was a foster kid and didn't have any family, and she'd been involved in community theater since she was a teen, so she was the perfect choice. Nobody to wonder where she was, and someone in desperate need of a family to fit into. She even got that fleur-de-lis tattoo on her arm, which makes me think she was hoping her role would be permanent. Robert fabricated her entire backstory and paid money to the right people to back it up. Police are looking for her, and hopefully she'll be brought back to New Orleans on fraud charges."

"What about the real Sunny, Felicity Hebert? Mimi was so frantic about you and your injuries when we spoke, I didn't want to add to her stress. And when I called Christopher, all he knew was that Felicity and Mimi had spoken in person, but he doesn't know what they discussed."

Beau nodded. "And all Mimi would tell me is that Felicity—as she still wants to be called—has gone back to New York and Michael went with her. She says she needs time to think, and I'm guessing that Michael does, too. Mimi also said that the authorities are now looking for Michael's parents, to find out what part they played in the abduction, and if they can corroborate Robert Sabatier's story about his wife's innocence."

I thought about Angelina and her kind smile, finding it very difficult to believe she had anything to do with any of it. "Angelina would have questioned the reappearance of her dead niece, right?"

Beau shrugged. "Robert said that Michael's parents had adopted a child right after their daughter's death, and Angelina found that acceptable. Or didn't ask too many questions because she was desperate to believe that she was being given two children that she sorely wanted."

"It's a sad story all around," I said. "Everyone loses something. And all because of one evil man. He's gone for good, right? It's a lot brighter here, and I no longer have PTSD when I go into the upstairs closet, but I wanted to check with you to be sure."

"He's gone. Promise. And hopefully my grandfather and mom, too. I'm not sure how all this works, but I still feel her presence."

I gently touched his arm. "That might not be a psychic thing. I feel my mom from time to time, too. Like when I'm stressed or need to make a big decision. I think it might be more of a mom thing than anything else."

A timer chimed inside. "First batch of cookies in the new oven! I'll let you take these home with you, Beau," Jolene said.

"Wait—what?"

"Don't get your panties in a twist, Nola. I've got enough dough here to make two more batches, and Beau's been through a lot."

"I was there, too, you know," I called back, but she had already ducked back inside, leaving Beau and me alone on the porch.

I moved to sit in the other rocking chair. "How are you really? Mimi's been keeping me updated, but I didn't want to bother you by texting. I did stop by the hospital, but Sam was there and I didn't want to intrude."

"I know. Mimi told me." He rocked back and forth. "My mom was there, too. I guess she wanted to make sure that I was okay."

"Did you thank her? For saving your life."

"Yeah. I told her she could go now. I told her that I forgave her." He gripped each arm of the rocker. "But I'm still angry."

"You were a little kid," I said. "It makes sense that you felt abandoned—and that it followed you into adulthood. Just remember—you weren't abandoned on purpose. It's just what happened as a result of a terrible catastrophe. Maybe that's what she meant by choosing what to fight for. You can hang on to something that happened in your past that you had no control over, or you can look forward to something new that will move you forward."

"Hmm," he said. "Easier for some people than others, I guess."

Before I could drill him on what he meant, he touched the scar on his head. "I need to properly thank Cooper for what he did. I thought about treating everyone to a nice dinner at Commander's. No expense spared. You can wear your new phone pouch if you really want to be fancy."

"Sounds like a plan."

He studied me closely, his eyes suddenly serious. "Nola?" He'd lowered his voice, and my blood may have run a bit faster.

"Yeah?"

"There are two things I need to tell you."

"Just two? I'm sure you have at least five just from my last driving lesson."

He grinned, pinching something in my gut like an arrow hitting its mark.

"The first is, thank you. Cooper couldn't have done what he did if you hadn't already done what you did. I owe you my life. I'm actually glad you didn't listen to me when I told you to leave."

I held up my phone. "Can I record you saying that so I have evidence?"

"Funny, but no."

"What's the second thing?"

He leaned toward me, reaching out his hand. I leaned toward him, too, aware of his broken ribs. "Nola?" he said, our faces only inches apart.

"Hmm?" My eyes were already half closed.

"You have a lot of blue-green paint chips stuck in your hair."

The air leaked out of my lungs in disappointment as I sat back in my chair. "Thanks. I'll wash it later."

He smiled, then leaned heavily on his arms as he pulled himself up to stand. "Good seeing you. I was thinking about calling Cooper to finally go look at the shotgun on Esplanade. I'll let you know when."

"Thanks," I said. "Just let me know."

Right on cue, Jolene came out with a covered plate of fresh-baked cookies. "Don't forget these! Just what the doctor ordered for a fast recovery."

Beau laughed, then said good-bye before heading back to his truck. Jolene watched his slow progress, waiting to speak until he'd closed his door.

"That boy is fine," she said, drawing out the last word into three syllables.

"Don't you have another batch of cookies to make?"

She was laughing as she shut the door behind her.

Long after the sound of Beau's truck had disappeared, I continued to sit on the porch, watching the cool November breeze tease the branches of the potted trees across the street, the strings of turkey lights and orange streamers shimmying in a dance choreographed by the wind.

I closed my eyes and took a deep breath of contentment until the sound of slow footsteps on the sidewalk forced them open. A woman with long dark hair streaked with gray stood looking up at me. Leathery skin sagged from her cheeks and jaw, and from beneath a forehead scored with heavy lines she stared out at me with clear, deep-set dark eyes. She wore an interesting mix of gauze skirts and strands of beads and large gold hoop earrings. I stared back as I tried to recall where I'd seen her before. Judging by her outfit, she could be one of my neighbors in the Marigny, well-known for its culturally eclectic residents. I'd probably stood behind her in line at Who Dat Coffee Cafe on my daily coffee run at some point.

"Good morning," I called, hoping she'd respond by introducing herself.

She smiled, revealing even white teeth, and not the missing or gold incisors I'd anticipated. Proving, once again, that you should never judge a book by its cover.

"Good morning, Nola," she said, her voice smooth, with a hint of an accent I didn't recognize.

I leaned forward. "Do I know you?"

"Not yet."

I stood and walked toward the edge of the porch. "Wait—I remember now. I saw you in Jackson Square, right? You had a crystal ball."

She dipped her head in acknowledgment.

When she didn't offer any more information, I prompted, "Do you live nearby?"

Instead of answering she said, "I have a message for Beau."

"You just missed him."

"I know. I wanted to give it to you first. He needs your counsel even though he would never admit it. He's stubborn, that one. Just like his father."

"You knew Buddy?"

She nodded. "That's why I'm here."

"Okay," I said slowly. "Can you tell me your name?"

"Madame Zoe. He won't know me, and he will fight the information he needs to know. Which is why I'm telling you."

I sighed, my sense of peace and respite evaporating like morning mist. "All right. Although I'm not sure he'll listen to me, either. He's . . . selective that way."

"He will. There is a connection between you two. He will hear you, although he might not listen at first. There's a difference, you know. That's why it needs to come from you. And when he's ready, you know where to find me."

"Can you be more specific? I'm not sure . . ."

But Madame Zoe had already begun to walk away. She shuffled off down the sidewalk, and I watched until she disappeared from view. I stood staring down the empty street for a long time before reaching for the putty knife to resume scraping. My hand froze in midair as I stared down at the recently scraped patch of floorboards. Next to the knife was a perfectly formed footprint, a water mark barely visible on the pale wood.

Straightening, I stepped back and saw that it was the first of several prints leading down the steps and across the street toward where Beau's truck had been parked. I sat down on the floor, watching as the footprints completely evaporated.

I continued scraping, mentally going over the long list of house projects still to be tackled and considering which I might start next. I'd discuss it with Thibaut, and Jorge, and maybe even Beau. Anything to keep from having to think about Madame Zoe or the personal demons I had thought I'd left behind.

If there was one thing that Melanie had taught me about besides spreadsheets and labeling guns, it was the belief that some problems did go away on their own. For those that didn't, well, that was what tomorrow was for. That's when I'd start to wonder why Adele was still here, and why my mother had chosen now to be worried about me. And what sort of bond I supposedly had with Beau. I pushed all those thoughts away. I'd think about them all tomorrow.

THE HOUSE ON PRYTANIA

KAREN WHITE

READERS GUIDE

Questions for Discussion

1. Were you surprised when Beau asked Nola to socialize under false pretenses with Michael Hebert? Do you think he was wrong to ask Nola?

2. Nola then had Sam ask her to do the same thing, but this time to protect Beau. Was Sam right or wrong in asking Nola?

3. Was Nola wrong to agree to see Michael again and reestablish their relationship? Do you think Nola should have given Michael a real chance at mending their relationship? Why or why not?

4. Why do you think Beau seems to be fighting against using his psychic abilities and is trying to block ghosts from communicating with him?

5. Readers get to see a lot of Melanie, the twins, and Jack in this book—do you think Nola regrets leaving Charleston and

buying her house in New Orleans? Why do you think she felt so strongly about living in New Orleans, away from her family, when she clearly loves and misses them?

6. Why do you think Beau still hosts a podcast defrauding psychic mediums when he knows both psychic mediums and ghosts are real?

7. Sarah, Nola's sister, has the same ability to communicate with ghosts as her mom and Beau do. Do you think it was wrong of both Sarah and Nola to utilize Sarah's ability when she's clearly affected by her contact with malevolent spirits?

8. Were you surprised when the truth of Sunny's identity was revealed? Why or why not?

9. Do you think Michael's aunt and uncle should go to prison for their decades-long deception? Why or why not?

10. Now that the family has Sunny back, why do you think the ghost of Beau's mother is still around Beau?

Read on for a preview of the next book
in the Royal Street series,

THE LADY ON ESPLANADE

A heavy early-November rain pummeled the windows and the roof of our town house on Broadway as pebble-sized drops fell on the streets and sidewalks, converting all flat surfaces to ankle-deep rivers. I stood inside the open front door as sheets of water cascaded down from the small overhang, splattering rain wetting my face as I breathed in the peculiar scent of moisture-laden air mixed with that of drenched asphalt and saturated dirt. Leftover jack-o-lanterns from a sodden Halloween remained perched on the fraternity house doorstep across the street, staring back at me with shriveled faces and jagged mouths black with mildew.

Hurricane season wasn't officially over until November thirtieth, and like all parts of the southeast that dipped its toes into the Gulf or Atlantic, the collective breath that had been held since the first of June wouldn't be completely expelled until December first. Names like Camille, Katrina, and Ida weren't mentioned out loud at all. I'd accidentally mentioned the K-word and Jolene—my force-of-nature redheaded roommate—had crossed herself and then told me that the following June she would take me to the Mass for hurricane protection, despite the fact that neither of us was Catholic.

I'd asked her if I could borrow her waders to explore this new underwater landscape, but she'd warned me about going outside during a gully-washer. Because when the water rises in New Orleans, it is anyone's guess what might rise with it. I closed the door, dulling the sounds and smells of the rain but not the tremor that crept over my skin at the thought of what the deluge might unbury.

I trudged up the bare wood steps and opened the single French door to our upstairs apartment. I was greeted enthusiastically by Mardi, my adopted gray and white fur ball, despite having been absent for less than five minutes. The dog's origins and bloodline were a mystery, but he was unquestionably mine despite Jolene's favorite-aunt status, which allowed her to dress him in seasonally themed sweaters and bandanas despite my protests and Mardi's resigned acceptance. Being a Mississippi native and more Southern than Dolly Parton, my roommate believed in accessorizing and monogramming everything. Including my dog.

"Still raining," I announced to the empty living room. "I hope the flooding is at least drowning the next generation of flying cockroaches."

"Honey, those evil critters would survive a nuclear explosion. I think the chemical pollution in the rain makes them bigger and gives them the kind of confidence required to open a screen door," Jolene said as she emerged from the back hallway with a life-sized Barbie head tucked under her arm. If it had been anyone else, I would have been alarmed, but with Jolene I didn't even blink.

"What's that for?" I asked, indicating Barbie.

"I'm fixin' to send it to Charleston for Sarah, since she said she didn't have one. I wanted to style the hair first so she can use it as a model for her own. Y'all have the same hair, so I thought I'd practice on Barbie before I did your hair for tonight."

"Tonight?"

She raised her perfectly shaped eyebrows, a shade darker than her natural red hair. "I know you're just trying to yank my chain, Nola. I put it on your calendar and used my good lipstick to write it on the bathroom mirror, so don't pretend you have no idea what I'm talking about. I'm going to run your bath in half an hour, so just mentally prepare yourself to get all gussied up."

I sighed heavily. "But how are we supposed to get there? The streets are flooded. And you know what humidity does to my hair."

"Bubba can plow through anything, and I'll use superglue on your hair if I have to. Because until I hear otherwise, Commander's is open and we're going to be there come hell or high water."

I glanced out through the large double window over the sofa, where the unrelenting rain continued to hit against the glass. "But can Bubba float?" Jolene's vintage automobile was a menace on the road because of its size and was doubly threatening when Jolene was behind the wheel. I had calluses on my right hand from clutching the passenger-side door handle. I shuddered at the image of Bubba barreling down the narrow streets of New Orleans like a speedboat in a low-wake zone, taking out everything in its path.

"I think it would be safer staying home." I gave her a hopeful smile. "I'll let you give me one of your smelly facial masks and paint my toenails."

"Nice try, but no." Jolene looked at her watch. "You've now got twenty-five minutes. You can use the time to soak your hands in my moisturizing gloves. They look like you've been manually scraping paint from old plaster."

I looked down at my reddened knuckles and ragged fingernails. "That's because I have," I said, unable to keep the pride from my voice. I'd recently purchased a Creole cottage on the brink of demolition in the Marigny neighborhood as my first step toward starting over and adulting in a brand-new city.

In my defense, I said, "Everybody we're having dinner with knows what I spend my time doing. And Beau will accuse me of not pulling my weight if my hands are as soft as a baby's bottom."

Despite having a graduate degree in historic preservation, I would have been in way over my head if it hadn't been for the unsolicited interference of one Beau Ryan. Granted, he was a licensed contractor and knew the ins and outs of renovating old houses, but he was also an unwelcome reminder of the parts of my past I would have rather forgotten. And, as much as I liked to believe that the restless spirits that inhabited my new corner of the world didn't bother me, Beau had risked his life to eradicate an especially vengeful one from my new home. I had returned at least part of the favor—with unexpected help from his deceased mother—during an epic showdown in the attic of his family's house on Prytania Street.

Like my stepmother, Melanie Middleton Trenholm, Beau had the ability to communicate with spirits, despite his popular podcast, which he used as a platform to debunk the many so-called psychics who gleefully took money from the grief-stricken. As a previous victim, desperate to find his parents, who'd disappeared during Hurricane Katrina, he was dedicated to preventing the fleecing of the vulnerable while simultaneously hiding his own physic gift he'd inherited from his mother. A gift he feared, if only because he couldn't control it.

"Yes," Jolene said. "But luckily for you, you've got me, and I've got an arsenal of beauty products to fix whatever's broken, and my reputation is at stake if I allow you to walk out the door looking like your fingers got stuck in a cotton gin. Or in an electric socket." Her gaze flicked over my Brillo-like hair, frizzed by the few minutes I'd spent in the open doorway watching the rain. "Fortunately, I enjoy the challenge." She smiled. "I've got the perfect dress for you to wear. I found it on sale at Saks, but the color blue matches your eyes so I want you to have it. I'm sure Beau will notice."

"In case you've forgotten, Beau has a girlfriend, and Samantha will be there tonight. Besides, you know I'm not interested in him. We don't even like each other."

"Right," she said, letting out an inelegant snort. "And it's okay to wear white shoes before Easter." She rolled her eyes. "It's not a small thing that you saved his life. He's hosting tonight's dinner to thank you, so you're going to be the star of the show. Just accept it. And you now have twenty-one minutes." Jolene placed the Barbie head on the dining table, then walked toward the bathroom in the back hallway.

"Why don't you wear it, Jolene? Won't Jaxson be there tonight, too?" I regretted saying it before the words had even left my mouth. I didn't want to encourage her to believe that one day Jaxson would wake up and realize he was with the wrong woman. Jolene and I both knew that Jaxson had already bought an engagement ring for his long-term girlfriend, Carly, but only Jolene clung to the belief that she still had a chance as long as the ring wasn't on Carly's finger.

Jolene kept walking and didn't respond, but I knew better than to think she hadn't heard me. As sweet and kind as my roommate was, I knew it was only a matter of time before I'd find a severed Barbie head in my bed.

By some miracle, Jolene and I arrived at Commander's Palace restaurant only fifteen minutes late. Jolene was firmly of the belief that it was always better to arrive late than ugly, so there was no escape from her smoothing, teasing, plucking, moisturizing, and painting my face and/or hair. Despite my worries, Bubba performed as a certified land yacht and plowed through the streets, creating wakes usually reserved for bigger boats like aircraft carriers.

Beau had reserved the private Little Room at Commander's, an intimate space where ambient noise and the footsteps of waitstaff were muffled by padded carpet. Elegant framed mirrors hung on the walls and reflected the muted light shining through the French doors and from the sparkling crystal chandeliers. Small tables had been placed together in the center of the room beneath white tablecloths, and menus lay on top of the place settings. Any hope that I had that I could sneak in unnoticed and grab a chair at the far end of the table was quickly dispelled when I saw that a spot had been reserved to the right of Beau, who stood from his place at the head of the table when we entered.

"And finally—the guest of honor," he announced. Jaxson rose from his seat at the middle of the table and pulled out the chair next to him for Jolene. Carly, his longtime girlfriend, sat across from him and gave Jolene a calculating glance before reaching her hand across the table to touch Jaxson's fingers. It was the same as if she'd just slapped a label on him that read MINE. Jolene was too busy trying not to look smug at my proximity to Beau to notice.

I greeted Beau's grandmother Mimi Ryan with a kiss to her powdered cheek. "I'm glad you could make it," she said with a note of reproach, as expected from the family matriarch, her odd eyes—one green, one blue—crinkling at the corners and softening her words.

She sat at the opposite end of the table next to Samantha—Sam—Beau's girlfriend and podcast partner. Sam stood and greeted me with a hug and a warm smile, and I thought yet again that we could have been friends if not for Beau Ryan. Considering that I didn't even like him very much, this was an odd sentiment, and one that I didn't care to analyze too closely.

I was happy to see Cooper Ravenel, who rose from where he'd been seated directly across from me and wrapped me in a bear hug. Because of his job he traveled a lot, and I hadn't seen much of him since the night of the St. Louis Cathedral fundraiser at the Ryan's, when Beau had almost died. Cooper had been instrumental in saving Beau and me from the brink of disaster, which was one of the reasons why he was at the celebratory dinner.

"It's good to see you," he said, his voice and touch vibrating through me.

"Same," I said, feeling everyone's eyes on us. "I hope you're in town long enough for me to show you the house on Esplanade."

"That's what I'm planning on. I've asked for no travel this coming week, so I'm all yours."

Cooper had been my teenage crush and first heartbreak and had recently moved to New Orleans. I was concentrating on renovating my cottage and starting my new life, and wasn't interested in a relationship beyond friendship, but I'd be lying to myself if I said that I didn't feel an electric jolt every time I saw him. I'd yet to ask him about the scar on his face and his years in California. If there was anything I'd learned from my stepmother, sometimes not knowing was best.

"Sounds like a plan," I said as I pulled away.

Everyone took their seats except for Beau, who remained standing. He gently clinked his water glass—no wine or champagne on the table in deference to me, I guessed—to quiet the chatter.

"Thank you all for coming. It was important that I gather us all together to thank those of you who not only saved my life"—he glanced and me, and I knew we were both recalling his slipping over the edge of the attic walkway as I struggled to hold on before Cooper miraculously appeared—"but also helped us find my long-lost sister, Sunny. As I know you are all aware, she is still processing her newly discovered identity, but Mimi and I have great hopes that she will return to us when she's ready. And we will be waiting with open arms."

"Hear, hear." Christopher Benoit, family friend and the manager of the Ryan's antiques store on Royal Street, the Past Is Never Past, raised his water glass. The rest of us followed suit, and the sound of glasses clinking sang over the table as we turned toward our neighbors and toasted to the answer to the decades-old mystery of what had happened to two-year-old Sunny Ryan, and also to the miracle of Beau's survival.

As I sipped my water, I looked around at the smiling faces, knowing that, except for Carly—whose reason for being present at the table wasn't clear—I knew I'd found my family. Not a new family, but an extension of my beloved family back home in Charleston. Because as Melanie and my father, Jack, had reminded me time and again, no matter where I went, there I was. And as a recovering alcoholic who'd chosen a city known for its partying lifestyle as my new home, my family had known even before I did that I would require a support system while I tried to prove to everyone that I didn't need anyone's support but my own.

I was halfway through my dessert of crème brûlée—which I didn't enjoy as much as I should have because I was too busy watching Sam and Beau share the bananas Foster for two—when the lights flickered, followed quickly by a sharp crack of lightning. I looked up and met Beau's gaze, almost as if we were sharing the same unspoken thought: that just the two of us had noticed that the crystal chandelier over our table had been the only light in the restaurant with interrupted power.

Anyone who lives in the coastal South is used to sporadic storms, even in November. We were even used to the electricity going out with annoying frequency. But there was an odd static in the air, a frisson of something unknown that hovered in the room that only Beau and I appeared to notice.

The waitstaff continued to refill water and iced tea glasses and deliver coffee in delicate china cups as if nothing had changed. As if the room hadn't just inhaled and was holding its breath. I picked up my glass and held it against my cheek, trying to cool my suddenly hot skin.

I was concentrating on slowing my heartbeat and was barely aware of Jaxson pulling out his chair and moving toward Carly. I half stood from my chair as Jaxson got down on one knee and produced a black velvet box. I turned to look at Jolene, whose porcelain skin had gone even paler, the carefully applied blush on her cheeks almost garish in contrast.

Everyone was rising to their feet and clapping loudly as Carly threw her arms around Jaxson's neck before delivering an intimate kiss to his lips. Jolene began clapping, too, but it looked as if her frozen white fingers might snap. I moved to her side and rested my arm around her shoulders. For a brief moment she leaned against me before straightening and configuring a smile that even I thought looked real.

As Jaxson slid the ring onto Carly's finger, I turned to Beau to ask him why he hadn't given us some kind of warning so Jolene could have been prepared. But instead of watching Jaxson and Carly, Beau was staring at the floor.

Carly extended her left hand, bright prisms of light reflecting off her large pear-shaped diamond. "We need to have an engagement party!" Her gaze scanned the room before alighting on Jolene. "And I happen to know the best party planner—Jolene McKenna! If anyone can make it the party of the decade, she can!"

Jolene continued to smile, adding a nod as if agreeing to the ludicrous suggestion that she throw an engagement party for Jaxson and Carly. It was almost as unimaginable as LSU throwing a victory party for Ole Miss.

I turned back to Beau, his gaze lifting from the floor to meet mine. I held my breath in anticipation, knowing before I looked down that I would see a set of a woman's footprints, each step marked by smeared water spots as if the owner had just climbed out of a pool. Since I'd first met Beau in Charleston, I'd seen them often enough to know without a doubt to whom they belonged. Just as much as I knew that Beau would do everything possible to deny it.

My eyes met Beau's again. *She's still here.* The unspoken words ricocheted from his thoughts to mine, my heart sinking as I realized what those wet footprints meant. I'd seen the footprints only once since the incident in the Ryan's attic, and I'd hoped she'd come only to say good-bye. Apparently that wasn't the case. Despite her daughter, Sunny, having been found, Adele Ryan still had unfinished business. And she needed her son's help.

Photo by Marchet Butler

Karen White is the *New York Times* and *USA Today* bestselling author of more than thirty-four novels, including the Tradd Street series, *The Shop on Royal Street*, *The Last Night in London*, *Dreams of Falling*, *The Night the Lights Went Out*, *Flight Patterns*, *The Sound of Glass*, *A Long Time Gone*, and *The Time Between*. She is the coauthor of *The Lost Summers of Newport*, *All the Ways We Said Goodbye*, *The Glass Ocean*, and *The Forgotten Room* with *New York Times* bestselling authors Beatriz Williams and Lauren Willig. She grew up in London but now lives with her husband and a spoiled Havanese dog, dividing her time between Atlanta, Georgia, and the northwest coast of Florida. When not writing, she spends her time reading, playing piano, and avoiding cooking.

VISIT KAREN WHITE ONLINE

Karen-White.com

KarenWhiteAuthor

KarenWhiteWrite

NEW YORK TIMES BESTSELLING AUTHOR

KAREN WHITE

"This is storytelling of the highest order: the kind of book that leaves you both deeply satisfied and aching for more."

—*New York Times* bestselling author Beatriz Williams

For a complete list of titles,
please visit prh.com/karenwhite